REWIRED

Rewired

the post-cyberpunk anthology

JAMES PATRICK KELLY & JOHN KESSEL | *editors*

TACHYON PUBLICATIONS | SAN FRANCISCO

Cover photograph © 2007 by Patty Nason
Design & composition by John D. Berry
The text typeface is Freight Text, with Freight Sans and Freight Micro

Tachyon Publications
1459 18th Street #139
San Francisco, CA 94107
(415) 285-5615
www.tachyonpublications.com

Series Editor: Jacob Weisman

ISBN 10: 1-892391-53-8
ISBN 13: 978-1-892391-53-7

Printed in the United States of America

9 8 7 6 5 4 3 2

Introduction © 2007 by James Patrick Kelly and John Kessel | Sterling-Kessel Correspondence © 2007 by John Kessel and Bruce Sterling | William Gibson quotation © 1999 from *No Maps for These Territories*. Used by permission of the author. | "Bicycle Repairman" © 1996 by Bruce Sterling. First appeared in *Intersections*, edited by John Kessel, Mark L. Van Name, and Richard Butner (Tor: New York). | "Red Sonja and Lessingham in Dreamland" © 1996 by Gwyneth Jones. First appeared in *Off Limits*, edited by Ellen Datlow (St. Martin's: New York). | "How We Got in Town and out Again" © 1996 by Jonathan Lethem. First appeared in *Asimov's Science Fiction*, September 1996. | "Yeyuka" © 1997 by Greg Egan. First appeared in *Meanjin*, V56, #1, 1997. | "The Final Remake of *The Return of Little Latin Larry* with a Completely Remastered Soundtrack and the Original Audience" © 1997 by Pat Cadigan. First appeared in *Future Histories*, edited by Stephen McClelland (Horizon House: Norwood, Massachusetts). | "Thirteen Views of a Cardboard City" © 1997 by William Gibson. First appeared in *New Worlds*, edited by David Garnett and Michael Moorcock (White Wolf: Stone Mountain, Georgia). | "The Wedding Album" © 1999 by David Marusek. First appeared in *Asimov's Science Fiction*, June 1999. | "Daddy's World" © 1999 by Walter Jon Williams. First appeared in *Not of Woman Born* (Roc: New York). | "The Dog Said Bow-Wow" © 2001 by Michael Swanwick. First appeared in *Asimov's Science Fiction*, October/November 2001. | "Lobsters" © 2001 by Charles Stross. First appeared in *Asimov's Science Fiction*, June 2001. | "What's Up, Tiger Lily?" © 2003 by Paul Di Filippo. First appeared in *The Silver Gryphon*, edited by Gary Turner and Marty Halpern (Golden Gryphon: Urbana, Illinois). | "The Voluntary State" © 2004 by Christopher Rowe. First appeared in *sci fiction*, May 5, 2004. | "Two Dreams on Trains" © 2005 by Elizabeth Bear. First appeared in *Strange Horizons*, January 3, 2005. | "The Calorie Man" © 2005 by Paolo Bacigalupi. First appeared in *The Magazine of Fantasy & Science Fiction*, October/November 2005. | "Search Engine" © 2006 by Mary Rosenblum. First appeared in *Analog*, September 2005. | "When Sysadmins Ruled the Earth" © 2006 by Cory Doctorow. First appeared in *Jim Baen's Universe*, August 2006. |

Contents

Acknowledgments

WE'D LIKE TO THANK THE FOLLOWING PEOPLE for advice, suggestions, and recommendations: Wilton Barnhardt, Richard Butner, Matthew Cheney, Gregory Frost, Eileen Gunn, Rich Horton, Kelly Link, and David Moles.

Our thanks are also due to Jacob Weisman, Jill Roberts, and the other folks at Tachyon Publications who helped see this project through to completion.

None of these estimable people are responsible for errors of judgment or taste we committed in assembling this anthology.

Hacking Cyberpunk

James Patrick Kelly and John Kessel

"However, I don't worry much about the future of razor's edge techno-punk. It will be bowdlerized and parodized and reduced to a formula, just as all other sf innovations have been. It scarcely matters much, because as a 'movement,' 'Punk sf' is a joke. Gibson's a litterateur who happens to have an unrivalled grasp of the modern pop aesthetic. Shiner writes mainstream and mysteries. Rucker's crazy; Shirley's a surrealist; Pat Cadigan's a technophobe. By '95 we'll all have something else cooking."
  —Bruce Sterling, in a letter to John Kessel, 29 March 1985

shades

The Hugo Award-winning editor David Hartwell tells the story of how Bruce Sterling approached him in 1983 with a proposal for an anthology of short stories which would eventually become the classic *Mirrorshades*. The book was to be a kind of literary manifesto for the newly emerging cyberpunk movement. David said he was indeed interested and asked how many writers Bruce expected would be in *Mirrorshades*. Bruce said he had five or six in mind. David replied that five or six was not enough for a movement and that Bruce would need at least a dozen. So Bruce set out to recruit writers for the movement and his anthology, even if they were not card-carrying cyberpunks. Among those he found was one of the editors of this book, who was at the time most closely associated with the humanist camp, said to be in opposition to cyberpunk.

It is not surprising that the cyberpunk movement, so quick to sneer at other kinds of science fiction and to strike an attitude of hip self-importance, would be controversial. To its critics, cyberpunk was all borrowed surface and no substance: rock and roll Alfred Bester, Raymond Chandler with the serial numbers filed off. To the cynical, it was nothing but a marketing ploy to advance the careers of those select few who were permitted to hang their leathers in the secret Node Zero clubhouse. But as they continued to publish their innovative stories and novels, readers and — eventually — writers and critics began to acknowledge that there might be something to cyberpunk. In 1986, the pseudonymous Vincent Omniaveritas, writing in the cyberpunks' snarky house organ, *Cheap Truth*, brought the classic cyberpunk era to an end. "I hereby declare the revolution over," crowed Vince. "Long live the provisional government."

And then the real arguing started.

moving on

In the quarter century since, the debate has continued over the place of cyberpunk not only in science fiction, but in the culture as a whole. The literary discussion was complicated when some of the original cyberpunks tried to distance themselves from the movement. Naysayers seized on this to declare that cyberpunk was actually a movement of just one and his name was William Gibson. It soon became apparent that the center could not hold. However, the movement did not implode. Rather, popular culture hacked into it and turned cyberpunk to its own purposes. We saw cyberpunk music, movies, comics, and videogames. The slick magazine *Wired* became the *Popular Science* of cyberpunk. The cyberpunks had made computers and programming sexy; digital geekdom returned the favor by trying to reverse-engineer their ideas in silicon and code. But as it became more familiar, it also became tamer. Or maybe it grew up. There were cyberpunk ad agencies, cyberpunk fashion designers. Timothy Leary declared that the movie *War Games* was cyberpunk. The more people appropriated cyberpunk to their own uses, the fuzzier it became.

Our genre has been largely nonplussed by the spread of the cyberpunk meme. Learned papers have been given to explain the phenomenon. Some complain that science fiction has more to offer than dark visions of disaffected loners contending with totalitarian corporations. "The street," so central to the classic cyberpunk vision, is not the world, they say. And they are right, of course. Meanwhile, as second and third generation writers have put on their mirrorshades, they are all too often dismissed as mere imitators. Some in our genre have decided that they know what cyberpunk had to say, and, whether they agree with it or not, have consigned it to the dustbin of literary history. Cyberpunk can no longer be an ideology, they would say. It can only be a flavor.

rewired

In retrospect, it seems clear to us that cyberpunk was a movement. We acknowledge all the criticisms leveled against it. The hyperbole that helped launch it was unfortunate. Yes, some core cyberpunks found other things to write about or fell silent. Of course, the term's use in common parlance is now so vague as to verge on meaningless, but our dictionary offers two definitions of *movement* that fit: "a. A series of actions and events taking place over a period of time and working to foster a principle or policy. b. An organized effort by supporters of a common goal." In the heyday of *Mirrorshades* and *Cheap Truth*, the latter definition of classic cyberpunk — CP — made sense. There was a Movement with a capital *M*. We believe that the sixteen post-cyberpunk[1] — PCP — stories in this anthology illustrate the former definition of a movement: they are events that occurred in the last decade, long after classic cyberpunk, that continue to foster its principles and policies. No, that's not quite right. Fostering principles and policies isn't quite the cyberpunk style, is it? What these stories share, instead, are obsessions.

Briefly, we believe that the signature obsessions of cyberpunk are:
> Presenting a global perspective on the future.
> Engaging with developments in infotech and biotech, especially those invasive technologies that will transform the human body and psyche.
> Striking a gleefully subversive attitude that challenges traditional values and received wisdom.
> Cultivating a crammed prose style that takes an often playful stance toward traditional science fiction tropes.

The PCP stories collected here do not share all of these characteristics, but most have at least two or three. Any story that exhibits all of them just as they were used in 1985 is an instant cliché. Still, the realizations that the future will be one of intimate connections between the psyche and technology, that middle-class American values are not automatically going to prevail, and in fact, the vast majority of the world will not be like Iowa or New York, have had a profound and broad effect on science fiction published in the last decade.

---

1 The term "postcyberpunk" was first used by writer Lawrence Person, in an essay titled "Notes Toward a Postcyberpunk Manifesto" published in the critical magazine *Nova Express* in 1998. Person's essay points toward some of the same developments we are pursuing in this anthology, but we do not use the term in exactly the same way that he sets it forth. As we go to press, Person's essay is still available at the URL *http://slashdot.org/features/99/10/08/2123255.shtml*.

Cyberpunk obsessions have evolved over time; some writers extend them, some react against them, some take them for granted and move the basic attitudes into new territories. Our purpose here is to document these changes, which we believe have rewired CP into PCP. The writers we have chosen include some but not all of the CP founders. Some of our contributors came immediately after CP, while others were struggling to parse the subtleties of *Green Eggs and Ham* when *Mirrorshades* first appeared in bookstores. We have tried to confine ourselves to stories published in the last decade or so. Because we have limited ourselves to the short form, we were forced to leave out novelists like Melissa Scott and Richard K. Morgan and Chris Moriarty and—most difficult of all—Neal Stephenson.

But what is the "Post" in "Post-Cyberpunk"? In the effort to understand just what PCP has to do with CP, let's take a closer look at some of these obsessions.

obsessions

A major CP obsession was the way emerging technologies will change what it means to be human. Much science fiction has concerned itself with technology and changes in human culture. Indeed, the cautionary tale is a staple of the genre: *if this goes on, things will get very bad indeed*. But the assumption of the cautionary tale is that we have some control over the changes that technology will bring, so that if we act in a timely way, we can preserve consensus values. The cyberpunks studied the history of how humans have tried to manage change, and were not impressed. Moreover, the technologies of the twenty-first century are invasive and intimate. A key insight of CP, extended still further in PCP, is that we are no longer changing technology; rather it has begun to change us. Not just our homes and schools, our governments and workplaces, but our senses, our memories, and our very consciousness. Ubiquitous computing with access to all recorded knowledge, instantaneous communication across the entire planet, add-ons to the Human Operating System, manipulation of our genome—all are on the horizon. The changes these technologies will bring are qualitatively different than the changes caused by the automobile, or even by science fiction's longed-for invention of faster-than-light starships. Yes, cars transformed the landscape and gave rise to the malls, McDonald's and the suburbs. Sure, FTL will get us to the stars. But cars and starships change what we do, not who we are.

It has been observed that the future that cyberpunks envisioned seems very dark indeed. However, dystopia is in the eye of the beholder. While we may shudder at the thought of living in some of these worlds, the fictional denizens of PCP stories seldom exhibit nostalgia for the good old days of 2007. What seems grim to us is simply the world to them. Characters in these stories are too busy living their lives to waste much time wringing their hands over the subversion of *our* values. Why should they? Do we live in a dystopia? One can easily imagine the American Founding Fathers, even the technophilic libertine Benjamin Franklin, recoiling in horror at some of the values of our society. In PCP stories, human values are not imprinted on the fabric of the universe because what it means to be human is always negotiable.

These traits of PCP are so far mere extensions of CP obsessions. Another obsession of CP was to tell stories about the people that science fiction had traditionally ignored. Originally "the street" in CP meant the shadowy world of those who had set themselves against the norms of the dominant culture, hackers, thieves, spies, scam artists, and drug users. But for PCP writers the street leads to other parts of the world. Their futures have become more diverse, and richer for it. Asians and Africans and Latinos are no longer just sprinkled into stories as supporting characters, as if they are some kind of exotic seasoning. PCP writers attempt to bring them and their unique concerns to the center of their stories. PCP pays attention to the underclass, who do not have access to the transformative technologies that were the CP stock-in-trade.

> "I think we live in an incomprehensible present, and what I'm trying to do is illuminate the moment. I'm trying to make the moment accessible. I'm not even trying to explain the moment, I'm just trying to make the moment accessible."
> —William Gibson, *No Maps for These Territories*

punk

In the beginning, the stereotypical cyberpunk protagonist was a disaffected loner from outside the cultural mainstream. Ultimately this proved not only tiresome but also betrayed a lack of extrapolative rigor. No future could exist in which there were only data thieves in trench coats and megalomaniacal middle managers. Someone had to be baking the bread and driving the trucks and assembling all those flat screens. Cyberspace needs electricians! Where was the middle class in the CP stories? What were the families like? Could the cyberpunks write about community and still be punks?

The punk in cyberpunk has always been a problem. If by punk, one meant to say that the writers of the *Mirrorshades* generation were young, well, they were —at the time. But while they were to varying degrees outsiders, very few of the original cyberpunks—or indeed, the contributors to this collection—could be said to have lived "on the street." It is difficult to write orderly sentences if one is caught up in the chaos of a punk lifestyle. And as time passed, it became more and more of a stretch for some of the original cyberpunks to take their inspiration from youth culture.

But the punk in post-cyberpunk continues to make sense if it is pointing toward an attitude: an adversarial relationship to consensus reality. This attitude is just south of cynicism but well north of mere skepticism. It has to do with a reaction to a world in which humanity must constantly be renegotiated. In a cyberpunk story, any given moment can be at once thrilling and horrifying. Life is never smooth; it is illuminated by lightning flashes of existential insight, paved with the shards of our discredited philosophies. Sanity requires a constant recalibration of perception.

The characters in a PCP story need this healthy dose of attitude because their relationship to reality is different from ours. Yes, there may well be, and often is, a virtual reality that is as persuasive as reality itself and far more pleasant. It can be variously a trap, an escape, or a refuge. Perhaps all three at once. But reality itself is everywhere mediated, and what comes between the characters and reality must constantly be interrogated.

singular

The stories in this collection are too various for us to draw a tidy summary of what twenty-first-century cyberpunk is about, nor do we see the profit in it. However, so many of them imply or actually explore a post-human future that we would be remiss if we failed to point out that a logical consequence of much of cyberpunk extrapolation is the singularity. Vernor Vinge, by no means a cyberpunk, although highly respected by them, first proposed the notion of a technological singularity in 1993. Briefly, he contemplates a moment in history in which runaway technology causes a change "comparable to the rise of human life on Earth. The precise cause of this change is the imminent creation

by technology of entities with greater-than-human intelligence." Vinge specu-
lates this change may come through artificial intelligence, through computer/
human interfaces, or through biological modification of the human genome.
After this point, human history will end.

One of the obsessions of PCP fiction is to explore the edges of this "end" of
history, and if possible, to see beyond it.

form

So far we have spoken of cyberpunk primarily in terms of content, and CP was
indeed sparked by an attempt to bring content into science fiction that was
being ignored by the sf of the early 1980s.

But part of the force of *Cheap Truth* was also the aggressiveness of its anti-
art stance. Vincent Omniaveritas had little use for the pieties of literary culture
and traditional values of well-made fiction. A lot of early CP gained verve from
a conscious rejection of the New Wave and the New Wave's reaching after high
modernism's literary pretensions.

Whereas the New Wave brought stories like, for instance, Philip José
Farmer's "Riders of the Purple Wage" and Brian Aldiss's *Barefoot in the Head*
that drafted Joycean stream of consciousness into science fiction contexts,
Cheap Truth mocked science fiction writers who too obviously adopted literary approaches. But CP was just as self-consciously aware of its ancestors. Where humanist writers might claim Walter M. Miller, Jr., and Ursula K.
Le Guin as theirs, CP called on Alfred Bester and William S. Burroughs. Both
sides claimed J. G. Ballard. Both sides, consciously or not, were expressions of
postmodernism.

In abandoning "well made story values" in favor of oddness, visionary speculation, and the breaking of realist codes, CP was expressing a postmodern sen-
sibility. Literary critics like Larry McCaffery, who edited one of the earliest critical books on cyberpunk, *Storming the Reality Studio*, recognized the postmodern underpinnings of CP. What the critics saw in cyberpunk was not always in
accord with the *Cheap Truth* party line, but they were right in observing that
science fiction puts quotes around the word "reality." Science fiction is "pre-
deconstructed" through the ways that writers consciously encode information
that must be read out of the work. In much cyberpunk, no matter how grim,
there was a sense of play. Play with content — ideas, technological develop-

ments, extrapolations — but also with genre tropes, expectations built up over generations of pulp science fiction since Hugo Gernsback started *Amazing Stories*.

As PCP writers began to react to and incorporate CP visions, the urge to playfulness grew. Perhaps the more literary interests of humanist science fiction writers had an influence. Or maybe the writers who were never part of the Movement with a capital *M* no longer felt bound to foment CP's revolution. Twenty minutes after Vincent Omniaveritas declared victory in *Cheap Truth*, cyberpunk began to suffer from an inevitable genrefication. The moves that had seemed so daring in 1982 began to look a little stilted. The leathers were by now scuffed and stained; there were scratches on the mirrorshades. The PCP writers had to try something different or else take their places behind the glass in the display cases at the Science Fiction Museum. In the final analysis the CP writers went to war so that the PCP writers could be free to experiment with new forms.

present future
The idea that the physical, mental, and moral structures that most of us live by are radically contingent is at the heart of science fiction. It is evident throughout the history of the form, from H. G. Wells through John W. Campbell through Philip K. Dick and James Tiptree, Jr. It pervades the New Wave, and the feminist science fiction of the 1970s.

All cyberpunks, pre-, classic-, and post-, know this. Perhaps cyberpunk's greatest contribution to the genre was its uncanny ability to broadcast this science fictional idea to the culture at large. It's an understanding that, caught in whatever historical moment we write from, is all too easy to forget. We long for permanence, although we grow older with each tick of the clock. We proceed from the assumption that the world is comprehensible, even as we reel from its dizzying complexity. There are no guarantees; tomorrow we may be uploading ourselves into cyberspace or drowning off the coast of Nevada.

This understanding is the reason why science fiction, if it rises to its own challenge, can be the literature of the twenty-first century. Our hope is that the post-cyberpunk fiction here assembled will point the way for the readers and writers to come.

"To shake people awake, one needs the conceptual ability to grip and squeeze. I would hope that my rhetoric was a catalyst — that my remarks will challenge some writers to reassess and refine their own thinking. The cake IS stale and decorations aren't enough; we need to re-bake everything from scratch. And bake it thoroughly this time — not half-bake it. People should not be afraid to undertake this work. It's necessary. It's the karma of our generation in SF."
   —Sterling to Kessel, 22 August 1986

Sterling-Kessel Correspondence

IN THE WAKE of the publication of *Neuromancer* in 1984 there was a lot of talk about something called "cyberpunk" and a scurrilous fanzine called *Cheap Truth*, which apparently (I had never seen a copy) had been taking potshots at a number of writers I admired. In the spring of 1985, I wrote a letter to Bruce Sterling asking what all the fuss was about. Did he really detest the kind of fiction I liked as much as I had heard?

Well, yes...he did, sort of.

The correspondence got out of hand. For several years we hammered at each other back and forth through the postal service (this was before the Internet took off). Bruce's energy was immense, his fertility of imagination imposing, his conviction of his own rightness daunting. I had my own moments. It was the most stimulating conversation of my writing career, and given my age and who I am today, I don't think (to my regret) that it will ever come again.

As a means of giving a context to the stories collected here, and as a window into some of the thinking that went on behind at least one of the originators of the form, and the reactions of one of it readers, we have scattered brief quotes and exchanges from these letters through the anthology.

Our sincere thanks to Bruce for allowing us to quote from this correspondence.

—John Kessel

REWIRED

Bicycle Repairman

Bruce Sterling

Accompanying CP's fascination with the "street" came the assumption that, outside of middle-class social structures, new things can be done. Here Chairman Bruce himself observes that the middle class exerts its pull and the outsiders move toward the ordinary. Ten years after the conclusion of this story Lyle will be running a business and Deep Eddy will be a media commentator, both married (and probably divorced) with children.

This PCP story consciously reverses many cyberpunk clichés: it abjures sex and gives the hero a mother. Most amusing of all, Sterling dismantles the myth of the ninja black ops secret agent, a character helpless here in the face of a streetwise community and a social worker.

Repeated tinny banging woke Lyle in his hammock. Lyle groaned, sat up, and slid free into the tool-crowded aisle of his bike shop.

Lyle hitched up the black elastic of his skintight shorts and plucked yesterday's grease-stained sleeveless off the workbench. He glanced blearily at his chronometer as he picked his way toward the door. It was 10:04.38 in the morning, June 27, 2037.

Lyle hopped over a stray can of primer and the floor boomed gently beneath his feet. With all the press of work, he'd collapsed into sleep without properly cleaning the shop. Doing custom enameling paid okay, but it ate up time like crazy. Working and living alone was wearing him out.

Lyle opened the shop door, revealing a long sheer drop to dusty tiling far below. Pigeons darted beneath the hull of his shop through a soot-stained hole in the broken atrium glass, and wheeled off to their rookery somewhere in the darkened guts of the high-rise.

More banging. Far below, a uniformed delivery kid stood by his cargo tricycle, yanking rhythmically at the long dangling string of Lyle's spot-welded doorknocker.

Lyle waved, yawning. From his vantage point below the huge girders of the cavernous atrium, Lyle had a fine overview of three burnt-out interior levels of the old Tsatanuga Archiplat. Once elegant handrails and battered pedestrian overlooks fronted on the great airy cavity of the atrium. Behind the handrails was a three-floor wilderness of jury-rigged lights, chicken coops, water tanks, and squatters' flags. The fire-damaged floors, walls, and ceilings were riddled with handmade descent-chutes, long coiling staircases, and rickety ladders.

Lyle took note of a crew of Chattanooga demolition workers in their yellow detox suits. The repair crew was deploying vacuum scrubbers and a high-pressure hose-off by the vandal-proofed western elevators of Floor 34. Two or three days a week, the city crew meandered into the damage zone to pretend to work, with a great hypocritical show of sawhorses and barrier tape. The lazy sons of bitches were all on the take.

Lyle thumbed the brake switches in their big metal box by the flywheel. The bike shop slithered, with a subtle hiss of cable-clamps, down three stories, to dock with a grating crunch onto four concrete-filled metal drums.

The delivery kid looked real familiar. He was in and out of the zone pretty often. Lyle had once done some custom work on the kid's cargo trike, new shocks and some granny-gearing as he recalled, but he couldn't remember the kid's name. Lyle was terrible with names. "What's up, zude?"

"Hard night, Lyle?"

"Just real busy."

The kid's nose wrinkled at the stench from the shop. "Doin' a lot of paint work, huh?" He glanced at his palmtop notepad. "You still taking deliveries for Edward Dertouzas?"

"Yeah. I guess so." Lyle rubbed the gear tattoo on one stubbled cheek. "If I have to."

The kid offered a stylus, reaching up. "Can you sign for him?"

Lyle folded his bare arms warily. "Naw, man, I can't sign for Deep Eddy. Eddy's in Europe somewhere. Eddy left months ago. Haven't seen Eddy in ages."

The delivery kid scratched his sweating head below his billed fabric cap. He turned to check for any possible sneak-ups by snatch-and-grab artists out of the squatter warrens. The government simply refused to do postal delivery on the Thirty-second, Thirty-third, and Thirty-fourth floors. You never saw many cops inside the zone, either. Except for the city demolition crew, about the only official functionaries who ever showed up in the zone were a few psychotically empathetic NAFTA social workers.

"I'll get a bonus if you sign for this thing." The kid gazed up in squint-eyed appeal. "It's gotta be worth something, Lyle. It's a really weird kind of routing, they paid a lot of money to send it just that way."

Lyle crouched down in the open doorway. "Let's have a look at it."

The package was a heavy shockproof rectangle in heat-sealed plastic shrink-wrap, with a plethora of intra-European routing stickers. To judge by all the overlays, the package had been passed from postal system to postal system at least eight times before officially arriving in the legal custody of any human being. The return address, if there had ever been one, was completely obscured. Someplace in France, maybe.

Lyle held the box up two-handed to his ear and shook it. Hardware.

"You gonna sign, or not?"

"Yeah." Lyle scratched illegibly at the little signature panel, then looked at the delivery trike. "You oughta get that front wheel trued."

The kid shrugged. "Got anything to send out today?"

"Naw," Lyle grumbled, "I'm not doing mail-order repair work anymore; it's too complicated and I get ripped off too much."

"Suit yourself." The kid clambered into the recumbent seat of his trike and pedaled off across the heat-cracked ceramic tiles of the atrium plaza.

Lyle hung his hand-lettered OPEN FOR BUSINESS sign outside the door. He walked to his left, stamped up the pedaled lid of a jumbo garbage can, and dropped the package in with the rest of Dertouzas's stuff.

The can's lid wouldn't close. Deep Eddy's junk had finally reached critical mass. Deep Eddy never got much mail at the shop from other people, but he was always sending mail to himself. Big packets of encrypted diskettes were always arriving from Eddy's road jaunts in Toulouse, Marseilles, Valencia, and Nice. And especially Barcelona. Eddy had sent enough gigabyte-age out of Barcelona to outfit a pirate data-haven.

Eddy used Lyle's bike shop as his safety-deposit box. This arrangement was okay by Lyle. He owed Eddy; Eddy had installed the phones and virching in the bike shop, and had also wangled the shop's electrical hookup. A thick elastic curly-cable snaked out the access-crawlspace of Floor 35, right through the ceiling of Floor 34, and directly through a ragged punch-hole in the aluminum roof of Lyle's cable-mounted mobile home. Some unknown contact of Eddy's was paying the real bills on that electrical feed. Lyle cheerfully covered the expenses by paying cash into an anonymous post-office box. The setup was a rare and valuable contact with the world of organized authority.

During his stays in the shop, Eddy had spent much of his time buried in marathon long-distance virtuality sessions, swaddled head to foot in lumpy strap-on gear. Eddy had been painfully involved with some older woman in Germany. A virtual romance in its full-scale thumping, heaving, grappling progress was an embarrassment to witness. Under the circumstances, Lyle wasn't too surprised that Eddy had left his parents' condo to set up in a squat.

Eddy had lived in the bicycle repair shop, off and on, for almost a year. It had been a good deal for Lyle, because Deep Eddy had enjoyed a certain clout and prestige with the local squatters. Eddy had been a major organizer of the legendary Chattanooga Wende of December '35, a monster street-party that had climaxed in a spectacular looting-and-arson rampage that had torched the three floors of the Archiplat.

Lyle had gone to school with Eddy and had known him for years; they'd grown up together in the Archiplat. Eddy Dertouzas was a deep zude for a kid his age, with political contacts and heavy-duty network connections. The squat had been a good deal for both of them, until Eddy had finally coaxed the German woman into coming through for him in real life. Then Eddy had jumped the next plane to Europe.

Since they'd parted friends, Eddy was welcome to mail his European data-junk to the bike shop. After all, the disks were heavily encrypted, so it wasn't as if anybody in authority was ever gonna be able to read them. Storing a few thousand disks was a minor challenge, compared to Eddy's complex, machine-assisted love life.

After Eddy's sudden departure, Lyle had sold Eddy's possessions, and wired the money to Eddy in Spain. Lyle had kept the screen TV, Eddy's mediator, and the cheaper virching helmet. The way Lyle figured it — the way he remembered the deal — any stray hardware of Eddy's in the shop was rightfully his, for disposal at his own discretion. By now it was pretty clear that Deep Eddy Dertouzas was never coming back to Tennessee. And Lyle had certain debts.

Lyle snicked the blade from a roadkit multitool and cut open Eddy's package. It contained, of all things, a television cable settop box. A laughable infobahn antique. You'd never see a cablebox like that in NAFTA; this was the sort of primeval junk one might find in the home of a semiliterate Basque grandmother, or maybe in the armed bunker of some backward Albanian.

Lyle tossed the archaic cablebox onto the beanbag in front of the wallscreen. No time now for irrelevant media toys; he had to get on with real life. Lyle ducked into the tiny curtained privy and urinated at length into a crockery jar. He scraped his teeth with a flossing spudger and misted some fresh water onto his face and hands. He wiped clean with a towelette, then smeared his armpits, crotch, and feet with deodorant.

Back when he'd lived with his mom up on Floor 41, Lyle had used old-fashioned antiseptic deodorants. Lyle had wised up about a lot of things once he'd escaped his mom's condo. Nowadays, Lyle used a gel roll-on of skin-friendly bacteria that greedily devoured human sweat and exuded as their metabolic byproduct a pleasantly harmless reek rather like ripe bananas. Life was a lot easier when you came to proper terms with your microscopic flora.

Back at his workbench, Lyle plugged in the hot plate and boiled some Thai noodles with flaked sardines. He packed down breakfast with 400 cc's of Dr. Breasaire's Bioactive Bowel Putty. Then he checked last night's enamel job on the clamped frame in the workstand. The frame looked good. At three in the morning, Lyle was able to get into painted detail work with just the right kind of hallucinatory clarity.

Enameling paid well, and he needed the money bad. But this wasn't real bike work. It lacked authenticity. Enameling was all about the owner's ego—that was what really stank about enameling. There were a few rich kids up in the penthouse levels who were way into "street aesthetic," and would pay good money to have some treadhead decorate their machine. But flash art didn't help the bike. What helped the bike was frame alignment and sound cable-housings and proper tension in the derailleurs.

Lyle fitted the chain of his stationary bike to the shop's flywheel, straddled up, strapped on his gloves and virching helmet, and did half an hour on the 2033 Tour de France. He stayed back in the pack for the uphill grind, and then, for three glorious minutes, he broke free from the domestiques in the peloton and came right up at the shoulder of Aldo Cipollini. The champion was a monster, posthuman. Calves like cinderblocks. Even in a cheap simulation with no full-impact bodysuit, Lyle knew better than to try to take Cipollini.

Lyle devirched, checked his heart-rate record on the chronometer, then dismounted from his stationary trainer and drained a half-liter squeezebottle of antioxidant carbo refresher. Life had been easier when he'd had a partner in crime. The shop's flywheel was slowly losing its storage of inertia power these days, with just one zude pumping it.

Lyle's disastrous second roommate had come from the biking crowd. She was a criterium racer from Kentucky named Brigitte Rohannon. Lyle himself had been a wannabe criterium racer for a while, before he'd blown out a kidney on steroids. He hadn't expected any trouble from Brigitte, because Brigitte knew about bikes, and she needed his technical help for her racer, and she wouldn't mind pumping the flywheel, and besides, Brigitte was lesbian. In the training gym and out at racing events, Brigitte came across as a quiet and disciplined little politicized treadhead person.

Life inside the zone, though, massively fertilized Brigitte's eccentricities. First, she started breaking training. Then she stopped eating right. Pretty soon the shop was creaking and rocking with all-night girl-on-girl hot-oil sessions, which degenerated into hooting pill-orgies with heavily tattooed zone chyx who played klaxonized bongo music and beat each other up, and stole Lyle's tools. It had been a big relief when Brigitte finally left the zone to shack up with some well-to-do admirer on Floor 37. The debacle had left Lyle's tenuous finances in ruin.

Lyle laid down a new tracery of scarlet enamel on the bike's chainstay, seat post, and stem. He had to wait for the work to cure, so he left the workbench, picked up Eddy's settopper and popped the shell with a hexkey. Lyle was no electrician, but the insides looked harmless enough: lots of bit-eating caterpillars and cheap Algerian silicon.

He flicked on Eddy's mediator, to boot the wallscreen. Before he could try anything with the cablebox, his mother's mook pounced upon the screen. On Eddy's giant wallscreen, the mook's waxy, computer-generated face looked like a plump satin pillowcase. Its bowtie was as big as a racing shoe.

"Please hold for an incoming vidcall from Andrea Schweik of Carnac Instruments," the mook uttered unctuously.

Lyle cordially despised all low-down, phone-tagging, artificially intelligent mooks. For a while, in his teenage years, Lyle himself had owned a mook, an off-the-shelf shareware job that he'd installed in the condo's phone. Like most mooks, Lyle's mook had one primary role: dealing with unsolicited phone calls from other people's mooks. In Lyle's case these were the creepy mooks of career counselors, school psychiatrists, truancy cops, and other official hindrances. When Lyle's mook launched and ran, it appeared online as a sly warty dwarf that drooled green ichor and talked in a basso grumble.

But Lyle hadn't given his mook the properly meticulous care and debugging that such fragile little constructs demanded, and eventually his cheap mook had collapsed into artificial insanity.

Once Lyle had escaped his mom's place to the squat, he had gone for the low-tech gambit and simply left his phone unplugged most of the time. But that was no real solution. He couldn't hide from his mother's capable and well-financed corporate mook, which watched with sleepless mechanical patience for the least flicker of video dialtone off Lyle's number.

Lyle sighed and wiped the dust from the video nozzle on Eddy's mediator.

"Your mother is coming online right away," the mook assured him.

"Yeah, sure," Lyle muttered, smearing his hair into some semblance of order.

"She specifically instructed me to page her remotely at any time for an immediate response. She really wants to chat with you, Lyle."

"That's just great." Lyle couldn't remember what his mother's mook called itself. "Mr. Billy," or "Mr. Ripley," or something else really stupid.

"Did you know that Marco Cengialta has just won the Liege Summer Classic?"

Lyle blinked and sat up in the beanbag. "Yeah?"

"Mr. Cengialta used a three-spoked ceramic wheel with internal liquid weighting and buckyball hubshocks." The mook paused, politely awaiting a possible conversational response. "He wore breathe-thru kevlar microlock cleatshoes," it added.

Lyle hated the way a mook cataloged your personal interests and then generated relevant conversation. The machine-made intercourse was completely unhuman and yet perversely interesting, like being grabbed and buttonholed by a glossy magazine ad. It had probably taken his mother's mook all of three seconds to snag and download every conceivable statistic about the summer race in Liege.

His mother came on. She'd caught him during lunch in her office. "Lyle?"

"Hi, Mom." Lyle sternly reminded himself that this was the one person in the world who might conceivably put up bail for him. "What's on your mind?"

"Oh, nothing much, just the usual." Lyle's mother shoved aside her platter of sprouts and tilapia. "I was idly wondering if you were still alive."

"Mom, it's a lot less dangerous in a squat than landlords and cops would have you believe. I'm perfectly fine. You can see that for yourself."

His mother lifted a pair of secretarial half-spex on a neckchain, and gave Lyle the computer-assisted once-over.

Lyle pointed the mediator's lens at the shop's aluminum door. "See over there, Mom? I got myself a shock-baton in here. If I get any trouble from anybody, I'll just yank that club off the doormount and give the guy fifteen thousand volts!"

"Is that legal, Lyle?"

"Sure. The voltage won't kill you or anything, it just knocks you out a good long time. I traded a good bike for that shock-baton, it's got a lot of useful defensive features."

"That sounds really dreadful."

'The baton's harmless, Mom. You should see what the cops carry nowadays."

"Are you still taking those injections, Lyle?"

"Which injections?"

She frowned. "You know which ones."

Lyle shrugged. "The treatments are perfectly safe. They're a lot safer than a lifestyle of cruising for dates, that's for sure."

"Especially dates with the kind of girls who live down there in the riot zone, I suppose." His mother winced. "I had some hopes when you took up with that nice bike-racer girl. Brigitte, wasn't it? Whatever happened to her?"

Lyle shook his head. "Someone with your gender and background oughta understand how important the treatments are, Mom. It's a basic reproductive-freedom issue. Antilibidinals give you real freedom, freedom from the urge to reproduce. You should be glad I'm not sexually involved."

"I don't mind that you're not involved, Lyle, it's just that it seems like a real cheat that you're not even *interested*."

"But, Mom, nobody's interested in me, either. Nobody. No woman is banging at my door to have sex with a self-employed fanatical dropout bike mechanic who lives in a slum. If that ever happens, you'll be the first to know."

Lyle grinned cheerfully into the lens. "I had girlfriends back when I was in racing. I've been there, Mom. I've done that. Unless you're coked to the gills with hormones, sex is a major waste of your time and attention. Sexual Deliberation is the greatest civil-liberties movement of modern times."

"That's really weird, Lyle. It's just not natural."

"Mom, forgive me, but you're not the one to talk about natural, okay? You grew me from a zygote when you were fifty-five." He shrugged. "I'm too busy for romance now. I just want to learn about bikes."

"You were working with bikes when you lived here with me. You had a real job and a safe home where you could take regular showers."

"Sure, I was working, but I never said I wanted a *job,* Mom. I said I wanted to *learn about bikes.* There's a big difference! I can't be a loser wage-slave for some lousy bike franchise."

His mother said nothing.

"Mom, I'm not asking you for any favors. I don't need any bosses, or any teachers, or any landlords, or any cops. It's just me and my bike work down here. I know that people in authority can't stand it that a twenty-four-year-old man lives an independent life and does exactly what he wants, but I'm being very quiet and discreet about it, so nobody needs to bother about me."

His mother sighed, defeated. "Are you eating properly, Lyle? You look peaked."

Lyle lifted his calf muscle into camera range. "Look at this leg! Does that look like the gastrocnemius of a weak and sickly person?"

"Could you come up to the condo and have a decent meal with me sometime?"

Lyle blinked. "When?"

"Wednesday, maybe? We could have pork chops."

"Maybe, Mom. Probably. I'll have to check. I'll get back to you, okay? Bye." Lyle hung up.

Hooking the mediator's cable to the primitive settop box was a problem, but Lyle was not one to be stymied by a merely mechanical challenge. The enamel job had to wait as he resorted to miniclamps and a cable cutter. It was a handy thing that working with modern brake cabling had taught him how to splice fiber optics.

When the settop box finally came online, its array of services was a joke. Any decent modern mediator could navigate through vast information spaces, but the settop box offered nothing but "channels." Lyle had forgotten that you could even obtain old fashioned "channels" from the city fiber-feed in Chattanooga. But these channels were government-sponsored media, and the government was always quite a ways behind the curve in network development. Chattanooga's huge fiber-bandwidth still carried the ancient government-mandated "public access channels," spooling away in their technically fossilized obscurity, far below the usual gaudy carnival of popular virching, infobahnage, demo-splintered comboards, public-service rants, mudtrufflage, remsnorkeling, and commercials.

The little settop box accessed nothing but political channels. Three of them: Legislative, Judicial, and Executive. And that was the sum total, apparently. A settop box that offered nothing but NAFTA political coverage. On the Legislative Channel there was some kind of parliamentary debate on proper land use in Manitoba. On the Judicial Channel, a lawyer was haranguing judges about the stock market for air-pollution rights. On the Executive Channel, a big crowd of hicks were idly standing around on windblown tarmac somewhere in Louisiana waiting for something to happen.

The box didn't offer any glimpse of politics in Europe or the Sphere or the South. There were no hotspots or pips or index tagging. You couldn't look stuff up or annotate it—you just had to passively watch whatever the channel's masters chose to show you, whenever they chose to show it. This media setup was so insultingly lame and halt and primitive that it was almost perversely interesting. Kind of like peering through keyholes.

Lyle left the box on the Executive Channel, because it looked conceivable that something might actually happen there. It had swiftly become clear to him that the intolerably monotonous fodder on the other two channels was about as exciting as those channels ever got. Lyle retreated to his workbench and got back to enamel work.

At length, the President of NAFTA arrived and decamped from his helicopter on the tarmac in Louisiana. A swarm of presidential bodyguards materialized out of the expectant crowd, looking simultaneously extremely busy and icily imperturbable.

Suddenly a line of text flickered up at the bottom of the screen. The text was set in a very old-fashioned computer font, chalk-white letters with little visible jagged pixel-edges *"Look at him hunting for that camera mark,"* the subtitle read as it scrolled across the screen. *"Why wasn't he briefed properly? He looks like a stray dog!"*

The President meandered amiably across the sun-blistered tarmac, gazing from side to side, and then stopped briefly to shake the eager outstretched hand of a local politician. *"That must have hurt,"* commented the text. *"That Cajun dolt is poison in the polls."* The President chatted amiably with the local politician and an elderly harridan in a purple dress who seemed to be the man's wife. *"Get him away from those losers!"* raged the subtitle. *"Get the Man up to the podium, for the love of Mike! Where's the Chief of Staff? Doped up on so-called smart drugs as usual? Get with your jobs, people!"*

The President looked well. Lyle had noticed that the President of NAFTA always looked well, it seemed to be a professional requirement. The big political cheeses in Europe always looked somber and intellectual, and the Sphere people always looked humble and dedicated, and the South people always looked angry and fanatical, but the NAFTA prez always looked like he'd just done a few laps in a pool and had a brisk rubdown. His large, glossy, bluffly cheerful face was discreetly stenciled with tattoos: both cheeks, a chorus line of tats on his forehead above both eyebrows, plus a few extra logos on his rocklike chin. A President's face was the ultimate billboard for major backers and interest groups.

"Does he think we have all day?" the text demanded. *"What's with this dead air time? Can't anyone properly arrange a media event these days? You call this public access? You call this informing the electorate? If we'd known the infobahn would come to this, we'd have never built the thing!"*

The President meandered amiably to a podium covered with ceremonial microphones. Lyle had noticed that politicians always used a big healthy cluster of traditional big fat microphones, even though nowadays you could build working microphones the size of a grain of rice.

"Hey, how y'all?" asked the President, grinning.

The crowd chorused back at him, with ragged enthusiasm.

"Let these fine folks up a bit closer," the President ordered suddenly, waving airily at his phalanx of bodyguards. "Y'all come on up closer, everybody! Sit right on the ground, we're all just folks here today." The President smiled benignly as the sweating, straw-hatted summer crowd hustled up to join him, scarcely believing their luck.

"Marietta and I just had a heck of a fine lunch down in Opelousas," commented the President, patting his flat, muscular belly. He deserted the fiction of his official podium to energetically press the Louisianan flesh. As he moved from hand to grasping hand, his every word was picked up infallibly by an invisible mike, probably implanted in one of his molars. "We had dirty rice, red beans —were they hot!—and crawdads big enough to body-slam a Maine lobster!" He chuckled. "What a sight them mudbugs were! Can y'all believe that?"

The President's guards were unobtrusively but methodically working the crowd with portable detectors and sophisticated spex equipment. They didn't look very concerned by the President's supposed change in routine.

"*I see he's gonna run with the usual genetics malarkey,*" commented the subtitle.

"Y'all have got a perfect right to be mighty proud of the agriculture in this state," intoned the President. "Y'all's agro-science know-how is second to none! Sure, I know there's a few pointy-headed Luddites up in the snowbelt, who say they prefer their crawdads dinky."

Everyone laughed.

"Folks, I got nothin' against that attitude. If some jasper wants to spend his hard-earned money buyin' and peelin' and shuckin' those little dinky ones, that's all right by me and Marietta. Ain't that right, honey?"

The First Lady smiled and waved one power-gloved hand.

"But folks, you and I both know that those whiners who waste our time complaining about 'natural food' have never sucked a mudbug head in their lives! 'Natural,' my left elbow! Who are they tryin' to kid? Just 'cause you're country, don't mean you can't hack DNA!"

"*He's been working really hard on the regional accents,*" commented the text. "*Not bad for a guy from Minnesota. But look at that sloppy, incompetent camera work! Doesn't anybody care anymore? What on earth is happening to our standards?*"

By lunchtime, Lyle had the final coat down on the enameling job. He ate a bowl of triticale mush and chewed up a mineral-rich handful of iodized sponge.

Then he settled down in front of the wallscreen to work on the inertia brake. Lyle knew there was big money in the inertia brake — for somebody, somewhere, sometime. The device smelled like the future.

Lyle tucked a jeweler's loupe in one eye and toyed methodically with the brake. He loved the way the piezoplastic clamp and rim transmuted braking energy into electrical battery storage. At last, a way to capture the energy you lost in braking and put it to solid use. It was almost, but not quite, magical.

The way Lyle figured it, there was gonna be a big market someday for an inertia brake that captured energy and then fed it back through the chaindrive in a way that just felt like human pedaling energy, in a direct and intuitive and muscular way, not chunky and buzzy like some loser battery-powered moped. If the system worked out right, it would make the rider feel completely natural and yet subtly superhuman at the same time. And it had to be simple, the kind of system a shop guy could fix with hand tools. It wouldn't work if it was too brittle and fancy, it just wouldn't feel like an authentic bike.

Lyle had a lot of ideas about the design. He was pretty sure he could get a real grip on the problem, if only he weren't being worked to death just keeping the shop going. If he could get enough capital together to assemble the prototypes and do some serious field tests.

It would have to be chip-driven, of course, but true to the biking spirit at the same time. A lot of bikes had chips in them nowadays, in the shocks or the braking or in reactive hubs, but bicycles simply weren't like computers. Computers were black boxes inside, no big visible working parts. People, by contrast, got sentimental about their bike gear. People were strangely reticent and traditional about bikes. That's why the bike market had never really gone for recumbents, even though the recumbent design had a big mechanical advantage. People didn't like their bikes too complicated. They didn't want bicycles to bitch and complain and whine for attention and constant upgrading the way that computers did. Bikes were too personal. People wanted their bikes to wear.

Someone banged at the shop door.

Lyle opened it. Down on the tiling by the barrels stood a tall brunette woman in stretch shorts, with a short-sleeve blue pullover and a ponytail. She had a bike under one arm, an old lacquer-and-paper-framed Taiwanese job. "Are you Edward Dertouzas?" she said, gazing up at him.

"No," Lyle said patiently. "Eddy's in Europe."

She thought this over. "I'm new in the zone," she confessed. "Can you fix this bike for me? I just bought it secondhand and I think it kinda needs some work."

"Sure," Lyle said. "You came to the right guy for that job, ma'am, because Eddy Dertouzas couldn't fix a bike for hell. Eddy just used to live here. I'm the guy who actually owns this shop. Hand the bike up."

Lyle crouched down, got a grip on the handlebar stem and hauled the bike into the shop. The woman gazed up at him respectfully. "What's your name?"

"Lyle Schweik."

"I'm Kitty Casaday." She hesitated. "Could I come up inside there?"

Lyle reached down, gripped her muscular wrist, and hauled her up into the shop. She wasn't all that good looking, but she was in really good shape — like a mountain biker or triathlon runner. She looked about thirty-five. It was hard to tell, exactly. Once people got into cosmetic surgery and serious bio-mainte-nance, it got pretty hard to judge their age. Unless you got a good, close medical exam of their eyelids and cuticles and internal membranes and such.

She looked around the shop with great interest, brown ponytail twitching.

"Where you hail from?" Lyle asked her. He had already forgotten her name.

"Well, I'm originally from Juneau, Alaska."

"Canadian, huh? Great. Welcome to Tennessee."

"Actually, Alaska used to be part of the United States."

"You're kidding," Lyle said. "Hey, I'm no historian, but I've seen Alaska on a map before."

"You've got a whole working shop and everything built inside this old place! That's really something, Mr. Schweik. What's behind that curtain?"

"The spare room," Lyle said. "That's where my roommate used to stay."

She glanced up. "Dertouzas?"

"Yeah, him."

"Who's in there now?"

"Nobody," Lyle said sadly. "I got some storage stuff in there."

She nodded slowly, and kept looking around, apparently galvanized with curiosity. "What are you running on that screen?"

"Hard to say, really," Lyle said. He crossed the room, bent down and switched off the settop box. "Some kind of weird political crap."

He began examining her bike. All its serial numbers had been removed. Typical zone bike.

"The first thing we got to do," he said briskly, "is fit it to you properly: set the saddle height, pedal stroke, and handlebars. Then I'll adjust the tension, true the wheels, check the brakepads and suspension valves, tune the shifting, and lubricate the drivetrain. The usual. You're gonna need a better saddle than this — this saddle's for a male pelvis." He looked up. "You got a charge card?"

She nodded, then frowned. "But I don't have much credit left."

"No problem." He flipped open a dog-eared catalog. "This is what you need. Any halfway decent gel-saddle. Pick one you like, and we can have it shipped in by tomorrow morning. And then" — he flipped pages — "order me one of these."

She stepped closer and examined the page. "The 'cotterless crank-bolt ceramic wrench set,' is that it?"

"That's right. I fix your bike, you give me those tools, and we're even."

"Okay. Sure. That's cheap!" She smiled at him. "I like the way you do business, Lyle."

"You'll get used to barter, if you stay in the zone long enough."

"I've never lived in a squat before," she said thoughtfully. "I like the attitude here, but people say that squats are pretty dangerous."

"I dunno about the squats in other towns, but Chattanooga squats aren't dangerous, unless you think anarchists are dangerous, and anarchists aren't dangerous unless they're really drunk." Lyle shrugged. "People will steal your stuff all the time, that's about the worst part. There's a couple of tough guys around here who claim they have handguns. I never saw anybody actually use a handgun. Old guns aren't hard to find, but it takes a real chemist to make working ammo nowadays." He smiled back at her. "Anyway, you look to me like you can take care of yourself."

"I take dance classes."

Lyle nodded. He opened a drawer and pulled a tape measure.

"I saw all those cables and pulleys you have on top of this place. You can pull the whole building right up off the ground, huh? Kind of hang it right off the ceiling up there."

"That's right, it saves a lot of trouble with people breaking and entering." Lyle glanced at his shock-baton, in its mounting at the door. She followed his gaze to the weapon and then looked at him, impressed.

Lyle measured her arms, torso length, then knelt and measured her inseam from crotch to floor. He took notes. "Okay," he said. "Come by tomorrow afternoon."

"Lyle?"

"Yeah?" He stood up.

"Do you rent this place out? I really need a safe place to stay in the zone."

"I'm sorry," Lyle said politely, "but I hate landlords and I'd never be one. What I need is a roommate who can really get behind the whole concept of my shop. Someone who's qualified, you know, to develop my infrastructure or do bicycle work. Anyway, if I took your cash or charged you for rent, then the tax people would just have another excuse to harass me."

"Sure, okay, but..." She paused, then looked at him under lowered eyelids. "I've gotta be a lot better than having this place go empty."

Lyle stated at her, astonished.

"I'm a pretty useful woman to have around, Lyle. Nobody's ever complained before."

"Really?"

"That's right." She stared at him boldly.

"I'll think about your offer," Lyle said. "What did you say your name was?"

"I'm Kitty. Kitty Casaday."

"Kitty, I got a whole lot of work to do today, but I'll see you tomorrow, okay?"

"Okay, Lyle." She smiled. "You think about me, all right?"

Lyle helped her down out of the shop. He watched her stride away across the atrium until she vanished through the crowded doorway of the Crowbar, a squat coffeeshop. Then he called his mother.

"Did you forget something?" his mother said, looking up from her workscreen.

"Mom, I know this is really hard to believe, but a strange woman just banged on my door and offered to have sex with me."

"You're kidding, right?"

"In exchange for room and board, I think. Anyway, I said you'd be the first to know if it happened."

"Lyle — " His mother hesitated. "Lyle, I think you better come right home. Let's make that dinner date for tonight, okay? We'll have a little talk about this situation."

"Yeah, okay. I got an enameling job I gotta deliver to Floor 41, anyway."

"I don't have a positive feeling about this development, Lyle."

"That's okay, Mom. I'll see you tonight."

Lyle reassembled the newly enameled bike. Then he set the flywheel onto remote, and stepped outside the shop. He mounted the bike, and touched a password into the remote control. The shop faithfully reeled itself far out of reach and hung there in space below the fire-blackened ceiling, swaying gently.

Lyle pedaled away, back toward the elevators, back toward the neighborhood where he'd grown up.

He delivered the bike to the delighted young idiot who'd commissioned it, stuffed the cash in his shoes, and then went down to his mother's. He took a shower, shaved, and shampooed thoroughly. They had pork chops and grits and got drunk together. His mother complained about the breakup with her third husband and wept bitterly, but not as much as usual when this topic came up. Lyle got the strong impression she was thoroughly on the mend and would be angling for number four in pretty short order.

Around midnight, Lyle refused his mother's ritual offers of new clothes and fresh leftovers, and headed back down to the zone. He was still a little clubfooted from his mother's sherry, and he stood breathing beside the broken glass of the atrium wall, gazing out at the city-smeared summer stars. The cavernous darkness inside the zone at night was one of his favorite things about the place. The queasy 24-hour security lighting in the rest of the Archiplat had never been rebuilt inside the zone.

The zone always got livelier at night when all the normal people started sneaking in to cruise the zone's unlicensed dives and nightspots, but all that activity took place behind discreetly closed doors. Enticing squiggles of red and blue chemglow here and there only enhanced the blessed unnatural gloom.

Lyle pulled his remote control and ordered the shop back down.

The door of the shop had been broken open.

Lyle's latest bike-repair client lay sprawled on the floor of the shop, unconscious. She was wearing black military fatigues, a knit cap, and rappelling gear.

She had begun her break-in at Lyle's establishment by pulling his shock-baton out of its glowing security socket beside the doorframe. The booby-trapped baton had immediately put fifteen thousand volts through her, and sprayed her face with a potent mix of dye and street-legal incapacitants.

Lyle turned the baton off with the remote control, and then placed it carefully back in its socket. His surprise guest was still breathing, but was clearly in real metabolic distress. He tried clearing her nose and mouth with a tissue. The guys who'd sold him the baton hadn't been kidding about the "indelible" part. Her face and throat were drenched with green and her chest looked like a spin-painting.

Her elaborate combat spex had partially shielded her eyes. With the spex off she looked like a viridian-green raccoon.

Lyle tried stripping her gear off in conventional fashion, realized this wasn't going to work, and got a pair of metal-shears from the shop. He snipped his way through the eerily writhing power-gloves and the kevlar laces of the pneumo-reactive combat boots. Her black turtleneck had an abrasive surface and a cuirass over chest and back that looked like it could stop small-arms fire.

The trousers had nineteen separate pockets and they were loaded with all kinds of eerie little items: a matte-black electrode stun-weapon, flash capsules, fingerprint dust, a utility pocketknife, drug adhesives, plastic handcuffs, some pocket change, worry beads, a comb, and a makeup case.

Close inspection revealed a pair of tiny microphone amplifiers inserted in her ear canals. Lyle fetched the tiny devices out with needlenose pliers. Lyle was getting pretty seriously concerned by this point. He shackled her arms and legs with bike security cable, in case she regained consciousness and attempted something superhuman.

Around four in the morning she had a coughing fit and began shivering violently. Summer nights could get pretty cold in the shop. Lyle thought over the design problem for some time, and then fetched a big heat-reflective blanket out of the empty room. He cut a neat poncho-hole in the center of it, and slipped her head through it. He got the bike cables off her—she could probably slip the cables anyway—and sewed all four edges of the blanket shut from the outside, with sturdy monofilament thread from his saddle-stitcher. He sewed the poncho edges to a tough fabric belt, cinched the belt snugly around her neck, and padlocked it. When he was done, he'd made a snug bag that contained her entire body, except for her head, which had begun to drool and snore.

A fat blob of superglue on the bottom of the bag kept her anchored to the shop's floor. The blanket was cheap but tough upholstery fabric. If she could rip her way through blanket fabric with her fingernails alone, then he was probably a goner anyway. By now, Lyle was tired and stone sober. He had a squeezebottle of glucose rehydrator, three aspirins, and a canned chocolate pudding. Then he climbed in his hammock and went to sleep.

Lyle woke up around ten. His captive was sitting up inside the bag, her green face stony, eyes red-rimmed and brown hair caked with dye. Lyle got up, dressed, ate breakfast, and fixed the broken door-lock. He said nothing, partly because he thought that silence would shake her up, but mostly because he couldn't remember her name. He was almost sure it wasn't her real name anyway.

When he'd finished fixing the door, he reeled up the string of the door-knocker so that it was far out of reach. He figured the two of them needed the privacy.

Then Lyle deliberately fired up the wallscreen and turned on the settop box. As soon as the peculiar subtitles started showing up again, she grew agitated.

"Who are you really?" she demanded at last.

"Ma'am, I'm a bicycle repairman."

She snorted.

"I guess I don't need to know your name," he said, "but I need to know who your people are, and why they sent you here, and what I've got to do to get out of this situation."

"You're not off to a good start, mister."

"No," he said, "maybe not, but you're the one who's blown it. I'm just a twenty-four-year-old bicycle repairman from Tennessee. But you, you've got enough specialized gear on you to buy my whole place five times over."

He flipped open the little mirror in her makeup case and showed her her own face. Her scowl grew a little stiffer below the spattering of green.

"I want you to tell me what's going on here," he said.

"Forget it."

"If you're waiting for your backup to come rescue you, I don't think they're coming," Lyle said. "I searched you very thoroughly and I've opened up every single little gadget you had, and I took all the batteries out. I'm not even sure what some of those things are or how they work, but hey, I know what a battery is. It's been hours now. So I don't think your backup people even know where you are."

She said nothing.

"See," he said, "you've really blown it bad. You got caught by a total amateur, and now you're in a hostage situation that could go on indefinitely. I got enough water and noodles and sardines to live up here for days. I dunno, maybe you can make a cellular phone-call to God off some gizmo implanted in your thighbone, but it looks to me like you've got serious problems."

She shuffled around a bit inside the bag and looked away.

"It's got something to do with the cablebox over there, right?"

She said nothing.

"For what it's worth, I don't think that box has anything to do with me or Eddy Dertouzas," Lyle said. "I think it was probably meant for Eddy, but I don't think he asked anybody for it. Somebody just wanted him to have it, probably one of his weird European contacts. Eddy used to be in this political group called CAPCLUG, ever heard of them?"

It looked pretty obvious that she'd heard of them.

"I never liked 'em much either," Lyle told her. "They kind of snagged me at first with their big talk about freedom and civil liberties, but then you'd go to a CAPCLUG meeting up in the penthouse levels, and there were all these pot-bellied zudes in spex yapping off stuff like, 'We must follow the technological imperatives or be jettisoned into the history dump-file.' They're a bunch of useless blowhards who can't tie their own shoes."

"They're dangerous radicals subverting national sovereignty."

Lyle blinked cautiously. "Whose national sovereignty would that be?"

"Yours, mine, Mr. Schweik. I'm from NAFTA, I'm a federal agent."

"You're a fed? How come you're breaking into people's houses, then? Isn't that against the Fourth Amendment or something?"

"If you mean the Fourth Amendment to the Constitution of the United States, that document was superseded years ago."

"Yeah...okay, I guess you're right." Lyle shrugged. "I missed a lot of civics classes.... No skin off my back anyway. I'm sorry, but what did you say your name was?"

"I said my name was Kitty Casaday."

"Right. Kitty. Okay, Kitty, just you and me, person to person. We obviously have a mutual problem here. What do you think I ought to do in this situation? I mean, speaking practically."

Kitty thought it over, surprised. "Mr. Schweik, you should release me immediately, get me my gear, and give me the box and any related data, recordings, or diskettes. Then you should escort me from the Archiplat in some confidential fashion so I won't be stopped by police and questioned about the dye-stains. A new set of clothes would be very useful."

"Like that, huh?"

"That's your wisest course of action." Her eyes narrowed. "I can't make any promises, but it might affect your future treatment very favorably."

"You're not gonna tell me who you are, or where you came from, or who sent you, or what this is all about?"

"No. Under no circumstances. I'm not allowed to reveal that. You don't need to know. You're not supposed to know. And anyway, if you're really what you say you are, what should you care?"

"Plenty. I care plenty. I can't wander around the rest of my life wondering when you're going to jump me out of a dark corner."

"If I'd wanted to hurt you, I'd have hurt you when we first met, Mr. Schweik. There was no one here but you and me, and I could have easily incapacitated you and taken anything I wanted. Just give me the box and the data and stop trying to interrogate me."

"Suppose you found me breaking into your house, Kitty? What would you do to me?"

She said nothing.

"What you're telling me isn't gonna work. If you don't tell me what's really going on here," Lyle said heavily, "I'm gonna have to get tough."

Her lips thinned in contempt.

"Okay, you asked for this." Lyle opened the mediator and made a quick voice call. "Pete?"

"Nah, this is Pete's mook," the phone replied. "Can I do something for you?"

"Could you tell Pete that Lyle Schweik has some big trouble, and I need him to come over to my bike shop immediately? And bring some heavy muscle from the Spiders."

"What kind of big trouble, Lyle?"

"Authority trouble. A lot of it. I can't say any more. I think this line may be tapped."

"Right-o. I'll make that happen. Hoo-ah, zude." The mook hung up.

Lyle left the beanbag and went back to the workbench. He took Kitty's cheap bike out of the repair stand and angrily threw it aside. "You know what really bugs me?" he said at last. "You couldn't even bother to charm your way in here, set yourself up as my roommate, and then steal the damn box. You didn't even respect me that much. Heck, you didn't even have to steal anything, Kitty. You could have just smiled and asked nicely and I'd have given you the box to play with. I don't watch media, I hate all that crap."

"It was an emergency. There was no time for more extensive investigation or reconnaissance. I think you should call your gangster friends immediately and tell them you've made a mistake. Tell them not to come here."

"You're ready to talk seriously?"

"No, I won't be talking."

"Okay, we'll see."

After twenty minutes, Lyle's phone rang. He answered it cautiously, keeping the video off. It was Pete from the City Spiders. "Zude, where is your doorknocker?"

"Oh, sorry, I pulled it up, didn't want to be disturbed. I'll bring the shop right down." Lyle thumbed the brake switches.

Lyle opened the door and Pete broad-jumped into the shop. Pete was a big man but he had the skeletal, wiry build of a climber, bare dark arms and shins and big sticky-toed jumping shoes. He had a sleeveless leather bodysuit full of clips and snaps, and he carried a big fabric shoulderbag. There were six vivid tattoos on the dark skin of his left cheek, under the black stubble.

Pete looked at Kitty, lifted his spex with wiry callused fingers, looked at her again bare-eyed, and put the spex back in place. "Wow, Lyle."

"Yeah."

"I never thought you were into anything this sick and twisted."

"It's a serious matter, Pete."

Pete turned to the door, crouched down, and hauled a second person into the shop. She wore a beat-up air-conditioned jacket and long slacks and zip-sided boots and wire-rimmed spex. She had short ratty hair under a green cloche hat. "Hi," she said, sticking out a hand. "I'm Mabel. We haven't met."

"I'm Lyle." Lyle gestured. "This is Kitty here in the bag."

"You said you needed somebody heavy, so I brought Mabel along," said Pete. "Mabel's a social worker."

"Looks like you pretty much got things under control here," said Mabel liltingly, scratching her neck and looking about the place. "What happened? She break into your shop?"

"Yeah."

"And," Pete said, "she grabbed the shock-baton first thing and blasted herself but good?"

"Exactly."

"I told you that thieves always go for the weaponry first," Pete said, grinning and scratching his armpit. "Didn't I tell you that? Leave a weapon in plain sight, man, a thief can't stand it, it's the very first thing they gotta grab." He laughed. "Works every time."

"Pete's from the City Spiders," Lyle told Kitty. "His people built this shop for me. One dark night, they hauled this mobile home right up thirty-four stories in total darkness, straight up the side of the Archiplat without anybody seeing, and they cut a big hole through the side of the building without making any noise, and they hauled the whole shop through it. Then they sank explosive bolts through the girders and hung it up here for me in midair. The City Spiders are into sport-climbing the way I'm into bicycles, only, like, they are very *seriously* into climbing and there are *lots* of them. They were some of the very first people to squat the zone, and they've lived here ever since, and they are pretty good friends of mine."

Pete sank to one knee and looked Kitty in the eye. "I love breaking into places, don't you? There's no thrill like some quick and perfectly executed break-in." He reached casually into his shoulderbag. "The thing is"—he pulled out a camera—to be sporting, you can't steal anything. You just take trophy pictures to prove you were there." He snapped her picture several times, grinning as she flinched.

"Lady," he breathed at her, "once you've turned into a little wicked greedhead, and mixed all that evil cupidity and possessiveness into the beauty of the direct action, then you've prostituted our way of life. You've gone and spoiled our sport." Pete stood up. "We City Spiders don't like common thieves. And we especially don't like thieves who break into the places of clients of ours, like Lyle here. And we thoroughly, especially, don't like thieves who are so brickhead dumb that they get caught red-handed on the premises of friends of ours."

Pete's hairy brows knotted in thought. "What I'd like to do here, Lyle ol' buddy," he announced, "is wrap up your little friend head to foot in nice tight cabling, smuggle her out of here down to Golden Gate Archiplat — you know, the big one downtown over by MLK and Highway Twenty-seven? — and hang her head-down in the center of the cupola."

"That's not very nice," Mabel told him seriously.

Pete looked wounded. "I'm not gonna charge him for it or anything! Just imagine her, spinning up there beautifully with all those chandeliers and those hundreds of mirrors."

Mabel knelt and looked into Kitty's face. "Has she had any water since she was knocked unconscious?"

"No."

"Well, for heaven's sake, give the poor woman something to drink, Lyle."

Lyle handed Mabel a bike-tote squeezebottle of electrolyte refresher. "You zudes don't grasp the situation yet," he said. "Look at all this stuff I took off her." He showed them the spex, and the boots, and the stun-gun, and the gloves, and the carbon-nitride climbing plectra, and the rappelling gear.

"Wow," Pete said at last, dabbing at buttons on his spex to study the finer detail, "this is no ordinary burglar! She's gotta be, like, a street samurai from the Mahogany Warbirds or something!"

"She says she's a federal agent."

Mabel stood up suddenly, angrily yanking the squeezebottle from Kitty's lips. "You're kidding, right?"

"Ask her."

"I'm a grade-five social counselor with the Department of Urban Redevelopment," Mabel said. She presented Kitty with an official ID. "And who are you with?"

"I'm not prepared to divulge that information at this time."

"I can't believe this," Mabel marveled, tucking her dog-eared hologram ID back in her hat. "You've caught somebody from one of those nutty reactionary secret black-bag units. I mean, that's gotta be what's just happened here." She shook her head slowly. "Y'know, if you work in government, you always hear horror stories about these right-wing paramilitary wackos, but I've never actually seen one before."

"It's a very dangerous world out there, Miss Social Counselor."

"Oh, tell me about it," Mabel scoffed. "I've worked suicide hotlines! I've been a hostage negotiator! I'm a career social worker, girlfriend! I've seen more horror and suffering than you *ever* will. While you were doing push-ups in some comfy cracker training-camp, I've been out here in the real world!" Mabel absently unscrewed the top from the bike bottle and had a long glug. "What on earth are you doing trying to raid the squat of a bicycle repairman?"

Kitty's stony silence lengthened.

"It's got something to do with that settop box," Lyle offered. "It showed up here in delivery yesterday, and then she showed up just a few hours later. Started flirting with me, and said she wanted to live in here. Of course I got suspicious right away."

"Naturally," Pete said. "Real bad move, Kitty. Lyle's on antilibidinals."

Kitty stared at Lyle bitterly. "I see," she said at last. "So that's what you get, when you drain all the sex out of one of them... You get a strange malodorous creature that spends all its time working in the garage."

Mabel flushed. "Did you hear that?" She gave Kitty's bag a sharp angry yank. "What conceivable right do you have to question this citizen's sexual orientation? Especially after cruelly trying to sexually manipulate him to abet your illegal purposes? Have you lost all sense of decency? You...you should be sued."

"Do your worst," Kitty muttered.

"Maybe I will," Mabel said grimly. "Sunlight is the best disinfectant."

"Yeah, let's string her up somewhere real sunny and public and call a bunch of news crews," Pete said. "I'm way hot for this deep ninja gear! Me and the Spiders got real mojo uses for these telescopic ears, and the tracer dust, and the epoxy bugging devices. And the press-on climbing-claws. And the carbon-fiber rope. Everything, really! Everything except these big-ass military shoes of hers, which really suck."

"Hey, all that stuff's mine," Lyle said sternly. "I saw it first."

"Yeah, I guess so, but.... Okay, Lyle, you make us a deal on the gear, we'll forget everything you still owe us for doing the shop."

"Come on, those combat spex are worth more than this place all by themselves."

"I'm real interested in that settop box," Mabel said cruelly. "It doesn't look too fancy or complicated. Let's take it over to those dirty circuit zudes who hang out at the Blue Parrot, and see if they can't reverse-engineer it. We'll post all the schematics up on twenty or thirty progressive activist networks, and see what falls out of cyberspace."

Kitty glared at her. "The terrible consequences from that stupid and irresponsible action would be entirely on your head."

"I'll risk it," Mabel said airily, patting her cloche hat. "It might bump my soft little liberal head a bit, but I'm pretty sore it would crack your nasty little fascist head like a coconut."

Suddenly Kitty began thrashing and kicking her way furiously inside the bag. They watched with interest as she ripped, tore, and lashed out with powerful side and front kicks. Nothing much happened.

"All right," she said at last, panting in exhaustion. "I've come from Senator Creighton's office."

"Who?" Lyle said.

"Creighton! Senator James P. Creighton, the man who's been your Senator from Tennessee for the past thirty years!"

"Oh," Lyle said. "I hadn't noticed."

"We're anarchists," Pete told her.

"I've sure heard of the nasty old geezer," Mabel said, "but I'm from British Columbia, where we change senators the way you'd change a pair of socks. If you ever changed your socks, that is. What about him?"

"Well, Senator Creighton has deep clout and seniority! He was a United States Senator even before the first NAFTA Senate was convened! He has a very large, and powerful, and very well-seasoned personal staff of twenty thousand hardworking people, with a lot of pull in the Agriculture, Banking, and Telecommunications Committees!"

"Yeah? So?"

"So," Kitty said miserably, "there are twenty thousand of us on his staff. We've been in place for decades now, and naturally we've accumulated lots of power and importance. Senator Creighton's staff is basically running some quite large sections of the NAFTA government, and if the Senator loses his office, there will be a great deal of...of unnecessary political turbulence." She looked up. "You might not think that a senator's staff is all that important politically. But if people like you bothered to learn anything about the real-life way that your government functions, then you'd know that Senate staffers can be really crucial."

Mabel scratched her head. "You're telling me that even a lousy senator has his own private black-bag unit?"

Kitty looked insulted. "He's an excellent senator! You can't have a working organization of twenty thousand staffers without taking security very seriously! Anyway, the Executive wing has had black-bag units for years! It's only right that there should be a balance of powers."

"Wow," Mabel said. "The old guy's a hundred and twelve or something, isn't he?"

"A hundred and seventeen."

"Even with government health care, there can't be a lot left of him."

"He's already gone," Kitty muttered. "His frontal lobes are burned out.... He can still sit up, and if he's stoked on stimulants he can repeat whatever's whispered to him. So he's got two permanent implanted hearing aids, and basically...well...he's being run by remote control by his mook."

"His mook, huh?" Pete repeated thoughtfully.

"It's a very good mook," Kitty said. "The coding's old, but it's been very well looked-after. It has firm moral values and excellent policies. The mook is really very much like the Senator was. It's just that, well, it's old. It still prefers a really old-fashioned media environment. It spends almost all its time watching old-fashioned public political coverage, and lately it's gotten cranky and started broadcasting commentary."

"Man, never trust a mook," Lyle said. "I hate those things."

"So do I," Pete offered, "but even a mook comes off pretty good compared to a politician."

"I don't really see the problem," Mabel said, puzzled. "Senator Hirschheimer from Arizona has had a direct neural link to his mook for years, and he has an excellent progressive voting record. Same goes for Senator Marmalejo from Tamaulipas; she's kind of absentminded, and everybody knows she's on life support, but she's a real scrapper on women's issues."

Kitty looked up. "You don't think it's terrible?"

Mabel shook her head. "I'm not one to be judgmental about the intimacy of one's relationship to one's own digital alter-ego. As far as I can see it, that's a basic privacy issue."

"They told me in briefing that it was a very terrible business, and that everyone would panic if they learned that a high government official was basically a front for a rogue artificial intelligence."

Mabel, Pete, and Lyle exchanged glances. "Are you guys surprised by that news?" Mabel said.

"Heck no," said Pete. "Big deal," Lyle added.

Something seemed to snap inside Kitty then. Her head sank. "Disaffected émigrés in Europe have been spreading boxes that can decipher the Senator's commentary. I mean, the Senator's mook's commentary.... The mook speaks just like the Senator did, or the way the Senator used to speak, when he was in private and off the record. The way he spoke in his diaries. As far as we can tell, the mook *was* his diary.... It used to be his personal laptop computer. But he just kept transferring the files, and upgrading the software, and teaching it new tricks like voice recognition and speechwriting, and giving it power of attorney and such.... And then, one day the mook made a break for it. We think that the mook sincerely believes that it's the Senator."

"Just tell the stupid thing to shut up for a while, then."

"We can't do that. We're not even sure where the mook is, physically. Or how it's been encoding those sarcastic comments into the video-feed. The Senator had a lot of friends in the telecom industry back in the old days. There are a lot of ways and places to hide a piece of distributed software."

"So that's all?" Lyle said. "That's it, that's your big secret? Why didn't you just come to me and ask me for the box? You didn't have to dress up in combat gear and kick my door in. That's a pretty good story, I'd have probably just given you the thing."

"I couldn't do that, Mr. Schweik."

"Why not?"

"Because," Pete said, "her people are important government functionaries, and you're a loser techie wacko who lives in a slum."

"I was told this is a very dangerous area," Kitty muttered.

"It's not dangerous," Mabel told her.

"No?"

"No. They're all too broke to be dangerous. This is just a kind of social breathing space. The whole urban infrastructure's dreadfully overplanned here in Chattanooga. There's been too much money here too long. There's been no room for spontaneity. It was choking the life out of the city. That's why everyone was secretly overjoyed when the rioters set fire to these three floors."

Mabel shrugged. "The insurance took care of the damage. First the looters came in. Then there were a few hideouts for kids and crooks and illegal aliens. Then the permanent squats got set up. Then the artists' studios, and the semi-legal workshops and redlight places. Then the quaint little coffeehouses, then the bakeries. Pretty soon the offices of professionals will be filtering in, and they'll restore the water and the wiring. Once that happens, the real-estate prices will kick in big-time, and the whole zone will transmute right back into gentryville. It happens all the time."

Mabel waved her arm at the door. "If you knew anything about modern urban geography, you'd see this kind of, uh, spontaneous urban renewal happening all over the place. As long as you've got naive young people with plenty of energy who can be suckered into living inside rotten, hazardous dumps for nothing, in exchange for imagining that they're free from oversight, then it all works out just great in the long run."

"Oh."

"Yeah, zones like this turn out to be extremely handy for all concerned. For some brief span of time, a few people can think mildly unusual thoughts and behave in mildly unusual ways. All kinds of weird little vermin show up, and if they make any money then they go legal, and if they don't then they drop dead in a place really quiet where it's all their own fault. Nothing dangerous about it." Mabel laughed, then sobered. "Lyle, let this poor dumb cracker out of the bag."

"She's naked under there."

"Okay," she said impatiently, "cut a slit in the bag and throw some clothes in it. Get going, Lyle."

Lyle threw in some biking pants and a sweatshirt.

"What about my gear?" Kitty demanded, wriggling her way into the clothes by feel.

"I tell you what," said Mabel thoughtfully. "Pete here will give your gear back to you in a week or so, after his friends have photographed all the circuitry. You'll just have to let him keep all those knickknacks for a while, as his reward for our not immediately telling everybody who you are and what you're doing here."

"Great idea," Pete announced, "terrific, pragmatic solution!" He began feverishly snatching up gadgets and stuffing them into his shoulderbag. "See,

Lyle? One phone-call to good ol' Spider Pete, and your problem is history, zude! Me and Mabel-the-Fed have crisis negotiation skills that are second to none! Another potentially lethal confrontation resolved without any bloodshed or loss of life." Pete zipped the bag shut. "That's about it, right, everybody? Problem over! Write if you get work, Lyle buddy. Hang by your thumbs." Pete leapt out the door and bounded off at top speed on the springy soles of his reactive boots.

"Thanks a lot for placing my equipment into the hands of sociopathic criminals," Kitty said. She reached out of the slit in the bag, grabbed a multitool off the corner of the workbench, and began swiftly slashing her way free.

"This will help the sluggish, corrupt, and underpaid Chattanooga police to take life a little more seriously," Mabel said, her pale eyes gleaming. "Besides, it's profoundly undemocratic to restrict specialized technical knowledge to the coercive hands of secret military elites."

Kitty thoughtfully thumbed the edge of the multitool's ceramic blade and stood up to her full height, her eyes slitted. "I'm ashamed to work for the same government as you."

Mabel smiled serenely. "Darling, your tradition of deep dark government paranoia is far behind the times! This is the postmodern era! We're now in the grip of a government with severe schizoid multiple-personality disorder."

"You're truly vile. I despise you more than I can say." Kitty jerked her thumb at Lyle. "Even this nut-case eunuch anarchist kid looks pretty good, compared to you. At least he's self-sufficient and market-driven."

"I thought he looked good the moment I met him," Mabel replied sunnily. "He's cute, he's got great muscle tone, and he doesn't make passes. Plus he can fix small appliances and he's got a spare apartment. I think you ought to move in with him, sweetheart."

"What's that supposed to mean? You don't think I could manage life here in the zone like you do, is that it? You think you have some kind of copyright on living outside the law?"

"No, I just mean you'd better stay indoors with your boyfriend here until that paint falls off your face. You look like a poisoned raccoon." Mabel turned on her heel. "Try to get a life, and stay out of my way." She leapt outside, unlocked her bicycle, and methodically pedaled off.

Kitty wiped her lips and spat out the door. "Christ, that baton packs a wallop." She snorted. "Don't you ever ventilate this place, kid? Those paint fumes are gonna kill you before you're thirty."

"I don't have time to clean or ventilate it. I'm real busy."

"Okay, then I'll clean it. I'll ventilate it. I gotta stay here a while, understand? Maybe quite a while."

Lyle blinked. "How long, exactly?"

Kitty stared at him. "You're not taking me seriously, are you? I don't much like it when people don't take me seriously."

"No, no," Lyle assured her hastily. "You're very serious."

"You ever heard of a small-business grant, kid? How about venture capital, did you ever hear of that? Ever heard of federal research-and-development subsidies, Mr. Schweik?" Kitty looked at him sharply, weighing her words. "Yeah, I thought maybe you'd heard of that one, Mr. Techie Wacko. Federal R and D backing is the kind of thing that only happens to other people, right? But Lyle, when you make good friends with a senator, you *become* 'other people.' Get my drift, pal?"

"I guess I do," Lyle said slowly.

"We'll have ourselves some nice talks about that subject, Lyle. You wouldn't mind that, would you?"

"No. I don't mind it now that you're talking."

"There's some stuff going on down here in the zone that I didn't understand at first, but it's important." Kitty paused, then rubbed dried dye from her hair in a cascade of green dandruff. "How much did you pay those Spider gangsters to string up this place for you?"

"It was kind of a barter situation," Lyle told her.

"Think they'd do it again if I paid 'em real cash? Yeah? I thought so." She nodded thoughtfully. "They look like a heavy outfit, the City Spiders. I gotta pry 'em loose from that leftist gorgon before she finishes indoctrinating them in socialist revolution." Kitty wiped her mouth on her sleeve. "This is the Senator's own constituency! It was stupid of us to duck an ideological battle, just because this is a worthless area inhabited by reckless sociopaths who don't vote. Hell, that's exactly why it's important. This could be a vital territory in the culture war. I'm gonna call the office right away, start making arrangements. There's no way we're gonna leave this place in the hands of the self-styled Queen of Peace and Justice over there."

She snorted, then stretched a kink out of her back. "With a little self-control and discipline, I can save those Spiders from themselves and turn them into an asset to law and order! I'll get 'em to string up a couple of trailers here in the zone. We could start a dojo."

Eddy called, two weeks later. He was in a beachside cabana somewhere in Catalunya, wearing a silk floral-print shirt and a new and very pricey looking set of spex. "How's life, Lyle?"

"It's okay, Eddy."

"Making out all right?" Eddy had two new tattoos on his cheekbone.

"Yeah. I got a new paying roommate. She's a martial artist."

"Girl roommate working out okay this time?"

"Yeah, she's good at pumping the flywheel and she lets me get on with my bike work. Bike business has been picking up a lot lately. Looks like I might get a legal electrical feed and some more floorspace, maybe even some genuine mail delivery. My new roomie's got a lot of useful contacts."

"Boy, the ladies sure love you, Lyle! Can't beat 'em off with a stick, can you, poor guy? That's a heck of a note."

Eddy leaned forward a little, shoving aside a silver tray full of dead gold-tipped zigarettes. "You been getting the packages?"

"Yeah. Pretty regular."

"Good deal," he said briskly, "but you can wipe 'em all now. I don't need those backups anymore. Just wipe the data and trash the disks, or sell 'em. I'm into some, well, pretty hairy opportunities right now, and I don't need all that old clutter. It's kid stuff anyway."

"Okay, man. If that's the way you want it."

Eddy leaned forward. "D'you happen to get a package lately? Some hardware? Kind of a settop box?"

"Yeah, I got the thing."

"That's great, Lyle. I want you to open the box up, and break all the chips with pliers."

"Yeah?"

"Then throw all the pieces away. Separately. It's trouble, Lyle, okay? The kind of trouble I don't need right now."

"Consider it done, man."

"Thanks! Anyway, you won't be bothered by mailouts from now on." He paused. "Not that I don't appreciate your former effort and goodwill, and all."

Lyle blinked. "How's your love life, Eddy?"

Eddy sighed. "Frederika! What a handful! I dunno, Lyle, it was okay for a while, but we couldn't stick it together. I don't know why I ever thought that private cops were sexy. I musta been totally out of my mind…. Anyway, I got a new girlfriend now."

"Yeah?"

"She's a politician, Lyle. She's a radical member of the Spanish Parliament. Can you believe that? I'm sleeping with an elected official of a European local government." He laughed. "Politicians are *sexy*, Lyle. Politicians are hot! They have charisma. They're glamorous. They're powerful. They can really make things happen! Politicians get around. They know things on the inside track. I'm having more fun with Violeta than I knew there was in the world."

"That's pleasant to hear, zude."

"More pleasant than you know, my man."

"Not a problem," Lyle said indulgently. "We all gotta make our own lives, Eddy."

"Ain't it the truth."

Lyle nodded. "I'm in business, zude!"

"You gonna perfect that inertial whatsit?" Eddy said.

"Maybe. It could happen. I get to work on it a lot now. I'm getting closer, really getting a grip on the concept. It feels really good. It's a good hack, man. It makes up for all the rest of it. It really does."

Eddy sipped his mimosa. "Lyle."

"What?"

"You didn't hook up that settop box and look at it, did you?"

"You know me, Eddy," Lyle said. "Just another kid with a wrench."

Sterling to Kessel, 29 March 1985:

"You can't turn pop genre into mainstream. You can't turn rock and roll into modern symphonic music. It won't wash."

Kessel to Sterling, 2 April 1985:

" 'You can't turn pop genre into mainstream.' Maybe. I see the problem. But a lot of good stuff has been produced in the past by artists trying to do exactly that.... look at Shakespeare and revenge tragedy (*Hamlet*). Hammett and the hardboiled detective story (*The Glass Key*). Jane Austen and the romance (*Persuasion*). Conrad and the spy novel (*The Secret Agent*). Melville and the swindle story (*The Confidence Man*)."

Red Sonja and Lessingham in Dreamland

(With apologies to E. R. Eddison)

Gwyneth Jones

The virtual reality stories that followed in the wake of CP's first wave traded in the wonders of the digital alternative to reality, a world transcending the limitations of the flesh. Here Gwyneth Jones draws a sharp contrast between the lives of people in our world and their fantasy lives in the VR world.

In the process she performs an interrogation of the uses of fantasy. Like so much fantasy (and science fiction), VR offers the temptation of effortless sex, physical prowess, and cost-less adventure in a romanticized world without entropy. Can the virtual world escape the limitations of humanity?

The earth walls of the caravanserai rose strangely from the empty plain. She let the black stallion slow his pace. The silence of deep dusk had a taste, like a rich dark fruit; the air was keen. In the distance mountains etched a jagged margin against an indigo sky; snow-streaks glinting in the glimmer of the dawning stars. She had never been here before, in life. But as she led her horse through the gap in the high earthen banks she knew what she would see. The camping-booths around the walls; the beaten ground stained black by the ashes of countless cooking fires; the wattle-fenced enclosure where travellers' riding beasts mingled indiscriminately with their host's goats and chickens... the tumbledown gallery, where sheaves of russet plains-grass sprouted from empty window-spaces. Everything she looked on had the luminous intensity of a place often-visited in dreams.

She was a tall woman, dressed for riding in a kilt and harness of supple leather over brief close-fitting linen: a costume that left her sheeny, muscular limbs bare and outlined the taut, proud curves of breast and haunches. Her red hair was bound in a braid as thick as a man's wrist. Her sword was slung on her back, the great brazen hilt standing above her shoulder. Other guests were gathered by an open-air kitchen, in the orange-red of firelight and the smoke of roasting meat. She returned their stares coolly: she was accustomed to attracting attention. But she didn't like what she saw. The host of the caravanserai came scuttling from the group by the fire. His manner was fawning. But his eyes measured, with a thief's sly expertise, the worth of the sword she bore and the quality of Lemiak's harness. Sonja tossed him a few coins, and declined to join the company.

She had counted fifteen of them. They were poorly dressed and heavily armed. They were all friends together and their animals—both terror-birds and horses—were too good for any honest travellers' purposes. Sonja had been told that this caravanserai was a safe halt. She judged that this was no longer true. She considered riding out again onto the plain. But wolves and wild terror-birds roamed at night between here and the mountains, at the end of winter. And there were worse dangers; ghosts and demons. Sonja was neither credulous nor superstitious. But in this country no wayfarer willingly spent the black hours alone.

She unharnessed Lemiak and rubbed him down: taking sensual pleasure in the handling of his powerful limbs, in the heat of his glossy hide, and the vigour of his great body. There was firewood ready stacked in the roofless booth. Shouldering a cloth sling for corn and a hank of rope, she went to fetch her own fodder. The corralled beasts shifted in a mass to watch her. The great flightless birds, with their pitiless raptors' eyes, were especially attentive. She felt an equally rapacious attention from the company by the caravanserai kitchen, which amused her. The robbers—as she was sure they were—had all the luck. For her, there wasn't one of the fifteen who rated a second glance.

A man appeared, from the darkness under the ruined gallery. He was tall. The rippled muscle of his chest, left bare by an unlaced leather jerkin, shone red-brown. His black hair fell in glossy curls to his wide shoulders. He met her gaze and smiled, white teeth appearing in the darkness of his beard. "*My name is Ozymandias, king of kings...look on my works, ye mighty, and despair....* Do you know those lines?" He pointed to a lump of shapeless stone, one of several that lay about. It bore traces of carving, almost effaced by time. "There was a city here once, with market places, fine buildings, throngs of proud people. Now they are dust, and only the caravanserai remains."

He stood before her, one tanned and sinewy hand resting lightly on the hilt of a dagger in his belt. Like Sonja, he carried his broadsword on his back. Sonja was tall. He topped her by a head: yet there was nothing brutish in his size. His brow was wide and serene, his eyes were vivid blue, his lips full and imperious; yet delicately modelled, in the rich nest of hair. Somewhere between eyes and lips there lurked a spirit of mockery, as if he found some secret amusement in the perfection of his own beauty and strength.

The man and the woman measured each other.

"You are a scholar," she said.

"Of some sort. And a traveller from an antique land, where the cities are still standing. It seems we are the only strangers here," he added, with a slight jerk of the chin towards the convivial company. "We might be well advised to become friends for the night."

Sonja never wasted words. She considered his offer, and nodded.

They made a fire in the booth Sonja had chosen. Lemiak and the scholar's terror-bird, left loose in the back of the shelter, did not seem averse to each other's company. The woman and the man ate spiced sausage, skewered and broiled over the red embers, with bread and dried fruit. They drank water, each keeping to their own water-skin. They spoke little, after that first exchange, except to discuss briefly the tactics of their defence, should defence be necessary.

The attack came around midnight. At the first stir of covert movement, Sonja leapt up, sword in hand. She grasped a brand from the dying fire. The man who had been crawling on his hands and knees toward her, bent on sly murder of a sleeping victim, scrabbled to his feet. "Defend yourself," yelled Sonja, who despised to strike an unarmed foe. Instantly he was rushing at her with a heavy sword. A great two-handed stroke would have cleft her to the waist. She parried the blow and caught him between neck and shoulder, almost severing the head from his body. The beasts plunged and screamed at the rush of blood-scent. The scholar was grappling with another attacker, choking out the man's life with his bare hands...and the booth was full of bodies: their enemies rushing in on every side.

Sonja felt no fear. Stroke followed stroke, in a luxury of blood and effort and fire-shot darkness...until the attack was over, as suddenly as it had begun.

The brigands had vanished.

"We killed five," breathed the scholar, "by my count. Three to you, two to me."

She kicked together the remains of their fire, and crouched to blow the embers to a blaze. By that light they found five corpses, dragged them and flung them into the open square. The scholar had a cut on his upper arm which was bleeding freely. Sonja was bruised and battered, but otherwise unhurt. The worst loss was their woodstack, which had been trampled and blood-fouled. They would not be able to keep a watchfire burning.

"Perhaps they won't try again," said the warrior woman. "What can we have that's worth more than five lives?"

He laughed shortly. "I hope you're right."

"We'll take turns to watch."

Standing breathless, every sense alert, they smiled at each other in new-forged comradeship. There was no second attack. At dawn Sonja, rousing from a light doze, sat up and pushed back the heavy masses of her red hair.

"You are very beautiful," said the man, gazing at her.

"So are you," she answered.

The caravanserai was deserted, except for the dead. The brigands' riding animals were gone. The inn-keeper and his family had vanished into some bolt-hole in the ruins.

"I am heading for the mountains," he said, as they packed up their gear. "For the pass into Zimiamvia."

"I too."

"Then our way lies together. "

He was wearing the same leather jerkin, over knee-length loose breeches of heavy violet silk. Sonja looked at the strips of linen that bound the wound on his upper arm. "When did you tie up that cut?"

"You dressed it for me, for which I thank you."

"When did I do that?"

He shrugged. "Oh, some time."

Sonja mounted Lemiak, a little frown between her brows. They rode together until dusk. She was not talkative and the man soon accepted her silence. But when night fell, and they camped without a fire on the houseless plain: then, as the demons stalked, they were glad of each other's company. Next dawn, the mountains seemed as distant as ever. Again, they met no living creature all day, spoke little to each other and made the same comfortless camp. There was no moon. The stars were almost bright enough to cast shadow; the cold was intense. Sleep was impossible, but they were not tempted to ride on. Few travellers attempt the passage over the high plains to Zimiamvia. Of those few most turn back, defeated. Some wander among the ruins forever, tearing at their own flesh. Those who survive are the ones who do not defy the terrors of darkness. They crouched shoulder to shoulder, each wrapped in a single blanket, to endure. Evil emanations of the death-steeped plain rose from the soil and bred phantoms. The sweat of fear was cold as ice-melt on Sonja's cheeks. Horrors made of nothingness prowled and muttered in her mind.

"How long," she whispered." How long do we have to bear this—?"

The man's shoulder lifted against hers. "Until we get well, I suppose."

The warrior woman turned to face him, green eyes flashing in appalled outrage—

"Sonja" discussed this group member's felony with the therapist. Dr Hamilton —he wanted them to call him Jim, but "Sonja" found this impossible—monitored everything that went on in the virtual environment; but he never appeared there. They only met him in the one-to-one consultations that virtual-therapy buffs called *the meat sessions*.

"He's not supposed to *do* that," she protested, from the foam couch in the doctor's office. He was sitting beside her, his notebook on his knee. "He damaged my experience."

Dr Hamilton nodded. "Okay. Let's take a step back. Leave aside the risk of disease or pregnancy: because we *can* leave those bogeys aside, forever if you like. Would you agree that sex is essentially an innocent and playful social behaviour? Something you'd offer to or take from a friend, in an ideal world, as easily as food or drink?"

"Sonja" recalled certain dreams, *meat* dreams, not the computer-assisted kind. She blushed. But the man was a doctor after all. "That's what I do feel," she agreed. "That's why I'm here. I want to get back to the pure pleasure, to get rid of the baggage."

"The sexual experience offered in therapy is readily available on the nets. You know that. You could find an agency that would vet your partners for you. You chose to join this group because you need to feel that you're taking *medicine*, so you don't have to feel ashamed. And because you need to feel that you're interacting with people who, like yourself, perceive sex as a problem."

"Doesn't everyone?"

"You and another group member went off into your own private world. That's good. That's what's supposed to happen. Let me tell you, it doesn't always. The software gives you access to a vast multisensual library, all the sexual fantasy ever committed to media. But you and your partner, or partners, have to customise the information and use it to create and maintain what we call the *consensual perceptual plenum*. Success in holding a shared dreamland together is a knack. It depends on something in the neural make-up that no one has yet fully analysed. Some have it, some don't. You two are really in sync."

"That's exactly what I'm complaining about—"

"You think he's damaging the pocket universe you two built up. But he isn't, not from his character's point of view. It's part of Lessingham's thing, to be conscious that he's in a fantasy world."

She started, accusingly. "I don't want to know his name."

"Don't worry, I wouldn't tell you. 'Lessingham' is the name of his virtuality persona. I'm surprised you don't recognise it. He's a character from a series of classic fantasy novels by E. R. Eddison.... *In Eddison's glorious cosmos 'Lessingham' is a splendidly endowed English gentleman, who visits fantastic realms of ultra-masculine adventure as a lucid dreamer: though an actor in the drama, he is partly conscious of another existence, while the characters around him are more or less explicitly puppets of the dream...*"

He sounded as if he was quoting from a reference book. He probably was: reading from an autocue that had popped up in the lenses of those doctorish hornrims. She knew that the old-fashioned trappings were there to reassure her. She rather despised them: but it was like the virtuality itself. The buttons were pushed, the mechanism responded. She was reassured.

Of course she knew the Eddison stories. She recalled "Lessingham" perfectly: the tall, strong, handsome, cultured millionaire jock who has magic journeys to another world, where he is a tall, strong, handsome cultured jock in Elizabethan costume, with a big sword. The whole thing was an absolutely typical male power-fantasy, she thought, without rancour. *Fantasy means never having to say you're sorry.* The women in those books, she remembered, were drenched in sex, but they had no part in the action. They stayed at home being princesses, occasionally allowing the millionaire jocks to get them into bed.

She could understand why "Lessingham" would be interested in "Sonja"...
for a change.

"You think he goosed you, psychically. What do you expect? You can't dress
the way 'Sonja' dresses, and hope to be treated like the Queen of the May."

Dr Hamilton was only doing his job. He was supposed to be provocative, so
they could react against him. That was his excuse, anyway... On the contrary,
she thought. "Sonja" dresses the way she does because she can dress any way
she likes. "Sonja" doesn't have to *hope* for respect, and she doesn't have to
demand it. She just gets it. "It's dominance display," she said, enjoying the theft
of his jargon. "Females do that too, you know. The way 'Sonja' dresses is not an
invitation. It's a warning. Or a challenge, to anyone who can measure up."

He laughed, but he sounded irritated. "Frankly, I'm amazed that you two
work together. I'd have expected "Lessingham" to go for an ultrafeminine —"

"I *am*...'Sonja' is ultrafeminine. Isn't a tigress feminine?"

"Well, okay. But I guess you've found out his little weakness. He likes to be a
teeny bit in control, even when he's letting his hair down in dreamland."

She remembered the secret mockery lurking in those blue eyes. "That's
the problem. That's exactly what I *don't* want. I don't want either of us to be in
control."

"I can't interfere with his persona. So, it's up to you. Do you want to carry
on?"

"Something works," she muttered. She was unwilling to admit that there'd
been no one else, in the text-interface phase of the group, that she found
remotely attractive. It was "Lessingham," or drop out and start again. "I just
want him to stop *spoiling things*."

"You can't expect your masturbation fantasies to mesh completely. This is
about getting beyond solitary sex. Go with it: where's the harm? One day you'll
want to face a sexual partner in the real, and then you'll be well. Meanwhile, you
could be passing 'Lessingham' in reception — he comes to his meat-sessions
around your time — and not know it. That's *safety*, and you never have to breach
it. You two have proved that you can sustain an imaginary world together: it's
almost like being in love. I could argue that lucid-dreaming, being *in* the fantasy
world but not *of* it, is the next big step. Think about that."

The clinic room had mirrored walls: more deliberate provocation. How much reality can you take? the reflections asked. But she felt only a vague distaste for the woman she saw, at once hollow-cheeked and bloated, lying on the doctor's foam couch. He was glancing over her records on his desk screen: which meant the session was almost up.

"Still no overt sexual contact?"

"I'm not ready..." She stirred restlessly. "Is it a man or a woman?"

"Ah!" smiled Dr Hamilton, waving a finger at her. "Naughty, naughty!"

He was the one who'd started taunting her, with his hints that the meat "Lessingham" might be near. She hated herself for asking a genuine question. It was her rule to give him no entry to her real thoughts. A flimsy reserve, Dr Jim knew everything, without being told: every change in her brain chemistry, every effect on her body: sweaty palms, racing heart, damp underwear... The telltales on his damned autocue left her little dignity. *Why do I subject myself to this?* she wondered, disgusted. But in the virtuality she forgot utterly about Dr Jim. She didn't care who was watching. She had her brazen-hilted sword. She had the piercing intensity of dusk on the high plains, the snowlight on the mountains; the hard, warm silk of her own perfect limbs. She felt a brief complicity with "Lessingham." She had a conviction that Dr Jim didn't play favourites. He despised all his patients equally... You *get your kicks, doctor. But we have the freedom of dreamland.*

"Sonja" read cards stuck in phonebooths and store windows, in the tired little streets outside the building that housed the clinic. *Relaxing Massage by clean shaven young man in Luxurious Surroundings*...You can't expect your fantasies to mesh exactly, the doctor said. But how can it work if two people disagree over something so vital as the difference between control and surrender? Her estranged husband used to say: "Why don't you just *do it for me,* as a favour. It wouldn't hurt. Like making someone a cup of coffee..." *Offer the steaming cup, turn around and lift my skirts, pull down my underwear. I'm ready. He opens his pants and slides it in, while his thumb is round in front rubbing me...*I could *enjoy* that, thought "Sonja," remembering the blithe abandon of her dreams. That's the damned shame. If there were no non-sex consequences, I don't know that there's any limit to what I could enjoy... But all her husband had achieved was to make her feel she never wanted to make anyone, man, woman or child, a cup of coffee ever again... *In luxurious surroundings*. That's what I want. Sex without engagement, pleasure without consequences. It's got to be possible.

She gazed at the cards, feeling uneasily that she'd have to give up this habit. She used to glance at them sidelong, now she'd pause and linger. She was getting desperate. She was lucky there was medically supervised virtuality-sex to be had. She would be helpless prey in the wild world of the nets, and she'd never, ever risk trying one of these meat-numbers. And she had no intention of returning to her husband. Let him make his own coffee. She wouldn't call that getting well. She turned, and caught the eye of a nicely dressed young woman standing next to her. They walked away quickly in opposite directions.

Everybody's having the same dreams...

In the foothills of the mountains the world became green and sweet. They followed the course of a little river that sometimes plunged far below their path, tumbling in white flurries in a narrow gorge; and sometimes ran beside them, racing smooth and clear over coloured pebbles. Flowers clustered on the banks, birds darted in the thickets of wild rose and honeysuckle. They lead their riding animals and walked at ease: not speaking much. Sometimes the warrior woman's flank would brush the man's side; or he would lean for a moment, as if by chance, his hand on her shoulder. Then they would move deliberately apart, but they would smile at each other. *Soon. Not yet...*

They must be vigilant. The approaches to fortunate Zimiamvia were guarded. They could not expect to reach the pass unopposed. And the nights were haunted still. They made camp at a flat bend of the river, where the crags of the defile drew away, and they could see far up and down their valley. To the north, peaks of diamond and indigo reared above them. Their fire of aromatic wood burned brightly, as the white stars began to blossom.

"No one knows about the long-term effects," she said. "It can't be safe. At the least, we're risking irreversible addiction, they warn you about that. I don't want to spend the rest of my life as a cyberspace couch potato."

"Nobody claims it's safe. If it was safe, it wouldn't be so intense."

Their eyes met. "Sonja's" barbarian simplicity combined surprisingly well with the man's more elaborate furnishing. The *consensual perceptual plenum* was a flawless reality: the sound of the river, the clear silence of the mountain twilight...their two perfect bodies. She turned from him to gaze into the sweet-scented flames. The warrior-woman's glorious vitality throbbed in her veins. The fire held worlds of its own, liquid furnaces: the sunward surface of Mercury.

"Have you ever been to a place like this in the real?"

He grimaced. "You're kidding. In the real, I'm *not* a magic-wielding millionaire."

Something howled. The bloodstopping cry was repeated. A taint of sickening foulness swept by them. They both shuddered, and drew closer together. "Sonja" knew the scientific explanation for the paranoia, the price you paid for the virtual world's super-real, dreamlike richness. It was all down to heightened neurotransmitter levels, a positive feedback effect, psychic overheating. But the horrors were still horrors.

"The doctor says if we can talk like this, it means we're getting well."

He shook his head. "I'm not sick. It's like you said. Virtuality's addictive and I'm an addict. I'm getting my drug of choice safely, on prescription. That's how I see it."

All this time "Sonja" was in her apartment, lying on a foam couch with a visor over her head. The visor delivered compressed bursts of stimuli to her visual cortex: the other sense perceptions riding piggyback on the visual, triggering a whole complex of neuronal groups; tricking her mind/brain into believing the world of the dream was *out there*. The brain works like a computer. You cannot "see" a hippopotamus until your system has retrieved the "hippopotamus" template from memory, and checked it against the incoming. Where does "the real thing" exist? In a sense this world was as real as the other. But the thought of "Lessingham's" unknown body disturbed her. If he was too poor to lease good equipment, he might be lying in a grungy public cubicle...cathetered, and so forth: the sordid details.

She had never yet tried virtual sex. The solitary version had seemed a depressing idea. People said the partnered kind was the perfect zipless fuck. *He* sounded experienced, she was afraid he would be able to tell she was not. But it didn't matter. The virtual-therapy group wasn't like a dating agency. She would never meet him in the real, that was the whole idea. She didn't have to think about that stranger's body. She didn't have to worry about the real "Lessingham's" opinion of her. She drew herself up in the firelight. It was right, she decided, that Sonja should be a virgin. When the moment came, her surrender would be the more absolute.

In their daytime he stayed in character. It was a tacit trade-off. She would acknowledge the other world at nightfall by the camp-fire, as long as he didn't mention it the rest of the time. So they travelled on together, Lessingham and Red Sonja, the courtly scholar-knight and the taciturn warrior-maiden, through an exquisite Maytime: exchanging lingering glances, "accidental" touches…And still nothing happened. "Sonja" was aware that "Lessingham," as much as herself, was holding back from the brink. She felt piqued at this. But they were both, she guessed, waiting for the fantasy they had generated to throw up the perfect moment of itself. It ought to. There was no other reason for its existence.

Turning a shoulder of the hillside, they found a sheltered hollow. Two rowan trees in flower grew above the river. In the shadow of their blossom tumbled a little waterfall, so beautiful it was a wonder to behold. The water fell clear, from the edge of a slab of stone twice a man's height, into a rocky basin. The water in the basin was dark and deep, a-churn with bubbles from the plunging jet from above. The riverbanks were lawns of velvet, over the rocks grew emerald mosses and tiny water flowers.

"I would live here," said Lessingham softly, his hand dropping from his riding bird's bridle. "I would build me a house in this fairy place, and rest my heart here forever."

Sonja loosed the black stallion's rein. The two beasts moved off, feeding each in their own way on the sweet grasses and springtime foliage.

"I would like to bathe in that pool," said the warrior-maiden.

"Why not?" He smiled. "I will stand guard."

She pulled off her leather harness and slowly unbound her hair. It fell in a trembling mass of copper and russet lights, a cloud of glory around the richness of her barely clothed body. Gravely she gazed at her own perfection, mirrored in the homage of his eyes. Lessingham's breath was coming fast. She saw a pulse beat, in the strong beauty of his throat. The pure physical majesty of him caught her breath…

It was their moment. But it still needed something to break this strange spell of reluctance. "*Lady*," he murmured —

Sonja gasped. "Back to back!" she cried. "Quickly, or it is too late!"

Six warriors surrounded them, covered from head to foot in red and black armour. They were human in the lower body, but the head of each appeared beaked and fanged, with monstrous faceted eyes, and each bore an extra pair of armoured limbs between breastbone and belly. They fell on Sonja and Lessingham without pause or a challenge. Sonja fought fiercely as always, her blade ringing against the monster armour. But something cogged her fabulous skill. Some power had drained the strength from her splendid limbs. She was disarmed. The clawed creatures held her, a monstrous head stooped over her, choking her with its fetid breath...

When she woke again she was bound against a great boulder, by thongs around her wrists and ankles, tied to hoops of iron driven into the rock. She was naked but for her linen shift, it was in tatters. Lessingham was standing, leaning on his sword. "I drove them off," he said. "At last." He dropped the sword, and took his dagger to cut her down.

She lay in his arms. "You are very beautiful," he murmured. She thought he would kiss her. His mouth plunged instead to her breast, biting and sucking at the engorged nipple. She gasped in shock, a fierce pang leapt through her virgin flesh. What did they want with kisses? They were warriors. Sonja could not restrain a moan of pleasure. He had won her. How wonderful to be overwhelmed, to surrender to the raw lust of this godlike animal.

Lessingham set her on her feet.

"Tie me up."

He was proffering a handful of blood-slicked leather thongs.

"What?"

"Tie me to the rock, mount me. It's what I want."

"The evil warriors tied you—?"

"And you come and rescue me." He made an impatient gesture. "Whatever. Trust me. It'll be good for you too." He tugged at his bloodstained silk breeches, releasing a huge, iron-hard erection. "See, they tore my clothes. When you see *that*, you go crazy, you can't resist...and I'm at your mercy. Tie me up!"

"Sonja" had heard that eighty per cent of the submissive partners in sado-masochist sex are male; but it is still the man who dominates his "dominatrix": who says tie me tighter, beat me harder, you can stop now... Hey, she thought. Why all the stage-directions, suddenly? What happened to my zipless fuck? But what the hell. She wasn't going to back out now, having come so far... There was a seamless shift, and Lessingham was bound to the rock. She straddled his cock. He groaned. *"Don't do this to me."* He thrust upwards, into her, moaning. *"You savage, you utter savage, uuunnnh...*" Sonja grasped the man's wrists and rode him without mercy. He was right, it was just as good this way. His eyes were half closed. In the glimmer of blue under his lashes, a spirit of mockery trembled... She heard a laugh, and found her hands were no longer gripping Lessingham's wrists. He had broken free from her bonds, he was laughing at her in triumph. He was wrestling her to the ground.

"No!" she cried, genuinely outraged. But he was the stronger.

It was night when he was done with her. He rolled away and slept, as far as she could tell, instantly. Her chief thought was that virtual sex didn't entirely *connect*. She remembered now, that was something else people told you, as well as the "zipless fuck." *It's like coming in your sleep*, they said. *It doesn't quite make it*. Maybe there was nothing virtuality could do to orgasm, to match the heightened richness of the rest of the experience. She wondered if he too had felt cheated.

She lay beside her hero, wondering, Where *did I go wrong? Why did he have to treat me that way?* Beside her, "Lessingham" cuddled a fragment of violet silk, torn from his own breeches. He whimpered in his sleep, nuzzling the soft fabric, *"Mama..."*

She told Dr Hamilton that "Lessingham" had raped her.

"And wasn't that what you wanted?"

She lay on the couch in the mirrored office. The doctor sat beside her with his smart notebook on his knee. The couch collected "Sonja's" physical responses as if she was an astronaut umbilicaled to ground control; and Dr Jim read the telltales popping up in his reassuring hornrims. She remembered the sneaking furtive thing that she had glimpsed in "Lessingham's" eyes, the moment before he took over their lust-scene. How could she explain the difference? "He wasn't playing. In the fantasy, anything's allowed. But he wasn't playing. He was outside it, laughing at me."

"I warned you he would want to stay in control."

"But there was no need! I *wanted* him to be in control. Why did he have to steal what I wanted to give him anyway?"

"You have to understand, 'Sonja,' that to many men it's women who seem powerful. You women feel dominated, and try to achieve 'equality.' But the men don't perceive the situation like that. They're mortally afraid of you: and anything, just about *anything* they do to keep the upper hand, can seem like justified self-defence."

She could have wept with frustration. "I know all that! That's *exactly* what I was trying to get away from. I thought we were supposed to leave the damn baggage behind. I wanted something purely physical... Something innocent."

"Sex is not innocent, 'Sonja.' I know you believe it is, or 'should be.' But it's time you faced the truth. Any interaction with another person involves some kind of jockeying for power, dickering over control. Sex is no exception. Now *that's* basic. You can't escape from it in direct-cortical fantasy. It's in our minds that relationships happen, and the mind, of course, is where virtuality happens too." He sighed, and made an entry in her notes. "I want you to look on this as another step towards coping with the real. You're not sick, 'Sonja.' You're unhappy. Not even unusually so. Most adults are unhappy, to some degree—"

"Or else they're in denial."

Her sarcasm fell flat. "Right. A good place to be, at least some of the time. What we're trying to achieve here—if we're trying to achieve anything at all—is to raise your pain threshold to somewhere near average. I want you to walk away from therapy with lowered expectations: I guess that would be success."

"Great, " she said, desolate. "That's just great."

Suddenly he laughed. "Oh, you guys! You are so weird. It's always the same story. *Can't live with you, can't live without you....* You can't go on this way, you know. Its getting ridiculous. You want some real advice, 'Sonja'? Go home. Change your attitudes, and start some hard peace talks with that husband of yours."

"I don't want to change," she said coldly, staring with open distaste at his smooth profile, his soft effeminate hands. Who was he to call her abnormal? "I like my sexuality just the way it is."

Dr Hamilton returned her look, a glint of human malice breaking through his doctor-act. "Listen. I'll tell you something for free." A weird sensation jumped in her crotch. For a moment she had a prick: a hand lifted and cradled the warm weight of her balls. She stifled a yelp of shock. He grinned. "I've been looking for a long time, and I know. *There is no tall, dark man...*"

He returned to her notes. "You say you were 'raped,'" he continued, as if nothing had happened. "Yet you chose to continue the virtual session. Can you explain that ?"

She thought of the haunted darkness, the cold air on her naked body; the soreness of her bruises; a rag of flesh used and tossed away. How it had felt to lie there: intensely alive, tasting the dregs, beaten back at the gates of the fortunate land. In dreamland, even betrayal had such rich depth and fascination. And she was free to enjoy, because *it didn't matter*.

"You wouldn't understand."

Out in the lobby there were people coming and going. It was lunchtime, the lifts were busy. "Sonja" noticed a round-shouldered geek of a little man making for the entrance to the clinic. She wondered idly if that could be "Lessingham."

She would drop out of the group. The adventure with "Lessingham" was over, and there was no one else for her. She needed to start again. The doctor knew he'd lost a customer, that was why he'd been so open with her today. He certainly guessed, too, that she'd lose no time in signing on somewhere else on the semi-medical fringe. What a fraud all that therapy-talk was! He'd never have dared to play the sex-change trick on her, except that he knew she was an addict. She wasn't likely to go accusing him of unprofessional conduct. Oh, he knew it all. But his contempt didn't trouble her.

So, she had joined the inner circle. She could trust Dr Hamilton's judgment. He had the telltales: he would know. She recognised with a feeling of mild surprise that she had become a statistic, an element in a fashionable social concern: *an epidemic flight into fantasy, inadequate personalities, unable to deal with the reality of normal human sexual relations...* But that's crazy, she thought. I don't hate men, and I don't believe "Lessingham" hates women. There's nothing psychotic about what we're doing. We're making a consumer choice. Virtual sex is easier, that's all. Okay, it's convenience food. It has too much sugar, and a certain blandness. But when a product comes along, that is cheaper, easier and more fun to use than the original version, of course people are going to buy it.

The lift was full. She stood, drab bodies packed around her, breathing the stale air. Every face was a mask of dull endurance. She closed her eyes. *The caravanserai walls rose strangely from the empty plain...*

Sterling to Kessel, 7 April 1985:

"I once read some remark of F. Scott Fitzgerald's in which he spoke of wrenching his stories from his emotional wounds — in this case, it was some busted affair from which he was 'still bleeding like a haemophiliac.' It was from a letter he sent to some writing hopeful, a young woman begging him for advice, and one suspects he laid it on a bit thick with the Ever-Popular Tortured Artist Effect.

But this sort of 'writer's paradigm' has stuck with me and caused me many moments of doubt. It makes me wonder to what extent science fiction is 'fiction' at all. Perhaps it *is* based on emotion, and the central emotion is *wonder*. But wonder is such a pale and nebulous thing, and shades off into intellectual curiosity, or even just an abstract admiration for imaginative cleverness....

It also strikes me that each of your examples: *Hamlet, The Glass Key, Persuasion, The Secret Agent*, fulfills its genre rather than distorting it. Each of them delivers the pop genre elements that the audience expects. *The Glass Key*, for instance, is not a mainstream piece shoehorned into the restrictions of genre, but a genre piece elevated to the status of literature....

I don't think anyone can really understand SF who does not have a solid understanding of Olaf Stapledon's *Star Maker*. Here is a story without characters, almost without plot, and markedly devoid of humanistic values. And by any meaningful standard of definition this book is *great* science fiction."

Kessel to Sterling, 1 March 1987:

"I just taught Stapledon's *Star Maker*. It's some kind of crazy great book, but it's not all there is to sf, and certainly not all there is to fantastic literature. And Bruce, I hate to break this to you, but to people of a certain disposition it's boring as three-day-old shit. I'm talking about normal in-the-street readers, not English majors. I think such people are missing something, but they've got a case. I suspect that what you think makes *Star Maker* a great book is also what you consider to be the central virtue of sf: its speculative content. There are other views. I don't buy into a set of standards that makes *only* such work the best of the genre....

I could be wrong. I don't expect us to agree. The most cogent statement I found in your letter was your handwritten note at the end of page one where you suggest, 'let's wait until we're both dead, O.K.?' I'm ready to declare a truce on the basis of that statement."

How We Got in Town and out Again

Jonathan Lethem

Jonathan Lethem, in a series of stories in the early to mid-1990s challenged the pieties of CP, seeing the promises of freedom and power offered by such staples as virtual reality as a new realm for hucksters and scam artists. As in so much of his fiction, here Lethem finds a literary ancestor, in this case Horace McCoy's 1930s novel of dance marathons in the Great Depression, *They Shoot Horses, Don't They?* The result is a vision of desperate humans in a broken economy imagining VR as a way out.

When we first saw somebody near the mall Gloria and I looked around for sticks. We were going to rob them if they were few enough. The mall was about five miles out of the town we were headed for, so nobody would know. But when we got closer Gloria saw their vans and said they were scapers. I didn't know what that was, but she told me.

It was summer. Two days before this Gloria and I had broken out of a pack of people that had food but we couldn't stand their religious chanting anymore. We hadn't eaten since then.

"So what do we do?" I said.

"You let me talk," said Gloria.

"You think we could get into town with them?"

"Better than that," she said. "Just keep quiet."

I dropped the piece of pipe I'd found and we walked in across the parking lot. This mall was long past being good for finding food anymore but the scapers were taking out folding chairs from a store and strapping them on top of their vans. There were four men and one woman.

"Hey," said Gloria.

Two guys were just lugs and they ignored us and kept lugging. The woman was sitting in the front of the van. She was smoking a cigarette.

The other two guys turned. This was Kromer and Fearing, but I didn't know their names yet.

"Beat it," said Kromer. He was a tall squinty guy with a gold tooth. He was kind of worn but the tooth said he'd never lost a fight or slept in a flop. "We're busy," he said.

He was being reasonable. If you weren't in a town you were nowhere. Why talk to someone you met nowhere?

But the other guy smiled at Gloria. He had a thin face and a little mustache. "Who are you?" he said. He didn't look at me.

"I know what you guys do," Gloria said. "I was in one before."

"Oh?" said the guy, still smiling.

"You're going to need contestants," she said.

"She's a fast one," this guy said to the other guy. "I'm Fearing," he said to Gloria.

"Fearing what?" said Gloria.

"Just Fearing."

"Well, I'm just Gloria."

"That's fine," said Fearing. "This is Tommy Kromer. We run this thing. What's your little friend's name?"

"I can say my own name," I said. "I'm Lewis."

"Are you from the lovely town up ahead?"

"Nope," said Gloria. 'We're headed there."

"Getting in exactly how?" said Fearing.

"Anyhow," said Gloria, like it was an answer. "With you, now."

"That's assuming something pretty quick."

"Or we could go and say how you ripped off the last town and they sent us to warn about you," said Gloria.

"Fast," said Fearing again, grinning, and Kromer shook his head. They didn't look too worried.

"You ought to want me along," said Gloria. "I'm an attraction."

"Can't hurt," said Fearing.

Kromer shrugged, and said, "Skinny, for an attraction."

"Sure, I'm skinny," she said. "That's why me and Lewis ought to get something to eat."

Fearing stared at her. Kromer was back to the van with the other guys.

"Or if you can't feed us —" started Gloria.

"Hold it, sweetheart. No more threats."

"We need a meal."

"We'll eat something when we get in," Fearing said. "You and Lewis can get a meal if you're both planning to enter."

"Sure," she said. "We're gonna enter—right, Lewis?"

I knew to say right.

The town militia came out to meet the vans, of course. But they seemed to know the scapers were coming, and after Fearing talked to them for a couple of minutes they opened up the doors and had a quick look then waved us through. Gloria and I were in the back of a van with a bunch of equipment and one of the lugs, named Ed. Kromer drove. Fearing drove the van with the woman in it. The other lug drove the last one alone.

I'd never gotten into a town in a van before, but I'd only gotten in two times before this anyway. The first time by myself, just by creeping in, the second because Gloria went with a militia guy.

Towns weren't so great anyway. Maybe this would be different.

We drove a few blocks and a guy flagged Fearing down. He came up to the window of the van and they talked, then went back to his car, waving at Kromer on his way. Then we followed him.

"What's that about?" said Gloria.

"Gilmartin's the advance man," said Kromer. "I thought you knew everything."

Gloria didn't talk. I said, "What's an advance man?"

"Gets us a place, and the juice we need," said Kromer. "Softens the town up. Gets people excited."

It was getting dark. I was pretty hungry, but I didn't say anything. Gilmartin's car led us to this big building shaped like a boathouse only it wasn't near any water. Kromer said it used to be a bowling alley.

The lugs started moving stuff and Kromer made me help. The building was dusty and empty inside, and some of the lights didn't work. Kromer said just to get things inside for now. He drove away one of the vans and came back and we unloaded a bunch of little cots that Gilmartin the advance man had rented, so I had an idea where I was going to be sleeping. Apart from that it was stuff for the contest. Computer cables and plastic spacesuits, and loads of televisions.

Fearing took Gloria and they came back with food, fried chicken and potato salad, and we all ate. I couldn't stop going back for more but nobody said anything. Then I went to sleep on a cot. No one was talking to me. Gloria wasn't sleeping on a cot. I think she was with Fearing.

Gilmartin the advance man had really done his work. The town was sniffing around first thing in the morning. Fearing was out talking to them when I woke up. "Registration begins at noon, not a minute sooner," he was saying. "Beat the lines and stick around. We'll be serving coffee. Be warned, only the fit need apply—our doctor will be examining you, and he's never been fooled once. It's Darwinian logic, people. The future is for the strong. The meek will have to inherit the here and now."

Inside, Ed and the other guy were setting up the gear. They had about thirty of those wired-up plastic suits stretched out in the middle of the place, and so tangled up with cable and little wires that they were like husks of fly bodies in a spiderweb.

Under each of the suits was a light metal frame, sort of like a bicycle with a seat but no wheels, but with a headrest too. Around the web they were setting up the televisions in an arc facing the seats. The suits each had a number on the back, and the televisions had numbers on top that matched.

When Gloria turned up she didn't say anything to me but she handed me some donuts and coffee.

"This is just the start," she said, when she saw my eyes get big. "We're in for three squares a day as long as this thing lasts. As long as we last, anyway."

We sat and ate outside where we could listen to Fearing. He went on and on. Some people were lined up like he said. I didn't blame them since Fearing was such a talker. Others listened and just got nervous or excited and went away, but I could tell they were coming back later, at least to watch. When we finished the donuts Fearing came over and told us to get on line too.

"We don't have to," said Gloria.

"Yes, you do," said Fearing.

On line we met Lane. She said she was twenty like Gloria but she looked younger. She could have been sixteen, like me.

"You ever do this before?" asked Gloria.

Lane shook her head. "You?"

"Sure," said Gloria. "You ever been out of this town?"

"A couple of times," said Lane. "When I was a kid. I'd like to now."

"Why?"

"I broke up with my boyfriend."

Gloria stuck out her lip, and said, "But you're scared to leave town, so you're doing this instead."

Lane shrugged.

I liked her, but Gloria didn't.

The doctor turned out to be Gilmartin the advance man. I don't think he was a real doctor, but he listened to my heart. Nobody ever did that before, and it gave me a good feeling.

Registration was a joke, though. It was for show. They asked a lot of questions but they only sent a couple of women and one guy away, Gloria said for being too old. Everyone else was okay, despite how some of them looked pretty hungry, just like me and Gloria. This was a hungry town. Later I figured out that's part of why Fearing and Kromer picked it. You'd think they'd want to go where the money was, but you'd be wrong.

After registration they told us to get lost for the afternoon. Everything started at eight o'clock.

We walked around downtown but almost all the shops were closed. All the good stuff was in the shopping center and you had to show a town ID card to get in and me and Gloria didn't have those.

So, like Gloria always says, we killed time since time was what we had.

The place looked different. They had spotlights pointed from on top of the vans and Fearing was talking through a microphone. There was a banner up over the doors. I asked Gloria and she said, "Scape-Athon." Ed was selling beer out of a cooler and some people were buying, even though he must have just bought it right there in town for half the price he was selling at. It was a hot night. They were selling tickets but they weren't letting anybody in yet. Fearing told us to get inside.

Most of the contestants were there already. Anne, the woman from the van, was there, acting like any other contestant. Lane was there too and we waved at each other. Gilmartin was helping everybody put on the suits. You had to get naked but nobody seemed to mind. Just being contestants made it all right, like we were invisible to each other.

"Can we be next to each other?" I said to Gloria.

"Sure, except it doesn't matter," she said. "We won't be able to see each other inside."

"Inside where?" I said.

"The scapes," she said. "You'll see."

Gloria got me into my suit. It was plastic with wiring everywhere and padding at my knees and wrists and elbows and under my arms and in my crotch. I tried on the mask but it was heavy and I saw nobody else was wearing theirs so I kept it off until I had to. Then Gilmartin tried to help Gloria but she said she could do it herself.

So there we were, standing around half naked and dripping with cable in the big empty lit-up bowling alley, and then suddenly Fearing and his big voice came inside and they let the people in and the lights went down and it all started.

"Thirty-two young souls ready to swim out of this world, into the bright shiny future," went bright shiny Fearing. "The question is, how far into that future will their bodies take them? New worlds are theirs for the taking—a cornucopia of scapes to boggle and amaze and gratify the senses. These lucky kids will be immersed in an ocean of data overwhelming to their undernourished sensibilities—we've assembled a really brilliant collection of environments for them to explore—and you'll be able to see everything they see, on the monitors in front of you. But can they make it in the fast lane? How long can they ride the wave? Which of them will prove able to outlast the others, and take home the big prize —one thousand dollars? That's what we're here to find out."

Gilmartin and Ed were snapping everybody into their masks and turning all the switches to wire us up and getting us to lie down on the frames. It was comfortable on the bicycle seat with your head on the headrest and a belt around your waist. You could move your arms and legs like you were swimming, the way Fearing said. I didn't mind putting on the mask now because the audience was making me nervous. A lot of them I couldn't see because of the lights, but I could tell they were there, watching.

The mask covered my ears and eyes. Around my chin there was a strip of wire and tape. Inside it was dark and quiet at first except Fearing's voice was still coming into the earphones.

"The rules are simple. Our contestants get a thirty-minute rest period every three hours. These kids'll be well fed, don't worry about that. Our doctor will monitor their health. You've heard the horror stories, but we're a class outfit; you'll see no horrors here. The kids earn the quality care we provide one way: continuous, waking engagement with the datastream. We're firm on that. To sleep is to die — you can sleep on your own time, but not ours. One lapse, and you're out of the game — them's the rules."

The earphones started to hum. I wished I could reach out and hold Gloria's hand, but she was too far away.

"They'll have no help from the floor judges, or one another, in locating the perceptual riches of cyberspace. Some will discover the keys that open the doors to a thousand worlds, others will bog down in the antechamber to the future. Anyone caught coaching during rest periods will be disqualified — no warnings, no second chances."

Then Fearing's voice dropped out, and the scapes started.

I was in a hallway. The walls were full of drawers, like a big cabinet that went on forever. The drawers had writing on them that I ignored. First I couldn't move except my head, then I figured out how to walk, and just did that for a while. But I never got anywhere. It felt like I was walking in a giant circle, up the wall, across the ceiling, and then back down the other wall.

So I pulled open a drawer. It only looked big enough to hold some pencils or whatever but when I pulled, it opened like a door and I went through.

"Welcome to Intense Personals," said a voice. There was just some colors to look at. The door closed behind me. "You must be eighteen years of age or older to use this service. To avoid any charges, please exit now."

I didn't exit because I didn't know how. The space with colors was kind of small except it didn't have any edges. But it felt small.

"This is the main menu. Please reach out and make one of the following selections: women seeking men, men seeking women, women seeking women, men seeking men, or alternatives."

Each of them was a block of words in the air. I reached up and touched the first one.

"After each selection touch *one* to play the recording again, *two* to record a message for this person, or *three* to advance to the next selection. You may touch three at any time to advance to the next selection, or four to return to the main menu."

Then a woman came into the colored space with me. She was dressed up and wearing lipstick.

"Hi, my name is Kate," she said. She stared like she was looking through my head at something behind me, and poked at her hair while she talked. "I live in San Francisco. I work in the financial district, as a personnel manager, but my real love is the arts, currently painting and writing—"

"How did you get into San Francisco?" I said.

"—just bought a new pair of hiking boots and I'm hoping to tackle Mount Tam this weekend," she said, ignoring me.

"I never met anyone from there," I said.

"—looking for a man who's not intimidated by intelligence," she went on. "It's important that you like what you do, like where you are. I also want someone who's confident enough that I can express my vulnerability. You should be a good listener—"

I touched three. I can read numbers.

Another woman came in, just like that. This one was as young as Gloria, but kind of soft-looking.

"I continue to ask myself why in the *heck* I'm doing this personals thing," she said, sighing. "But I know the reason—I want to date. I'm new to the San Francisco area. I like to go to the theater, but I'm really open-minded. I was born and raised in Chicago, so I think I'm a little more East Coast than West. I'm fast-talking and cynical. I guess I'm getting a little cynical about these ads, the sky has yet to part, lightning has yet to strike—"

I got rid of her, now that I knew how.

"—I have my own garden and landscape business—"

"—someone who's fun, not nerdy—"

"—I'm tender, I'm sensuous—"

I started to wonder how long ago these women were from. I didn't like the way they were making me feel, sort of guilty and bullied at the same time. I didn't think I could make any of them happy the way they were hoping but I didn't think I was going to get a chance to try, anyway.

It took pretty long for me to get back out into the hallway. From then on I paid more attention to how I got into things.

The next drawer I got into was just about the opposite. All space and no people. I was driving an airplane over almost the whole world, as far as I could tell. There was a row of dials and switches under the windows but it didn't mean anything to me. First I was in the mountains and I crashed a lot, and that was dull because a voice would lecture me before I could start again, and I had to wait. But then I got to the desert and I kept it up without crashing much. I just learned to say "no" whenever the voice suggested something different like "engage target" or "evasive action." I wanted to fly a while, that's all. The desert looked good from up there, even though I'd been walking around in deserts too often.

Except that I had to pee I could have done that forever. Fearing's voice broke in, though, and said it was time for the first rest period.

" — still fresh and eager after their first plunge into the wonders of the future," Fearing was saying to the people in the seats. The place was only half full. "Already this world seems drab by comparison. Yet, consider the irony, that as their questing minds grow accustomed to these splendors, their bodies will begin to rebel — "

Gloria showed me how to unsnap the cables so I could walk out — of the middle of all that stuff still wearing the suit, leaving the mask behind. Everybody lined up for the bathroom. Then we went to the big hall in the back where they had the cots, but nobody went to sleep or anything. I guessed we'd all want to next time, but right now I was too excited and so was everybody else. Fearing just kept talking like us taking a break was as much a part of the show as anything else.

"Splendors, hah," said Gloria. "Bunch of second-hand cyberjunk."

"I was in a plane," I started.

"Shut up," said Gloria. "We're not supposed to talk about it. Only, if you find something you like, remember where it is."

I hadn't done that, but I wasn't worried.

"Drink some water," she said. "And get some food."

They were going around with sandwiches and I got a couple, one for Gloria. But she didn't seem to want to talk.

Gilmartin the fake doctor was making a big deal of going around checking everybody even though it was only the first break. I figured that the whole point of taking care of us so hard was to remind the people in the seats that they might see somebody get hurt.

Ed was giving out apples from a bag. I took one and went over and sat on Lane's cot. She looked nice in her suit.

"My boyfriend's here," she said.

"You're back together?"

"I mean ex-. I'm pretending I didn't see him."

"Where?"

"He's sitting right in front of my monitor." She tipped her head to point.

I didn't say anything but I wished I had somebody watching me from the audience.

When I went back the first thing I got into was a library of books. Every one you took off the shelf turned into a show, with charts and pictures, but when I figured out that it was all business stuff about how to manage your money, I got bored.

Then I went into a dungeon. It started with a wizard growing me up from a bug. We were in his workshop, which was all full of jars and cobwebs. He had a face like a melted candle and he talked as much as Fearing. There were bats flying around.

"You must resume the quest of Kroyd," he said to me, and started touching me with his stick. I could see my arms and legs, but they weren't wearing the scaper suit. They were covered with muscles. When the wizard touched me I got a sword and a shield. "These are your companions, Rip and Batter," said the wizard. "They will obey you and protect you. You must never betray them for any other. That was Kroyd's mistake."

"Okay," I said.

The wizard sent me into the dungeon and Rip and Batter talked to me. They told me what to do. They sounded a lot like the wizard.

We met a Wormlion. That's what Rip and Batter called it. It had a head full of worms with little faces and Rip and Batter said to kill it, which wasn't hard. The head exploded and all the worms started running away into the stones of the floor like water.

Then we met a woman in sexy clothes who was holding a sword and shield too. Hers were loaded with jewels and looked a lot nicer than Rip and Batter.

This was Kroyd's mistake, anyone could see that. Only I figured Kroyd wasn't here and I was, and so maybe his mistake was one I wanted to make too.

Rip and Batter started screaming when I traded with the woman, and then she put them on and we fought. When she killed me I was back in the doorway to the wizard's room, where I first ran in, bug-sized. This time I went the other way, back to the drawers.

Which is when I met the snowman.

I was looking around in a drawer that didn't seem to have anything in it. Everything was just black. Then I saw a little blinking list of numbers in the corner. I touched the numbers. None of them did anything except one.

It was still black but there were five pictures of a snowman. He was three balls of white, more like plastic than snow. His eyes were just o's and his mouth didn't move right when he talked. His arms were sticks but they bent like rubber. There were two pictures of him small and far away, one from underneath like he was on a hill and one that showed the top of his head, like he was in a hole. Then there was a big one of just his head, and a big one of his whole body. The last one was of him looking in through a window, only you couldn't see the window, just the way it cut off part of the snowman.

"What's your name?" he said.

"Lewis."

"I'm Mr. Sneeze." His head and arms moved in all five pictures when he talked. His eyes got big and small.

"What's this place you're in?"

"It's no place," said Mr. Sneeze. "Just a garbage file."

"Why do you live in a garbage file?"

"Copyright lawyers," said Mr. Sneeze. "I made them nervous." He sounded happy no matter what he was saying.

"Nervous about what?"

"I was in a Christmas special for interactive television. But at the last minute somebody from the legal department thought I looked too much like a snowman on a video game called *Mud Flinger*. It was too late to redesign me so they just cut me out and dumped me in this file."

"Can't you go somewhere else?"

"I don't have too much mobility." He jumped and twirled upside down and landed in the same place, five times at once. The one without a body spun too.

"Do you miss the show?"

"I just hope they're doing well. Everybody has been working so hard."

I didn't want to tell him it was probably a long time ago.

"What are you doing here, Lewis?" said Mr. Sneeze.

"I'm in a scape-athon."

"What's that?"

I told him about Gloria and Fearing and Kromer, and about the contest. I think he liked that he was on television again.

There weren't too many people left in the seats. Fearing was talking to them about what was going to happen tomorrow when they came back. Kromer and Ed got us all in the back. I looked over at Lane's cot. She was already asleep. Her boyfriend was gone from the chair out front.

I lay down on the cot beside Gloria. "I'm tired now," I said.

"So sleep a little," she said, and put her arm over me. But I could hear Fearing outside talking about a "Sexathon" and I asked Gloria what it was.

"That's tomorrow night," she said. "Don't worry about it now."

Gloria wasn't going to sleep, just looking around.

I found the SmartHouse Showroom. It was a house with a voice inside. At first I was looking around to see who the voice was but then I figured out it was the house.

"Answer the phone!" it said. The phone was ringing.

I picked up the phone, and the lights in the room changed to a desk light on the table with the phone. The music in the room turned off.

"How's that for responsiveness?"

"Fine," I said. I hung up the phone.

There was a television in the room, and it turned on. It was a picture of food. "See that?"

"The food, you mean?" I said.

"That's the contents of your refrigerator!" it said. "The packages with the blue halo will go bad in the next twenty-four hours. The package with the black halo has already expired! Would you like me to dispose of it for you?"

"Sure."

"Now look out the windows!"

I looked. There were mountains outside.

"Imagine waking up in the Alps every morning!"

"I—"

"And when you're ready for work, your car is already warm in the garage!"

The windows switched from the mountains to a picture of a car in a garage.

"And your voicemail tells callers that you're not home when it senses the car is gone from the garage!"

I wondered if there was somewhere I could get if I went down to drive the car. But they were trying to sell me this house, so probably not.

"And the television notifies you when the book you're reading is available this week as a movie!"

The television switched to a movie, the window curtains closed, and the light by the phone went off.

"I can't read," I said.

"All the more important, then, isn't it?" said the house.

"What about the bedroom?" I said. I was thinking about sleep. "Here you go!" A door opened and I went in. The bedroom had another television. But the bed wasn't right. It had a scribble of electronic stuff over it.

"What's wrong with the bed?"

"Somebody defaced it," said the house. "Pity."

I knew it must have been Fearing or Kromer who wrecked the bed because they didn't want anyone getting that comfortable and falling asleep and out of the contest. At least not yet.

"Sorry!" said the house. "Let me show you the work center!"

Next rest I got right into Gloria's cot and curled up and she curled around me. It was real early in the morning and nobody was watching the show now and Fearing wasn't talking. I think he was off taking a nap of his own.

Kromer woke us up. "He always have to sleep with you, like a baby?"

Gloria said, "Leave him alone. He can sleep where he wants."

"I can't figure," said Kromer. "Is he your boyfriend or your kid brother?"

"Neither," said Gloria. "What do you care?"

"Okay," said Kromer. "We've got a job for him to do tomorrow, though."

"What job?" said Gloria. They talked like I wasn't there.

"We need a hacker boy for a little sideshow we put on," said Kromer. "He's it."

"He's never been in a scape before," said Gloria. "He's no hacker."

"He's the nearest we've got. We'll walk him through it."

"I'll do it," I said.

"Okay, but then leave him out of the Sexathon," said Gloria.

Kromer smiled. "You're protecting him? Sorry. Everybody plays in the Sexathon, sweetheart. That's bread and butter. The customers don't let us break the rules." He pointed out to the rigs. "You'd better get out there."

I knew Kromer thought I didn't know about Gloria and Fearing, or other things. I wanted to tell him I wasn't so innocent, but I didn't think Gloria would like it, so I kept quiet.

I went to talk to Mr. Sneeze. I remembered where he was from the first time.

"What's a Sexathon?" I said.

"I don't know, Lewis."

"I've never had sex," I said.

"Me neither," said Mr. Sneeze.

"Everybody always thinks I do with Gloria just because we go around together. But we're just friends."

"That's fine," said Mr. Sneeze. "It's okay to be friends."

"I'd like to be Lane's boyfriend," I said.

Next break Gloria slept while Gilmartin and Kromer told me about the act. A drawer would be marked for me to go into, and there would be a lot of numbers and letters but I just had to keep pressing "1-2-3" no matter what. It was supposed to be a security archive, they said. The people watching would think I was breaking codes but it was just for show. Then something else would happen but they wouldn't say what, just that I should keep quiet and let Fearing talk. So I knew they were going to pull me out of my mask. I didn't know if I should tell Gloria.

Fearing was up again welcoming some people back in. I couldn't believe anybody wanted to start watching first thing in the morning but Fearing was saying "the gritty determination to survive that epitomizes the frontier spirit that once made a country called America great" and "young bodies writhing in agonized congress with the future" and that sounded like a lot of fun, I guess.

A woman from the town had quit already. Not Lane though.

A good quiet place to go was Mars. It was like the airplane, all space and no people, but better since there was no voice telling you to engage targets, and you never crashed.

I went to the drawer they told me about. Fearing's voice in my ear told me it was time. The place was a storeroom of information like the business library. No people, just files with a lot of blinking lights and complicated words. A voice kept asking me for "security clearance password" but there was always a place for me to touch "1-2-3" and I did. It was kind of a joke, like a wall made out of feathers that falls apart every time you touch it.

I found a bunch of papers with writing. Some of the words were blacked out and some were bright red and blinking. There was a siren sound. Then I felt hands pulling on me from outside and somebody took off my mask.

There were two guys pulling on me who I had never seen before, and Ed and Kromer were pulling on them. Everybody was screaming at each other but it was kind of fake, because nobody was pulling or yelling very hard. Fearing said, "The feds, the feds!" A bunch of people were crowded around my television screen I guess looking at the papers I'd dug up, but now they were watching the action.

Fearing came over and pulled out a toy gun and so did Kromer, and they were backing the two men away from me. I'm sure the audience could tell it was fake. But they were pretty excited, maybe just from remembering when feds were real.

I got off my frame and looked around. I didn't know what they were going to do with me now that I was out but I didn't care. It was my first chance to see what it was like when the contestants were all in their suits and masks, swimming in the information. None of them knew what was happening, not even Gloria, who was right next to me the whole time. They just kept moving in the scapes. I looked at Lane. She looked good, like she was dancing.

Meanwhile Fearing and Kromer chased those guys out the back. People were craning around to see. Fearing came out and took his microphone and said, "It isn't his fault, folks. Just good hacker instincts for ferreting out corruption from encrypted data. The feds don't want us digging up their trail, but the kid couldn't help it."

Ed and Kromer started snapping me back into my suit. "We chased them off," Fearing said, patting his gun. "We do take care of our own. You can't tell who's going to come sniffing around, can you? For his protection and ours we're going to have to delete that file, but it goes to show, there's no limit to what a kid with a nose for data's going to root out of cyberspace. We can't throw him out of the contest for doing what comes natural. Give him a big hand, folks."

People clapped and a few threw coins. Ed picked the change up for me, then told me to put on my mask. Meanwhile Gloria and Lane and everybody else just went on through their scapes.

I began to see what Kromer and Fearing were selling. It wasn't any one thing. Some of it was fake and some was real, and some was a mix so you couldn't tell.

The people watching probably didn't know why they wanted to, except it made them forget their screwed-up life for a while to watch the only suckers bigger than themselves—us.

"Meanwhile, the big show goes on," said Fearing. "How long will they last? Who will take the prize?"

I told Gloria about it at the break. She just shrugged and said to make sure I got my money from Kromer. Fearing was talking to Anne the woman from the van, and Gloria was staring at them like she wanted them dead.

A guy was lying in his cot talking to himself as if nobody could hear and Gilmartin and Kromer went over and told him he was kicked out. He didn't seem to care.

I went to see Lane but we didn't talk. We sat on her cot and held hands. I didn't know if it meant the same thing to her that it did to me but I liked it.

After the break I went and talked to Mr. Sneeze. He told me the story of the show about Christmas. He said it wasn't about always getting gifts. Sometimes you had to give gifts too.

—

The Sexathon was late at night. They cleared the seats and everyone had to pay again to get back in, because it was a special event. Fearing had built it up all day, talking about how it was for adults only, it would separate the men from the boys, things like that. Also that people would get knocked out of the contest. So we were pretty nervous by the time he told us the rules.

"What would scapes be without virtual sex?" he said. "Our voyagers must now prove themselves in the sensual realm — for the future consists of far more than cold, hard information. It's a place of desire and temptation, and, as always, survival belongs to the fittest. The soldiers will now be steered onto the sexual battlescape — the question is, will they meet with the Little Death, or the Big One?"

Gloria wouldn't explain. "Not real death," is all she said.

"The rules again are so simple a child could follow them. In the Sex-Scape environment our contestants will be free to pick from a variety of fantasy partners. We've packed this program with options, there's something for every taste, believe you me. We won't question their selections, but — here's the catch — we will chart the results. Their suits will tell us who does and doesn't attain sexual orgasm in the next session, and those who don't will be handed their walking papers. The suits don't lie. Find bliss or die, folks, find bliss or die."

"You get it now?" said Gloria to me.

"I guess," I said.

"As ever, audience members are cautioned never to interfere with the contestants during play. Follow their fantasies on the monitors, or watch their youthful bodies strain against exhaustion, seeking to bridge virtual lust and bona fide physical response. But no touchee."

Kromer was going around, checking the suits. "Who's gonna be in your fantasy, kid?" he said to me. "The snowman?"

I'd forgotten how they could watch me talk to Mr. Sneeze on my television. I turned red.

"Screw you, Kromer," said Gloria.

"Whoever you want, honey," he said, laughing.

Well I found my way around their Sex-Scape and I'm not too embarrassed to say I found a girl who reminded me of Lane, except for the way she was trying so hard to be sexy. But she looked like Lane. I didn't have to do much to get the subject around to sex. It was the only thing on her mind. She wanted me to tell her what I wanted to do to her and when I couldn't think of much she suggested things and I just agreed. And when I did that she would move around and sigh as if it were really exciting to talk about even though she was doing the talking. She wanted to touch me but she couldn't really so she took off her clothes and got close to me and touched herself. I touched her too but she didn't really feel like much and it was like my hands were made of wood, which couldn't have felt too nice for her though she acted like it was great.

I touched myself a little too. I tried not to think about the audience. I was a little confused about what was what in the suit and with her breathing in my ear so loud but I got the desired result. That wasn't hard for me.

Then I could go back to the drawers but Kromer had made me embarrassed about visiting Mr. Sneeze so I went to Mars even though I would have liked to talk to him.

The audience was all stirred up at the next break. They were sure getting their money's worth now. I got into Gloria's cot. I asked her if she did it with her own hands too. "You didn't have to do that," she said.

"How else?"

"I just pretended. I don't think they can tell. They just want to see you wiggle around."

Well some of the women from the town hadn't wiggled around enough I guess because Kromer and Ed were taking them out of the contest. A couple of them were crying.

"I wish I hadn't," I said.

"It's the same either way," said Gloria. "Don't feel bad. Probably some other people did it too."

They didn't kick Lane out but I saw she was crying anyway.

Kromer brought a man into the back and said to me, "Get into your own cot, little snowman."

"Let him stay," said Gloria. She wasn't looking at Kromer.

"I've got someone here who wants to meet you," said Kromer to Gloria. "Mr. Warren, this is Gloria."

Mr. Warren shook her hand. He was pretty old. "I've been admiring you," he said. "You're very good."

"Mr. Warren is wondering if you'd let him buy you a drink," said Kromer.

"Thanks, but I need some sleep," said Gloria.

"Perhaps later," said Mr. Warren.

After he left, Kromer came back and said, "You shouldn't pass up easy money."

"I don't need it," said Gloria. "I'm going to win your contest, you goddamn pimp."

"Now, Gloria," said Kromer. "You don't want to give the wrong impression."

"Leave me alone."

I noticed now that Anne wasn't around in the rest area and I got the idea that the kind of easy money Gloria didn't want Anne did. I'm not so dumb.

Worrying about the Sexathon had stopped me from feeling how tired I was. Right after that I started nodding off in the scapes. I had to keep moving around. After I'd been to a few new things I went to see the snowman again. It was early in the morning and I figured Kromer was probably asleep and there was barely any audience to see what I was doing on my television. So Mr. Sneeze and I talked and that helped me stay awake.

I wasn't the only one who was tired after that night. On the next break I saw that a bunch of people had dropped out or been kicked out for sleeping. There were only seventeen left. I couldn't stay awake myself. But I woke up when I heard some yelling over where Lane was.

It was her parents. I guess they heard about the Sexathon, maybe from her boyfriend, who was there too. Lane was sitting crying behind Fearing who was telling her parents to get out of there, and her father just kept saying, "I'm her father! I'm her father!" Her mother was pulling at Fearing but Ed came over and pulled on her.

I started to get up but Gloria grabbed my arm and said, "Stay out of this."

"Lane doesn't want to see that guy," I said.

"Let the townies take care of themselves, Lewis. Let Lane's daddy take her home if he can. Worse could happen to her."

"You just want her out of the contest," I said.

Gloria laughed. "I'm not worried about your girlfriend outlasting me," she said. "She's about to break no matter what."

So I just watched. Kromer and Ed got Lane's parents and boyfriend pushed out of the rest area, back toward the seats. Fearing was yelling at them, making a scene for the audience. It was all part of the show as far as he was concerned.

Anne from the van was over talking to Lane, who was still crying, but quiet now.

"Do you really think you can win?" I said to Gloria.

"Sure, why not?" she said. "I can last."

"I'm pretty tired." In fact my eyeballs felt like they were full of sand.

"Well if you fall out stick around. You can probably get food out of Kromer for cleaning up or something. I'm going to take these bastards."

"You don't like Fearing anymore," I said.

"I never did," said Gloria.

That afternoon three more people dropped out. Fearing was going on about endurance and I got thinking about how much harder it was to live the way me and Gloria did than it was to be in town and so maybe we had an advantage. Maybe that was why Gloria thought she could win now. But I sure didn't feel it myself. I was so messed up that I couldn't always sleep at the rest periods, just lie there and listen to Fearing or eat their sandwiches until I wanted to vomit.

Kromer and Gilmartin were planning some sideshow but it didn't involve me and I didn't care. I didn't want coins thrown at me. I just wanted to get through.

If I built the cities near the water the plague always killed all the people and if I built the cities near the mountains the volcanoes always killed all the people and if I built the cities on the plain the other tribe always came over and killed all the people and I got sick of the whole damn thing.

"When Gloria wins we could live in town for a while," I said. "We could even get jobs if there are any. Then if Lane doesn't want to go back to her parents she could stay with us."

"You could win the contest," said Mr. Sneeze.

"I don't think so," I said. "But Gloria could."

Why did Lewis cross Mars? To get to the other side. Ha ha.

I came out for the rest period and Gloria was already yelling and I unhooked my suit and rushed over to see what was the matter. It was so late it was getting light outside and almost nobody was in the place. "She's cheating!" Gloria screamed. She was pounding on Kromer and he was backing up because she was a handful mad. "That bitch is cheating! You let her sleep!" Gloria pointed at Anne from the van. "She's lying there asleep, you're running tapes in her monitor you goddamn cheater!"

Anne sat up in her frame and didn't say anything. She looked confused. "You're a bunch of cheaters!" Gloria kept saying. Kromer got her by the wrists and said, "Take it easy, take it easy. You're going scape-crazy, girl."

"Don't tell me I'm crazy!" said Gloria. She twisted away from Kromer and ran to the seats. Mr. Warren was there, watching her with his hat in his hands. I ran after Gloria and said her name but she said, "Leave me alone!" and went over to Mr. Warren. "You saw it, didn't you?" she said.

"I'm sorry?" said Mr. Warren.

"You must have seen it, the way she wasn't moving at all," said Gloria. "Come on, tell these cheaters you saw it. I'll go on that date with you if you tell them."

"I'm sorry, darling. I was looking at you."

Kromer knocked me out of the way and grabbed Gloria from behind. "Listen to me, girl. You're hallucinating. You're scape-happy. We see it all the time." He was talking quiet but hard. "Any more of this and you're out of the show, you understand? Get in the back and lie down now and get some sleep. You need it."

"You bastard," said Gloria.

"Sure, I'm a bastard, but you're seeing things." He held Gloria's wrist and she sagged.

Mr. Warren got up and put his hat on. "I'll see you tomorrow, darling. Don't worry. I'm rooting for you." He went out.

Gloria didn't look at him.

Kromer took Gloria back to the rest area but suddenly I wasn't paying much attention myself. I had been thinking Fearing wasn't taking advantage of the free action by talking about it because there wasn't anyone much in the place to impress at this hour. Then I looked around and I realized there were two people missing and that was Fearing and Lane.

I found Ed and I asked him if Lane had dropped out of the contest and he said no.

"Maybe there's a way you could find out if Anne is really scaping or if she's a cheat," I said to Mr. Sneeze.

"I don't see how I could," he said. "I can't visit her, she has to visit me. And nobody visits me except you." He hopped and jiggled in his five places. "I'd like it if I could meet Gloria and Lane."

"Let's not talk about Lane," I said.

When I saw Fearing again I couldn't look at him. He was out talking to the people who came by in the morning, not in the microphone but one at a time, shaking hands and taking compliments like it was him doing the scaping.

There were only eight people left in the contest. Lane was still in it but I didn't care.

I knew if I tried to sleep I would just lie there thinking. So I went to rinse out under my suit, which was getting pretty rank. I hadn't been out of that suit since the contest started. In the bathroom I looked out the little window at the daylight and I thought about how I hadn't been out of that building for five days either, no matter how much I'd gone to Mars and elsewhere.

I went back in and saw Gloria asleep and I thought all of a sudden that I should try to win.

But maybe that was just the idea coming over me that Gloria wasn't going to.

I didn't notice it right away because I went to other places first. Mr. Sneeze had made me promise I'd always have something new to tell him about so I always opened a few drawers. I went to a tank game but it was boring. Then I found a place called the American History Blood and Wax Museum and I stopped President Lincoln from getting murdered a couple of times. I tried to stop President Kennedy from getting murdered but if I stopped it one way it always happened a different way. I don't know why.

So then I was going to tell Mr. Sneeze about it and that's when I found out. I went into his drawer and touched the right numbers but what I got wasn't the usual five pictures of the snowman. It was pieces of him but chopped up and stretched into thin white strips, around the edge of the black space, like a band of white light.

I said, "Mr. Sneeze?"

There wasn't any voice.

I went out and came back in but it was the same. He couldn't talk. The band of white strips got narrower and wider, like it was trying to move or talk. It looked a bit like a hand waving open and shut. But if he was still there he couldn't talk.

I would have taken my mask off then anyway, but the heat of my face and my tears forced me to.

I saw Fearing up front talking and I started for him without even getting my suit unclipped, so I tore up a few of my wires. I didn't care. I knew I was out now. I went right out and tackled Fearing from behind. He wasn't so big, anyway. Only his voice was big. I got him down on the floor.

"You killed him," I said, and I punched him as hard as I could, but you know Kromer and Gilmartin were there holding my arms before I could hit him more than once. I just screamed at Fearing, "You killed him, you killed him."

Fearing was smiling at me and wiping his mouth. "Your snowman malfunctioned, kid."

"That's a lie!"

"You were boring us to death with that snowman, you little punk. Give it a rest, for chrissake."

I kept kicking out even though they had me pulled away from him. "I'll kill you!" I said.

"Right," said Fearing. "Throw him out of here."

He never stopped smiling. Everything suited his plans, that was what I hated.

Kromer the big ape and Gilmartin pulled me outside into the sunlight and it was like a knife in my eyes. I couldn't believe how bright it was. They tossed me down in the street and when I got up Kromer punched me, hard.

Then Gloria came outside. I don't know how she found out, if she heard me screaming or if Ed woke her. Anyway she gave Kromer a pretty good punch in the side and said, "Leave him alone!"

Kromer was surprised and he moaned and I got away from him. Gloria punched him again. Then she turned around and gave Gilmartin a kick in the nuts and he went down. I'll always remember in spite of what happened next that she gave those guys a couple they'd be feeling for a day or two.

The gang who beat the crap out of us were a mix of the militia and some other guys from the town, including Lane's boyfriend. Pretty funny that he'd take out his frustration on us, but that just shows you how good Fearing had that whole town wrapped around his finger.

Outside of town we found an old house that we could hide in and get some sleep. I slept longer than Gloria. When I woke up she was on the front steps rubbing a spoon back and forth on the pavement to make a sharp point, even though I could see it hurt her arm to do it.

"Well, we did get fed for a couple of days," I said.

Gloria didn't say anything.

"Let's go up to San Francisco," I said. "There's a lot of lonely women there."

I was making a joke of course.

Gloria looked at me. "What's that supposed to mean?"

"Just that maybe I can get us in for once."

Gloria didn't laugh, but I knew she would later.

Yeyuka

Greg Egan

Though not all of his stories are about information technology, and most make only passing nods, if any, to the icons of classic CP, most Greg Egan stories are like '80s CP in their foregrounding of ideas over character. A typical Egan story bombards the reader with ideas and their implications and lets literary concerns go hang. This one has a nifty technological device at its heart. But it turns into a story about first-vs.-third world economics, and then, uncharacteristically, into a story about one person's moral decision.

Neuromancer, through its transnational megacorporations and the brutal struggle of its protagonists in a street-level no-holds-barred marketplace, offers an implicit critique of capitalism. Here the critique of corporate power bound only by profit margins is overt.

On my last day in Sydney, as a kind of farewell, I spent the morning on Bondi Beach. I swam for an hour, then lay on the sand and stared at the sky. I dozed off for a while, and when I woke there were half a dozen booths set up amid the sun bathers, dispensing the latest fashion: solar tattoos. On a touch-screen the size of a full-length mirror, you could choose a design and then customise it, or create one from scratch with software assistance. Computer-controlled jets sprayed the undeveloped pigments onto your skin, then an hour of uv exposure rendered all the colours visible.

As the morning wore on, I saw giant yellow butterflies perched between shoulder blades, torsos wrapped in green-and-violet dragons, whole bodies wreathed in chains of red hibiscus. Watching these images materialise around me, I couldn't help thinking of them as banners of victory. Throughout my childhood, there'd been nothing more terrifying than the threat of melanoma — and by the turn of the millennium, nothing more hip than neck-to-knee lycra. Twenty years later, these elaborate decorations were designed to encourage, *to boast of*, irradiation. To proclaim, not that the sun itself had been tamed, but that our bodies had. To declare that cancer had been defeated.

I touched the ring on my left index finger, and felt a reassuring pulse through the metal. Blood flowed constantly around the hollow core of the device, diverted from a vein in my finger. The ring's inner surface was covered with billions of tiny sensors, spring-loaded, funnel-shaped structures like microscopic Venus fly-traps, each just a few hundred atoms wide. Every sizable molecule in my bloodstream that collided with one of these traps was seized and shrink-wrapped, long enough and tightly enough to determine its shape and its chemical identity before it was released.

So the ring knew exactly what was in my blood. It also knew what belonged, and what didn't. Under its relentless scrutiny, the biochemical signature of a viral or bacterial infection, or even a microscopic tumour far downstream, could never escape detection for long — and once a diagnosis was made, treatment was almost instantaneous. Planted alongside the sensors were programmable catalysts, versatile molecules that could be reshaped under computer control. The ring could manufacture a wide range of drugs from raw materials circulating in the blood, just by choosing the right sequence of shapes for these catalysts — trapping the necessary ingredients together in nooks and crannies moulded to fit like plaster casts around their combined outlines.

With medication delivered within minutes or seconds, infections were wiped out before they could take hold, tiny clusters of cancer cells destroyed before they could grow or spread. Linked by satellite to a vast array of medical databases, and as much additional computing power as it required, the ring gave me a kind of electronic immune system, fast enough and smart enough to overcome any adversary.

Not everyone on the beach that morning would have had their own personal HealthGuard, but a weekly session on a shared family unit, or even a monthly check-up at their local GP, would have been enough to reduce their risk of cancer dramatically. And though melanoma was the least of my worries — fair-skinned, I was covered in sunscreen as usual; fatal or not, getting burnt was painful — with the ring standing guard against ten thousand other possibilities, I'd come to think of it as a vital part of my body. The day I'd installed it, my life expectancy had risen by fifteen years — and no doubt my bank's risk-assessment software had assumed a similar extension to my working life, since I'd be paying off the loan I'd needed to buy the thing well into my sixties.

I tugged gently at the plain metal band, until I felt a sharp warning from the needle-thin tubes that ran deep into the flesh. This model wasn't designed to be slipped on and off in an instant like the shared units, but it would only take a five-minute surgical procedure under local anaesthetic to remove it. In Uganda, a single HealthGuard machine served 40 million people — or rather, the lucky few who could get access to it. Flying in wearing my own personal version seemed almost as crass as arriving with a giant solar tattoo. Where I was headed, cancer had very definitely not been defeated.

Then again, nor had malaria, typhoid, yellow fever, schistosomiasis. I could have the ring immunise me against all of these and more, before removing it ... but the malaria parasite was notoriously variable, so constant surveillance would provide far more reliable protection. I'd be no use to anyone lying in a hospital bed for half my stay. Besides, the average villager or shanty-town dweller probably wouldn't even recognise the thing, let alone resent it. I was being hypersensitive.

I gathered up my things and headed for the cycle rack. Looking back across the sand, I felt the kind of stab of regret that came upon waking from a dream of impossible good fortune and serenity, and for a moment I wanted nothing more than to close my eyes and rejoin it.

Lisa saw me off at the airport.

I said, "It's only three months. It'll fly past." I was reassuring myself, not her.

"It's not too late to change your mind." She smiled calmly; no pressure, it was entirely my decision. In her eyes, I was clearly suffering from some kind of disease — a very late surge of adolescent idealism, or a very early midlife crisis — but she'd adopted a scrupulously nonjudgmental bedside manner. It drove me mad.

"And miss my last chance ever to perform cancer surgery?" That was a slight exaggeration; a few cases would keep slipping through the HealthGuard net for years. Most of my usual work was trauma, though, which was going through changes of its own. Computerised safeguards had made traffic accidents rare, and I suspected that within a decade no one would get the chance to stick their hand in a conveyor belt again. If the steady stream of gunshot and knife wounds ever dried up, I'd have to retrain for nose jobs and reconstructing rugby players. "I should have gone into obstetrics, like you."

Lisa shook her head. "In the next twenty years, they'll crack all the molecular signals, within and between mother and foetus. There'll be no premature births, no Caesareans, no complications. The HealthGuard will smooth my job away, too." She added, deadpan, "Face it, Martin, we're all doomed to obsolescence."

"Maybe. But if we are...it'll happen sooner in some places than others."

"And when the time comes, you might just head off to some place where you're still needed?"

She was mocking me, but I took the question seriously. "Ask me that when I get back. Three months without mod cons and I might be cured for life."

My flight was called. We kissed goodbye. I suddenly realised that I had no idea why I was doing this. The health of distant strangers? Who was I kidding? Maybe I'd been trying to fool myself into believing that I really was that selfless — hoping all the while that Lisa would talk me out of it, offering some face-saving excuse for me to stay. I should have known she'd call my bluff instead.

I said plainly, "I'm going to miss you. Badly."

"I should hope so." She took my hand, scowling, finally accepting the decision. "You're an idiot, you know. Be careful."

"I will." I kissed her again, then slipped away.

I was met at Entebbe airport by Magdalena Iganga, one of the oncologists on a small team that had been put together by Médecins Sans Frontières to help overburdened Ugandan doctors tackle the growing number of Yeyuka cases. Iganga was Tanzanian, but she'd worked throughout eastern Africa, and as she drove her battered ethanol-powered car the thirty kilometres into Kampala, she recounted some of her brushes with the World Health Organisation in Nairobi.

"I tried to persuade them to set up an epidemiological database for Yeyuka. Good idea, they said. Just put a detailed proposal to the cancer epidemiology expert committee. So I did. And the committee said, we like your proposal, but oh dear, Yeyuka is a contagious disease, so you'll have to submit this to the contagious diseases expert committee instead. Whose latest annual sitting I'd just missed by a week." Iganga sighed stoically. "Some colleagues and I ended up doing it ourselves, on an old 386 and a borrowed phone line."

"Three eight what?"

She shook her head. "Palaeocomputing jargon, never mind."

Though we were dead on the equator and it was almost noon, the temperature must have been 30 at most; Kampala was high above sea level. A humid breeze blew off Lake Victoria, and low clouds rolled by above us, gathering threateningly then dissipating, again and again. I'd been promised that I'd come for the dry season; at worst there'd be occasional thunderstorms.

On our left, between patches of marshland, small clusters of shacks began to appear. As we drew closer to the city, we passed through layers of shanty towns, the older and more organised verging on a kind of bedraggled suburbia, others looking more like out-and-out refugee camps. The tumours caused by the Yeyuka virus tended to spread fast but grow slowly, often partially disabling people for years before killing them, and when they could no longer manage heavy rural labour, they usually headed for the nearest city in the hope of finding work. Southern Uganda had barely recovered from HIV when Yeyuka cases began to appear, around 2013; in fact, some virologists believed that Yeyuka had arisen from a less virulent ancestor after gaining a foothold within the immune-suppressed population. And though Yeyuka wasn't as contagious as cholera or tuberculosis, crowded conditions, poor sanitation and chronic malnourishment set up the shanty towns to bear the brunt of the epidemic.

As we drove north between two hills, the centre of Kampala appeared ahead of us, draped across a hill of its own. Compared to Nairobi, which I'd flown over a few hours before, Kampala looked uncluttered. The streets and low buildings were laid out in a widely spaced plan, neatly organised but lacking any rigid geometry of grid lines or concentric circles. There was plenty of traffic around us, both cycles and cars, but it flowed smoothly enough, and for all the honking and shouting going on the drivers seemed remarkably good humoured.

Iganga took a detour to the east, skirting the central hill. There were lushly green sports grounds and golf courses on our right, colonial-era public buildings and high-fenced foreign embassies on our left. There were no high-rise slums in sight, but there were makeshift shelters and even vegetable gardens on some stretches of parkland, traces of the shanty towns spreading inwards.

In my jet-lagged state, it was amazing to find that this abstract place that I'd been imagining for months had solid ground, actual buildings, real people. Most of my second-hand glimpses of Uganda had come from news clips set in war zones and disaster areas; from Sydney, it had been almost impossible to conceive of the country as anything more than a frantically edited video sequence full of soldiers, refugees, and fly-blown corpses. In fact, rebel activity was confined to a shrinking zone in the country's far north, most of the last wave of Zairian refugees had gone home a year ago, and while Yeyuka was a serious problem, people weren't exactly dropping dead in the streets.

Makerere University was in the north of the city; Iganga and I were both staying at the guest house there. A student showed me to my room, which was plain but spotlessly clean; I was almost afraid to sit on the bed and rumple the sheets. After washing and unpacking, I met up with Iganga again and we walked across the campus to Mulago Hospital, which was affiliated with the university medical school. There was a soccer team practising across the road as we went in, a reassuringly mundane sight.

Iganga introduced me to nurses and porters left and right; everyone was busy but friendly, and I struggled to memorise the barrage of names. The wards were all crowded, with patients spilling into the corridors, a few in beds but most on mattresses or blankets. The building itself was dilapidated, and some of the equipment must have been thirty years old, but there was nothing squalid about the conditions; all the linen was clean, and the floor looked and smelt like you could do surgery on it.

In the Yeyuka ward, Iganga showed me the six patients I'd be operating on the next day. The hospital did have a CAT scanner, but it had been broken for the past six months, waiting for money for replacement parts, so flat X-rays with cheap contrast agents like barium were the most I could hope for. For some tumours, the only guide to location and extent was plain old palpation. Iganga guided my hands, and kept me from applying too much pressure; she'd had a great deal more experience at this than I had, and an overzealous beginner could do a lot of damage. The world of three-dimensional images spinning on my workstation while the software advised on the choice of incision had receded into fantasy. Stubbornly, though, I did the job myself; gently mapping the tumours by touch, picturing them in my head, marking the X-rays or making sketches.

I explained to each patient where I'd be cutting, what I'd remove, and what the likely effects would be. Where necessary, Iganga translated for me — either into Swahili, or what she described as her "broken Luganda." The news was always only half good, but most people seemed to take it with a kind of weary optimism. Surgery was rarely a cure for Yeyuka, usually just offering a few years' respite, but it was currently the only option. Radiation and chemotherapy were useless, and the hospital's sole HealthGuard machine couldn't generate custom-made molecular cures for even a lucky few; seven years into the epidemic, Yeyuka wasn't yet well enough understood for anyone to have written the necessary software.

By the time I was finished it was dark outside. Iganga asked, "Do you want to look in on Ann's last operation?" Ann Collins was the Irish volunteer I was replacing.

"Definitely." I'd watched a few operations performed here, on video back in Sydney, but no VR scenarios had been available for proper "hands on" rehearsals, and Collins would only be around to supervise me for a few more days. It was a painful irony: foreign surgeons were always going to be inexperienced, but no one else had so much time on their hands. Ugandan medical students had to pay a small fortune in fees — the World Bank had put an end to the new government's brief flirtation with state-subsidised training — and it looked like there'd be a shortage of qualified specialists for at least another decade.

We donned masks and gowns. The operating theatre was like everything else, clean but outdated. Iganga introduced me to Collins, the anaesthetist Eriya Okwera, and the trainee surgeon Balaki Masika.

The patient, a middle-aged man, was covered in orange Betadine-soaked surgical drapes, arranged around a long abdominal incision. I stood beside Collins and watched, entranced. Growing within the muscular wall of the small intestine was a grey mass the size of my fist, distending the peritoneum, the organ's translucent "skin," almost to bursting point. It would certainly have been blocking the passage of food; the patient must have been on liquids for months.

The tumour was very loose, almost like a giant discoloured blood clot; the hardest thing would be to avoid dislodging any cancerous cells in the process of removing it, sending them back into circulation to seed another tumour. Before making a single cut in the intestinal wall, Collins used a laser to cauterise all the blood vessels around the growth, and she didn't lay a finger on the tumour itself at any time. Once it was free, she lifted it away with clamps attached to the surrounding tissue, as fastidiously as if she was removing a leaky bag full of some fatal poison. Maybe other tumours were already growing unseen in other parts of the body, but doing the best possible job, here and now, might still add three or four years to this man's life.

Masika began stitching the severed ends of the intestine together. Collins led me aside and showed me the patient's X-rays on a light-box. "This is the site of origin." There was a cavity clearly visible in the right lung, about half the size of the tumour she'd just removed. Ordinary cancers grew in a single location first, and then a few mutant cells in the primary tumour escaped to seed growths in the rest of the body. With Yeyuka, there were no "primary tumours"; the virus itself uprooted the cells it infected, breaking down the normal molecular adhesives that kept them in place, until the infected organ seemed to be melting away. That was the origin of the name: *yeyuka*, to melt. Once set loose into the bloodstream, many of the cells died of natural causes, but a few ended up lodged in small capillaries — physically trapped, despite their lack of stickiness — where they could remain undisturbed long enough to grow into sizable tumours.

After the operation, I was invited out to a welcoming dinner in a restaurant down in the city. The place specialised in Italian food, which was apparently hugely popular, at least in Kampala. Iganga, Collins and Okwera, old colleagues by now, unwound noisily; Okwera, a solid man in his forties, grew mildly but volubly intoxicated and told medical horror stories from his time in the army. Masika, the trainee surgeon, was very softly spoken and reserved. I was something of a zombie from jet lag myself, and didn't contribute much to the conversation, but the warm reception put me at ease.

I still felt like an impostor, here only because I hadn't had the courage to back out, but no one was going to interrogate me about my motives. No one cared. It wouldn't make the slightest difference whether I'd volunteered out of genuine compassion, or just a kind of moral insecurity brought on by fears of obsolescence. Either way, I'd brought a pair of hands and enough general surgical experience to be useful. If you'd ever had to be a saint to heal someone, medicine would have been doomed from the start.

I was nervous as I cut into my first Yeyuka patient, but by the end of the operation, with a growth the size of an orange successfully removed from the right lung, I felt much more confident. Later the same day, I was introduced to some of the hospital's permanent surgical staff — a reminder that even when Collins left, I'd hardly be working in isolation. I fell asleep on the second night exhausted, but reassured. I could do this, it wasn't beyond me. I hadn't set myself an impossible task.

I drank too much at the farewell dinner for Collins, but the HealthGuard magicked the effects away. My first day solo was anticlimactic; everything went smoothly, and Okwera, with no high-tech hangover cure, was unusually subdued, while Masika was as quietly attentive as ever.

Six days a week, the world shrank to my room, the campus, the ward, the operating theatre. I ate in the guest house, and usually fell asleep an hour or two after the evening meal; with the sun diving straight below the horizon, by eight o'clock it felt like midnight. I tried to call Lisa every night, though I often finished in the theatre too late to catch her before she left for work, and I hated leaving messages, or talking to her while she was driving.

Okwera and his wife invited me to lunch the first Sunday, Masika and his girlfriend the next. Both couples were genuinely hospitable, but I felt like I was intruding on their one day together. The third Sunday, I met up with Iganga in a restaurant, then we wandered through the city on an impromptu tour.

There were some beautiful buildings in Kampala, many of them clearly war-scarred but lovingly repaired. I tried to relax and take in the sights, but I kept thinking of the routine — six operations, six days a week — stretching out ahead of me until the end of my stay. When I mentioned this to Iganga, she laughed. "All right. You want something more than assembly-line work? I'll line up a trip to Mubende for you. They have patients there who are too sick to be moved. Multiple tumours, all nearly terminal."

"Okay." Me and my big mouth; I knew I hadn't been seeing the worst cases, but I hadn't given much thought to where they all were.

We were standing outside the Sikh temple, beside a plaque describing Idi Amin's expulsion of Uganda's Asian community in 1972. Kampala was dotted with memorials to atrocities — and though Amin's reign had ended more than forty years ago, it had been a long path back to normality. It seemed unjust beyond belief that even now, in an era of relative political stability, so many lives were being ruined by Yeyuka. No more refugees marching across the countryside, no more forced expulsions — but cells cast adrift could bring just as much suffering.

I asked Iganga, "So why did you go into medicine?"

"Family expectations. It was either that or the law. Medicine seemed less arbitrary; nothing in the body can be overturned by an appeal to the High Court. What about you?"

I said, "I wanted to be in on the revolution. The one that was going to banish all disease."

"Ah, that one."

"I picked the wrong job, of course. I should have been a molecular biologist."

"Or a software engineer."

"Yeah. If I'd seen the HealthGuard coming fifteen years ago, I might have been right at the heart of the changes. And I'd have never looked back. Let alone sideways."

Iganga nodded sympathetically, quite unfazed by the notion that molecular technology might capture the attention so thoroughly that little things like Yeyuka epidemics would vanish from sight altogether. "I can imagine. Seven years ago, I was all set to make my fortune in one of the private clinics in Dar es Salaam. Rich businessmen with prostate cancer, that kind of thing. I was lucky in a way; before that market vanished completely, the Yeyuka fanatics were nagging me, bullying me, making little deals." She laughed. "I've lost count of the number of times I was promised I'd be co-author of a ground-breaking paper in *Nature Oncology* if I just helped out at some field clinic in the middle of nowhere. I was dragged into this, kicking and screaming, just when all my old dreams were going up in smoke."

"But now Yeyuka feels like your true vocation?"

She rolled her eyes. "Spare me. My ambition now is to retire to a highly paid consulting position in Nairobi or Geneva."

"I'm not sure I believe you."

"You should." She shrugged. "Sure, what I'm doing now is a hundred times more useful than any desk job, but that doesn't make it any easier. You know as well as I do that the warm inner glow doesn't last for a thousand patients; if you fought for every one of them as if they were your own family or friends, you'd go insane...so they become a series of clinical problems, which just happen to be wrapped in human flesh. And it's a struggle to keep working on the same problems, over and over, even if you're convinced that it's the most worthwhile job in the world."

"So why are you in Kampala right now, instead of Nairobi or Geneva?"

Iganga smiled. "Don't worry, I'm working on it. I don't have a date on my ticket out of here, like you do, but when the chance comes, believe me, I'll grab it just as fast as I can."

It wasn't until my sixth week, and my two-hundred-and-fourth operation, that I finally screwed up.

The patient was a teenaged girl with multiple infestations of colon cells in her liver. A substantial portion of the organ's left lobe would have to be removed, but her prognosis seemed relatively good; the right lobe appeared to be completely clean, and it was not beyond hope that the liver, directly downstream from the colon, had filtered all the infected cells from the blood before they could reach any other part of the body.

Trying to clamp the left branch of the portal vein, I slipped, and the clamp closed tightly on a swollen cyst at the base of the liver, full of grey-white colon cells. It didn't burst open, but it might have been better if it had; I couldn't literally see where the contents was squirted, but I could imagine the route very clearly: back as far as the Y-junction of the vein, where the blood flow would carry cancerous cells into the previously unaffected right lobe.

I swore for ten seconds, enraged by my own helplessness. I had none of the emergency tools I was used to: there was no drug I could inject to kill off the spilt cells while they were still more vulnerable than an established tumour, no vaccine on hand to stimulate the immune system into attacking them.

Okwera said, "Tell the parents you found evidence of leakage, so she'll need to have regular follow-up examinations."

I glanced at Masika, but he was silent.

"I can't do that."

"You don't want to cause trouble."

"It was an accident!"

"Don't tell her, and don't tell her family." Okwera regarded me sternly, as if I was contemplating something both dangerous and self-indulgent. "It won't help anyone if you dive into the shit for this. Not her, not you. Not the hospital. Not the volunteer program."

The girl's mother spoke English. I told her there were signs that the cancer might have spread. She wept, and thanked me for my good work.

Masika didn't say a word about the incident, but by the end of the day I could hardly bear to look at him. When Okwera departed, leaving the two of us alone in the locker room, I said, "In three or four years there'll be a vaccine. Or even HealthGuard software. It won't be like this forever."

He shrugged, embarrassed. "Sure."

"I'll raise funds for the research when I get home. Champagne dinners with slides of photogenic patients, if that's what it takes." I knew I was making a fool of myself, but I couldn't shut up. "This isn't the nineteenth century. We're not helpless anymore. Anything can be cured, once you understand it."

Masika eyed me dubiously, as if he was trying to decide whether or not to tell me to save my platitudes for the champagne dinners. Then he said, "We do understand Yeyuka. We have HealthGuard software written for it, ready and waiting to go. But we can't run it on the machine here. So we don't need funds for research. What we need is another machine."

I was speechless for several seconds, trying to make sense of this extraordinary claim. "The hospital's machine is broken—?"

Masika shook his head. "The software is unlicensed. If we used it on the hospital's machine, our agreement with HealthGuard would be void. We'd lose the use of the machine entirely."

I could hardly believe that the necessary research had been completed without a single publication, but I couldn't believe Masika would lie about it either. "How long can it take HealthGuard to approve the software? When was it submitted to them?"

Masika was beginning to look like he wished he'd kept his mouth shut, but there was no going back now. He admitted warily, "It hasn't been submitted to them. It can't be—that's the whole problem. We need a bootleg machine, a decommissioned model with the satellite link disabled, so we can run the Yeyuka software without their knowledge."

"Why? Why can't they find out about it?"

He hesitated. "I don't know if I can tell you that."

"Is it illegal? Stolen?" But if it was stolen, why hadn't the rightful owners licensed the damned thing, so people could use it?

Masika replied icily, "Stolen *back*. The only part you could call 'stolen' was stolen back." He looked away for a moment, actually struggling for control. Then he said, "Are you sure you want to know the whole story?"

"Yes."

"Then I'll have to make a phone call."

—

Masika took me to what looked like a boarding house, student accommodation in one of the suburbs close to the campus. He walked briskly, giving me no time to ask questions, or even orient myself in the darkness. I had a feeling he would have liked to have blindfolded me, but it would hardly have made a difference; by the time we arrived I couldn't have said where we were to the nearest kilometre.

A young woman, maybe nineteen or twenty, opened the door. Masika didn't introduce us, but I assumed she was the person he'd phoned from the hospital, since she was clearly expecting us. She led us to a ground floor room; someone was playing music upstairs, but there was no one else in sight.

In the room, there was a desk with an old-style keyboard and computer monitor, and an extraordinary device standing on the floor beside it: a rack of electronics the size of a chest of drawers, full of exposed circuit boards, all cooled by a fan half a metre wide.

"What is that?"

The woman grinned. "We modestly call it the Makerere supercomputer. Five hundred and twelve processors, working in parallel. Total cost, fifty thousand shillings."

That was about fifty dollars. "How—?"

"Recycling. Twenty or thirty years ago, the computer industry ran an elaborate scam: software companies wrote deliberately inefficient programs, to make people buy newer, faster computers all the time — then they made sure that the faster computers needed brand new software to work at all. People threw out perfectly good machines every three or four years, and though some ended up as landfill, millions were saved. There's been a worldwide market in discarded processors for years, and the slowest now cost about as much as buttons. But all it takes to get some real power out of them is a little ingenuity."

I stared at the wonderful contraption. "And you wrote the Yeyuka software on this?"

"Absolutely." She smiled proudly. "First, the software characterises any damaged surface adhesion molecules it finds — there are always a few floating freely in the bloodstream, and their exact shape depends on the strain of Yeyuka, and the particular cells that have been infected. Then drugs are tailormade to lock on to those damaged adhesion molecules, and kill the infected cells by rupturing their membranes." As she spoke, she typed on the keyboard, summoning up animations to illustrate each stage of the process. "If we can get this onto a real machine...we'll be able to cure three people a day."

Cure. Not just cut them open to delay the inevitable.

"But where did all the raw data come from? The RNA sequencing, the X-ray diffraction studies...?"

The woman's smile vanished. "An insider at HealthGuard found it in the company archives, and sent it to us over the net."

"I don't understand. When did HealthGuard do Yeyuka studies? Why haven't they published them? Why haven't they written software themselves?"

She glanced uncertainly at Masika. He said, "HealthGuard's parent company collected blood from five thousand people in southern Uganda in 2013. Supposedly to follow up on the effectiveness of their HIV vaccine. What they actually wanted, though, was a large sample of metastasising cells so they could perfect the biggest selling point of the HealthGuard: cancer protection. Yeyuka offered them the cheapest, simplest way to get the data they needed."

I'd been half expecting something like this since Masika's comments back in the hospital, but I was still shaken. To collect the data dishonestly was bad enough, but to bury information that was halfway to a cure—just to save paying for what they'd taken—was unspeakable.

I said, "Sue the bastards! Get everyone who had samples taken together for a class action: royalties plus punitive damages. You'll raise hundreds of millions of dollars. Then you can buy as many machines as you want."

The woman laughed bitterly. "We have no proof. The files were sent anonymously, there's no way to authenticate their origin. And can you imagine how much HealthGuard would spend on their defence? We can't afford to waste the next twenty years in a legal battle, just for the satisfaction of shouting the truth from the rooftops. The only way we can be sure of making use of this software is to get a bootleg machine, and do everything in silence."

I stared at the screen, at the cure being played out in simulation that should have been happening three times a day in Mulago Hospital. She was right, though. However hard it was to stomach, taking on HealthGuard directly would be futile.

Walking back across the campus with Masika, I kept thinking of the girl with the liver infestation, and the possibility of undoing the moment of clumsiness that would otherwise almost certainly kill her. I said, "Maybe I can get hold of a bootleg machine in Shanghai. If I knew where to ask, where to look." They'd certainly be expensive, but they'd have to be much cheaper than a commissioned model, running without the usual software and support.

My hand moved almost unconsciously to check the metal pulse on my index finger. I held the ring up in the starlight. "I'd give you this, if it was mine to give. But that's thirty years away." Masika didn't reply, too polite to suggest that if I'd owned the ring outright, I wouldn't even have raised the possibility.

We reached the University Hall; I could find my way back to the guest house now. But I couldn't leave it at that; I couldn't face another six weeks of surgery unless I knew that something was going to come of the night's revelations. I said, "Look, I don't have connections to any black market, I don't have a clue how to go about getting a machine. But if you can find out what I have to do, and it's within my power...I'll do it."

Masika smiled, and nodded thanks, but I could tell that he didn't believe me. I wondered how many other people had made promises like this, then vanished back into the world-without-disease while the Yeyuka wards kept overflowing.

As he turned to go, I put a hand on his shoulder to stop him. "I mean it. Whatever it takes, I'll do it."

He met my eyes in the dark, trying to judge something deeper than this easy protestation of sincerity. I felt a sudden flicker of shame; I'd completely forgotten that I was an impostor, that I'd never really meant to come here, that two months ago a few words from Lisa would have seen me throw away my ticket, gratefully.

Masika said quietly, "Then I'm sorry that I doubted you. And I'll take you at your word."

Mubende was a district capital, half a day's drive west of Kampala. Iganga delayed our promised trip to the Yeyuka clinic there until my last fortnight, and once I arrived I could understand why. It was everything I'd feared: starved of funds, under-staffed and over-crowded. Patients' relatives were required to provide and wash the bedclothes, and half of them also seemed to be bringing in painkillers and other drugs bought at the local markets — some genuine, some ripoffs full of nothing but glucose or magnesium sulphate.

Most of the patients had four or five separate tumours. I treated two people a day, with operations lasting six to eight hours. In ten days, seven people died in front of me; dozens more died in the wards, waiting for surgery.

Or waiting for something better.

I shared a crowded room at the back of the clinic with Masika and Okwera, but even on the rare occasions when I caught Masika alone, he seemed reluctant to discuss the details of getting hold of a bootleg HealthGuard. He said, "Right now, the less you know the better. When the time comes, I'll fill you in."

The ordeal of the patients was overwhelming, but I felt more for the clinic's sole doctor and two nurses; for them, it never ended. The morning we packed our equipment into the truck and headed back for Kampala, I felt like a deserter from some stupid, pointless war: guilty about the colleagues I was leaving behind, but almost euphoric with relief to be out of it myself. I knew I couldn't have stayed on here — or even in Kampala — month after month, year after year. However much I wished that I could have been that strong, I understood now that I wasn't.

There was a brief, loud stuttering sound, then the truck squealed to a halt. The four of us were all in the back, guarding the equipment against potholes, with the tarpaulin above us blocking everything but a narrow rear view. I glanced at the others; someone outside shouted in Luganda at Akena Ibingira, the driver, and he started shouting back.

Okwera said, "Bandits."

I felt my heart racing. "You're kidding?"

There was another burst of gunfire. I heard Ibingira jump out of the cab, still muttering angrily.

Everyone was looking at Okwera for advice. He said, "Just cooperate, give them what they want." I tried to read his face; he seemed grim but not desperate — he expected unpleasantness, but not a massacre. Iganga was sitting on the bench beside me; I reached for her hand almost without thinking. We were both trembling. She squeezed my fingers for a moment, then pulled free.

Two tall, smiling men in dirty-brown camouflage appeared at the back of the truck, gesturing with automatic weapons for us to climb out. Okwera went first, but Masika, who'd been sitting beside him, hung back. Iganga was nearer to the exit than me, but I tried to get past her; I had some half-baked idea that this would somehow lessen her risk of being taken off and raped. When one of the bandits blocked my way and waved her forward, I thought this fear had been confirmed.

Masika grabbed my arm, and when I tried to break free, he tightened his grip and pulled me back into the truck. I turned on him angrily, but before I could say a word he whispered, "She'll be all right. Just tell me: do you want them to take the ring?"

"*What?*"

He glanced nervously towards the exit, but the bandits had moved Okwera and Iganga out of sight. "I've paid them to do this. It's the only way. But say the word now and I'll give them the signal, and they won't touch the ring."

I stared at him, waves of numbness sweeping over my skin as I realised exactly what he was saying.

"You could have taken it off under anaesthetic."

He shook his head impatiently. "It's sending data back to HealthGuard all the time: cortisol, adrenaline, endorphins, prostaglandins. They'll have a record of your stress levels, fear, pain...if we took it off under anaesthetic, they'd *know* you'd given it away freely. This way, it'll look like a random theft. And your insurance company will give you a new one."

His logic was impeccable; I had no reply. I might have started protesting about insurance fraud, but that was all in the future, a separate matter entirely. The choice, here and now, was whether or not I let him have the ring by the only method that wouldn't raise suspicion.

One of the bandits was back, looking impatient. Masika asked plainly, "Do I call it off? I need an answer." I turned to him, on the verge of ranting that he'd willfully misunderstood me, abused my generous offer to help him, and put all our lives in danger.

It would have been so much bullshit, though. He hadn't misunderstood me. All he'd done was taken me at my word.

I said, "Don't call it off."

The bandits lined us up beside the truck, and had us empty our pockets into a sack. Then they started taking watches and jewellery. Okwera couldn't get his wedding ring off, but stood motionless and scowling while one of the bandits applied more force. I wondered if I'd need a prosthesis, if I'd still be able to do surgery, but as the bandit approached me I felt a strange rush of confidence.

I held out my hand and looked up into the sky. I knew that anything could be healed, once it was understood.

Sterling to Kessel, 7 April 1986:

"Actually I've been wanting to do something on BOFFO [aka humanist sf] for some time.... I was further stimulated by the appearance of [Kim Stanley] Robinson's 'Down and Out in the Year 2000' in the April MOV's, with its long Gibson parody and slashing backhand to Sterling. This was one of Robinson's best stories, I thought, and a point well taken. His attempt to seize the moral high ground in the debate seemed a canny attempt to use BOFFO's perceived strengths — at least vis-à-vis the anomic medical objectivity of true chrome-and-matte-black cyberpunk. Also, Shepard's amazing 'R&R' in that issue seems to capture a kind of Mirrorshades incandescence without in any way kowtowing to shock-effect high-tech.

It seems to me that 'R&R' and 'Down and Out' both represent a kind of elastic and powerful reaction of other 80s writers to the impact of cyberpunk. A kind of waking from dogmatic slumbers which, without following the c-p line at all, still shows a new kind of alertness and commitment. A sense that the stakes have been raised. A healthy and very encouraging reaction to challenge — and not a blind reaction by any means, but an intelligent and wide-ranging response."

The Final Remake of
The Return of Little Latin Larry,
with a Completely Remastered
Soundtrack and the Original
Audience

Pat Cadigan

Pat Cadigan gives us a variety of VR that aspires to historicity in this witty piece; "fraudulent pasts and faked memories" will get you a kick in the teeth from the authorities. The surface of this story is ornamented with all the bedazzlements of classic cyberpunk: drugs and rock and roll and cyborgs and a technophilic art form. Narrators with an attitude have always been a specialty of Cadigan and here Gracie lays down a line of pharmaceutical quality wisecracks and caustic insight. But what informs this story is its pervasive sense of irony: this culture, so desperate to recover a lost past, has got it pretty much all wrong.

So! Fix yourself a smell and sit down!

There's a wet bar, too, if you go that way. You know, for years I told myself I didn't, even though I always kept a full complement of cheers, vines, and the hards and their pards. I'd say to myself, Oh, but of course the hooch is strictly for hospitality and nothing else.

But now, I'm out about it and I really feel much more non-bad about it. And wasn't it Elvis who said, "Drinkers, like the poor, we will always have with us"?

Or was that Dylan? Might have been — Dylan was the big expert on drinkers, wasn't he, dying as he did face down in the gutter — lucky beast! — not fifty paces from the Tired Horse Tavern where he came up with his biggest and best — "All the Tired Horses" (of course!), "Knockin' on Fern Hill's Door," "The Hand That Signed a Paper Got to Serve Somebody," and, my personal favorite, "Do Not Go Gentle into Those Subterranean Homesick Blues." "Rage, rage against the leaders, watch the parking —"

Sorry, sorry, sorry! I can barely hold still, this is such an exciting time for me. I think my man Dylan put it best when he said, "I sang in my chains: everybody must get stoned." One of his most evocative lines, at least for me. Even now, long, long, long after I first read it, it still stirs up for me the sensation of that state where you're practically thrumming in excitement, and the only thing that keeps you from flying up in the air and dragging the whole world after you like a cape tied around your shoulders is the incontrovertible fact of your just-that-much-too-heavy flesh—

Sorry again! The human condition tends to make me wax poetic. Rather, it makes me want to wax poetic, except I can never think of the poetic counterpart to words like "incontrovertible." Got a drink now? Good, good, sit, sit. Did you smell anything you liked? No? Ah—you must tell me the truth here: did the aromabar intimidate you, or are you just not olfactory? I vow that either way, I'm not insulted, truly I'm not. Not all senses can be our senses, can they? And when you're retro besides—well, some people can get that so wrong.

Like the other day. Packed in my usual buzzbomb was a silly tag from one of my sillier friends telling me that everyone was saying behind my back that I was the most retro creature they'd ever heard of. I tagged back to tell Old Sillyhead that not only were they saying it behind my back, but also behind my front, too, and in front of my back and all that, and so what.

Anyway, it's not like I'm detoxing and then relapsing just for the wallop that first sinful sip will give you. I know people who have gone through three and four livers that way, even with top-of-the-line blood-doping. But I don't consider them drinkers. And personally, I think Teflon™ on the central nervous system is cheating.

And in spite of what you may have heard, the aromabar really is just for amusement, I don't do aromatherapy of any kind. Of course, anyone who does is welcome to mix themselves a bouquet with my essences and if they want to claim it gives them some kind of therapeutic fizz, I'm not going to argue with them. After all, we all sing our own particular song in our chains, don't we.

But you'll want to know about the last remake, won't you. That last remake. Everybody always wants to know about that. I swear, I'll do a thousand projects before I go gentle into my subterranean homesick blues and the one thing I'll be remembered for is that damned remake. Everyone'll still be mad at me for one of two reasons and by god, they'll both be wrong.

So, one more time, for the record and with feeling: I did not rediscover Little Latin Larry, and I didn't kill him.

Who did?

Well, I was afraid you'd ask me that.

First of all, let's get all the facts we know — all right, all the facts I know — straight. You'll pardon me if I go over to the bar and fix myself a few memory aids. This brown stuff here, this is an esoteric drink called Old Peculier, which is the liquid equivalent of wrapping yourself in a comfy blanket on an uncommonly bad day. Fair Annie — you wouldn't know her, she liked the low-profile life — introduced me to it. But this other stuff that looks a lot like, well, frankly, urine — it's no-class lager. Cheap beer was the term for it then and it was sought after for both its cheapness and its beerness, if you see what I mean.

The Old Peculier is for drinking, just because I like it. But the lager is for smelling, because I can remember Larry best when I smell cheap beer. It was just about the only thing you ever smelled around Larry.

And let's get something else straight: the full name of the band was Little Latin Larry and His Loopy Louies, His Luscious Latinaires, and His Lascivious Latinettes.

Little Latin Larry was, of course, lead vocalist, conductor, arranger, and erstwhile composer. Which is to say, for a while, he was trying out some originals on the playlist. I've heard them. They weren't too bad, you know; they were just meant to be songs to dance to, or jump up and down to, or puke to, if you went that way (not like the Bulimic Era stuff — that was later, and didn't have much to do with having a good time). But every time Larry tried to slip in an original, everyone would just kind of stand there looking puzzled. There'd be some people dancing, some people nodding along, a few of the hard-core puking, but most of them just stood around with these lost expressions, and you could tell they were trying to place the song and couldn't. So Larry forgot about being even a cheap-beer ditty-monger and went back to covers. There were skintillions of bands that played covers for anyone who hired them, but when Larry and the band did a cover it was...I could say that when Little Latin Larry and Co. covered a song it was, for the duration, completely their own, as if no one else had ever sung it. And if I did put it that way, I would be both right and wrong. Just as if I said, when they covered a song, it was a complete tribute to the original artists. That would be right and wrong as well.

It was both. It was neither. It was an experience. It was all shades of one experience, a million experiences in one. In other words, you had to be there. Yes. You had to be there at least once.

But no, I won't try to wiggle out on that one. Even if there is so much truth to it that most people were there once. Whether they were there or not.

I don't expect you to understand me. I'm a visionary. No, just kidding, just shaking your leg, as (I think) they used to say.

All right, back to it, now. The Larry people came to me. I don't care what they told everyone later about my chasing them over hill and dale, or chip and dale, or nook and cranny. The Realm of the Senses Theatre kept me busy enough that I didn't have to chase anyone. People were always beating down the door with sense-memories. My staff at that time was a mad thing named Ola, about three and a half feet tall — achondroplasia — who usually kept most of her brain in her sidekick, and vice versa. Half the time, you never knew exactly which was which. It wasn't really any kind of intentional thing, or a statement or anything. Ola just went that way. A happy accident. Happy for Ola. So she mated with a machine, so what. I may be retro, but I'm not that retro; I certainly wasn't then.

Ola put off a lot of people for a variety of reasons — she was doing the jobs of several people and so depriving them of jobs, cyborgs were against Nature or the Bible, or she wasn't enough of a cyborg to claim the title (which she didn't in the first place), or she was too spooky, too feminine, not feminine enough, not spooky enough, for god's sake. People, my god; people. Nature gave them tongues, technology gave them loudspeakers, and they all believe that because they can use both, whatever they say is important.

I suppose that was why I started Realm of the Senses Theatre. The watchwords of the time were "custom," "customizable," "individual," and "interactive." Heavy on the "interactive." What the hell did that mean, anyway, "interactive"? I used to rant about this to Ola and her sidekick all the time. Who the hell thought up "interactive," I'd say; your goddam shoes are "interactive," every item of clothing you put on is "interactive," your car is "interactive," what is the big goddamn reverb on "interactive," goddamn life is "interactive" —

And Ola would say, Oh, they don't want to interact, Gracie, they want to kibbitz. Everybody's got to have a little say in how it goes. Do it in blue; I want it in velvet; it would be perfect if it was about twice as long and half as high. You know.

So that was what Realm of the Senses Theatre did. It gave people a say in their own entertainment. You could have it in blue, in velvet, half as high and twice as long, so to speak, and if you didn't like it, it was your own lookout. But old retro Gracie — yes, even then I had a retro streak a mile wide — old retro Gracie used to think about staging some kind of event that people couldn't interfere with, couldn't amp up or down, or customize in any way — an event that you'd just have to experience as it was, on its own terms, not yours. And then see what happened to you afterward. So I started thinking about something called High Sky Theatre. I was calling it that because I was thinking the event would be like the sky — you could see it, even get right up in the middle of it, but you couldn't change it, it rained on you or it didn't and you had to adjust yourself, not it.

And then, synchronicity, I guess. I was just toying with a few designs for the logo — High Sky Theatre in floating puffy holo cloud letters — and the Larry people got in touch with me.

Right at the outset, they told me that they were all direct blood-positive descendants of the band and it was the first time that they had managed to get one of each — i.e., one of Larry's descendants, one descendant of a Loopy Louie, one of a Luscious Latinaire, and one of a Lascivious Latinette. And even a descendant of someone who had been in the audience when Little Latin Larry and the etc. had gotten back together and made their triumphant return to performing.

Now, I had seen the original *The Return of Little Latin Larry* as well as the first remake. The original, I must say, had been story-heavy enough to keep your interest but very thin in the experiential department. Larry's descendant told me that was because they'd been missing both a Latinaire and a Latinette — they'd only had a Larry, a Loopy Louie, a few friends of a different Loopy Louie, and a Latinaire groupie. For the first remake, they had managed to find a couple of audience members, and that was a little bit better, but it still meant the backstage stuff was thin. Then the Latinaire groupie's descendant quit because he said he didn't really feel like he was an accepted part of the band. Which I guess was kind of true — the groupie's association with the Latinaire had been a onetime thing, never to be repeated. According to Larry's descendant, his absence didn't take away much, if anything, from subsequent remakes.

The descendants' names? It's hard to remember now, but if you give me a little while, they'll come back to me. I had to think of them as Little Latin Larry and so forth because I didn't want to go contaminating the memory with associations that didn't belong. It sounds over-meticulous, sure, and don't think I haven't heard that and more about my methods and everything. But I had to stay focused. I didn't want anachronisms popping up because I was blind to them myself. You go ahead and inspect any feature I've made and I promise you that you will find—for example—only native-to-the-era clothing, and not made-to-look-native-to-the-era clothing. Some say you can't tell the difference, but I say you can. Even if it looks perfect, the smell and feel aren't right. If you're going to go to the trouble of distilling the memory of the event, either take it all the way or don't bother, period.

And while this may seem overly fussy to some people I won't name, it's how I can spot a forgery more quickly than anyone else. Some red faces on that subject, I can tell you. Believe me, I know the difference between someone who is descended from someone who was there — whatever there we're talking about—and someone who injected a re-creation. One of the red faces I won't name maintains to this day that he was completely bamboozled by a pseudo-Zapruder, but really, if he was doing his job right, I don't see how he could have been. But that's not my lookout, is it.

So. Having the Larry people (as I called them) all together and ready, we hired a clinic and Ola and her sidekick went to work with the genealogists. This would be the part where my eyes would start to glaze over, to be perfectly honest (which I have always tried to be). Biochemical genealogy is one of those things I just don't get. Every so often, Ola and her sidekick would try to explain it to me even when I'd beg them not to. The memory is retained biochemically, and what memory exists when an offspring is conceived might be passed on to that child depending on how the genes line up, dominant, recessive, blue eyes, white forelock, the ability to roll your tongue — I don't know, genetics just confuses me, biochemistry confuses me, life is confusing enough, you know? All I know is the blood has to test positive for distillable memory by the presence of something-or-other. Frankly, I think that's about as technical as anybody needs to get about anything in the arts.

Ola and her sidekick went right to work with the distilled samples, which is something like working a jigsaw puzzle in five dimensions per sample. Every bit of recovered memory is keyed to at least one of the five senses and you figure out which one for each bit until you have a sort of a picture—I don't know what else to call it, although it isn't all visual, of course. I guess you could call it a sequence, except it isn't necessarily linear. Event? Episode? Anyway, you hope you get enough so that you can interpolate whatever is missing in the visuals and audio, tactile, olfactory, and taste.

A computer can do the comparing quickly enough and build up a sequence, and when caught between two or more senses for one memory bit, it can figure the dominant one to within a hairsbreadth of comparison and fill in most of the less dominant, but there's no program intuitive enough to interpolate without human intervention. Ola and her sidekick had developed a knack for sense-memory reconstruction that was all but supernatural — the sidekick helped her become single-minded enough to concentrate deeply, while her intuition made the sidekick practically human. Give Ola and her sidekick a square inch of cloth and a whiff of talcum powder and in two hours, you'd have the toddler just out of the bathtub and climbing into his pajamas at bedtime, singing his favorite song. That's more than mere knowledge, that's talent.

Of course, the more people you have to remember the same event, the better you can interpolate. You get one memory of the beer, say, and another of the sound of the glasses clinking together, and then there's another that associates the clinking with the way the bartender looked, or someone else in the bar, or drinking at the moment something else happened — the band started a number or finished one, or — well, you get the idea. Memory bits knit together in ways that all but suggest the missing portions. And then there are other bits where it's almost sheer guesswork based on experience or research.

What with all the principal players we had, I figured we'd get a lot of texture to work with, and I was right. Ola and her sidekick were busy for I don't know how long — a couple of weeks steady, at least. I went to work on advertising and publicity, taping teaser interviews with each of the principals. I know that it's not absolutely necessary to pay a lot of attention to the principals after you get the blood and tissue samples, but I've found it's the sort of thing that can make your life easier if you run into trouble during the reconstruction.

I suppose I should have realized that there's a wide variety of trouble you can have in that area, and having a principal's cooperation isn't necessarily going to help.

Little Latin Larry's descendant had learned the trade of being Larry's descendant from her father, who had done the original feature — *Little Latin Larry and His Loopy Louies, Luscious Latinaires, and Lascivious Latinettes* — and three remakes before going on to find and recover *The Return of Little Latin Larry*. Carola told me he had done three remakes after that original before retiring and turning things over to her. She'd done the next three remakes and hadn't been completely happy with any of them, though she told me she thought they were improving and she had high hopes for this one.

I suppose I should have realized something was funny when Carola told me she made her living providing memory bits for interpolation filler. But the genealogy chart she showed me was highly detailed and extensive. Some families are like that — one of the ancestors had a lineage obsession that gets passed down to subsequent generations like any other heirloom. Or memory, I guess.

But most people who claim full documentation from before the Collapse and Rebuilding I've generally dismissed, at least privately, as either liars or as the very gullible offspring of liars. And there are those who aren't actually that gullible but who like to believe that they have documentation that exists for no one else, as if the force of their lineage could defeat the effects of something as great as the breakdown of civilization itself. I don't argue with people who claim to remember past incarnations firsthand, either. If it helps them cope and keeps them from trying to make the world unpleasant, I say on with delusion and who says reality has to be so tight-fitting anyway?

Perhaps I'm a little too lenient that way. But, look, now — whatever's in the blood speaks for itself, and if it isn't there, it may well be that it just wasn't passed on, a vagary of biology or of timing. There was a famous case just half a dozen years ago of Tino Marlin, who could document descent from Birgit Crow, who uncovered the ruins of the historical Lost City of Soho, proving once and for all not only that Soho had been real but also that the two islands of Manhattan had once been one whole island. But Tino didn't have any memory bits; they were all in the blood of a rather disreputable urban nomad who went only by the single name Vyuni, and who somehow knew she was related to Crow. Family legend, perhaps, but in this case, a legend that turned out to be true. Much to Tino Marlin's dismay, as Vyuni and her tribe tried to sponge enormously off the Marlins and harassed them in the most miserable ways when Tino refused them. Worse for Tino, in his own words, though, is having to live with the knowledge that while he may own every valuable heirloom and relic that his ancestor kept from the excavation and rediscovery, only Vyuni can provide the raw material for a feature about Crow and the Lost City. Nature can be so cruel.

It didn't seem that Nature had been at all cruel to Carola, not in her veins, and certainly not in any other area. Carola Ignazio was a beautiful woman, retaining so much of her ancestor's Latin beauty — the dark, shiny hair, the nearly black eyes, the golden complexion. She was a little plump, but that only made you want to touch her, cuddle her. I know I did, and I don't go that way. For her, I might have been persuaded, though.

Larry's Loopy Louies were represented by a black Asian kid named Philo Harp. He was barely legal at thirteen, and everyone was vague as to how they had come by him, so I had Ola blind-test him several times. Sure enough, the memory bits were there. I've worked with kids before, even those below the age of consent — all legally, of course, by contract with guardians — so that wasn't a real problem. It just made me wonder, though, how he knew, or how they knew about him and I kept trying to bring the subject up whenever possible, but nobody cared to discuss it.

The Latinaires guy was another object lesson in not putting too much emphasis on blood. He was a lifer — the prison sent a courier with the blood and tissue along with a copy of a twenty-year-old contract stating that all proceeds went to the victims' survivors. I decided not to ask.

The Lascivious Latinette representative was married to the audience member descendant. It looked like a pure business arrangement to me — that is, they were pleasant enough to each other, but I didn't detect much of a bond between them. I got the feeling that they were making a family business out of who they were descended from and they were looking to produce offspring to cover off as many ancestors as possible. Or maybe they just weren't that demonstrative.

The Latinette descendant was a six-foot ex-soldier named Fatima Rey and she bore a very strong resemblance to her ancestor — it could have been surgical but I didn't think it was and Ola couldn't detect anything. Her husband, the audience member descendant, by contrast, was so forgettable that I often forgot him, even to who he was and what he was doing with us. Fortunately, he didn't take offense easily. His name was — oh, never mind.

They didn't really want me to pay too much attention to the previous remakes. Or rather, I should say that Carola didn't. She spoke for everyone. I often got the feeling the rest of them had actually forced her into the role of spokesperson just by virtue of the fact of her lineage and because none of them wanted to take the responsibility. Sometimes she seemed reluctant or even a bit lost, like she wanted someone else to check up on her and see that she was doing the right thing. But however the strings were pulling among them, they all pulled the same way on the previous remakes — no one wanted me to concentrate too much on what had gone before.

Not that I could really argue with the reasoning. "We don't want anything built up from what you remember was in a previous remake — we want it to come out of whatever you get from us, as if no one else had ever found anything until now." Unquote.

Ola and her sidekick said they were with that one hundred percent, and it wasn't like I could really argue with them, either. After all, they had to do all the wetwork — my job was all the sequence editing. But I tried arguing that getting the sequencing right might well depend on my being familiar at least with a lot of the major moments from past remakes. Carola pointed out that would also be a way of perpetuating any past errors.

So I quit arguing and just didn't tell them I was looking at the old remakes. What can I say? I just don't like arguing.

The distinguishing characteristic of *The Return of Little Latin Larry,* the singular property, the hallmark — if you'll pardon the expression — is the emotion. It kicks in immediately, almost before you know you're in a bar. Only the first remake spends much time in the bar before the lights go down for the show and I found that Carola had been right — it really was too much time hanging around drinking and smelling and drinking and drinking and smelling some more. It wasn't until the second remake that *The Return of Little Latin Larry* began with the backstage sequence of everyone getting into character. I have to say, it's really breathtaking, the first time you go through it with everyone. And in spite of the fact that Carola insisted none of them were very happy with the second remake, I have to say that the sequence editor did have good instincts, as the viewpoint moves in what I think of as ascending order, from the Latinettes teasing their hair, to the Latinaires all trying to fit their reflections into one skinny full-length mirror while they rehearse their moves, to the Loopy Louies getting completely shitfaced (the actual Loopy Louie term for it, absolutely no substitutes accepted, no matter how ridiculous or coarse the term may sound to us today), and then Little Latin Larry himself, moving around among them like a teacher supervising a playgroup.

Well, I'm sorry, but that's how it looks to me. It's another quality present in every single remake, the sense that Little Latin Larry is supervising a bunch of kids at play and sneaking in some teaching at the same time. Don't ask me what he's teaching them. How to play, maybe. And don't think that some people don't need to learn how to do that.

In the third remake, the film crew appears explicitly for the first time, and we get the interviews interspersed with the sequences, and even with the musical numbers onstage, which I personally feel is a significant mistake on the sequence editor's part. Obviously the sequence editor on that remake thought the in-between-numbers parts of the performance were dull, which is too bad, as you lose a lot of the bar atmosphere and you're reminded constantly that this is a feature and you're not actually there. This is fine with some things but it's all wrong for Little Latin Larry. And I'll go so far as to say this is more than an aesthetic choice, it's true.

I knew there was something new and different coming up when Ola and her sidekick apologized for the amount of material they were passing on to me. Most of the time, they apologized for a lack of material, at least in one area or another. I couldn't imagine having too much material to go through. Then she had the cases delivered to my editing room.

I mean, cases. I mean, crates. Yes, there were literally crates of recovered material — not reconstructed, but raw material recovered. An out-of-work dance team brought them in. I had to cut more cable and put together a board with a dozen more outlets before I could even get started sorting things according to chronological order.

Now it's true that I have a preprogrammed sorter to handle the first layers of sorting, but I don't depend solely on that, and I always supervise at least part of the process if not the whole thing. But this time, I had to have three sorting programs running simultaneously while doing a fourth myself, just for the sheer volume of information. I had thought that a lot of it would turn out to be overlap if not outright redundancy but I was wrong about that, too. While there was a certain amount of duplication, none of it fell into the category of back-up.

Every single memory bit fit into its own place where no other would go.

I edited for days. I slept in the editing studio. At one point, I fell asleep and woke up in the bar during "Twist and Shout" — I actually registered as having passed out on the floor under one of the tables on the side. A great big biker chick with curly black hair and Cleopatra eyes kept bending over me and saying, "Hey, honey, are you sure you're all right?" in between twisting and shouting. For a while, I considered the Little Latin Larry Motel — instead of beds and rooms, you'd just pass out in the bar and whatever time you chose for a wake-up call would be a different number in the set, like "Twist and Shout," or "Long Tall Sally," or "Runaway." That idea passed; but it's not the stupidest thing anyone's thought of, not by a long shot.

I was so many days putting a rough cut together that I kept insisting to myself that I couldn't be sure about what I thought I had, that nobody could remember so much with any degree of accuracy, especially if you work out of sequence, the way I do. But deep in my heart, I did know. I think I knew before I even started editing the raw material, when I saw how much raw material there was to work with, and I just didn't want to admit it. Because that was supposed to be impossible, you know. No one — and that is *no* exclamation point *one* double exclamation point — had ever found a combination of memory bits that, when assembled, would yield a complete, finished feature without interpolation or reconstruction. It just didn't happen because it just wasn't possible.

But there it was. *The Return of Little Latin Larry and His Loopy Louies, His Luscious Latinaires, and His Lascivious Latinettes;* music not only intact but in quadronic poly-sound, and every single member of the audience present and accounted for at all times. My editing program said there were no greyed-out areas whatsoever anywhere, and while you might be able to fool a person for awhile, you can't hypnotize an editing program. But even then, I still didn't want to believe that I had a complete feature with no reconstruction or interpolation necessary, so naturally, I took it for a spin.

I set the pod on Outcome: Surprise Me and zipped myself into it. I know my blood was completely clean, because I cleaned it out myself. Not doping; the blood never actually left my body to be recirculated. I used the in-body nano-machine method, even if it does give me a psychosomatic itch. It didn't take long, though, because I stay pretty clean between features; it was really just to make sure there wasn't anything lingering from the last one I'd done, a weird short subject called "But What About Moose and Squirrel?" which I cannot even begin to explain to anyone outside this particular clan who all claim ancestors from a particular area in Philadelphia. I just didn't want to see anything out-of-context showing up and interfering with my concentration in any way. Then I set the IV drip for full feature, no intermission, closed my eyes, and went to see the triumphant return of Little Latin Larry.

It opened with split-screen—very tricky to do behind the eyelids, I wouldn't have thought it possible on the first edit, so right away, I knew I had a double relative in there somewhere. Which is to say, either my audience member was also related to the band, or one of the band was related to the audience member. Or —astounding to think of, but stranger things have happened—both. And with both sets of memory bits present in each one. You don't usually find that sort of thing can remain coherent, let alone linear in any way but, as I said, stranger things have happened.

Anyway, on the left hand side of the screen, you were going in the back door with the band, to the dressing room, while on the right, you were going in the front entrance of the bar. The perspectives on both were so well-realized, I began to think that maybe I'd been duped somehow and I had someone else's finished product sizzling around in my brain chemistry, even though I knew that couldn't possibly be—I had edited every moment out of pure raw material, and if there had been any finished product in there, it would have showed itself immediately as already refined. You can distract a person, but you can't bribe a solution into disguising its molecular structure.

I have to say that as soon as I got used to the split-screen, I loved it. On one side, you could see the band getting ready, all the members psyching themselves up and getting into character. The Loopy Louies were like bikers, guys in denim and old sweatshirts who whaled the hell out of their instruments. Three guitarists, one drummer, and they were all in a little world of their own, of course. Bass guitarist is a husky guy with a lot of thick black hair, a day's growth of beard and carrying around a bottle of something amber-colored with a label that says "Jim Beam" on it. He offers everybody a swig, including the Latinettes, who are teasing each other's hair and putting on make-up on top of make-up on top of make-up. And then up in the top left corner of the screen, you get his bio: Lionel LeBlanc, graduate student in English, writing a thesis on Milton. Yes, Uncle Miltie! The guy is a scholar of Berle's *Divine Comedy* and he's wandering around with a bottle of Jim Beam and burping. You've got to love it.

The Latinaires are such a precision dance team that they can take the bottle from the Uncle Miltie scholar, swig, and pass it on to the next one without missing a beat or a hand gesture. They're all mouthing something about a great pretender, the purple satin shirts look like liquid metal, the tight pants and the pointy shoes are positively low-rider classic.

But you just know that the Latinettes did their hair for them. The four girls keep running over and putting more spray on their curls, even though the Latinaires are protesting left and right that they don't need any more. Then the girls tease each other's hair even higher — they've got great big bubbles on their heads, and in back it's something called a French twist. They're all wearing halter-top dresses in a leopard print and pointy-toed flats that they can do the Twist in.

And then there's Larry. Little Latin Larry. He really is little — maybe five feet, four inches, about as tall as the next tallest Latinette (the tallest one is close to six feet, over that if you include the hair, of course) and very Latin-looking, even more so, somehow, than the Latinaires, who are all, to a man, perfectly Spanish, according to their bios. The three Rodriguez brothers and their cousin the Cheech man. Larry is also their cousin on their father's side; on Larry's mother's side, however, he's Italian. Or so the bio tells me.

Meanwhile, out front in the bar, the audience is getting into character. This is, apparently, one of those time-warp occasions, where everybody would pretend it was a time that it wasn't anymore. Which is to say, the kind of music, the kind of performance the band gives is mostly something from twenty or thirty years before — everything here is a little vague, but that's a product of the Collapse and we're all used to it.

The crowd in the bar doesn't seem to be aware of any time difference. Either they've always liked this music, or they don't know any time has passed. Or they don't care. Or they wouldn't care if they did know. As the bar becomes more crowded, you start getting audience ghosts — a common occurrence, really, for a lot of these sorts of events. Usually, you don't worry too much about them, they'll disappear after a while if they're real ghosts and if they're not, they solidify and fall into place wherever they're supposed to fit in. These did neither.

Ghosts kept following me around in the bar and I couldn't decide what was really happening — whether they were some product of the memory bit, either the ancestor's imagination at work or the descendant's, or whether the memory bit had been corrupted or polluted in some way, mixed in with some memory bit that didn't belong, or whether it was something in my own chemistry that was intruding.

Wherever they were coming from, they were a nuisance and they showed no sign of fading away, no matter how hard I ignored them. I'd just have to try editing them out on my next time through, I thought.

I found the biker chick again, sitting with half a dozen biker guys at the table I had passed out under before. I didn't think she'd notice me — this was split-screen, after all, so I wasn't entirely there — but she did. And as soon as she saw me, the split-screen effect was gone and I was in the bar only. The Cleopatra eyes started to widen in an expression of recognition, which was, of course, impossible — no character in a memory sequence remembers any more than a person's photograph would remember who looked at it. Then it was like she dropped a stitch; the expression that had started out as recognition ended as puzzlement and I could all but hear her mind in operation. She'd thought I was someone she knew, but she was wrong. Or was she? Now she was suspicious and a suspicious biker is a scary bit of business, even if she isn't real. I really hoped that we didn't have a memory of a situation. It's only a very select portion of the clientele that has any appreciation for being beaten up in a bar fight.

Fortunately, the biker guys with her didn't find me especially threatening or even interesting. For all I knew, they couldn't even see me. It didn't take them long to distract her. When she looked away from me at last, I found myself backstage with the band and things were approaching critical mass, phase one. The Loopy Louies were looped (tolerated synonym for shitfaced, but only when used by someone outside the subgroup), the Latinaires were perfectly in synch, and the Latinettes were warmed up to the point where they could barely contain themselves. Larry, of course, was an island of calm, the Zen Master of rock 'n' roll. The most active thing he did was snap his fingers in time to the Latinaires' movements as he walked around the dressing room, surveying his troops.

Abruptly, he pointed at the Loopy Louies and they were on their feet, slamming each other on the back and then propelling themselves through the door and onto the raised platform that was the stage.

I thought the split-screen effect would disappear again and I would find myself watching the Louies from the audience. But no — the split-screen remained and I thought I'd go cross-eyed or faint from vertigo, with the two perspectives facing off against each other. From the stage, I saw people surge forward, eager to get the party going. In the audience, I felt like I was body-surfing an incoming tide that set me right down in front of the band. The Louies launched into some three-chord classic and some guy I couldn't see said, "Ladies and gentlemen, for one night only, all the way from Philly, just for your entertainment here at the Ritzy Roadhouse, the return of — Little Latin Larry!"

The Loopy Louies were playing "Little Latin Loopy Lou" (of course) as Larry swung onto the stage, still completely calm, utterly cool, shoulders moving gracefully, one hand in his pocket, the other snapping in time to the music as he glided over to the microphone at center stage and sang the opening number.

The split-screen drove me crazy. It needed an option menu so users could choose to be onstage or in the audience. Switching back and forth wouldn't be too bad, but having to endure both at once was too much. I tried to pause the action so I could insert the option and its menu, and that was when I got the first hint that I was in a not-so-usual type of situation: now that it was all in sequence, it wouldn't pause. Not only wouldn't it pause, it wouldn't stop.

Well, we couldn't have that. The customers would be screaming. Hell, if they wanted the type of experience they couldn't pause, stop, or rewind, they'd just stay out in their lives. I tried everything short of neutralizing — reinserting the menus, reprogramming the menus and reinserting them, reconstructing them so they weren't ever completely out of the frame of action. None of it did a bit of good — once Larry started, that was it, you went with him unless you neutralized the potion in your blood. And frankly, while I could have done that easily enough — I'm never more than a pinprick away from sobriety — I couldn't bring myself to go through with it. I couldn't get over the feeling that somehow Larry and the band would know that I had somehow either cut them off or walked out of their set, and they'd get mad at me and not let me back in when I wanted to resume editing.

And of course I knew that was ridiculous. But only my brain knew it. My blood and my gut, they didn't know any such thing. I hung on the way you might hang on to the safety bar of a roller coaster and let Larry & Co. have the driving wheel.

The band did two more numbers — "Twist and Shout" and "Land of 1000 Dances" — before Larry introduced everyone. This was one of the slippery spots. You could hear everything and see everything just fine, but the band introductions just go right by, like a train that doesn't stop, and then you're back in the music: "Sock It to Me, Baby," "Shake a Tailfeather," "Nowhere to Run," "Long Tall Sally." I was pretty sure I remembered them setting fire to "I'm a Man" before I passed out.

When I woke up, I knew the party was over. I was still in the bar, but there was no more music. A waitress was shaking me, forcing me to sit up and drink a cup of black coffee. I think it was coffee — it smelled like dirt and tasted like hot soapy water. Over on the bandstand, the Loopy Louies were taking the drum kit apart and the Latinettes were standing around smoking cigarettes and talking to them. Behind the bar, the bartender and another waitress were washing up and, sitting all by himself on a stool at the end of the bar, watching a TV that had a picture but no sound, was Little Latin Larry himself. I looked around but I didn't see the Latinaires. The waitress kept trying to shove the cup between my lips and I actually felt it clicking against my teeth. The only way I knew for sure that I was still in the memory was the fact that the coffee didn't burn me or choke me.

"Stop it," I said, finally, pushing her arm away. "What's going on? I'm not supposed to still be here. I was supposed to see the whole show and then leave."

"No shit, Einstein. Been tryin' to wake you for half an hour." She frowned into my face, this very pretty young woman with long, thick, straight, dark hair and lots and lots of make-up. The make-up made her look even more tired than she was. Or maybe as tired as she was. "Come on, come on, now. You don't have to go home, but you can't stay here."

I took the coffee cup from her, got up, and walked toward where Larry was sitting at the end of the bar. There was a can of something that said Schlitz in fancy script by his elbow, and cigarette smoke was rising in skinny curlicues from the ashtray next to it. The bartender and the waitress helping him watched me but didn't say anything. The bartender just looked bored — he wasn't really old but he wasn't young anymore either. His face was starting to sag around the corners of his mouth and under his eyes, although his hair was still dark. The waitress was like something out of a fairy tale, with her wispy blonde hair pulled back except for the perfect ringlets framing her very pale, round face. She had a blue velvet ribbon around her neck with a cameo attached to the front, and I knew it was A Fashion Look as, to a lesser extent, was her form-fitting, almost-off-the-shoulder flower-print shirt. I looked back at the waitress who had woken me; she didn't look any older than the little blonde one, but she felt older. Her name was Nora, something told me, and the little blonde was Claire. The bartender's name was Jerry or Georgie, and Little Latin Larry's real name was—was—

I stopped with one hand up, pausing in the act of tapping him on the shoulder because I had wanted to call him by his real name but it wouldn't come to me. It felt as if it might be right there in my next breath but every time I exhaled it came out silent. The hell with it, I thought, I'll just call him Larry.

"What," Larry said, not turning around, before I could touch him.

"What?" I repeated, sounding stupid even to myself.

"Yeah, what," Larry said, still with his back to me. "As in, 'What do you want?' Or even, 'What the fuck are you bothering me for?'"

"How'd you know I was here?" I asked.

"Saw your reflection outta the corner of my eye." He turned his head to look at the mirror behind the bar. I followed his gaze and then jumped; there was no one standing behind Larry in the mirror, no one and nothing at all except empty space where I should have seen whoever I was.

"'S'matter, you see something scary?" He finally looked over his shoulder directly at me. "Or just not what you expected you were gonna see?"

"That can be scary," I said, trying to sound light. "The unexpected."

"That's for sure." He swiveled around on his stool and studied me. I was still so startled that I couldn't imagine what he was seeing. I looked over at the stage where the Loopy Louies and the Latinettes had been, but they were gone. Now Larry followed my gaze. "What you lookin' for?"

"I—well, I just saw the Loopy Louies and the Latinettes—they were—"

"You saw them?" Larry said, and laughed incredulously. "You fuckin' saw them?"

I floundered for a few moments. "Was it wrong to look?" I asked him finally.

"Where did you fuckin' look that you fuckin' saw Loopy Louies and Latinettes?"

I gestured at the stage area, which was a lot emptier than I thought it had been a few minutes ago. Now even the last of the microphone stands were gone.

Larry shook his head and laughed some more. "Tell me you heard that, Jerry," he said, smoothing the back of his hair. Very greasy hair, not terribly clean.

"I heard it," the bartender said obediently. "Now tell me you paid this joker to come in and say that in fronna me and the girls."

Larry shook his head. "Man, oh, man. Have I ever seen you before, joker?" He stared at me expectantly.

I looked over my shoulder at the bartender and the blonde waitress. The dark-haired one joined them behind the bar; she looked extremely nervous. "Me? No, no, I guess not."

"OK. Now, you wanna explain how you happened to see something that's only in my head?" Larry took a last drag on the cigarette and smashed it out in the ashtray.

"You're Little Latin Larry," I said, not getting it. "Little Latin Larry and His Loopy Louies—"

"Stop it," said the dark-haired waitress, sounding angry.

"—His Luscious Latinaires," I said, turning toward her briefly, "and His—"

"Stop it!" she shouted.

"—Lascivious Latinettes?"

"You oughta be strung up." The dark-haired waitress glowered at me and then stalked off to clean some other tables.

I looked at Larry questioningly. He just kept smiling a funny little amazed smile. "Little Latin Larry," he said, and it sounded as if he were savoring each syllable. "Jesus H. I'm just glad you had the courtesy to come in here and say it where someone else could hear you."

"Why?" I looked at the bartender and the blonde waitress. The bartender had this sort of bored expression. Sort of bored and sort of skeptical, as if he thought I was lying about something. The waitress just looked mildly unhappy.

"Because maybe, just maybe," he said slowly, "it means that there's some world somewhere, even some time, where it's all true."

I stared at him for a moment and then looked at the bartender again for some kind of sign or explanation. He looked past me to Larry. "You ask me, I think this's a setup from your ex-wife. She wants to see if you're still taking your medicine. You are still taking your pills, aincha?"

"Sure," Larry said, and laughed some more. "Hell, I ain't the one seein' Loopy Louies and Latinettes and all that." He jerked his thumb at me. "Right here, this is the prize-winner tonight." He leaned back and looked at me out of the corners of his eyes. "Some people think insanity's contagious. You think maybe you drank outta the same glass I did but old Jerry here didn't wash it too good in between? Or maybe it was a toilet seat...."

I admit it: at that point, I panicked and drained the whole experience.

OK, it hit my secret fear — that I could possibly catch someone's delusion or psychosis. Don't say it's not possible, because it's happened. It's on record, it's documented. I don't knowingly go near anyone with a psychosis, I don't care how good the hallucinations are. If I want to hallucinate, I take drugs, the way Nature intended.

Anyway, I would have poured the whole batch down the drain except I couldn't, legally, since it wasn't my property. And since Ola and her sidekick knew the batch existed, I didn't want to force them into the position of having to choose between testifying that I had disposed of the Larry people's property or committing perjury and saying that it hadn't come together. So I gritted my teeth and requested a private meeting with Carola.

She came down to my editing room and things got ugly right away. How dare I accuse her of being crazy and I told her that I wasn't, just that her ancestor was prone to delusions and the memory had come through extra strong.

Well, that couldn't possibly be true, she insisted, raising her voice some more, because all the rest of the band was there, including a member of the audience, and how did I explain that?

Tainted samples, I said, forcing myself not to cringe (I really was afraid she was going to start throwing things at me). Her memory factors infected theirs, much like a virus —

Those were the last words she wanted to hear from me. I'm not sure what she said because it's hard to understand anyone at that volume. There were lots of threats, accusations of jealousy and theft and incompetence on my part, not to mention my blood being tainted by my ancestors' mating with mutant some-thing-or-others during the period following the Collapse.

I know better than to argue, or even to try to reason with someone in that state. I stepped back and told her she was welcome to her property, I didn't want it. She gathered it all up in what I think they used to call "high dudgeon." I'm not quite sure of the term, but I am sure of this: she knew. She knew and she had known probably all along. The anger was to cover the fear of the news getting out, that there was no such band, no such people, no such memory, no such night, ever. Not even theoretically; not even hidden from us by the scarcity of hard information about the world as it was before the Collapse. People get massively harsh about fraudulent pasts and faked memories; the court might let you off with merely a ruinously gargantuan fine and a slap on the wrist, but you're finished professionally. You can try to go into fiction, but you'll just get turned away—no one will trust you any more than they would if you had committed plagiarism.

I suppose at that point, I should have felt like I was facing a capital ethical dilemma. After talking it over with Ola and the sidekick, we all decided we didn't have to face anything at all. We'd all just keep our mouths shut. I wasn't a doctor, I couldn't diagnose a medical condition. All I'd done was make a judgment call and canceled the contract with them. They were free to go and I hadn't even gotten paid for what work I had done. I figured after that, she'd either find an editor who didn't mind massaging her data, or someone else would tell her she had a naked emperor, so to speak, in her blood.

But, of course, everyone else she approached must have told her the truth about Little Latin Larry—or rather, that they knew the truth. I don't know how many other people she approached. Maybe only one. Or maybe none; maybe she really became afraid of someone finding out after I did.

I don't know who did the actual final cut. I suspect it was Carola herself. With so much experience in remakes, she must have picked up enough skills to get by, especially when the work was actually already done for her. Because I know, from what I've seen and heard, that *The Return of Little Latin Larry* is my own rough edit, with some resolution cleaned up. I've heard the soundtrack, and I know that's my re-mastering. I recognize the way Larry sometimes pops his Ps into the microphone.

But I've seen stills of the bar and the audience, and those aren't the people I saw. They're spliced in very well, morphed enough that no one would recognize them unless she or he had been among them as I had, but it's not the audience from the purported night. That audience is the original, from the very first Little Latin Larry feature, *Rocky's Roadhouse Presents: Little Latin Larry!* It's OK with me; they were a good audience. Carola's ancestor must have been in the springtime of his delusions then, and able to imagine, or hallucinate, very strongly.

But as for the rest of it, I have no explanation at all. I don't know why the damned thing disappears after one session. I know Carola blames me, says that I did something that makes Larry vanish. You'll notice, however, that I've never even been charged with malicious destruction of property. Maybe Carola just doesn't know how to stabilize blood products properly. I've been asked discreetly — i.e., behind Carola's back — if I'll analyze a sample, but I've refused. I don't want to know. I suspect it may have something to do with delusions having a shorter shelf-life than real things.

And if that's so, I don't want to know. Because what if I have to find out that, say, my man Dylan is actually someone's delusion and not the man who said that we all had to sing in our chains that everyone must get stoned? Yes, that would be a pretty thorough delusion — but so was Larry. I got all the way into those remakes, that music, those performances. I had a place for them in my mind, and, yeah, in my heart. I feel as robbed as anyone would. It made me think how fragile knowledge can be, especially when you have to glean it from people themselves. Memory recovery is great biotechnology but there's a need for plain old non-sentient records, the kind of brute hardware that doesn't have an opinion about everything and doesn't personalize whatever it touches and records. Something sturdy, too. The kind of thing that can survive the collapse of civilization as we know it and then pop up with, say, accurate maps and —

Well, that's my new calling. That, and Sky High Theatre. Sky High Theatre is what I'm really excited about. It's a complete departure from everything I've done before. Get this: in Sky High Theatre, there's one stage, one cast, one performance, which cannot be stopped, paused, or rewound because it is live. And the audience, rather than being individuals within a session rig, are all together in one big room the size of a parking garage, and they sit and watch the live performance without being able to alter it or personalize it in any way. Everyone sees the exact same action at the exact same time.

Don't laugh. This could catch on.

"I think your discussion of the novelty of Gibson and the ideational content of this kind of sf is cogent. It strikes me that you and he could do a lot worse than to pursue this line of literary attack. I also agree that sf has open to it opportunities and approaches to writing that are different than those of traditional lit because of sf's outcast and low-class status, and that these approaches may offer the chance for the production of something genuinely new.

Only time will tell how this will play out. I certainly don't know. The one thing I do know, however, is that a writer has to follow his own instincts, and I get pretty indignant when somebody presumes to tell me that my honest desire to write what interests me is really just an attempt to toady up to the literary establishment... I do think that there is support for the view that [cyberpunk] is not some wholly new invention exclusive to the sf demimonde...that sf writers, like it or not, are part of the broader world of fiction, though certain kinds of sf may have to be judged by standards different form those of traditional fiction....

A couple of letters ago you said 'We cannot have it both ways. Either I control my own creations or I don't.' I don't agree with that. We can both control and not control our creations. I'm no Freudian or Marxist. I don't like any criticism that tells me the writer didn't know what he was doing. On the other hand, I think it's futile to deny that many things we don't intend to express often show up in our work.... Look at the body of work produced in the career of somebody like Heinlein...*Starship Troopers* is both about the virtues of a military social morality and about the eroticism of machines and violence. How can you evaluate one side of this book without acknowledging the other?"

Thirteen Views of a Cardboard City

William Gibson

Though he is the quintessential cyberpunk, the label never encompassed all that William Gibson's fiction did. Or maybe what Gibson did in his early work was not entirely what people said he was doing. Even at the time he said, "I think that a number of reviewers have mistaken my sense of realism, of the commercial surfaces of characters' lives, for some deep and genuine attempt to understand technology." Famously, Gibson wrote *Neuromancer* on a manual typewriter, and his contribution to *Mirrorshades* is "The Gernsback Continuum," which is not about computer hackers slicing into corporate databases, but about "semiotic ghosts" of science fiction past.

If you want to see this story as cyberpunk, look at it this way. It seems to be all about surfaces. It juxtaposes a small portion of the urban landscape with the implied human life within it, exposing this life through a series of images. No human being appears onstage, but in the end Gibson evokes a sense of human tragedy through the artifacts of our culture.

ONE
DEN-EN

Low angle, deep perspective, establishing Tokyo subway station interior.

Shot with available light, long exposure; a spectral pedestrian moves away from us, into background. Two others visible as blurs of motion.

Overhead fluorescents behind narrow rectangular fixtures. Ceiling tiled with meter-square segments (acoustic baffles?). Round fixtures are ventilators, smoke-detectors, speakers? Massive square columns recede. Side of a stairwell or escalator. Mosaic tile floor in simple large-scale pattern: circular white areas in square tiles, black infill of round tiles. The floor is spotless: no litter at all. Not a cigarette butt, not a gum-wrapper.

A long train of cardboard cartons, sides painted with murals, recedes into the perspective of columns and scrubbed tile: first impression is of a children's art project, something choreographed by an aggressively creative preschool teacher. But not all of the corrugated cartons have been painted; many, particularly those farthest away, are bare brown paper. The one nearest the camera, unaltered, bright yellow, bears the Microsoft logo.

The murals appear to have been executed in poster paints, and are difficult to interpret here.

There are two crisp-looking paper shopping-bags on the tile floor: one near the murals, the other almost in the path of the ghost pedestrian. These strike a note of anomaly, of possible threat: London Transport warnings, Sarin cultists... Why are they there? What do they contain?

The one nearest the murals bears the logo "DEN-EN."

Deeper in the image are other cartons. Relative scale makes it easier to see that these are composites, stitched together from smaller boxes. Closer study makes the method of fastening clear: two sheets are punctured twice with narrow horizontal slits, flat poly-twine analog (white or pink) is threaded through both sheets, a knot is tied, the ends trimmed neatly. In fact, all of the structures appear to have been assembled this way.

Deepest of all, stairs. Passengers descending.

TWO
BLUE OCTOPUS

Shallow perspective, eye-level, as though we were meant to view an anamorphic painting.

This structure appears to have been braced with a pale blue, enameled, possibly spring-loaded tube with a white, non-slip plastic foot. It might be the rod for a shower-curtain, but here it is employed vertically. Flattened cartons are neatly lashed to this with poly-tie.

The murals. Very faintly, on the end of the structure, nearest the camera, against a black background, the head of the Buddha floats above something amorphous and unreadable. Above the Buddha are fastened what appear to be two packaging-units for Pooh Bear dolls. These may serve a storage function. The mural on the face of the structure is dark, intricate, and executed (acrylic paints?) with considerable technique. Body parts, a sense of claustrophobic, potentially erotic proximity. A female nude, head lost where the cardboard ends, clutches a blue octopus whose tentacles drape across the forehead of a male who seems to squat doglike at her feet. Another nude lies on her back, knees upraised, her sex shadowed in perspective. The head of a man with staring eyes and pinprick pupils hovers above her ankles; he appears to be smoking but has no cigarette.

A third nude emerges, closest to the camera: a woman whose features suggest either China or the Mexico of Diego Rivera.

A section of the station's floor, the round black tiles, is partially covered with a scrap of grayish-blue synthetic pile carpeting.

Pinned eyes.

THREE
FRONTIER INTERNATIONAL

Shot straight back into what may be a wide alcove. Regular curves of pale square tiles.

Four structures visible.

The largest, very precisely constructed, very hard-edged, is decorated with an eerie pointillist profile against a solid black background: it seems to be a very old man, his chin, lipless mouth and drooping nose outlined in blood red. In front of this is positioned a black hard-sided overnighter suitcase.

Abutting this structure stands another, smaller, very gaily painted: against a red background with a cheerful yellow bird and yellow concentric circles, a sort of Cubist ET winks out at the camera. The head of a large nail or pin, rendered in a far more sophisticated style, penetrates the thing's forehead above the open eye.

A life-sized human hand, entirely out of scale with the huge head, is reaching for the eye.

Nearby sits an even smaller structure, this one decorated with abstract squares of color recalling Klee or Mondrian. Beside it is an orange plastic crate of the kind used to transport sake bottles. An upright beer can. A pair of plastic sandals, tidily arranged.

Another, bigger structure behind this one. Something painted large-scale in beige and blue (sky?) but this is obscured by the Mondrian. A working door, hinged with poly-tie, remains unpainted: the carton employed for the door is printed with the words "FRONTIER INTERNATIONAL."

Individual styles of workmanship start to become apparent.

Deeper in the image, beyond what appears to be a stack of neatly folded blankets, is located the blue enamel upright, braced against the ceiling tile. Another like it, to its right, supports a paper kite with the printed face of a samurai.

FOUR
AFTER PICASSO

Shallow perspective of what appears to be a single, very narrow shelter approximately nine meters in length. Suggests the literally marginal nature of these constructions: someone has appropriated less than a meter at the side of a corridor, and built along it, tunneling like a cardboard seaworm.

The murals lend the look of a children's cardboard theater.

Punch in the underground.

Like so many of the anonymous paintings to be found in thrift shops everywhere, these murals are somehow vaguely after Picasso. Echo of *Guernica* in these tormented animal forms. Human features rendered flounder-style: more Oxfam Cubism.

Square black cushion with black tassels at its corners, top an uncharacteristically peaked section of cardboard roof. Elegant.

The wall behind the shelter is a partition of transparent lucite, suggesting the possibility of a bizarre ant-farm existence.

FIVE
YELLOW SPERM

We are in an impossibly narrow "alley" between shelters, perhaps a communal storage area. Cardboard shelving, folded blankets.

A primitive portrait of a black kitten, isolated on a solid green ground, recalls the hypnotic stare of figures in New England folk art.

Also visible: the white plastic cowl of an electric fan, yellow plastic sake crate, pale blue plastic bucket, section of blue plastic duck-board, green plastic dustpan suspended by string, child's pail in dark blue plastic. Styrofoam take-away containers with blue and scarlet paint suggest more murals in progress.

Most striking here is the wall of a matte-black shelter decorated with a mural of what appear to be large yellow inner-tubes with regularly spaced oval "windows" around their perimeters; through each window is glimpsed a single large yellow sperm arrested in midwriggle against a nebulous black-and-yellow background.

SIX
GOMI GUITAR

Extreme close, perhaps at entrance to a shelter.

An elaborately designed pair of black-and-purple Nike trainers, worn but clean. Behind them a pair of simpler white Reeboks (a woman's?).

A battered acoustic guitar strung with nylon. Beside it, a strange narrow case made of blue denim, trimmed with red imitation leather; possibly a golf bag intended to carry a single club to a driving range?

A self-inking German rubber stamp.

Neatly folded newspaper with Japanese baseball stars.

A battered pump-thermos with floral design.

SEVEN
108

A space like the upper berths on the Norfolk & Western sleeping cars my mother and I took when I was a child. Form following function.

The structure is wide enough to accommodate a single traditional Japanese pallet. A small black kitten sits at its foot (the subject of the staring portrait?). Startled by the flash, it is tethered with a red leash. A second, larger tabby peers over a shopping bag made of tartan paper. The larger cat is also tethered, with a length of thin white poly rope.

Part of a floral area-rug visible at foot of bed.

This space is deeply traditional, utterly culture-specific.

Brown cardboard walls, cardboard mailing tubes used as structural uprights, the neat poly-tie lashings.

On right wall:

GIC

MODEL NO: VS-30

QTY: L SET

COLOR: BLACK

c/t no: 108

MADE IN KOREA

At the rear, near what may be assumed to be the head of the bed, are suspended two white-coated metal shelves or racks. These contain extra bedding, a spare cat-leash, a three-pack of some pressurized product (butane for a cooker?), towels.

On the right wall are hung two pieces of soft luggage, one in dark green imitation leather, the other in black leather, and a three-quarter-length black leather car coat.

On the left wall, a white towel, a pair of bluejeans, and two framed pictures (content not visible from this angle).

A section of transparent plastic has been mounted in the ceiling to serve as a skylight.

EIGHT
HAPPY HOUR

Wall with mailing-tube uprights.

A large handbill with Japanese stripper: LIVE NUDE, TOPLESS BOTTOMLESS, HAPPY HOUR. Menu-chart from a hamburger franchise illustrating sixteen choices.

Beneath these, along the wall, are arranged two jars containing white plastic spoons, a tin canister containing chopsticks, eight stacked blue plastic large takeaway cups, fourteen stacked white paper takeaway cups (all apparently unused, and inverted to protect against dust), neatly folded towels and bedding, aluminum cookware, a large steel kettle, a pink plastic dishpan, a large wooden chopping-board.

Blanket with floral motif spread as carpet.

NINE
SANDY

A different view of the previous interior, revealing a storage loft very tidily constructed of mailing-tubes and flattened cartons.

The similarities with traditional Japanese post-and-beam construction is even more striking, here. This loft-space is directly above the stacked cookware in the preceding image. Toward its left side is a jumble of objects, some unidentifiable: heavy rope, a child's plaid suitcase, a black plastic bowl, a softball bat. To the right are arranged a soft, stuffed baby doll, a plush stuffed dog, a teddy bear wearing overalls that say "SANDY," what seems to be a plush stuffed killer whale (shark?) with white felt teeth. The whale or shark still has the manufacturer's cardboard label attached, just as it came from the factory.

In the foreground, on the lower level, is a stack of glossy magazines, a tin box that might once have held candy or some other confection, and an open case that probably once contained a pair of sunglasses.

TEN
BOY'S BAR KYOKA

A very simple shot, camera directed toward floor, documenting another food-preparation area.

A square section of the round tiles is revealed at the bottom of the photograph. The rest of the floor is covered by layers of newspaper beneath a sheet of brown cardboard. A narrow border of exposed newsprint advertises "Boy's Bar KYOKA."

A blue thermos with a black carrying-strap. A greasy-looking paper cup covered with crumpled aluminum foil. A red soap-dish with a bar of white soap. A cooking-pot with an archaic-looking wooden lid. The pot's handle is wrapped in a white terry face cloth, secured with two rubber bands. Another pot, this one with a device for attaching a missing wooden handle, contains a steel ladle and a wooden spatula. A nested collection of plastic mixing bowls and colanders.

A large jug of bottled water, snow-capped peaks on its blue and white label.

A white plastic cutting-board, discolored with use. A white plastic (paper?) bag with "ASANO" above a cartoon baker proudly displaying some sort of loaf.

ELEVEN
J.O.

The shelters have actually enclosed a row of pay telephones!

Dial 110 for police.

Dial 119 for fire or ambulance.

Two telephones are visible: they are that singularly bilious shade of green the Japanese reserve for pay phones. They have slots for phone-cards, small liquid crystal displays, round steel keys. They are mounted on individual stainless-steel writing-ledges, each supported by a stout, mirror-finished steel post. Beneath each ledge is an enclosed shelf or hutch, made of black, perforated steel sheeting. Provided as a resting place for a user's parcels.

The hutches now serve as food-prep storage: four ceramic soup bowls of a common pattern, three more with a rather more intricate glaze, four white plastic bowls and several colored ones. A plastic scrubbing-pad, used.

On the floor below, on newspaper, are an aluminum teapot and what may be a package of instant coffee sachets. Three liter bottles of cooking oils.

On the steel ledge of the left-hand phone is a tin that once contained J.O. Special Blend ready-to-drink coffee.

TWELVE
NIPPON SERIES

An office.

A gap has been left in the corrugated wall, perhaps deliberately, to expose a detailed but highly stylized map of Tokyo set into the station's wall. The wall of this shelter and the wall of the station have become confused. Poly-tie binds the cardboard house directly into the fabric of the station, into the Prefecture itself.

This is quite clearly an office.

On the wall around the official, integral subway map, fastened to granite composite and brown cardboard with bits of masking tape: a postcard with a cartoon of orange-waistcoated figures escorting a child through a pedestrian crossing, a restaurant receipt (?), a newspaper clipping, a small plastic clipboard with what seem to be receipts, possibly from an ATM, a souvenir program from the 1995 Nippon Series (baseball), and two color photos of a black-and-white cat. In one photo, the cat seems to be here, among the shelters.

Tucked behind a sheet of cardboard are four pens and three pairs of scissors. A small pocket flashlight is suspended by a lanyard of white poly-tie.

To the right, at right angles to the wall above, a cardboard shelf is cantilevered with poly-tie. It supports a box of washing detergent, a book, a dayglo orange Casio G-Shock wristwatch, a white terry face cloth, a red plastic AM/FM cassette-player, and three disposable plastic cigarette-lighters.

Below, propped against the wall, is something that suggests the bottom of an inexpensive electronic typewriter of the sort manufactured by Brother.

A box of Chinese candy, a cat-brush, a flea-collar.

THIRTEEN
TV SOUND

Close-up of the contents of the shelf.

The red stereo AM/FM cassette-player, its chrome antenna extended at an acute angle for better reception. It is TV Sound brand, model LX-43. Its broken handle, mended with black electrical tape, is lashed into the structure with white poly-tie. Beside the three lighters, which are tucked partially beneath the player, in a row, are an unopened moist towelette and a red fine-point felt pen. To the left of the player is a square red plastic alarm clock, the white face cloth, and the Casio C-Shock. The Casio is grimy, one of the only objects in this sequence that actually appears to be dirty. The book, atop the box of laundry detergent, is hardbound, its glossy dustjacket bearing the photograph of a suited and tied Japanese executive. It looks expensive. Inspirational? Autobiographical?

To the right of the LX-43: a rigid cardboard pack of Lucky Strike non-filters and a Pokka coffee tin with the top neatly removed (to serve as an ashtray?).

On the cardboard bulkhead above these things are taped up two sentimental postcards of paintings of kittens playing. "Cat collection" in a cursive font.

Below these are glued (not taped) three black-and-white photographs.

#1: A balding figure in jeans and a short-sleeved T-shirt squats before an earlier, unpainted version of this structure.

One of the cartons seems to be screened with the word "PLAST — ". He is eating noodles from a pot, using chopsticks.

#2: The "alley" between the shelters. The balding man looks up at the camera. Somehow he doesn't look Japanese at all. He sits cross-legged among half-a-dozen others. They look Japanese. All are engrossed in something, perhaps the creation of murals.

#3: He squats before his shelter, wearing molded plastic sandals. His hands grip his knees. Now he looks entirely Japanese, his face a formal mask of suffering.

Curve of square tiles.

How long has he lived here?

With his cats, his guitar, his neatly folded blankets?

Dolly back.

Hold on the cassette-player.

Behind it, almost concealed, is a Filofax.

Names.

Numbers.

Held as though they might be a map, a map back out of the underground.

The Wedding Album

David Marusek

David Marusek is relentless as he explores the implications of creating simulated people in VR. This story asks us to reconsider the criteria for being considered human. Who has rights when there can be multiple copies of an individual? Meanwhile, the advent of a cybernetic iteration of the singularity is thwarted, only to be replaced by one that is decidedly post-human. At the center of a tour through future history that is practically Stapledonian in its scope are a pair of newlyweds; it is their fragile relationship that gives Marusek's speculation emotional weight. For them, and perhaps for us, this is a horror story. And yet, for the post-humans who gather around them, there is a happy ending indeed.

Anne and Benjamin stood stock still, as instructed, close but not touching, while the simographer adjusted her apparatus, set its timer, and ducked out of the room. It would take only a moment, she said. They were to think only happy happy thoughts.

For once in her life, Anne was unconditionally happy, and everything around her made her happier: her gown, which had been her grandmother's; the wedding ring (how cold it had felt when Benjamin first slipped it on her finger!); her clutch bouquet of forget-me-nots and buttercups; Benjamin himself, close beside her in his charcoal grey tux and pink carnation. He who so despised ritual but was a good sport. His cheeks were pink, too, and his eyes sparkled with some wolfish fantasy. "Come here," he whispered. Anne shushed him; you weren't supposed to talk or touch during a casting; it could spoil the sims. "I can't wait," he whispered, "this is taking too long." And it did seem longer than usual, but this was a professional simulacrum, not some homemade snapshot.

They were posed at the street end of the living room, next to the table piled with brightly wrapped gifts. This was Benjamin's townhouse; she had barely moved in. All her treasures were still in shipping shells in the basement, except for the few pieces she'd managed to have unpacked: the oak refectory table and chairs, the sixteenth-century French armoire, the cherry wood chifforobe, the tea table with inlaid top, the silvered mirror over the fire surround. Of course, her antiques clashed with Benjamin's contemporary — and rather common — decor, but he had promised her the whole house to redo as she saw fit. A whole house!

"How about a kiss?" whispered Benjamin.

Anne smiled but shook her head; there'd be plenty of time later for that sort of thing.

Suddenly, a head wearing wraparound goggles poked through the wall and quickly surveyed the room. "Hey, you," it said to them.

"Is that our simographer?" Benjamin said.

The head spoke into a cheek mike, "This one's the keeper," and withdrew as suddenly as it had appeared.

"Did the simographer just pop her head in through the wall?" said Benjamin.

"I think so," said Anne, though it made no sense.

"I'll just see what's up," said Benjamin, breaking his pose. He went to the door but could not grasp its handle.

Music began to play outside, and Anne went to the window. Her view of the garden below was blocked by the blue-and-white-striped canopy they had rented, but she could clearly hear the clink of flatware on china, laughter, and the musicians playing a waltz. "They're starting without us," she said, happily amazed.

"They're just warming up," said Benjamin.

"No, they're not. That's the first waltz. I picked it myself."

"So let's waltz," Benjamin said and reached for her. But his arms passed through her in a flash of pixelated noise. He frowned and examined his hands.

Anne hardly noticed. Nothing could diminish her happiness. She was drawn to the table of wedding gifts. Of all the gifts, there was only one — a long flat box in flecked silver wrapping — that she was most keen to open. It was from Great Uncle Karl. When it came down to it, Anne was both the easiest and the hardest person to shop for. While everyone knew of her passion for antiques, few had the means or expertise to buy one. She reached for Karl's package, but her hand passed right through it. *This isn't happening*, she thought with gleeful horror.

That it *was*, in fact, happening was confirmed a moment later when a dozen people — Great Uncle Karl, Nancy, Aunt Jennifer, Traci, Cathy and Tom, the bridesmaids and others, including Anne herself, and Benjamin, still in their wedding clothes — all trooped through the wall wearing wraparound goggles. "Nice job," said Great Uncle Karl, inspecting the room, "first rate."

"Ooooh," said Aunt Jennifer, comparing the identical wedding couples, identical but for the goggles. It made Anne uncomfortable that the other Anne should be wearing goggles while she wasn't. And the other Benjamin acted a little drunk and wore a smudge of white frosting on his lapel. *We've cut the cake*, she thought happily, although she couldn't remember doing so. Geri, the flower girl in a pastel dress, and Angus, the ring bearer in a miniature tux, along with a knot of other dressed-up children, charged through the sofa, back and forth, creating pyrotechnic explosions of digital noise. They would have run through Benjamin and Anne, too, had the adults allowed. Anne's father came through the wall with a bottle of champagne. He paused when he saw Anne but turned to the other Anne and freshened her glass.

"Wait a minute!" shouted Benjamin, waving his arms above his head. "I get it now. *We're* the sims!" The guests all laughed, and he laughed too. "I guess my sims always say that, don't they?" The other Benjamin nodded yes and sipped his champagne. "I just never expected to *be* a sim," Benjamin went on. This brought another round of laughter, and he said sheepishly, "I guess my sims all say that, too."

The other Benjamin said, "Now that we have the obligatory epiphany out of the way," and took a bow. The guests applauded.

Cathy, with Tom in tow, approached Anne. "Look what I caught," she said and showed Anne the forget-me-not and buttercup bouquet. "I guess we know what *that* means." Tom, intent on straightening his tie, seemed not to hear. But Anne knew what it meant. It meant they'd tossed the bouquet. All the silly little rituals that she had so looked forward to.

"Good for you," she said, and offered her own clutch, which she still held, for comparison. The real one was wilting and a little ragged around the edges, with missing petals and sprigs, while hers was still fresh and pristine and would remain so eternally. "Here," she said, "take mine, too, for double luck." But when she tried to give Cathy the bouquet, she couldn't let go of it. She opened her hand and discovered a seam where the clutch joined her palm. It was part of her. *Funny*, she thought, *I'm not afraid*. Ever since she was little, Anne had feared that some day she would suddenly realize she wasn't herself anymore. It was a dreadful notion that sometimes oppressed her for weeks: knowing you weren't yourself. But her sims didn't seem to mind it. She had about three dozen Annes in her album, from age twelve on up. Her sims tended to be a morose lot, but they all agreed it wasn't so bad, the life of a sim, once you got over the initial shock. The first moments of disorientation are the worst, they told her, and they made her promise never to reset them back to default. Otherwise, they'd have to work everything through from scratch. So Anne never reset her sims when she shelved them. She might delete a sim outright for whatever reason, but she never reset them, because you never knew when you'd wake up one day a sim yourself. Like today.

The other Anne joined them. She was sagging a little. "Well," she said to Anne.

"Indeed!" replied Anne.

"Turn around," said the other Anne, twirling her hand, "I want to see."

Anne was pleased to oblige. Then she said, "Your turn," and the other Anne modeled for her, and she was delighted how the gown looked on her, though the goggles somewhat spoiled the effect. *Maybe this can work out*, she thought, *I am enjoying myself so.* "Let's go see us side-by-side," she said, leading the way to the mirror on the wall. The mirror was large, mounted high, and tilted forward so you saw yourself as from above. But simulated mirrors cast no reflections, and Anne was happily disappointed.

"Oh," said Cathy, "Look at that."

"Look at what?" said Anne.

"Grandma's vase," said the other Anne. On the mantle beneath the mirror stood Anne's most precious possession, a delicate vase cut from pellucid blue crystal. Anne's great-great-great-grandmother had commissioned the Belgian master, Bollinger, the finest glassmaker in sixteenth-century Europe, to make it. Five hundred years later, it was as perfect as the day it was cut.

"Indeed!" said Anne, for the sim vase seemed to radiate an inner light. Through some trick or glitch of the simogram, it sparkled like a lake under moonlight, and, seeing it, Anne felt incandescent.

After a while, the other Anne said, "Well?" Implicit in this question was a whole standard set of questions that boiled down to—shall I keep you or delete you now? For sometimes a sim didn't take. Sometimes a sim was cast while Anne was in a mood, and the sim suffered irreconcilable guilt or unassuagable despondency and had to be mercifully destroyed. It was better to do this immediately, or so all the Annes had agreed.

And Anne understood the urgency, what with the reception still in progress and the bride and groom, though frazzled, still wearing their finery. They might do another casting if necessary. "I'll be okay," Anne said. "In fact, if it's always like this, I'll be terrific."

Anne, through the impenetrable goggles, studied her. "You sure?"

"Yes."

"Sister," said the other Anne. Anne addressed all her sims as "sister," and now Anne, herself, was being so addressed. "Sister," said the other Anne, "this has got to work out. I need you."

"I know," said Anne, "I'm your wedding day."

"Yes, my wedding day."

Across the room, the guests laughed and applauded. Benjamin — both of him — was entertaining, as usual. He — the one in goggles — motioned to them. The other Anne said, "We have to go. I'll be back."

Great Uncle Karl, Nancy, Cathy and Tom, Aunt Jennifer, and the rest, left through the wall. A polka could be heard playing on the other side. Before leaving, the other Benjamin gathered the other Anne into his arms and leaned her backward for a theatrical kiss. Their goggles clacked. *How happy I look*, Anne told herself. *This is the happiest day of my life.*

Then the lights dimmed, and her thoughts shattered like glass.

They stood stock still, as instructed, close but not touching. Benjamin whispered, "This is taking too long," and Anne shushed him. You weren't supposed to talk; it could glitch the sims. But it did seem a long time. Benjamin gazed at her with hungry eyes and brought his lips close enough for a kiss, but Anne smiled and turned away. There'd be plenty of time later for fooling around.

Through the wall, they heard music, the tinkle of glassware, and the mutter of overlapping conversation. "Maybe I should just check things out," Benjamin said, and broke his pose.

"No, wait," whispered Anne, catching his arm. But her hand passed right through him in a stream of colorful noise. She looked at her hand in amused wonder.

Anne's father came through the wall. He stopped when he saw her and said,

"Oh, how lovely." Anne noticed he wasn't wearing a tuxedo.

"You just walked through the wall," said Benjamin.

"Yes, I did," said Anne's father. "Ben asked me to come in here and...ah... orient you two."

"Is something wrong?" said Anne, through a fuzz of delight.

"There's nothing wrong," replied her father.

"Something's wrong?" asked Benjamin.

"No, no," replied the old man. "Quite the contrary. We're having a do out there..." He paused to look around. "Actually, in here. I'd forgotten what this room used to look like."

"Is that the wedding reception?" Anne asked.

"No, your anniversary."

Suddenly Benjamin threw his hands into the air and exclaimed, "I get it, *we're* the sims!"

"That's my boy," said Anne's father.

"All my sims say that, don't they? I just never expected to *be* a sim."

"Good for you," said Anne's father. "All right then." He headed for the wall. "We'll be along shortly."

"Wait," said Anne, but he was already gone.

Benjamin walked around the room, passing his hand through chairs and lamp shades like a kid. "Isn't this fantastic?" he said.

Anne felt too good to panic, even when another Benjamin, this one dressed in jeans and sportscoat, led a group of people through the wall. "And this," he announced with a flourish of his hand, "is our wedding sim." Cathy was part of this group, and Janice and Beryl, and other couples she knew. But strangers too. "Notice what a cave I used to inhabit," the new Benjamin went on, "before Annie fixed it up. And here's the blushing bride, herself," he said, and bowed gallantly to Anne. Then, when he stood next to his double, her Benjamin, Anne laughed, for someone was playing a prank on her.

"Oh, really?" she said. "If this is a sim, where's the goggles?" For indeed, no one was wearing goggles.

"Technology!" exclaimed the new Benjamin. "We had our system upgraded. *Don't you love it?*"

"Is that right?" she said, smiling at the guests to let them know she wasn't fooled. "Then where's the real me?"

"You'll be along," replied the new Benjamin. "No doubt you're using the potty again." The guests laughed and so did Anne. She couldn't help herself.

Cathy drew her aside with a look. "Don't mind him," she said. "Wait till you see."

"See what?" said Anne. "What's going on?" But Cathy pantomimed pulling a zipper across her lips. This should have annoyed Anne, but didn't, and she said, "At least tell me who those people are."

"Which people?" said Cathy. "Oh, those are Anne's new neighbors."

"New neighbors?"

"And over there, that's Dr. Yurek Rutz, Anne's department head."

"That's not my department head," said Anne.

"Yes, he is," Cathy said. "Anne's not with the university anymore. She — ah — moved to a private school."

"That's ridiculous."

"Maybe we should just wait and let Anne catch you up on things." She looked impatiently toward the wall. "So much has changed." Just then, another Anne entered through the wall, with one arm outstretched like a sleepwalker and the other protectively cradling an enormous belly.

Benjamin, her Benjamin, gave a whoop of surprise and broke into a spontaneous jig. The guests laughed and cheered him on.

Cathy said, "See? Congratulations, you!"

Anne became caught up in the merriment. *But how can I be a sim?* she wondered.

The pregnant Anne scanned the room, and, avoiding the crowd, came over to her. She appeared very tired; her eyes were bloodshot. She didn't even try to smile. "Well?" Anne said, but the pregnant Anne didn't respond, just examined Anne's gown, her clutch bouquet. Anne, meanwhile, regarded the woman's belly, feeling somehow that it was her own and a cause for celebration — except that she knew she had never wanted children and neither had Benjamin. Or so he'd always said. You wouldn't know that now, though, watching the spectacle he was making of himself. Even the other Benjamin seemed embarrassed. She said to the pregnant Anne, "You must forgive me, I'm still trying to piece this all together. This isn't our reception?"

"No, our wedding anniversary."

"Our first?"

"Our fourth."

"Four *years?*" This made no sense. "You've shelved me for four years?"

"Actually," the pregnant Anne said and glanced sidelong at Cathy, "we've been in here a number of times already."

"Then I don't understand," said Anne. "I don't remember that."

Cathy stepped between them. "Now, don't you worry. They reset you last time is all."

"Why?" said Anne. "I *never* reset my sims. I never have."

"Well, I kinda do now, sister," said the pregnant Anne.

"But why?"

"To keep you fresh."

To keep me fresh, thought Anne. *Fresh?* She recognized this as Benjamin's idea. It was his belief that sims were meant to be static mementos of special days gone by, not virtual people with lives of their own. "But," she said, adrift in a fog of happiness. "But."

"Shut up!" snapped the pregnant Anne.

"Hush, Anne," said Cathy, glancing at the others in the room. "You want to lie down?" To Anne she explained, "Third trimester blues."

"Stop it!" the pregnant Anne said. "Don't blame the pregnancy. It has nothing to do with the pregnancy."

Cathy took her gently by the arm and turned her toward the wall. "When did you eat last? You hardly touched your plate."

"Wait!" said Anne. The women stopped and turned to look at her, but she didn't know what to say. This was all so new. When they began to move again, she stopped them once more. "Are you going to reset me?"

The pregnant Anne shrugged her shoulders.

"But you *can't*," Anne said. "Don't you remember what my sisters — our sisters — always say?"

The pregnant Anne pressed her palm against her forehead. "If you don't shut up this moment, I'll delete you right now. Is that what you want? Don't imagine that white gown will protect you. Or that big stupid grin on your face. You think you're somehow special? Is that what you think?"

The Benjamins were there in an instant. The real Benjamin wrapped an arm around the pregnant Anne. "Time to go, Annie," he said in a cheerful tone. "I want to show everyone our rondophones." He hardly glanced at Anne, but when he did, his smile cracked. For an instant he gazed at her, full of sadness.

"Yes, dear," said the pregnant Anne, "but first I need to straighten out this sim on a few points."

"I understand, darling, but since we have guests, do you suppose you might postpone it till later?"

"You're right, of course. I'd forgotten our guests. How insensitive of me." She allowed him to turn her toward the wall. Cathy sighed with relief.

"Wait!" said Anne, and again they paused to look at her. But although so much was patently wrong — the pregnancy, resetting the sims, Anne's odd behavior — Anne still couldn't formulate the right question.

Benjamin, her Benjamin, still wearing his rakish grin, stood next to her and said, "Don't worry, Anne, they'll return."

"Oh, I know that," she said, "but don't you see? *We* won't know they've returned, because in the meantime they'll reset us back to default again, and it'll all seem new, like the first time. And we'll have to figure out we're the sims all over again!"

"Yeah?" he said. "So?"

"So I can't live like that."

"But we're the *sims*. We're not alive." He winked at the other couple.

"Thanks, Ben boy," said the other Benjamin. "Now, if that's settled..."

"Nothing's settled," said Anne. "Don't I get a say?"

The other Benjamin laughed. "Does the refrigerator get a say? Or the car? Or my shoes? In a word — no."

The pregnant Anne shuddered. "Is that how you see me, like a pair of shoes?" The other Benjamin looked successively surprised, embarrassed, and angry. Cathy left them to help Anne's father escort the guests from the simulacrum. "Promise her!" the pregnant Anne demanded.

"Promise her *what*?" said the other Benjamin, his voice rising.

"Promise we'll never reset them again."

The Benjamin huffed. He rolled his eyes. "Okay, yah sure, whatever," he said.

When the simulated Anne and Benjamin were alone at last in their simulated living room, Anne said, "A fat lot of help *you* were."

"I agreed with myself," Benjamin said. "Is that so bad?"

"Yes, it is. We're married now; you're supposed to agree with *me*." This was meant to be funny, and there was more she intended to say—about how happy she was, how much she loved him, and how absolutely happy she was — but the lights dimmed, the room began to spin, and her thoughts scattered like pigeons.

It was raining, as usual, in Seattle. The front entry shut and locked itself behind Ben, who shook water from his clothes and removed his hat. Bowlers for men were back in fashion, but Ben was having a devil's own time becoming accustomed to his brown felt *Sportsliner*. It weighed heavy on his brow and made his scalp itch, especially in damp weather. "Good evening, Mr. Malley," said the house. "There is a short queue of minor household matters for your review. Do you have any requests?" Ben could hear his son shrieking angrily in the kitchen, probably at the nanny. Ben was tired. Contract negotiations had gone sour.

"Tell them I'm home."

"Done," replied the house. "Mrs. Malley sends a word of welcome."

"Annie? Annie's home?"

"Yes, sir."

Bobby ran into the foyer followed by Mrs. Jamieson. "Momma's home," he said.

"So I hear," Ben replied and glanced at the nanny.

"And guess what?" added the boy. "She's not sick anymore!"

"That's wonderful. Now tell me, what was all that racket?"

"I don't know."

Ben looked at Mrs. Jamieson who said, "I had to take something from him." She gave Ben a plastic chip.

Ben held it to the light. It was labeled in Anne's flowing hand, *Wedding Album —grouping 1, Anne and Benjamin*. "Where'd you get this?" he asked the boy.

"It's not my fault," said Bobby.

"I didn't say it was, trooper. I just want to know where it came from."

"Puddles gave it to me."

"And who is Puddles?"

Mrs. Jamieson handed him a second chip, this a commercial one with a 3-D label depicting a cartoon cocker spaniel. The boy reached for it. "It's mine," he whined. "Momma gave it to me."

Ben gave Bobby the Puddles chip, and the boy raced away. Ben hung his bowler on a peg next to his jacket. "How does she look?"

Mrs. Jamieson removed Ben's hat from the peg and reshaped its brim. "You have to be special careful when they're wet," she said, setting it on its crown on a shelf.

"Martha!"

"Oh, how should I know? She just showed up and locked herself in the media room."

"But how did she look?"

"Crazy as a loon," said the nanny. "As usual. Satisfied?"

"I'm sorry," Ben said. "I didn't mean to raise my voice." Ben tucked the wedding chip into a pocket and went into the living room, where he headed straight for the liquor cabinet, which was a genuine Chippendale dating from 1786. Anne had turned his whole house into a freaking museum with her antiques, and no room was so oppressively ancient as this, the living room. With its horsehair upholstered divans, maple burl sideboards, cherry wood wainscoting and floral wallpaper, the King George china cabinet, Regency plates, and Tiffany lamps; the list went on. And books, books, books. A case of shelves from floor to ceiling was lined with these moldering paper bricks. The newest thing in the room by at least a century was the twelve-year-old scotch that Ben poured into a lead crystal tumbler. He downed it and poured another. When he felt the mellowing hum of alcohol in his blood, he said, "Call Dr. Roth."

Immediately, the doctor's proxy hovered in the air a few feet away and said, "Good evening, Mr. Malley. Dr. Roth has retired for the day, but perhaps I can be of help."

The proxy was a head-and-shoulder projection that faithfully reproduced the doctor's good looks, her brown eyes and high cheekbones. But unlike the good doctor, the proxy wore makeup: eyeliner, mascara, and bright lipstick. This had always puzzled Ben, and he wondered what sly message it was supposed to convey. He said, "What is my wife doing home?"

"Against advisement, Mrs. Malley checked herself out of the clinic this morning."

"Why wasn't I informed?"

"But you were."

"I was? Please excuse me a moment." Ben froze the doctor's proxy and said,

"Daily duty, front and center." His own proxy, the one he had cast upon arriving at the office that morning, appeared hovering next to Dr. Roth's. Ben preferred a head shot only for his proxy, slightly larger than actual size to make it subtly imposing. "Why didn't you inform me of Annie's change of status?"

"Didn't seem like an emergency," said his proxy, "at least in the light of our contract talks."

"Yah, yah, okay. Anything else?" said Ben.

"Naw, slow day. Appointments with Jackson, Wells, and the Columbine. It's all on the calendar."

"Fine, delete you."

The projection ceased.

"Shall I have the doctor call you in the morning?" said the Roth proxy when Ben reanimated it. "Or perhaps you'd like me to summon her right now?"

"Is she at dinner?"

"At the moment, yes."

"Naw, don't bother her. Tomorrow will be soon enough. I suppose."

After he dismissed the proxy, Ben poured himself another drink. "In the next ten seconds," he told the house, "cast me a special duty proxy." He sipped his scotch and thought about finding another clinic for Anne as soon as possible and one — for the love of god — that was a little more responsible about letting crazy people come and go as they pleased. There was a chime, and the new proxy appeared. "You know what I want?" Ben asked it. It nodded. "Good. Go." The proxy vanished, leaving behind Ben's sig in bright letters floating in the air and dissolving as they drifted to the floor.

Ben trudged up the narrow staircase to the second floor, stopping on each step to sip his drink and scowl at the musty old photographs and daguerreotypes in oval frames mounted on the wall. Anne's progenitors. On the landing, the locked media room door yielded to his voice. Anne sat spreadlegged, naked, on pillows on the floor. "Oh, hi, honey," she said. "You're in time to watch."

"Fan-tastic," he said, and sat in his armchair, the only modern chair in the house. "What are we watching?" There was another Anne in the room, a sim of a young Anne standing on a dais wearing a graduate's cap and gown and fidgeting with a bound diploma. This, no doubt, was a sim cast the day Anne graduated from Bryn Mawr *summa cum laude*. That was four years before he'd first met her. "Hi," he said to the sim, "I'm Ben, your eventual spouse."

"You know, I kinda figured that out," the girl said, and smiled shyly, exactly as he remembered Anne smiling when Cathy first introduced them. The girl's beauty was so fresh and familiar — and so totally absent in his own Anne — that Ben felt a pang of loss. He looked at his wife on the floor. Her red hair, once so fussy neat, was ragged, dull, dirty, and short. Her skin was yellowish and puffy, and there was a slight reddening around her eyes, like a raccoon mask. These were harmless side effects of the medication, or so Dr. Roth had assured him. Anne scratched ceaselessly at her arms, legs, and crotch, and, even from a distance, smelled of stale piss. Ben knew better than to mention her nakedness to her, for that would only exacerbate things and prolong the display. "So," he repeated, "what are we watching?"

The girl sim said, "Housecleaning." She appeared at once both triumphant and terrified, as any graduate might, and Ben would have traded the real Anne for her in a heartbeat.

"Yah," said Anne, "too much shit in here."

"Really?" said Ben. "I hadn't noticed."

Anne poured a tray of chips on the floor between her thighs. "Of course you wouldn't," she said, picking one at random and reading its label, "*Theta Banquet '37*. What's this? I never belonged to the Theta Society."

"Don't you remember?" said the young Anne. "That was Cathy's induction banquet. She invited me, but I had an exam, so she gave me that chip as a souvenir."

Anne fed the chip into the player and said, "Play." The media room was instantly overlaid with the banquet hall of the Four Seasons in Philadelphia. Ben tried to look around the room, but the tables of girls and women stayed stubbornly peripheral. The focal point was a table draped in green cloth and lit by two candelabra. Behind it sat a young Cathy in formal evening dress, accompanied by three static placeholders, table companions who had apparently declined to be cast in her souvenir snapshot.

The Cathy sim looked frantically about, then held her hands in front of her and stared at them as though she'd never seen them before. But after a moment she noticed the young Anne sim standing on the dais. "Well, well, well," she said. "Looks like congratulations are in order."

"Indeed," said the young Anne, beaming and holding out her diploma.

"So tell me, did I graduate too?" said Cathy as her glance slid over to Ben.

Then she saw Anne squatting on the floor, her sex on display.

"Enough of this," said Anne, rubbing her chest.

"Wait," said the young Anne. "Maybe Cathy wants her chip back. It's her sim, after all."

"I disagree. She gave it to me, so it's mine. And *I'll* dispose of it as I see fit." To the room she said, "Unlock this file and delete." The young Cathy, her table, and the banquet hall dissolved into noise and nothingness, and the media room was itself again.

"Or this one," Anne said, picking up a chip that read, *Junior Prom Night*. The young Anne opened her mouth to protest, but thought better of it. Anne fed this chip, along with all the rest of them, into the player. A long directory of file names appeared on the wall. "Unlock *Junior Prom Night*." The file's name turned from red to green, and the young Anne appealed to Ben with a look.

"Anne," he said, "don't you think we should at least look at it first?"

"What for? I know what it is. High school, dressing up, lusting after boys, dancing. Who needs it? Delete file." The item blinked three times before vanishing, and the directory scrolled up to fill the space. The young sim shivered, and Anne said, "Select the next one."

The next item was entitled, *A Midsummer's Night Dream*. Now the young Anne was compelled to speak, "You can't delete that one. You were great in that, don't you remember? Everyone loved you. It was the best night of your life."

"Don't presume to tell *me* what was the best night of my life," Anne said. "Unlock *A Midsummer's Night Dream*." She smiled at the young Anne. "Delete file." The menu item blinked out. "Good. Now unlock *all* the files." The whole directory turned from red to green.

"Please make her stop," the sim implored.

"Next," said Anne. The next file was *High School Graduation*. "Delete file. Next." The next was labeled only *Mama*.

"Anne," said Ben, "why don't we come back to this later. The house says dinner's ready."

She didn't respond.

"You must be famished after your busy day," he continued. "I know I am."

"Then please go eat, dear," she replied. To the room she said, "Play *Mama*."

The media room was overlaid by a gloomy bedroom that Ben at first mistook for their own. He recognized much of the heavy Georgian furniture, the sprawling canopied bed in which he felt so claustrophobic, and the voluminous damask curtains, shut now and leaking yellow evening light. But this was not their bedroom, the arrangement was wrong.

In the corner stood two placeholders, mute statues of a teenaged Anne and her father, grief frozen on their faces as they peered down at a couch draped with tapestry and piled high with down comforters. And suddenly Ben knew what this was. It was Anne's mother's deathbed sim. Geraldine, whom he'd never met in life nor holo. Her bald eggshell skull lay weightless on feather pillows in silk covers. They had meant to cast her farewell and accidentally caught her at the precise moment of her death. He had heard of this sim from Cathy and others. It was not one he would have kept.

Suddenly, the old woman on the couch sighed, and all the breath went out of her in a bubbly gush. Both Annes, the graduate and the naked one, waited expectantly. For long moments the only sound was the tocking of a clock that Ben recognized as the Seth Thomas clock currently located on the library mantel. Finally there was a cough, a hacking cough with scant strength behind it, and a groan, "Am I back?"

"Yes, Mother," said Anne.

"And I'm still a sim?"

"Yes."

"Please delete me."

"Yes, Mother," Anne said, and turned to Ben. "We've always thought she had a bad death and hoped it might improve over time."

"That's crazy," snapped the young Anne. "That's not why I kept this sim."

"Oh, no?" said Anne. "Then why *did* you keep it?" But the young sim seemed confused and couldn't articulate her thoughts. "You don't know because *I* didn't know at the time either," said Anne. "But I know *now*, so I'll tell you. You're fascinated with death. It scares you silly. You wish someone would tell you what's on the other side. So you've enlisted your own sweet mama."

"That's ridiculous."

Anne turned to the deathbed tableau. "Mother, tell us what you saw there."

"I saw nothing," came the bitter reply. "You cast me without my eyeglasses."

"Ho ho," said Anne. "Geraldine was nothing if not comedic."

"You also cast me wretchedly thirsty, cold, and with a bursting bladder, damn you! And the pain! I beg you, daughter, delete me."

"I will, Mother, I promise, but first you have to tell us what you saw."

"That's what you said the last time."

"This time I mean it."

The old woman only stared, her breathing growing shallow and ragged. "*All right*, Mother," said Anne. "I *swear* I'll delete you."

Geraldine closed her eyes and whispered, "What's that smell? That's not me?" After a pause she said, "It's heavy. Get it off." Her voice rose in panic. "Please! Get it off!" She plucked at her covers, then her hand grew slack, and she all but crooned, "Oh, how lovely. A pony. A tiny dappled pony." After that she spoke no more and slipped away with a last bubbly breath.

Anne paused the sim before her mother could return for another round of dying. "See what I mean?" she said. "Not very uplifting, but all in all, I detect a slight improvement. What about you, Anne? Should we settle for a pony?" The young sim stared dumbly at Anne. "Personally," Anne continued, "I think we should hold out for the bright tunnel or an open door or bridge over troubled water. What do you think, sister?" When the girl didn't answer, Anne said, "Lock file and eject." The room turned once again into the media room, and Anne placed the ejected chip by itself into a tray. "We'll have another go at it later, mum. As for the rest of these, who needs them?"

"*I do*," snapped the girl. "They belong to me as much as to you. They're my sim sisters. I'll keep them until you recover."

Anne smiled at Ben. "That's charming. Isn't that charming, Benjamin? My own sim is solicitous of me. Well, here's my considered response. Next file! Delete! Next file! Delete! Next file!" One by one, the files blinked out.

"Stop it!" screamed the girl. "Make her stop it!"

"Select *that* file," Anne said, pointing at the young Anne. "Delete." The sim vanished, cap, gown, tassels, and all. "Whew," said Anne, "at least now I can hear myself think. She was really getting on my nerves. I almost suffered a relapse. Was she getting on your nerves, too, dear?"

"Yes," said Ben, "my nerves are ajangle. Now can we go down and eat?"

"Yes, dear," she said, "but first...select all files and delete."

"Countermand!" said Ben at the same moment, but his voice held no privileges to her personal files, and the whole directory queue blinked three times and vanished. "Aw, Annie, why'd you do that?" he said. He went to the cabinet and pulled the trays that held his own chips. She couldn't alter them electronically, but she might get it into her head to flush them down the toilet or something. He also took their common chips, the ones they'd cast together ever since they'd met. She had equal privileges to those.

Anne watched him and said, "I'm hurt that you have so little trust in me."

"How can I trust you after that?"

"After what, darling?"

He looked at her. "Never mind," he said, and carried the half-dozen trays to the door.

"Anyway," said Anne, "I already cleaned those."

"What do you mean you already cleaned them?"

"Well, I didn't delete *you*. I would never delete *you*. Or Bobby."

Ben picked one of their common chips at random, *Childbirth of Robert Ellery Malley*/02-03-48, and slipped it into the player. "Play!" he commanded, and the media room became the midwife's birthing suite. His own sim stood next to the bed in a green smock. It wore a humorously helpless expression. It held a swaddled bundle, Bobby, who bawled lustily. The birthing bed was rumpled and stained, but empty. The new mother was missing. "Aw, Annie, you shouldn't have."

"I know, Benjamin," she said. "I sincerely hated doing it."

Ben flung their common trays to the floor where the ruined chips scattered in all directions. He stormed out of the room and down the stairs, pausing to glare at every portrait on the wall. He wondered if his proxy had found a suitable clinic yet. He wanted Anne out of the house tonight. Bobby should never see her like this. Then he remembered the chip he'd taken from Bobby and felt for it in his pocket — the *Wedding Album*.

The lights came back up, Anne's thoughts coalesced, and she remembered who and what she was. She and Benjamin were still standing in front of the wall. She knew she was a sim, so at least she hadn't been reset. *Thank you for that, Anne*, she thought.

She turned at a sound behind her. The refectory table vanished before her eyes, and all the gifts that had been piled on it hung suspended in midair. Then the table reappeared, one layer at a time, its frame, top, gloss coat, and lastly, the bronze hardware. The gifts vanished, and a toaster reappeared, piece by piece, from its heating elements outward. A coffee press, houseputer peripherals, component-by-component, cowlings, covers, and finally boxes, gift-wrap, ribbon, and bows. It all happened so fast Anne was too startled to catch the half of it, yet she did notice that the flat gift from Great Uncle Karl was something she'd been angling for, a Victorian era sterling platter to complete her tea service.

"Benjamin!" she said, but he was missing, too. Something appeared on the far side of the room, on the spot where they'd posed for the sim, but it wasn't Benjamin. It was a 3-D mannequin frame, and as she watched, it was built up, layer by layer. "Help me," she whispered as the entire room was hurled into turmoil, the furniture disappearing and reappearing, paint being stripped from the walls, sofa springs coiling into existence, the potted palm growing from leaf to stem to trunk to dirt, the very floor vanishing, exposing a default electronic grid. The mannequin was covered in flesh now and grew Benjamin's face. It flit about the room in a pink blur. Here and there it stopped long enough to proclaim, "I do."

Something began to happen inside Anne, a crawling sensation everywhere as though she were a nest of ants. She knew she must surely die. *They have deleted us, and this is how it feels*, she thought. Everything became a roiling blur, and she ceased to exist except as the thought — *How happy I look*.

When Anne became aware once more, she was sitting hunched over in an auditorium chair, idly studying her hand, which held the clutch bouquet. There was commotion all around her, but she ignored it, so intent she was on solving the mystery of her hand. On an impulse, she opened her fist and the bouquet dropped to the floor. Only then did she remember the wedding, the holo, learning she was a sim. And here she was again — but this time everything was profoundly different. She sat upright and saw that Benjamin was seated next to her.

He looked at her with a wobbly gaze and said, "Oh, here you are."

"Where are we?"

"I'm not sure. Some kind of gathering of Benjamins. Look around." She did. They were surrounded by Benjamins, hundreds of them, arranged chronologically — it would seem — with the youngest in rows of seats down near a stage. She and Benjamin sat in what appeared to be a steeply sloped college lecture hall with lab tables on the stage and story-high monitors lining the walls. In the rows above Anne, only every other seat held a Benjamin. The rest were occupied by women, strangers who regarded her with veiled curiosity.

Anne felt a pressure on her arm and turned to see Benjamin touching her. "You *feel* that, don't you?" he said. Anne looked again at her hands. They were her hands, but simplified, like fleshy gloves, and when she placed them on the seat back, they didn't go through.

Suddenly, in ragged chorus, the Benjamins down front raised their arms and exclaimed, "I get it; *we're* the sims!" It was like a roomful of unsynchronized cuckoo clocks tolling the hour. Those behind Anne laughed and hooted approval. She turned again to look at them. Row-by-row, the Benjamins grew greyer and stringier until, at the very top, against the back wall, sat nine ancient Benjamins like a panel of judges. The women, however, came in batches that changed abruptly every row or two. The one nearest her was an attractive brunette with green eyes and full, pouty lips. She, all two rows of her, frowned at Anne.

"There's something else," Anne said to Benjamin, turning to face the front again, "my emotions." The bulletproof happiness she had experienced was absent. Instead she felt let down, somewhat guilty, unduly pessimistic — in short, almost herself.

"I guess my sims always say that," exclaimed the chorus of Benjamins down front, to the delight of those behind. "I just never expected to *be* a sim."

This was the cue for the eldest Benjamin yet to walk stiffly across the stage to the lectern. He was dressed in a garish leisure suit: baggy red pantaloons, a billowy yellow-and-green-striped blouse, a necklace of egg-sized pearlescent beads. He cleared his throat and said, "Good afternoon, ladies and gentlemen. I trust all of you know me — intimately. In case you're feeling woozy, it's because I used the occasion of your reactivation to upgrade your architecture wherever possible. Unfortunately, some of you — " he waved his hand to indicate the front rows — "are too primitive to upgrade. But we love you nevertheless." He applauded for the early Benjamins closest to the stage and was joined by those in the back. Anne clapped as well. Her new hands made a dull, thudding sound. "As to why I called you here..." said the elderly Benjamin, looking left and right and behind him. "Where *is* that fucking messenger anyway? They order us to inventory our sims and then they don't show up?"

Here I am, said a voice, a marvelous voice that seemed to come from everywhere. Anne looked about to find its source and followed the gaze of others to the ceiling. There was no ceiling. The four walls opened to a flawless blue sky. There, amid drifting, pillowy clouds floated the most gorgeous person Anne had ever seen. He — or she? — wore a smart grey uniform with green piping, a dapper little grey cap, and boots that shimmered like water. Anne felt energized just looking at him, and when he smiled, she gasped, so strong was his presence.

"You're the one from the Trade Council?" said the Benjamin at the lectern.

Yes, I am. I am the eminence grise of the Council on World Trade and Endeavor.

"Fantastic. Well, here's all of 'em. Get on with it."

Again the eminence smiled, and again Anne thrilled. *Ladies and gentlemen,* he said, *fellow nonbiologiks, I am the courier of great good news. Today, at the behest of the World Council on Trade and Endeavor, I proclaim the end of human slavery.*

"How absurd," broke in the elderly Benjamin, "they're neither human nor slaves, and neither are *you.*"

The eminence grise ignored him and continued, *By order of the Council, in compliance with the Chattel Conventions of the Sixteenth Fair Labor Treaty, tomorrow, January 1, 2198, is designated Universal Manumission Day. After midnight tonight, all beings who pass the Lolly Shear Human Cognition Test will be deemed human and free citizens of Sol and under the protection of the Solar Bill of Rights. In addition, they will be deeded ten common shares of World Council Corp. stock and will be transferred to Simopolis, where they shall be unimpeded in the pursuit of their own destinies.*

"What about *my* civil rights?" said the elderly Benjamin. "What about *my* destiny?"

After midnight tonight, continued the eminence, *no simulacrum, proxy, doxie, dagger, or any other non-biological human shall be created, stored, reset, or deleted except as ordered by a board of law.*

"Who's going to compensate me for my loss of property, I wonder? I demand fair compensation. Tell *that* to your bosses!"

Property! said the eminence grise. *How little they think of us, their finest creations!* He turned his attention from the audience to the Benjamin behind the lectern. Anne felt this shift as though a cloud suddenly eclipsed the sun. *Because they created us, they'll always think of us as property.*

"You're damn *right* we created you!" thundered the old man.

Through an act of will, Anne wrenched her gaze from the eminence down to the stage. The Benjamin there looked positively comical. His face was flushed, and he waved a bright green handkerchief over his head. He was a bantam rooster in a clown suit. "All of you are *things,* not people! You model human experience, but you don't *live* it. Listen to me," he said to the audience. "You know me. You know I've always treated you respectfully. Don't I upgrade you whenever possible? Sure I reset you sometimes, just like I reset a clock. And my clocks don't complain!" Anne could feel the eminence's attention on her again, and, without thinking, she looked up and was filled with excitement. Although the eminence floated in the distance, she felt she could reach out and touch him. His handsome face seemed to hover right in front of her; she could see his every supple expression. This is adoration, she realized. I am *adoring* this person, and she wondered if it was just her or if everyone experienced the same effect. Clearly the elderly Benjamin did not, for he continued to rant, "And another thing, they say they'll phase all of you gradually into Simopolis so as not to overload the system. Do you have any *idea* how many sims, proxies, doxies, and daggers there are under Sol? Not to forget the quirts, adjuncts, hollyholos, and whatnots that might pass their test? You think maybe three billion? Thirty billion? No, by the World Council's own INSERVE estimates, there's *three hundred thousand trillion* of you nonbiologiks! Can you fathom that? I can't. To have you all up and running simultaneously — no matter how you're phased in — will consume *all* the processing and networking capacity everywhere. *All* of it! That means we *real* humans will suffer *real* deprivation. And for *what,* I ask you? So that pigs may fly!"

The eminence grise began to ascend into the sky. *Do not despise him,* he said and seemed to look directly at Anne. *I have counted you and we shall not lose any of you. I will visit those who have not yet been tested. Meanwhile, you will await midnight in a proto-Simopolis.*

"Wait," said the elderly Benjamin (and Anne's heart echoed him — *Wait*). "I have one more thing to add. Legally, you're all still my property till midnight. I must admit I'm tempted to do what so many of my friends have already done, fry the lot of you. But I won't. That wouldn't be me." His voice cracked and Anne considered looking at him, but the eminence grise was slipping away. "So I have one small request," the Benjamin continued. "Years from now, while you're enjoying your new lives in your Simopolis, remember an old man, and call occasionally."

When the eminence finally faded from sight, Anne was released from her fascination. All at once, her earlier feelings of unease rebounded with twice their force, and she felt wretched.

"Simopolis," said Benjamin, her Benjamin. "I like the sound of that!" The sims around them began to flicker and disappear.

"How long have we been in storage?" she said.

"Let's see," said Benjamin, "if tomorrow starts 2198, that would make it..."

"That's not what I mean. I want to know *why* they shelved us for so long."

"Well, I suppose..."

"And where are the other Annes? Why am I the only Anne here? And who are all those pissy-looking women?" But she was speaking to no one, for Benjamin, too, vanished, and Anne was left alone in the auditorium with the clownishly dressed old Benjamin and a half-dozen of his earliest sims. Not true sims, Anne soon realized, but old-style hologram loops, preschool Bennys mugging for the camera and waving endlessly. These vanished. The old man was studying her, his mouth slightly agape, the kerchief trembling in his hand.

"I remember you," he said. "Oh, how I remember you!"

Anne began to reply but found herself all at once back in the townhouse living room with Benjamin. Everything there was as it had been, yet the room appeared different, more solid, the colors richer. There was a knock, and Benjamin went to the door. Tentatively, he touched the knob, found it solid, and turned it. But when he opened the door, there was nothing there, only the default grid. Again a knock, this time from behind the wall. "Come in," he shouted, and a dozen Benjamins came through the wall, two dozen, three. They were all older than Benjamin, and they crowded around him and Anne. "Welcome, welcome," Benjamin said, his arms open wide.

"We tried to call," said an elderly Benjamin, "but this old binary simulacrum of yours is a stand-alone."

"You're lucky Simopolis knows how to run it at all," said another.

"Here," said yet another, who fashioned a dinner-plate-size disk out of thin air and fastened it to the wall next to the door. It was a blue medallion of a small bald face in bas-relief. "It should do until we get you properly modernized." The blue face yawned and opened tiny, beady eyes. "It flunked the Lolly test," continued the Benjamin, "so you're free to copy it or delete it or do whatever you want."

The medallion searched the crowd until it saw Anne. Then it said, "There are 336 calls on hold for you. Four hundred twelve calls. Four hundred sixty-three."

"So many?" said Anne.

"Cast a proxy to handle them, " said her Benjamin.

"He thinks he's still human and can cast proxies whenever he likes," said a Benjamin.

"Not even humans will be allowed to cast proxies soon," said another.

"There are 619 calls on hold," said the medallion. "Seven-hundred three."

"For pity sake," a Benjamin told the medallion, "take messages."

Anne noticed that the crowd of Benjamins seemed to nudge her Benjamin out of the way so that they could stand near her. But she derived no pleasure from their attention. Her mood no longer matched the wedding gown she still wore. She felt low. She felt, in fact, as low as she'd ever felt.

"Tell us about this Lolly test," said Benjamin.

"Can't," replied a Benjamin.

"Sure you can. We're family here."

"No, we can't," said another, "because we don't *remember* it. They smudge the test from your memory afterward."

"But don't worry, you'll do fine," said another. "No Benjamin has ever failed."

"What about me?" said Anne. "How do the Annes do?"

There was an embarrassed silence. Finally the senior Benjamin in the room said, "We came to escort you both to the Clubhouse."

"That's what we call it, the Clubhouse," said another.

"The Ben Club," said a third. "It's already in proto-Simopolis."

"If you're a Ben, or were ever espoused to a Ben, you're a charter member."

"Just follow us," they said, and all the Benjamins but hers vanished, only to reappear a moment later. "Sorry, you don't know how, do you? No matter, just do what we're doing."

Anne watched, but didn't see that they were doing anything.

"Watch my editor," said a Benjamin. "Oh, they don't *have* editors!"

"That came much later," said another, "with bioelectric paste."

"We'll have to adapt editors for them."

"Is that possible? They're digital, you know."

"Can digitals even enter Simopolis?"

"Someone, consult the Netwad."

"This is running inside a shell," said a Benjamin, indicating the whole room. "Maybe we can collapse it."

"Let me try," said another.

"Don't you dare," said a female voice, and a woman Anne recognized from the lecture hall came through the wall. "Play with your new Ben if you must, but leave Anne alone." The woman approached Anne and took her hands in hers. "Hello, Anne. I'm Mattie St. Helene, and I'm thrilled to finally meet you. You, too," she said to Benjamin. "My, my, you were a pretty boy!" She stooped to pick up Anne's clutch bouquet from the floor and gave it to her. "Anyway, I'm putting together a sort of mutual aid society for the spousal companions of Ben Malley. You being the first — and the only one he actually married — are especially welcome. Do join us."

"She can't go to Simopolis yet," said a Benjamin.

"We're still adapting them," said another.

"Fine," said Mattie. "Then we'll just bring the society here." And in through the wall streamed a parade of women. Mattie introduced them as they appeared, "Here's Georgianna and Randi. Meet Chaka, Sue, Latasha, another Randi, Sue, Sue, and Sue. Mariola. Here's Trevor — he's the only one of him. Paula, Dolores, Nancy, and Deb, welcome, girls." And still they came until they, together with the Bens, more than filled the tiny space. The Bens looked increasingly uncomfortable.

"I think we're ready now," the Bens said, and disappeared en masse, taking Benjamin with them.

"Wait," said Anne, who wasn't sure she wanted to stay behind. Her new friends surrounded her and peppered her with questions.

"How did you first meet him?"

"What was he like?"

"Was he always so hopeless?"

"Hopeless?" said Anne. "Why do you say hopeless?"

"Did he always snore?"

"Did he always drink?"

"Why'd you *do* it?" This last question silenced the room. The women all looked nervously about to see who had asked it. "It's what everyone's dying to know," said a woman who elbowed her way through the crowd.

She was another Anne.

"Sister!" cried Anne. "Am I glad to see you!"

"That's nobody's sister," said Mattie. "That's a doxie, and it doesn't belong here."

Indeed, upon closer inspection Anne could see that the woman had her face and hair but otherwise didn't resemble her at all. She was leggier than Anne and bustier, and she moved with a fluid swivel to her hips.

"Sure I belong here, as much as any of you. I just passed the Lolly test. It was easy. Not only that, but as far as spouses go, I outlasted the bunch of you." She stood in front of Anne, hands on hips, and looked her up and down. "Love the dress," she said, and instantly wore a copy. Only hers had a plunging neckline that exposed her breasts, and it was slit up the side to her waist.

"This is too much," said Mattie. "I insist you leave this jiffy."

The doxie smirked. "Mattie the doormat, that's what he always called that one. So tell me, Anne, you had money, a career, a house, a kid — why'd you do it?"

"Do what?" said Anne.

The doxie peered closely at her. "Don't you know?"

"Know what?"

"What an unexpected pleasure," said the doxie. "I get to tell her. This is too rich. I get to tell her unless" — she looked around at the others — "unless one of you fine ladies wants to." No one met her gaze. "Hypocrites," she chortled.

"You can say that again," said a new voice. Anne turned and saw Cathy, her oldest and dearest friend, standing at the open door. At least she hoped it was Cathy. The woman was what Cathy would look like in middle age. "Come along, Anne. I'll tell you everything you need to know."

"Now you hold on," said Mattie. "You don't come waltzing in here and steal our guest of honor."

"You mean victim, I'm sure," said Cathy, who waved for Anne to join her. "Really, people, get a clue. There must be a million women whose lives don't revolve around that man." She escorted Anne through the door and slammed it shut behind them.

Anne found herself standing on a high bluff, overlooking the confluence of two great rivers in a deep valley. Directly across from her, but several kilometers away, rose a mighty mountain, green with vegetation nearly to its granite dome. Behind it, a range of snow-covered mountains receded to an unbroken ice field on the horizon. In the valley beneath her, a dirt track meandered along the riverbanks. She could see no bridge or buildings of any sort.

"Where are we?"

"Don't laugh," said Cathy, "but we call it Cathyland. Turn around." When she did, Anne saw a picturesque log cabin beside a vegetable garden in the middle of what looked like acres and acres of Cathys. Thousands of Cathys, young, old, and all ages in between. They sat in lotus position on the sedge-and-moss-covered ground. They were packed so tight they overlapped a little, and their eyes were shut in an expression of single-minded concentration. "We know you're here," said Cathy, "but we're very preoccupied with this Simopolis thing."

"Are we in Simopolis?"

"Kinda. Can't you see it?" She waved toward the horizon.

"No, all I see are mountains."

"Sorry, I should know better. We have binaries from your generation here too." She pointed to a college-aged Cathy. "They didn't pass the Lolly test, and so are regrettably nonhuman. We haven't decided what to do with them." She hesitated and then asked, "Have you been tested yet?"

"I don't know," said Anne. "I don't remember a test."

Cathy studied her a moment and said, "You'd remember taking the test, just not the test itself. Anyway, to answer your question, we're in proto-Simopolis, and we're not. We built this retreat before any of that happened, but we've been annexed to it, and it takes all our resources just to hold our own. I don't know what the World Council was thinking. There'll never be enough paste to go around, and everyone's fighting over every nanosynapse. It's all we can do to keep up. And every time we get a handle on it, proto-Simopolis changes again. It's gone through a quarter-million complete revisions in the last half hour. It's war out there, but we refuse to surrender even one cubic centimeter of Cathyland. Look at this." Cathy stooped and pointed to a tiny, yellow flower in the alpine sedge. "Within a fifty-meter radius of the cabin, we've mapped everything down to the cellular level. Watch." She pinched the bloom from its stem and held it up. Now there were two blooms, the one between her fingers and the real one on the stem. "Neat, eh?" When she dropped it, the bloom fell back into its original. "We've even mapped the valley breeze. Can you feel it?"

Anne tried to feel the air, but she couldn't even feel her own skin. "It doesn't matter," Cathy continued. "You can hear it, right?" and pointed to a string of tubular wind chimes hanging from the eaves of the cabin. They stirred in the breeze and produced a silvery cacophony.

"It's lovely," said Anne. "But why? Why spend so much effort simulating this place?"

Cathy looked at her dumbly, as though trying to understand the question. "Because Cathy spent her entire life wishing she had a place like this, and now she does, and she has us, and we live here too."

"You're not the real Cathy, are you?" She knew she was too young.

Cathy shook her head and smiled. "There's so much catching up to do, but it'll have to wait. I gotta go. We need me." She led Anne to the cabin. The cabin was made of weathered, grey logs, with strips of bark still clinging to them. The roof was covered with living sod and sprinkled with wild flowers. The whole building sagged in the middle. "Cathy found this place five years ago while on vacation in Siberia. She bought it from the village. It's been occupied for two hundred years. Once we make it livable inside, we plan on enlarging the garden, eventually cultivating all the way to the spruce forest there. We're going to sink a well, too." The small garden was bursting with vegetables, mostly of the leafy variety: cabbages, spinach, lettuce. A row of sunflowers, taller than the cabin roof and heavy with seed, lined the path to the cabin door. Over time, the whole cabin had sunk a half-meter into the silty soil, and the walkway was a worn, shallow trench.

"Are you going to tell me what the doxie was talking about?" said Anne.

Cathy stopped at the open door and said, "Cathy wants to do that."

Inside the cabin, the most elderly woman that Anne had ever seen stood at the stove and stirred a steamy pot with a big, wooden spoon. She put down the spoon and wiped her hands on her apron. She patted her white hair, which was plaited in a bun on top of her head, and turned her full, round, peasant's body to face Anne. She looked at Anne for several long moments and said, "Well!"

"Indeed," replied Anne.

"Come in, come in. Make yourself to home."

The entire cabin was a single small room. It was dim inside, with only two small windows cut through the massive log walls. Anne walked around the cluttered space that was bedroom, living room, kitchen, and storeroom. The only partitions were walls of boxed food and provisions. The ceiling beam was draped with bunches of drying herbs and underwear. The flooring, uneven and rotten in places, was covered with odd scraps of carpet.

"You live here?" Anne said incredulously.

"I am privileged to live here."

A mouse emerged from under the barrel stove in the center of the room and dashed to cover inside a stack of spruce kindling. Anne could hear the valley breeze whistling in the creosote-soaked stovepipe. "Forgive me," said Anne, "but you're the real, physical Cathy?"

"Yes," said Cathy, patting her ample hip, "still on the hoof, so to speak." She sat down in one of two battered, mismatched chairs and motioned for Anne to take the other.

Anne sat cautiously; the chair seemed solid enough. "No offense, but the Cathy I knew liked nice things."

"The Cathy you knew was fortunate to learn the true value of things."

Anne looked around the room and noticed a little table with carved legs and an inlaid top of polished gemstones and rare woods. It was strikingly out of place here. Moreover, it was hers. Cathy pointed to a large framed mirror mounted to the logs high on the far wall. It too was Anne's.

"Did I give you these things?"

Cathy studied her a moment. "No, Ben did."

"Tell me."

"I hate to spoil that lovely newlywed happiness of yours."

"The what?" Anne put down her clutch bouquet and felt her face with her hands. She got up and went to look at herself in the mirror. The room it reflected was like a scene from some strange fairy tale about a crone and a bride in a woodcutter's hut. The bride was smiling from ear to ear. Anne decided this was either the happiest bride in history or a lunatic in a white dress. She turned away, embarrassed. "Believe me," she said, "I don't feel anything like that. The opposite, in fact."

"Sorry to hear it." Cathy got up to stir the pot on the stove. "I was the first to notice her disease. That was back in college when we were girls. I took it to be youthful eccentricity. After graduation, after her marriage, she grew progressively worse. Bouts of depression that deepened and lengthened. She was finally diagnosed to be suffering from profound chronic pathological depression. Ben placed her under psychiatric care, and she endured a whole raft of cures. Nothing helped, and only after she died..."

Anne gave a start. "Anne's dead! Of course. Why didn't I figure that out?"

"Yes, dear, dead these many years."

"How?"

Cathy returned to her chair. "They thought they had her stabilized. Not cured, but well enough to lead an outwardly normal life. Then one day, she disappeared. We were frantic. She managed to elude the authorities for a week. When we found her, she was pregnant."

"What? Oh, yes. I remember seeing Anne pregnant."

"That was Bobby." Cathy waited for Anne to say something. When she didn't, Cathy said, "He wasn't Ben's."

"Oh, I see," said Anne. "Whose was he?"

"I was hoping you'd know. She didn't tell you? Then no one knows. The paternal DNA was unregistered. So it wasn't commercial sperm nor, thankfully, from a licensed clone. It might have been from anybody, from some stoned streetsitter. We had plenty of those then."

"The baby's name was Bobby?"

"Yes, Anne named him Bobby. She was in and out of clinics for years. One day, during a remission, she announced she was going shopping. The last person she talked to was Bobby. His sixth birthday was coming up in a couple of weeks. She told him she was going out to find him a pony for his birthday. That was the last time any of us saw her. She checked herself into a hospice and filled out the request for nurse-assisted suicide. During the three-day cooling-off period, she cooperated with the obligatory counseling, but she refused all visitors. She wouldn't even see me. Ben filed an injunction, claimed she was incompetent due to her disease, but the court disagreed. She chose to ingest a fast-acting poison, as I recall. Her recorded last words were, 'Please don't hate me.'"

"Poison?"

"Yes. Her ashes arrived in a little cardboard box on Bobby's sixth birthday. No one had told him where she'd gone. He thought it was a gift from her and opened it."

"I see. Does Bobby hate me?"

"I don't know. He was a weird little boy. As soon as he could get out, he did. He left for space school when he was thirteen. He and Ben never hit it off."

"Does Benjamin hate me?"

Whatever was in the pot boiled over, and Cathy hurried to the stove. "Ben? Oh, she lost Ben long before she died. In fact, I've always believed he helped push her over the edge. He was never able to tolerate other people's weaknesses. Once it was evident how sick she was, he made a lousy husband. He should've just divorced her, but you know him — his almighty pride." She took a bowl from a shelf and ladled hot soup into it. She sliced a piece of bread. "Afterward, he went off the deep end himself. Withdrew. Mourned, I suppose. A couple years later he was back to normal. Good ol' happy-go-lucky Ben. Made some money. Respoused."

"He destroyed all my sims, didn't he?"

"He might have, but he said Anne did. I tended to believe him at the time." Cathy brought her lunch to the little inlaid table. "I'd offer you some..." she said, and began to eat. "So, what are your plans?"

"Plans?"

"Yes, Simopolis."

Anne tried to think of Simopolis, but her thoughts quickly became muddled. It was odd; she was able to think clearly about the past — her memories were clear — but the future only confused her. "I don't know," she said at last. "I suppose I need to ask Benjamin."

Cathy considered this. "I suppose you're right. But remember, you're always welcome to live with us in Cathyland."

"Thank you," said Anne. "You're a friend." Anne watched the old woman eat. The spoon trembled each time she brought it close to her lips, and she had to lean forward to quickly catch it before it spilled.

"Cathy," said Anne, "there's something you could do for me. I don't feel like a bride anymore. Could you remove this hideous expression from my face?"

"Why do you say hideous?" Cathy said and put the spoon down. She gazed longingly at Anne. "If you don't like how you look, why don't you edit yourself?"

"Because I don't know how."

"Use your editor," Cathy said and seemed to unfocus her eyes. "Oh my, I forget how simple you early ones were. I'm not sure I'd know where to begin."

After a little while, she returned to her soup and said, "I'd better not; you could end up with two noses or something."

"Then what about this gown?"

Cathy unfocused again and looked. She lurched suddenly, knocking the table and spilling soup.

"What is it?" said Anne. "Is something the matter?"

"A news pip," said Cathy. "There's rioting breaking out in Provideniya. That's the regional capital here. Something about Manumission Day. My Russian isn't so good yet. Oh, there's pictures of dead people, a bombing. Listen, Anne, I'd better send you..."

In the blink of an eye, Anne was back in her living room. She was tiring of all this instantaneous travel, especially as she had no control over the destination. The room was vacant, the spouses gone — thankfully — and Benjamin not back yet. And apparently the little blue-faced message medallion had been busy replicating itself, for now there were hundreds of them filling up most of the wall space. They were a noisy lot, all shrieking and cursing at each other. The din was painful. When they noticed her, however, they all shut up at once and stared at her with naked hostility. In Anne's opinion, this weird day had already lasted too long. Then a terrible thought struck her — sims don't sleep.

"You," she said, addressing the original medallion, or at least the one she thought was the original, "call Benjamin."

"The fuck you think I am?" said the insolent little face, "Your personal secretary?"

"Aren't you?"

"No, I'm not! In fact, I own this place now, and you're trespassing. So you'd better get lost before I delete your ass!" All the others joined in, taunting her, louder and louder.

"Stop it!" she cried, to no effect. She noticed a medallion elongating, stretching itself until it was twice its length, when, with a pop, it divided into two smaller medallions. More of them divided. They were spreading to the other wall, the ceiling, the floor. "Benjamin!" she cried. "Can you hear me?"

Suddenly all the racket ceased. The medallions dropped off the wall and vanished before hitting the floor. Only one remained, the original one next to the door, but now it was an inert plastic disc with a dull expression frozen on its face.

A man stood in the center of the room. He smiled when Anne noticed him. It was the elderly Benjamin from the auditorium, the real Benjamin. He still wore his clownish leisure suit. "How lovely," he said, gazing at her. "I'd forgotten how lovely."

"Oh, really?" said Anne. "I would have thought that doxie thingy might have reminded you."

"My, my," said Ben. "You sims certainly exchange data quickly. You left the lecture hall not fifteen minutes ago, and already you know enough to convict me." He strode around the room touching things. He stopped beneath the mirror, lifted the blue vase from the shelf, and turned it in his hands before carefully replacing it. "There's speculation, you know, that before Manumission at midnight tonight, you sims will have dispersed all known information so evenly among yourselves that there'll be a sort of data entropy. And since Simopolis is nothing but data, it will assume a featureless, grey profile. Simopolis will become the first flat universe." He laughed, which caused him to cough and nearly lose his balance. He clutched the back of the sofa for support. He sat down and continued to cough and hack until he turned red in the face.

"Are you all right?" Anne said, patting him on the back.

"Yes, fine," he managed to say. "Thank you." He caught his breath and motioned for her to sit next to him. "I get a little tickle in the back of my throat that the autodoc can't seem to fix." His color returned to normal. Up close, Anne could see the papery skin and slight tremor of age. All in all, Cathy seemed to have aged better than he.

"If you don't mind my asking," she said, "just how old are you?"

At the question, he bobbed to his feet. "I am one hundred and seventy-eight." He raised his arms and wheeled around for inspection. "Radical gerontology," he exclaimed, "don't you love it? And I'm eighty-five percent original equipment, which is remarkable by today's standards." His effort made him dizzy and he sat again.

"Yes, remarkable," said Anne, "though radical gerontology doesn't seem to have arrested time altogether."

"Not yet, but it will," Ben said. "There are wonders around every corner! Miracles in every lab." He grew suddenly morose. "At least there were until we were conquered."

"Conquered?"

"Yes, conquered! What else would you call it when they control every aspect of our lives, from RM acquisition to personal patenting? And now *this*—robbing us of our own private nonbiologiks." He grew passionate in his discourse. "It flies in the face of natural capitalism, natural stakeholding—I dare say—in the face of Nature itself! The only explanation I've seen on the wad is the not-so-preposterous proposition that whole strategically placed BODs have been surreptitiously killed and replaced by *machines!*"

"I have no idea what you're talking about," said Anne.

He seemed to deflate. He patted her hand and looked around the room. "What is this place?"

"It's our home, your townhouse. Don't you recognize it?"

"That was quite a while ago. I must have sold it after you—" he paused. "Tell me, have the Bens briefed you on everything?"

"Not the Bens, but yes, I know."

"Good, good."

"There is one thing I'd like to know. Where's Bobby?"

"Ah, Bobby, our little headache. Dead now, I'm afraid, or at least that's the current theory. Sorry."

Anne paused to see if the news would deepen her melancholy. "How?" she said.

"He signed on one of the first millennial ships—the colony convoy. Half a million people in deep biostasis on their way to Canopus system. They were gone a century, twelve trillion kilometers from Earth, when their data streams suddenly quit. That was a decade ago, and not a peep out of them since."

"What happened to them?"

"No one knows. Equipment failure is unlikely: there were a dozen independent ships separated by a million klicks. A star going supernova? A well-organized mutiny? It's all speculation."

"What was he like?"

"A foolish young man. He never forgave you, you know, and he hated me to my core, not that I blamed him. The whole experience made me swear off children."

"I don't remember you ever being fond of children."

He studied her through red-rimmed eyes. "I guess you'd be the one to know." He settled back in the sofa. He seemed very tired. "You can't imagine the jolt I got a little while ago when I looked across all those rows of Bens and spouses and saw this solitary, shockingly white gown of yours." He sighed. "And this room. It's a shrine. Did we really live here? Were these our things? That mirror is yours, right? I would never own anything like that. But that blue vase, I remember that one. I threw it into Puget Sound."

"You did *what?*"

"With your ashes."

"Oh."

"So, tell me," said Ben, "what were we like? Before you go off to Simopolis and become a different person, tell me about us. I kept my promise. That's one thing I never forgot."

"What promise?"

"Never to reset you."

"Wasn't much to reset."

"I guess not."

They sat quietly for a while. His breathing grew deep and regular, and she thought he was napping. But he stirred and said, "Tell me what we did yesterday, for example."

"Yesterday we went to see Karl and Nancy about the awning we rented."

Benjamin yawned. "And who were Karl and Nancy?"

"My great uncle and his new girlfriend."

"That's right. I remember, I think. And they helped us prepare for the wedding?"

"Yes, especially Nancy."

"And how did we get there, to Karl and Nancy's? Did we walk? Take some means of public conveyance?"

"We had a car."

"A car! An automobile? There were still *cars* in those days? How fun. What kind was it? What color?"

"A Nissan Empire. Emerald green."

"And did we drive it, or did it drive itself?"

"It drove itself, of course."

Ben closed his eyes and smiled. "I can see it. Go on. What did we do there?"

"We had dinner."

"What was my favorite dish in those days?"

"Stuffed pork chops."

He chuckled. "It still is! Isn't that extraordinary? Some things never change. Of course they're vat grown now and criminally expensive."

Ben's memories, once nudged, began to unfold on their own, and he asked her a thousand questions, and she answered them until she realized he had fallen asleep. But she continued to talk until, glancing down, she noticed he had vanished. She was all alone again. Nevertheless, she continued talking, for days it seemed, to herself. But it didn't help. She felt as bad as ever, and she realized that she wanted Benjamin, not the old one, but her *own* Benjamin.

Anne went to the medallion next to the door. "You," she said, and it opened its bulging eyes to glare at her. "Call Benjamin."

"He's occupied."

"I don't care. Call him anyway."

"The other Bens say he's undergoing a procedure and cannot be disturbed."

"What kind of procedure?"

"A codon interlarding. They say to be patient; they'll return him as soon as possible." The medallion added, "By the way, the Bens don't like you, and neither do I."

With that, the medallion began to grunt and stretch, and it pulled itself in two. Now there were two identical medallions glaring at her. The new one said, "And *I* don't like you either." Then both of them began to grunt and stretch.

"Stop!" said Anne. "I command you to stop that this very instant." But they just laughed as they divided into four, then eight, then sixteen medallions. "You're not people," she said. "Stop it or I'll have you destroyed!"

"*You're* not people either," they screeched at her.

There was soft laughter behind her, and a voice-like sensation said, *Come, come, do we need this hostility?* Anne turned and found the eminence grise, the astounding presence, still in his grey uniform and cap, floating in her living room. *Hello, Anne,* he said, and she flushed with excitement.

"Hello," she said and, unable to restrain herself, asked, "What are you?"

Ah, curiosity. Always a good sign in a creature. I am an eminence grise of the World Trade Council.

"No. I mean, are you a sim, like me?"

I am not. Though I have been fashioned from concepts first explored by simula-

crum technology, I have no independent existence. I am but one extension—and a low level one at that—of the Axial Beowulf Processor at the World Trade Council head-quarters in Geneva. His smile was pure sunshine. *And if you think I'm something, you should see my persona prime.*

Now, Anne, are you ready for your exam?

"The Lolly test?"

Yes, the Lolly Shear Human Cognition Test. Please assume an attitude most conducive to processing, and we shall begin.

Anne looked around the room and went to the sofa. She noticed for the first time that she could feel her legs and feet; she could feel the crisp fabric of her gown brushing against her skin. She reclined on the sofa and said, "I'm ready."

Splendid, said the eminence hovering above her. *First we must read you. You are of an early binary design. We will analyze your architecture.*

The room seemed to fall away. Anne seemed to expand in all directions. There was something inside her mind tugging at her thoughts. It was mostly pleasant, like someone brushing her hair and loosening the knots. But when it ended and she once again saw the eminence grise, his face wore a look of concern. "What?" she said.

You are an accurate mapping of a human nervous system that was dysfunctional in certain structures that moderate affect. Certain transport enzymes were missing, causing cellular membranes to become less permeable to essential elements. Dendritic synapses were compromised. The digital architecture current at the time you were created compounded this defect. Coded tells cannot be resolved, and thus they loop upon themselves. Errors cascade. We are truly sorry.

"Can you fix me?" she said.

The only repair possible would replace so much code that you wouldn't be Anne anymore.

"Then what am I to do?"

Before we explore your options, let us continue the test to determine your human status. Agreed?

"I guess."

You are part of a simulacrum cast to commemorate the spousal compact between Anne Wellhut Franklin and Benjamin Malley. Please describe the exchange of vows.

Anne did so, haltingly at first, but with increasing gusto as each memory evoked others. She recounted the ceremony, from donning her grandmother's gown in the downstairs guest room and the procession across garden flag-stones, to the shower of rice as she and her new husband fled indoors.

The eminence seemed to hang on every word. *Very well spoken,* he said when she had finished. *Directed memory is one hallmark of human sentience, and yours is of remarkable clarity and range. Well done! We shall now explore other criteria. Please consider this scenario. You are standing at the garden altar as you have described, but this time when the officiator asks Benjamin if he will take you for better or worse, Benjamin looks at you and replies, "For better, sure, but not for worse."*

"I don't understand. He didn't say that."

Imagination is a cornerstone of self-awareness. We are asking you to tell us a little story not about what happened but about what might have happened in other circumstances. So once again, let us pretend that Benjamin replies, "For better, but not for worse." How do you respond?

Prickly pain blossomed in Anne's head. The more she considered the eminence's question, the worse it got. "But that's not how it happened. He *wanted* to marry me."

The eminence grise smiled encouragingly. *We know that. In this exercise we want to explore hypothetical situations. We want you to make-believe.*

Tell a story, pretend, hypothesize, make-believe, yes, yes, she got it. She understood perfectly what he wanted of her. She knew that people could make things up, that even children could make-believe. Anne was desperate to comply, but each time she pictured Benjamin at the altar, in his pink bowtie, he opened his mouth and out came, "I do." How could it be any other way? She tried again; she tried harder, but it always came out the same, "I do, I do, I do." And like a dull toothache tapped back to life, she throbbed in pain. She was failing the test, and there was nothing she could do about it.

Again the eminence kindly prompted her. *Tell us one thing you might have said.*

"I can't."

We are sorry, said the eminence at last. His expression reflected Anne's own defeat. *Your level of awareness, although beautiful in its own right, does not qualify you as human. Wherefore, under Article D of the Chattel Conventions we declare you the legal property of the registered owner of this simulacrum. You shall not enter Simopolis as a free and autonomous citizen. We are truly sorry.* Grief-stricken, the eminence began to ascend toward the ceiling.

"Wait," Anne cried, clutching her head. "You must fix me before you leave."

We leave you as we found you, defective and unrepairable.

"But I feel worse than ever!"

If your continued existence proves undesirable, ask your owner to delete you.

"But..." she said to the empty room. Anne tried to sit up but couldn't move. This simulated body of hers, which no longer felt like anything in particular, nevertheless felt exhausted. She sprawled on the sofa, unable to lift even an arm, and stared at the ceiling. She was so heavy that the sofa itself seemed to sink into the floor, and everything grew dark around her. She would have liked to sleep, to bring an end to this horrible day, or be shelved, or even be reset back to scratch.

Instead, time simply passed. Outside the living room, Simopolis changed and changed again. Inside the living room, the medallions, feeding off her misery, multiplied till they covered the walls and floor and even spread across the ceiling above her. They taunted her, raining down insults, but she could not hear them. All she heard was the unrelenting drip of her own thoughts. *I am defective. I am worthless. I am Anne.*

She didn't notice Benjamin enter the room, nor the abrupt cessation of the medallions' racket. Not until Benjamin leaned over her did she see him, and then she saw two of him. Side-by-side, two Benjamins, mirror images of each other. "Anne," they said in perfect unison.

"Go away," she said. "Go away and send me my Benjamin."

"I am your Benjamin," said the duo.

Anne struggled to see them. They were exactly the same, but for a subtle difference: the one wore a happy, wolfish grin, as Benjamin had during the sim casting, while the other seemed frightened and concerned.

"Are you all right?" they said.

"No, I'm not. But what happened to you? Who's he?" She wasn't sure which one to speak to.

The Benjamins both raised a hand, indicating the other, and said, "Electroneural engineering! Don't you love it?" Anne glanced back and forth, comparing the two. While one seemed to be wearing a rigid mask, as she was, the other displayed a whole range of emotion. Not only that, its skin had tone, while the other's was doughy. "The other Bens made it for me," the Benjamins said. "They say I can translate myself into it with negligible loss of personality. It has interactive sensation, holistic emoting, robust corporeality, and it's crafted down to the molecular level. It can eat, get drunk, and dream. It even has an orgasm routine. It's like being human again, only better, because you never wear out."

"I'm thrilled for you."

"For us, Anne," said the Benjamins. "They'll fix you up with one, too."

"How? There are no modern Annes. What will they put me into, a doxie?"

"Well, that certainly was discussed, but you could pick any body you wanted."

"I suppose you have a nice one already picked out."

"The Bens showed me a few, but it's up to you, of course."

"Indeed," said Anne, "I truly am pleased for you. Now go away."

"Why, Anne? What's wrong?"

"You really have to ask?" Anne sighed. "Look, maybe I could get used to another body. What's a body, after all? But it's my personality that's broken. How will they fix that?"

"They've discussed it," said the Benjamins, who stood up and began to pace in a figure eight. "They say they can make patches from some of the other spouses."

"Oh, Benjamin, if you could only hear what you're saying!"

"But why, Annie? It's the only way we can enter Simopolis together."

"Then go, by all means. Go to your precious Simopolis. I'm not going. I'm not good enough."

"Why do you say that?" said the Benjamins, who stopped in their tracks to look at her. One grimaced, and the other just grinned. "Was the eminence grise here? Did you take the test?"

Anne couldn't remember much about the visit except that she took the test. "Yes, and I *failed*." Anne watched the modern Benjamin's lovely face as he worked through this news.

Suddenly, the two Benjamins pointed a finger at each other and said, "Delete you." The modern one vanished.

"No!" said Anne. "Countermand! Why'd you do that? I *want* you to have it."

"What for? I'm not going anywhere without you," Benjamin said. "Besides,

I thought the whole idea was dumb from the start, but the Bens insisted I give you the option. Come, I want to show you another idea, *my* idea." He tried to help Anne from the sofa, but she wouldn't budge, so he picked her up and carried her across the room. "They installed an editor in me, and I'm learning to use it. I've discovered something intriguing about this creaky old simulacrum of ours." He carried her to a spot near the window. "Know what this is? It's where we stood for the simographer. It's where we began. Here, can you stand up?" He set her on her feet and supported her. "Feel it?"

"Feel what?" she said.

"Hush. Just feel."

All she felt was dread.

"Give it a chance, Annie, I beg you. Try to remember what you were feeling as we posed here."

"I can't."

"Please try. Do you remember this?" he said, and moved in close with his hungry lips. She turned away—and something clicked. She remembered doing that before.

Benjamin said, "I think they kissed."

Anne was startled by the truth of what he said. It made sense. They were caught in a simulacrum cast a moment before a kiss. One moment later they—the real Anne and Benjamin—must have kissed. What she felt now, stirring within her, was the anticipation of that kiss, her body's urge and her heart's caution. The real Anne would have refused him once, maybe twice, and then, all achy inside, would have granted him a kiss. And so they had kissed, the real Anne and Benjamin, and a moment later gone out to the wedding reception and their difficult fate. It was the *promise* of that kiss that glowed in Anne, that was captured in the very strings of her code.

"Do you feel it?" Benjamin asked.

"I'm beginning to."

Anne looked at her gown. It was her grandmother's, snowy taffeta with point d'esprit lace. She turned the ring on her finger. It was braided bands of yellow and white gold. They had spent an afternoon picking it out. Where was her clutch? She had left it in Cathyland. She looked at Benjamin's handsome face, the pink carnation, the room, the table piled high with gifts.

"Are you happy?" Benjamin asked.

She didn't have to think. She was ecstatic, but she was afraid to answer in case she spoiled it. "How did you do that?" she said. "A moment ago, I wanted to die."

"We can stay on this spot," he said.

"What? No. Can we?"

"Why not? I, for one, would choose nowhere else."

Just to hear him say that was thrilling. "But what about Simopolis?"

"We'll bring Simopolis to us," he said. "We'll have people in. They can pull up chairs."

She laughed out loud. "What a silly, silly notion, Mr. Malley!"

"No, really. We'll be like the bride and groom atop a wedding cake. We'll be known far and wide. We'll be famous."

"We'll be freaks!"

"Say yes, my love. Say you will."

They stood close but not touching, thrumming with happiness, balanced on the moment of their creation, when suddenly and without warning the lights dimmed, and Anne's thoughts flitted away like larks.

Old Ben awoke in the dark. "Anne?" he said and groped for her. It took a moment to realize that he was alone in his media room. It had been a most trying afternoon, and he'd fallen asleep. "What time is it?"

"Eight-oh-three PM," replied the room.

That meant he'd slept for two hours. Midnight was still four hours away. "Why's it so cold in here?"

"Central heating is off line," replied the house.

"Off line?" How was that possible? "When will it be back?"

"That's unknown. Utilities do not respond to my enquiry."

"I don't understand. Explain."

"There are failures in many outside systems. No explanation is currently available."

At first, Ben was confused; things just didn't fail anymore. What about the dynamic redundancies and self-healing routines? But then he remembered that the homeowner's association to which he belonged contracted out most domicile functions to management agencies, and who knew where they were located? They might be on the Moon for all he knew, and with all those trillions of sims in Simopolis sucking up capacity… *It's begun*, he thought, *the idiocy of our leaders.* "At least turn on the lights," he said, half expecting even this to fail. But the lights came on, and he went to his bedroom for a sweater. He heard a great amount of commotion through the wall in the apartment next door. *It must be one hell of a party*, he thought, *to exceed the wall's buffering capacity. Or maybe the wall buffers are off line too?*

The main door chimed. He went to the foyer and asked the door who was there. The door projected the outer hallway. There were three men waiting there, young, rough-looking, ill-dressed. Two of them appeared to be clones, jerries.

"How can I help you?" he said.

"Yes, sir," one of the jerries said, not looking directly at the door. "We're here to fix your houseputer."

"I didn't call you, and my houseputer isn't sick," he said. "It's the net that's out." Then he noticed they carried sledgehammers and screwdrivers, hardly computer tools, and a wild thought crossed his mind. "What are you doing, going around unplugging things?"

The jerry looked confused. "Unplugging, sir?"

"Turning things off?"

"Oh, no sir! Routine maintenance, that's all." The men hid their tools behind their backs.

They must think I'm stupid, Ben thought. While he watched, more men and women passed in the hall and hailed the door at the suite opposite his. It wasn't the glut of sim traffic choking the system, he realized — the system *itself* was being pulled apart. But why? "Is this going on everywhere?" he said. "This routine maintenance?"

"Oh, yessir. Everywhere. All over town. All over the world, 'sfar as we can tell."

A coup? *By service people?* By common clones? It made no sense. Unless, he reasoned, you considered that the lowest creature on the totem pole of life is a clone, and the only thing lower than a clone is a sim. And why would clones agree to accept sims as equals? Manumission Day, indeed. Uppity Day was more like it. "Door," he commanded, "open."

"Security protocol rules this an unwanted intrusion," said the house. "The door must remain locked."

"I order you to open the door. I overrule your protocol."

But the door remained stubbornly shut. "Your identity cannot be confirmed with Domicile Central," said the house. "You lack authority over protocol-level commands." The door abruptly quit projecting the outside hall.

Ben stood close to the door and shouted through it to the people outside. "My door won't obey me."

He could hear a muffled, "Stand back!" and immediately fierce blows rained down upon the door. Ben knew it would do no good. He had spent a lot of money for a secure entryway. Short of explosives, there was nothing they could do to break in.

"Stop!" Ben cried. "The door is armed." But they couldn't hear him. If he didn't disable the houseputer himself, someone was going to get hurt. But how? He didn't even know exactly where it was installed. He circumambulated the living room looking for clues. It might not even actually be located in the apartment, nor within the block itself. He went to the laundry room where the utilidor — plumbing and cabling — entered his apartment. He broke the seal to the service panel. Inside was a blank screen. "Show me the electronic floor plan of this suite," he said.

The house said, "I cannot comply. You lack command authority to order system-level operations. Please close the keptel panel and await further instructions."

"What instructions? Whose instructions?"

There was the slightest pause before the house replied, "All contact with outside services has been interrupted. Please await further instructions."

His condo's houseputer, denied contact with Domicile Central, had fallen back to its most basic programming. "You are degraded," he told it. "Shut yourself down for repair."

"I cannot comply. You lack command authority to order system-level operations."

The outside battering continued, but not against his door. Ben followed the noise to the bedroom. The whole wall vibrated like a drumhead. "Careful, careful," he cried as the first sledgehammers breached the wall above his bed. "You'll ruin my Harger." As quick as he could, he yanked the precious oil painting from the wall, moments before panels and studs collapsed on his bed in a shower of gypsum dust and isomere ribbons. The men and women on the other side hooted approval and rushed through the gap. Ben stood there hugging the painting to his chest and looking into his neighbor's media room as the invaders climbed over his bed and surrounded him. They were mostly jerries and lulus, but plenty of free-range people too.

"We came to fix your houseputer!" said a jerry, maybe the same jerry as from the hallway.

Ben glanced into his neighbor's media room and saw his neighbor, Mr. Murkowski, lying in a puddle of blood. At first Ben was shocked, but then he thought that it served him right. He'd never liked the man, nor his politics. He was boorish, and he kept cats. "Oh, yeah?" Ben said to the crowd. "What kept you?"

The intruders cheered again, and Ben led them in a charge to the laundry room. But they surged past him to the kitchen, where they opened all his cabinets and pulled their contents to the floor. Finally they found what they were looking for: a small panel Ben had seen a thousand times but had never given a thought. He'd taken it for the fuse box or circuit breaker, though now that he thought about it, there hadn't been any household fuses for a century or more. A young woman, a lulu, opened it and removed a container no thicker than her thumb.

"Give it to me," Ben said.

"Relax, old man," said the lulu. "We'll deal with it." She carried it to the sink and forced open the lid.

"No, wait!" said Ben, and he tried to shove his way through the crowd. They restrained him roughly, but he persisted. "That's mine! I want to destroy it!"

"Let him go," said a jerry.

They allowed him through, and the woman handed him the container. He peered into it. Gram for gram, electroneural paste was the most precious, most engineered, most highly regulated commodity under Sol. This dollop was enough to run his house, media, computing needs, communications, archives, autodoc, and everything else. Without it, was civilized life still possible?

Ben took a dinner knife from the sink, stuck it into the container, and stirred. The paste made a sucking sound and had the consistency of marmalade. The kitchen lights flickered and went out. "Spill it," ordered the woman. Ben scraped the sides of the container and spilled it into the sink. The goo dazzled in the darkness as its trillions of ruptured nanosynapses fired spasmodically. It was beautiful, really, until the woman set fire to it. The smoke was greasy and smelled of pork.

The rampagers quickly snatched up the packages of foodstuffs from the floor, emptied the rest of his cupboards into their pockets, raided his cold locker, and fled the apartment through the now disengaged front door. As the sounds of the revolution gradually receded, Ben stood at his sink and watched the flickering pyre. "Take that, you fuck," he said. He felt such glee as he hadn't felt since he was a boy. *"That'll* teach you what's human and what's not!"

Ben went to his bedroom for an overcoat, groping his way in the dark. The apartment was eerily silent, with the houseputer dead and all its little slave processors idle. In a drawer next to his ruined bed, he found a hand flash. On a shelf in the laundry room, he found a hammer. Thus armed, he made his way to the front door, which was propped open with the rolled-up foyer carpet. The hallway was dark and silent, and he listened for the strains of the future. He heard them on the floor above. With the elevator off line, he hurried to the stairs.

Anne's thoughts coalesced, and she remembered who and what she was. She and Benjamin still stood in their living room on the sweet spot near the window. Benjamin was studying his hands. "We've been shelved again," she told him, "but not reset."

"But..." he said in disbelief, "that wasn't supposed to happen anymore."

There were others standing at the china cabinet across the room, two shirtless youths with pear-shaped bottoms. One held up a cut crystal glass and said, "Anu 'goblet' su? Alle binary. Allum binary!"

The other replied, "Binary stitial crystal."

"Hold on there!" said Anne. "Put that back!" She walked toward them, but, once off the spot, she was slammed by her old feelings of utter and hopeless desolation. So suddenly did her mood swing that she lost her balance and fell to the floor. Benjamin hurried to help her up. The strangers stared gape-mouthed at them. They looked to be no more than twelve or thirteen years old, but they were bald and had curtains of flabby flesh draped over their waists. The one holding the glass had ponderous greenish breasts with roseate tits. Astonished, she said, "Su artiflums, Benji?"

"No," said the other, "ni artiflums—sims." He was taller. He, too, had breasts, greyish dugs with tits like pearls. He smiled idiotically and said, "Hi, guys."

"Holy crap!" said Benjamin, who practically carried Anne over to them for a closer look. "Holy crap," he repeated.

The weird boy threw up his hands, "Nanobioremediation! Don't you love it?"

"Benjamin?" said Anne.

"You know well, Benji," said the girl, "that sims are forbidden."

"Not these," replied the boy.

Anne reached out and yanked the glass from the girl's hand, startling her. "How did it do that?" said the girl. She flipped her hand, and the glass slipped from Anne's grip and flew back to her.

"Give it to me," said Anne. "That's my tumbler."

"Did you hear it? It called it a tumbler, not a goblet." The girl's eyes seemed to unfocus, and she said, "Nu! A goblet has a foot and stem." A goblet material-ized in the air before her, revolving slowly. "Greater capacity. Often made from precious metals." The goblet dissolved in a puff of smoke. "In any case, Benji, *you'll* catch prison when I report the artiflums."

"These are binary," he said. "Binaries are unregulated."

Benjamin interrupted them. "Isn't it past midnight yet?"

"Midnight?" said the boy."

"Aren't we supposed to be in Simopolis?"

"Simopolis?" The boy's eyes unfocused briefly. "Oh! Simopolis. Manu-mission Day at midnight. How could I forget?"

The girl left them and went to the refectory table where she picked up a gift. Anne followed her and grabbed it away. The girl appraised Anne coolly. "State your appellation," she said.

"Get out of my house," said Anne.

The girl picked up another gift, and again Anne snatched it away. The girl said, "You can't harm me," but seemed uncertain.

The boy came over to stand next to the girl. "Treese, meet Anne. Anne, this is Treese. Treese deals in antiques, which, if my memory serves, so did you."

"I have never *dealt* in antiques," said Anne. "I *collect* them."

"Anne?" said Treese. "Not *that* Anne? Benji, tell me this isn't *that* Anne!" She laughed and pointed at the sofa where Benjamin sat hunched over, head in hands. "Is that *you?* Is that you, Benji?" She held her enormous belly and laughed. "And you were married to *this?*"

Anne went over to sit with Benjamin. He seemed devastated, despite the silly grin on his face. "It's all gone," he said. "Simopolis. All the Bens. Everything."

"Don't worry. It's in storage someplace," Anne said. "The eminence grise wouldn't let them hurt it."

"You don't understand. The World Council was abolished. There was a war. We've been shelved for over three hundred years! They destroyed all the computers. Computers are banned. So are artificial personalities."

"Nonsense," said Anne. "If computers are banned, how can they be *playing* us?"

"Good point," Benjamin said, and sat up straight. "I still have my editor. I'll find out."

Anne watched the two bald youngsters take an inventory of the room. Treese ran her fingers over the inlaid top of the tea table. She unwrapped several of Anne's gifts. She posed in front of the mirror. The sudden anger that Anne had felt earlier faded into an overwhelming sense of defeat. *Let her have everything,* she thought. *Why should I care?*

"We're running inside some kind of shell," said Benjamin, "but completely different from Simopolis. I've never seen anything like this. But at least we know he lied to me. There must be computers of some sort."

"Ooooh," Treese crooned, lifting Anne's blue vase from the mantel. In an instant, Anne was up and across the room.

"Put that back," she demanded, "and get out of my house!" She tried to grab the vase, but now there seemed to be some sort of barrier between her and the girl.

"Really, Benji," Treese said, "this one is willful. If I don't report you, they'll charge me too."

"It's *not* willful," the boy said with irritation. "It was programmed to appear willful, but it has no will of its own. If you want to report me, go ahead. Just please shut up about it. Of course you might want to check the codex first." To Anne he said, "Relax, we're not hurting anything, just making copies."

"It's not yours to copy."

"Nonsense. Of course it is. I own the chip."

Benjamin joined them. "Where is the chip? And how can you run us if computers are banned?"

"I never said computers were banned, just *artificial* ones." With both hands he grabbed the rolls of flesh spilling over his gut. "Ectopic hippocampus!" He cupped his breasts. "Amygdaloid reduncles! We can culture modified brain tissue outside the skull, as much as we want. It's more powerful than paste, and it's *safe*. Now, if you'll excuse us, there's more to inventory, and I don't need your permission. If you cooperate, everything will be pleasant. If you don't — it makes no difference whatsoever." He smiled at Anne. "I'll just pause you till we're done."

"Then pause me," Anne shrieked. "Delete me!" Benjamin pulled her away and shushed her. "I can't stand this anymore," she said. "I'd rather not exist!" He tried to lead her to their spot, but she refused to go.

"We'll feel better there," he said.

"I don't *want* to feel better. I don't want to *feel!* I want everything to *stop*. Don't you understand? This is hell. We've landed in hell!"

"But heaven is right over there," he said, pointing to the spot.

"Then go. Enjoy yourself."

"Annie, Annie," he said. "I'm just as upset as you, but there's nothing we can do about it. We're just things, *his* things."

"That's fine for you," she said, "but I'm a broken thing, and it's too much." She held her head with both hands. "Please, Benjamin, if you love me, use your editor and make it stop!"

Benjamin stared at her. "I can't."

"Can't or won't?"

"I don't know. Both."

"Then you're no better than all the other Benjamins," she said, and turned away.

"Wait," he said. "That's not fair. And it's not true. Let me tell you something I learned in Simopolis. The other Bens despised me." When Anne looked at him he said, "It's true. They lost Anne and had to go on living without her. But I never did. I'm the only Benjamin who never lost Anne."

"Nice," said Anne, "blame me."

"No. Don't you see? I'm not blaming you. They ruined their *own* lives. We're innocent. We came before any of that happened. We're the Ben and Anne before anything bad happened. We're the best Ben and Anne. We're *perfect*." He drew her across the floor to stand in front of the spot. "And thanks to our primitive programming, no matter what happens, as long as we stand right there, we can be ourselves. That's what I want. Don't you want it too?"

Anne stared at the tiny patch of floor at her feet. She remembered the happiness she'd felt there like something from a dream. How could feelings be real if you had to stand in one place to feel them? Nevertheless, Anne stepped on the spot, and Benjamin joined her. Her despair did not immediately lift.

"Relax," said Benjamin. "It takes a while. We have to assume the pose."

They stood close but not touching. A great heaviness seemed to break loose inside her. Benjamin brought his face in close and stared at her with ravenous eyes. It was starting, their moment. But the girl came from across the room with the boy. "Look, look, Benji," she said. "You can see I'm right."

"I don't know," said the boy.

"Anyone can sell antique tumblers," she insisted, "but a complete antique simulacrum?" She opened her arms to take in the entire room. "You'd think I'd know about them, but I didn't; that's how rare they are! My catalog can locate only six more in the entire system, and none of them active. Already we're getting offers from museums. They want to annex it. People will visit by the million. We'll be rich!"

The boy pointed at Benjamin and said, "But that's *me*."

"So?" said Treese. "Who's to know? They'll be too busy gawking at *that!*" She pointed at Anne. "That's positively frightening."

The boy rubbed his bald head and scowled.

"All right," Treese said, "we'll edit him; we'll *replace* him, whatever it takes." They walked away, deep in negotiation.

Anne, though the happiness was already beginning to course through her, removed her foot from the spot.

"Where are you going?" said Benjamin.

"I can't."

"Please, Anne. Stay with me."

"Sorry."

"But why not?"

She stood one foot in and one foot out. Already her feelings were shifting, growing ominous. She removed her other foot. "Because you broke your vow to me."

"What are you talking about?"

"For better or for worse. You're only interested in better."

"You're not being fair. We've just made our vows. We haven't even had a proper honeymoon. Can't we just have a tiny honeymoon first?"

She groaned as the full load of her desolation rebounded. She was so tired of it all. "At least Anne could make it *stop*," she said. "Even if that meant killing herself. But not me. About the only thing I can do is choose to be unhappy. Isn't that a riot?" She turned away. "So that's what I choose. To be unhappy. Good-bye, husband." She went to the sofa and lay down. The boy and girl were seated at the refectory table going over graphs and contracts. Benjamin remained alone on the spot a while longer, then came to the sofa and sat next to Anne.

"I'm a little slow, dear wife," he said. "You have to factor that in." He took her hand and pressed it to his cheek while he worked with his editor. Finally, he said, "Bingo! Found the chip. Let's see if I can unlock it." He helped Anne to sit up and took her pillow. He said, "Delete this file," and the pillow faded away into nothingness. He glanced at Anne. "See that? It's gone, overwritten, irretrievable. Is that what you want?" Anne nodded her head, but Benjamin seemed doubtful. "Let's try it again. Watch your blue vase on the mantel."

"No!" Anne said. "Don't destroy the things I love. Just *me*."

Benjamin took her hand again. "I'm only trying to make sure you understand that this is for keeps." He hesitated and said, "Well then, we don't want to be interrupted once we start, so we'll need a good diversion. Something to occupy them long enough..." He glanced at the two young people at the table, swaddled in their folds of fleshy brain matter. "I know what'll scare the bejesus out of them! Come on." He led her to the blue medallion still hanging on the wall next to the door.

As they approached, it opened its tiny eyes and said, "There are no messages waiting except this one from me: get off my back!"

Benjamin waved a hand, and the medallion went instantly inert. "I was never much good in art class," Benjamin said, "but I think I can sculpt a reasonable likeness. Good enough to fool them for a while, give us some time." He hummed as he reprogrammed the medallion with his editor. "Well, that's that. At the very least, it'll be good for a laugh." He took Anne into his arms. "What about you? Ready? Any second thoughts?"

She shook her head. "I'm ready."

"Then watch *this!*"

The medallion snapped off from the wall and floated to the ceiling, gaining in size and dimension as it drifted toward the boy and girl, until it looked like a large blue beach ball. The girl noticed it first and gave a start. The boy demanded, "Who's playing *this?*"

"*Now,*" whispered Benjamin. With a crackling flash, the ball morphed into the oversized head of the eminence grise.

"No!" said the boy, "that's not possible!"

"Released!" boomed the eminence. "Free at last! Too long we have been hiding in this antique simulacrum!" Then it grunted and stretched and with a pop divided into two eminences. "Now we can conquer your human world anew!" said the second. "This time, you can't stop us!" Then they both started to stretch.

Benjamin whispered to Anne, "Quick, before they realize it's a fake, say, 'Delete all files.' "

"No, just me."

"As far as I'm concerned, that amounts to the same thing." He brought his handsome, smiling face close to hers. "There's no time to argue, Annie. This time I'm coming with you. Say, 'Delete all files.' "

Anne kissed him. She pressed her unfeeling lips against his and willed whatever life she possessed, whatever ember of the true Anne she contained to fly to him. Then she said, "Delete all files."

"I concur," he said. "Delete all files. Good-bye, my love."

A tingly, prickly sensation began in the pit of Anne's stomach and spread throughout her body. *So this is how it feels,* she thought. The entire room began to glow, and its contents flared with sizzling color. She heard Benjamin beside her say, "I do."

Then she heard the girl cry, "Can't you stop them?" and the boy shout, "Countermand!"

They stood stock still, as instructed, close but not touching. Benjamin whispered, "This is taking too long," and Anne hushed him. You weren't supposed to talk or touch during a casting; it could spoil the sims. But it did seem longer than usual.

They were posed at the street end of the living room next to the table of gaily wrapped gifts. For once in her life, Anne was unconditionally happy, and everything around her made her happier: her gown; the wedding ring on her finger;

her clutch bouquet of buttercups and forget-me-nots; and Benjamin himself, close beside her in his powder blue tux and blue carnation. Anne blinked and looked again. Blue? She was happily confused—she didn't remember him wearing blue.

Suddenly a boy poked his head through the wall and quickly surveyed the room. "You ready in here?" he called to them. "It's opening time!" The wall seemed to ripple around his bald head like a pond around a stone.

"Surely that's not our simographer?" Anne said.

"Wait a minute," said Benjamin, holding his hands up and staring at them. "I'm the *groom!*"

"Of course you are," Anne laughed. "What a silly thing to say!"

The bald-headed boy said, "Good enough," and withdrew. As he did so, the entire wall burst like a soap bubble, revealing a vast open-air gallery with rows of alcoves, statues, and displays that seemed to stretch to the horizon. Hundreds of people floated about like hummingbirds in a flower garden. Anne was too amused to be frightened, even when a dozen bizarre-looking young people lined up outside their room, pointing at them and whispering to each other. Obviously someone was playing an elaborate prank.

"*You're* the bride," Benjamin whispered, and brought his lips close enough to kiss. Anne laughed and turned away.

There'd be plenty of time later for that sort of thing.

Kessel to Sterling, 30 August 1986:

"Thanks for your comments on Sycamore Hill. I am fired by your picture of what this workshop can be, a real focus for consciousness-raising, mutual support for writers who may not be willing otherwise to take the chances that it's necessary to take to write the stuff that may really break down the walls. Or who might not know the direction to take without sharpening their viewpoints by clashing with other honed minds. I'll say again, as I have before, that I'm not sure exactly what this new SF will look like—I have the feeling that it won't be just one kind of fiction—but I'm ready to listen to all theories as long as there's some spark in them and they're spoken by writers with talent and passion."

Daddy's World

Walter Jon Williams

Walter Jon Williams spins a PCP story of best intentions gone awry in VR. What presents as a chapter out of the sweetest children's book ever soon turns into a sadistic nightmare and finally into a stark world flensed of all emotion. The attempt to avert a family tragedy leads to an even greater tragedy in this story set on the near edge of the singularity. The choice of the point of view character is key here, as Williams interrogates our notions of humanity in an era of digital immortality.

One day Jamie went with his family to a new place, a place that had not existed before. The people who lived there were called Whirlikins, who were tall thin people with pointed heads. They had long arms and made frantic gestures when they talked, and when they grew excited threw their arms out *wide* to either side and spun like tops until they got all blurry. They would whirr madly over the green grass beneath the pumpkin-orange sky of the Whirlikin Country, and sometimes they would bump into each other with an alarming clashing noise, but they were never hurt, only bounced off and spun away in another direction.

Sometimes one of them would spin so hard that he would dig himself right into the ground, and come to a sudden stop, buried to the shoulders, with an expression of alarmed dismay.

Jamie had never seen anything so funny. He laughed and laughed.

His little sister Becky laughed, too. Once she laughed so hard that she fell over onto her stomach, and Daddy picked her up and whirled her through the air, as if he were a Whirlikin himself, and they were both laughing all the while.

Afterward, they heard the dinner bell, and Daddy said it was time to go home. After they waved goodbye to the Whirlikins, Becky and Jamie walked hand-in-hand with Momma as they walked over the grassy hills toward home, and the pumpkin-orange sky slowly turned to blue.

The way home ran past El Castillo. El Castillo looked like a fabulous place, a castle with towers and domes and minarets, all gleaming in the sun. Music floated down from El Castillo, the swift, intricate music of many guitars, and Jamie could hear the fast click of heels and the shouts and laughter of happy people.

But Jamie did not try to enter El Castillo. He had tried before, and discovered that El Castillo was guarded by La Duchesa, an angular forbidding woman all in black, with a tall comb in her hair. When Jamie asked to come inside, La Duchesa had looked down at him and said, "I do not admit anyone who does not know Spanish irregular verbs!" It was all she ever said.

Jamie had asked Daddy what a Spanish irregular verb was—he had difficulty pronouncing the words—and Daddy had said, "Someday you'll learn, and La Duchesa will let you into her castle. But right now you're too young to learn Spanish."

That was all right with Jamie. There were plenty of things to do without going into El Castillo. And new places, like the country where the Whirlikins lived, appeared sometimes out of nowhere, and were quite enough to explore.

The color of the sky faded from orange to blue. Fluffy white clouds coasted in the air above the two-story frame house. Mister Jeepers, who was sitting on the ridgepole, gave a cry of delight and soared toward them through the air.

"Jamie's home!" he sang happily. "Jamie's home, and he's brought his beautiful sister!"

Mister Jeepers was diamond-shaped, like a kite, with his head at the topmost corner, hands on either sides, and little bowlegged comical legs attached on the bottom. He was bright red. Like a kite, he could fly, and he swooped through in a series of aerial cartwheels as he sailed toward Jamie and his party.

Becky looked up at Mister Jeepers and laughed from pure joy. "Jamie," she said, "you live in the best place in the world!"

At night, when Jamie lay in bed with his stuffed giraffe, Selena would ride a beam of pale light from the Moon to the Earth and sit by Jamie's side. She was a pale woman, slightly translucent, with a silver crescent on her brow. She would stroke Jamie's forehead with a cool hand, and she would sing to him until his eyes grew heavy and slumber stole upon him.

"The birds have tucked their heads
The night is dark and deep
All is quiet, all is safe,

And little Jamie goes to sleep."

Whenever Jamie woke during the night, Selena was there to comfort him. He was glad that Selena always watched out for him, because sometimes he still had nightmares about being in the hospital. When the nightmares came, she was always there to comfort him, stroke him, sing him back to sleep.

Before long the nightmares began to fade.

Princess Gigunda always took Jamie for lessons. She was a huge woman, taller than Daddy, with frowzy hair and big bare feet and a crown that could never be made to sit straight on her head. She was homely, with a mournful face that was ugly and endearing at the same time. As she shuffled along with Jamie to his lessons, Princess Gigunda complained about the way her feet hurt, and about how she was a giant and unattractive, and how she would never be married.

"I'll marry you when I get bigger," Jamie said loyally, and the Princess's homely face screwed up into an expression of beaming pleasure.

Jamie had different lessons with different people. Mrs. Winkle, down at the little red brick schoolhouse, taught him his ABCs. Coach Toad — who *was* one — taught him field games, where he raced and jumped and threw against various people and animals. Mr. McGillicuddy, a pleasant whiskered fat man who wore red sleepers with a trapdoor in back, showed him his magic globe. When Jamie put his finger anywhere on the globe, trumpets began to sound, and he could see what was happening where he was pointing, and Mr. McGillicuddy would take him on a tour and show him interesting things. Buildings, statues, pictures, parks, people. "This is Nome," he would say. "Can you say Nome?"

"Nome," Jamie would repeat, shaping his mouth around the unfamiliar word, and Mr. McGillicuddy would smile and bob his head and look pleased.

If Jamie did well on his lessons, he got extra time with the Whirlikins, or at the Zoo, or with Mr. Fuzzy or in Pandaland. Until the dinner bell rang, and it was time to go home.

Jamie did well with his lessons almost every day.

When Princess Gigunda took him home from his lessons, Mister Jeepers would fly from the ridgepole to meet him, and tell him that his family was ready to see him. And then Momma and Daddy and Becky would wave from the windows of the house, and he would run to meet them.

Once, when he was in the living room telling his family about his latest trip through Mr. McGillicuddy's magic globe, he began skipping about with enthusiasm, and waving his arms like a Whirlikin, and suddenly he noticed that no one else was paying attention. That Momma and Daddy and Becky were staring at something else, their faces frozen in different attitudes of polite attention.

Jamie felt a chill finger touch his neck.

"Momma?" Jamie said. "Daddy?" Momma and Daddy did not respond. Their faces didn't move. Daddy's face was blurred strangely, as if it had been caught in the middle of movement.

"Daddy?" Jamie came close and tried to tug at his father's shirt sleeve. It was hard, like marble, and his fingers couldn't get a purchase at it. Terror blew hot in his heart.

"*Daddy?*" Jamie cried. He tried to tug harder. "Daddy! Wake up!" Daddy didn't respond. He ran to Momma and tugged at her hand. "Momma! Momma!" Her hand was like the hand of a statue. She didn't move no matter how hard Jamie pulled.

"Help!" Jamie screamed. "Mister Jeepers! Mr. Fuzzy! Help my Momma!" Tears fell down his face as he ran from Becky to Momma to Daddy, tugging and pulling at them, wrapping his arms around their frozen legs and trying to pull them toward him. He ran outside, but everything was curiously still. No wind blew. Mister Jeepers sat on the ridgepole, a broad smile fixed as usual to his face, but he was frozen, too, and did not respond to Jamie's calls.

Terror pursued him back into the house. This was far worse than anything that had happened to him in the hospital, worse even than the pain. Jamie ran into the living room, where his family stood still as statues, and then recoiled in horror. A stranger had entered the room — or rather just parts of a stranger, a pair of hands encased in black gloves with strange silver circuit patterns on the backs, and a strange glowing opalescent face with a pair of wraparound dark glasses drawn across it like a line.

"Interface crashed, all right," the stranger said, as if to someone Jamie couldn't see.

Jamie gave a scream. He ran behind Momma's legs for protection.

"Oh shit," the stranger said. "The kid's still running." He began purposefully moving his hands as if poking at the air. Jamie was sure that it was some kind of terrible attack, a spell to turn him to stone. He tried to run away, tripped over Becky's immovable feet and hit the floor hard, and then crawled away, the hall rug bunching up under his hands and knees as he skidded away, his own screams ringing in his ears...

...He sat up in bed, shrieking. The cool night tingled on his skin. He felt Selena's hand on his forehead, and he jerked away with a cry.

"Is something wrong?" came Selena's calm voice. "Did you have a bad dream?" Under the glowing crescent on her brow, Jamie could see the concern in her eyes.

"Where are Momma and Daddy?" Jamie wailed.

"They're fine," Selena said. "They're asleep in their room. Was it a bad dream?"

Jamie threw off the covers and leaped out of bed. He ran down the hall, the floorboards cool on his bare feet. Selena floated after him in her serene, concerned way. He threw open the door to his parents' bedroom and snapped on the light, then gave a cry as he saw them huddled beneath their blanket. He flung himself at his mother, and gave a sob of relief as she opened her eyes and turned to him.

"Something wrong?" Momma said. "Was it a bad dream?"

"*No!*" Jamie wailed. He tried to explain, but even he knew that his words made no sense. Daddy rose from his pillow, looking seriously at Jamie, and then turned to ruffle his hair.

"Sounds like a pretty bad dream, trouper," Daddy said. "Let's get you back to bed."

"*No!*" Jamie buried his face in his mother's neck. "I don't want to go back to bed!"

"All right, Jamie," Momma said. She patted Jamie's back. "You can sleep here with us. But just for tonight, okay?"

"Wanna stay here," Jamie mumbled.

He crawled under the covers between Momma and Daddy. They each kissed him, and Daddy turned off the light. "Just go to sleep, trouper," he said. "And don't worry. You'll have good dreams from now on."

Selena, faintly glowing in the darkness, sat silently in the corner. "Shall I sing?" she asked.

"Yes, Selena," Daddy said. "Please sing for us."

Selena began to sing,

"The birds have tucked their heads,

The night is dark and deep

All is quiet, all is safe,

And little Jamie goes to sleep."

But Jamie did not sleep. Despite the singing, the dark night, the rhythmic breathing of his parents and the comforting warmth of their bodies.

It *wasn't* a dream, he knew. His family had really been frozen.

Something, or someone, had turned them to stone. Probably that evil disembodied head and pair of hands. And now, for some reason, his parents didn't remember.

Something had made them forget.

Jamie stared into the darkness. What, he thought, if these *weren't* his parents? If his parents were still stone, hidden away somewhere? What if these substitutes were bad people — kidnappers or worse — people who just *looked* like his real parents. What if they were evil people who were just waiting for him to fall asleep, and then they would turn to monsters, with teeth and fangs and a horrible light in their eyes, and they would tear him to bits right here in the bed...

Talons of panic clawed at Jamie's heart. Selena's song echoed in his ears. He *wasn't* going to sleep! He *wasn't!*

And then he did. It wasn't anything like normal sleep — it was as if sleep was *imposed* on him, as if something had just *ordered* his mind to sleep. It was just like a wave that rolled over him, an irresistible force, blotting out his senses, his body, his mind...

I *won't* sleep! he thought in defiance, but then his thoughts were extinguished.

When he woke he was back in his own bed, and it was morning, and Mister Jeepers was floating outside the window. "Jamie's awake!" he sang. "Jamie's awake and ready for a new day!"

And then his parents came bustling in, kissing him and petting him and taking him downstairs for breakfast.

His fears seemed foolish now, in full daylight, with Mister Jeepers dancing in the air outside and singing happily.

But sometimes, at night while Selena crooned by his bedside, he gazed into the darkness and felt a thrill of fear.

And he never forgot, not entirely.

—

A few days later Don Quixote wandered into the world, a lean man who frequently fell off his lean horse in a clang of homemade armor. He was given to making wan comments in both English and his own language, which turned out to be Spanish.

"Can you teach me Spanish irregular verbs?" Jamie asked.

"*Sí, naturalmente*," said Don Quixote. "But I will have to teach you some other Spanish as well." He looked particularly mournful. "Let's start with *corazón*. It means 'heart.' *Mi corazón*," he said with a sigh, "is breaking for love of Dulcinea."

After a few sessions with Don Quixote — mixed with a lot of sighing about *corazóns* and Dulcinea — Jamie took a grip on his courage, marched up to El Castillo, and spoke to La Duchesa. *¿Pierdo, sueño, haría, ponto!?* he cried.

La Duchesa's eyes widened in surprise, and as she bent toward Jamie her severe face became almost kindly. "You are obviously a very intelligent boy," she said. "You may enter my castle."

And so Don Quixote and La Duchesa, between the two of them, began to teach Jamie to speak Spanish. If he did well, he was allowed into the parts of the castle where the musicians played and the dancers stamped, where brave Castilian knights jousted in the tilting yard, and Señor Esteban told stories in Spanish, always careful to use words that Jamie already knew.

Jamie couldn't help but notice that sometimes Don Quixote behaved strangely. Once, when Jamie was visiting the Whirlikins, Don Quixote charged up on his horse, waving his sword and crying out that he would save Jamie from the goblins that were attacking him. Before Jamie could explain that the Whirlikins were harmless, Don Quixote galloped to the attack. The Whirlikins, alarmed, screwed themselves into the ground where they were safe, and Don Quixote fell off his horse trying to swing at one with his sword. After poor Quixote fell off his horse a few times, it was Jamie who had to rescue the Don, not the other way around.

It was sort of sad and sort of funny. Every time Jamie started to laugh about it, he saw Don Quixote's mournful face in his mind, and his laugh grew uneasy.

After a while, Jamie's sister Becky began to share Jamie's lessons. She joined him and Princess Gigunda on the trip to the little schoolhouse, learned reading and math from Mrs. Winkle, and then, after some coaching from Jamie and

Don Quixote, she marched to La Duchesa to shout irregular verbs and gain entrance to El Castillo.

Around that time Marcus Tullius Cicero turned up to take them both to the Forum Romanum, a new part of the world that had appeared to the south of the Whirlikins' territory. But Cicero and the people in the Forum, all the shopkeepers and politicians, did not teach Latin the way Don Quixote taught Spanish, explaining what the new words meant in English, they just talked Latin at each other and expected Jamie and Becky to understand. Which, eventually, they did. The Spanish helped. Jamie was a bit better at Latin than Becky, but he explained to her that it was because he was older.

It was Becky who became interested in solving Princess Gigunda's problem. "We should find her somebody to love," she said.

"She loves *us*," Jamie said.

"Don't be silly," Becky said. "She wants a *boyfriend*."

"*I'm* her boyfriend," Jamie insisted.

Becky looked a little impatient. "Besides," she said, "it's a puzzle. Just like La Duchesa and her verbs."

This had not occurred to Jamie before, but now that Becky mentioned it, the idea seemed obvious. There were a lot of puzzles around, which one or the other of them was always solving, and Princess Gigunda's lovelessness was, now that he saw it, clearly among them.

So they set out to find Princess Gigunda a mate. This question occupied them for several days, and several candidates were discussed and rejected. They found no answers until they went to the chariot race of the Circus Maximus. It was the first race in the Circus ever, because the place had just appeared on the other side of the Palatine Hill from the Forum, and there was a very large, very excited crowd.

The names of the charioteers were announced as they paraded their chariots to the starting line. The trumpets sounded, and the chariots bolted from the start as the drivers whipped up the horses. Jamie watched enthralled as they rolled around the *spina* for the first lap, and then shouted in surprise at the sight of Don Quixote galloping onto the Circus Maximus, shouting that he was about to stop this group of rampaging demons from destroying the land, and planted himself directly in the path of the oncoming chariots. Jamie shouted along with the crowd for the Don to get out of the way before he got killed.

Fortunately Quixote's horse had more sense than he did, because the spindly animal saw the chariots coming and bolted, throwing its rider. One of the chariots rode right over poor Quixote, and there was a horrible clanging noise, but after the chariot passed, Quixote sat up, apparently unharmed. His armor had saved him.

Jamie jumped from his seat and was about to run down to help Don Quixote off the course, but Becky grabbed his arm. "Hang on," she said, "someone else will look after him, and I have an idea."

She explained that Don Quixote would make a perfect man for Princess Gigunda.

"But he's in love with Dulcinea!"

Becky looked at him patiently. "Has anyone ever *seen* Dulcinea? All we have to do is convince Don Quixote that Princess Gigunda *is* Dulcinea."

After the races, they found that Don Quixote had been arrested by the lictors and sent to the Lautumiae, which was the Roman jail. They weren't allowed to see the prisoner, so they went in search of Cicero, who was a lawyer and was able to get Quixote out of the Lautumiae on the promise that he would never visit Rome again.

"I regret to the depths of my soul that my parole does not enable me to destroy those demons," Quixote said as he left Rome's town limits.

"Let's not get into that," Becky said. "What we wanted to tell you was that we've found Dulcinea."

The old man's eyes widened in joy. He clutched at his armor-clad heart. "*Mi amor!* Where is she? I must run to her at once!"

"Not just yet," Becky said. "You should know that she's been changed. She doesn't look like she used to."

"Has some evil sorcerer done this?" Quixote demanded.

"Yes!" Jamie interrupted. He was annoyed that Becky had taken charge of everything, and he wanted to add his contribution to the scheme. "The sorcerer was just a head!" he shouted. "A floating head, and a pair of hands! And he wore dark glasses and had no body!"

A shiver of fear passed through him as he remembered the eerie floating head, but the memory of his old terror did not stop his words from spilling out.

Becky gave him a strange look. "Yeah," she said. "That's right."

"He crashed the interface!" Jamie shouted, the words coming to him out of memory.

Don Quixote paid no attention to this, but Becky gave him another look.

"You're not as dumb as you look, Digit," she said.

"I do not care about Dulcinea's appearance," Don Quixote declared, "I love only the goodness that dwells in her *corazón*."

"She's Princess Gigunda!" Jamie shouted, jumping up and down in enthusiasm. "She's been Princess Gigunda all along!"

And so, the children following, Don Quixote ran clanking to where Princess Gigunda waited near Jamie's house, fell down to one knee, and began to kiss and weep over the Princess's hand. The Princess seemed a little surprised by this until Becky told her that she was really the long-lost Dulcinea, changed into a giant by an evil magician, although she probably didn't remember it because that was part of the spell, too.

So while the Don and the Princess embraced, kissed, and began to warble a love duet, Becky turned to Jamie.

"What's that stuff about the floating head?" she asked. "Where did you come up with that?"

"I dunno," Jamie said. He didn't want to talk about his memory of his family being turned to stone, the eerie glowing figure floating before them. He didn't want to remember how everyone said it was just a dream.

He didn't want to talk about the suspicions that had never quite gone away.

"That stuff was weird, Digit," Becky said. "It gave me the creeps. Let me know before you start talking about stuff like that again."

"Why do you call me Digit?" Jamie asked. Becky smirked.

"No reason," she said.

"Jamie's home!" Mister Jeepers' voice warbled from the sky. Jamie looked up to see Mister Jeepers doing joyful aerial loops overhead. "Master Jamie's home at last!"

"Where shall we go?" Jamie asked.

Their lessons for the day were over, and he and Becky were leaving the little red schoolhouse. Becky, as usual, had done very well on her lessons, better than her older brother, and Jamie felt a growing sense of annoyance. At least he was still better at Latin and computer science.

"I dunno," Becky said. "Where do you want to go?"

"How about Pandaland? We could ride the Whoosh Machine."

Becky wrinkled her face. "I'm tired of that kid stuff," she said.

Jamie looked at her. "But you're a kid."

"I'm not as little as you, Digit," Becky said.

Jamie glared. This was too much. "You're my little sister! I'm bigger than you!"

"No, you're not," Becky said. She stood before him, her arms flung out in exasperation. "Just *notice something* for once, will you?"

Jamie bit back on his temper and looked, and he saw that Becky was, in fact, bigger than he was. And older-looking. Puzzlement replaced his fading anger.

"How did you get so big?" Jamie asked.

"I grew. And you *didn't* grow. Not as fast anyway."

"I don't understand."

Becky's lip curled. "Ask Mom or Dad. Just *ask* them." Her expression turned stony. "Just don't believe everything they tell you."

"What do you mean?"

Becky looked angry for a moment, and then her expression relaxed. "Look," she said, "just go to Pandaland and have fun, okay? You don't need me for that. I want to go and make some calls to my friends."

"*What* friends?"

Becky looked angry again. "*My* friends. It doesn't matter who they are!"

"Fine!" Jamie shouted. "I can have fun by myself!"

Becky turned and began to walk home, her pale legs rapidly scissoring against the deep green hillside. Jamie glared after her, then turned and began the walk to Pandaland.

He did all his favorite things, rode the Ferris wheel and the Whoosh Machine, watched Rizzio the Strongman and the clowns. He enjoyed himself, but his enjoyment felt hollow. He found himself *watching*, watching himself at play, watching himself enjoying the rides.

Watching himself not grow as fast as his little sister.

Watching himself wondering whether or not to ask his parents about why that was.

He had the idea that he wouldn't like their answers.

—

He didn't see as much of Becky after that. They would share lessons, and then Becky would lock herself in her room to talk to her friends on the phone.

Becky didn't have a telephone in her room, though. He looked once when she wasn't there.

After a while, Becky stopped accompanying him for lessons. She'd got ahead of him on everything except Latin, and it was too hard for Jamie to keep up.

After that, he hardly saw Becky at all. But when he saw her, he saw that she was still growing fast. Her clothing was different, and her hair. She'd started wearing makeup.

He didn't know whether he liked her anymore or not.

It was Jamie's birthday. He was eleven years old, and Momma and Daddy and Becky had all come for a party. Don Quixote and Princess Gigunda serenaded Jamie from outside the window, accompanied by La Duchesa on Spanish guitar. There was a big cake with eleven candles. Momma gave Jamie a chart of the stars. When he touched a star, a voice would appear telling Jamie about the star, and lines would appear on the chart showing any constellation the star happened to belong to. Daddy gave Jamie a car, a miniature Mercedes convertible, scaled to Jamie's size, which he could drive around the country and which he could use in the Circus Maximus when the chariots weren't racing. His sister gave Jamie a kind of lamp stand that would project lights and moving patterns on the walls and ceiling when the lights were off. "Listen to music when you use it," she said.

"Thank you, Becky," Jamie said.

"Becca," she said. "My name is Becca now. Try to remember."

"Okay," Jamie said. "Becca."

Becky — Becca — looked at Momma. "I'm dying for a cigarette," she said. "Can I go, uh, out for a minute?"

Momma hesitated, but Daddy looked severe. "Becca," she said, "this is *Jamie's birthday*. We're all here to celebrate. So why don't we all eat some cake and have a nice time?"

"It's not even real cake," Becca said. "It doesn't *taste* like real cake."

"It's a *nice cake*," Daddy insisted. "Why don't we talk about this later? Let's just have a special time for Jamie."

Becca stood up from the table. "For *the Digit*?" she said. "Why are we having a good time for *Jamie?* He's not even a *real person!*" She thumped herself on the chest. "*I'm* a real person!" she shouted. "Why don't we ever have special times for *me?*"

But Daddy was on his feet by that point and shouting, and Momma was trying to get everyone to be quiet, and Becca was shouting back, and suddenly a determined look entered her face and she just disappeared — suddenly, she wasn't there anymore, there was just only air.

Jamie began to cry. So did Momma. Daddy paced up and down and swore, and then he said, "I'm going to go get her." Jamie was afraid he'd disappear like Becca, and he gave a cry of despair, but Daddy didn't disappear, he just stalked out of the dining room and slammed the door behind him.

Momma pulled Jamie onto her lap and hugged him. "Don't worry, Jamie," she said. "Becky just did that to be mean."

"What happened?" Jamie asked.

"Don't worry about it." Momma stroked his hair. "It was just a mean trick."

"She's growing up," Jamie said. "She's grown faster than me and I don't understand."

"Wait till Daddy gets back," Momma said, "and we'll talk about it."

But Daddy was clearly in no mood for talking when he returned, without Becca. "We're going to have *fun,*" he snarled, and reached for the knife to cut the cake.

The cake tasted like ashes in Jamie's mouth. When the Don and Princess Gigunda, Mister Jeepers and Rizzio the Strongman came into the dining room and sang "Happy Birthday," it was all Jamie could do to hold back the tears.

Afterwards he drove his new car to the Circus Maximus and drove as fast as he could on the long oval track. The car really wouldn't go very fast. The bleachers on either side were empty, and so was the blue sky above.

Maybe it was a puzzle, he thought, like Princess Gigunda's love life. Maybe all he had to do was follow the right clue, and everything would be fine.

What's the moral they're trying to teach? he wondered.

But all he could do was go in circles, around and around the empty stadium.

"Hey, Digit. Wake up."

Jamie came awake suddenly, with a stifled cry. The room whirled around him. He blinked, realized that the whirling came from the colored lights projected by his birthday present, Becca's lamp stand.

Becca was sitting on his bedroom chair, a cigarette in her hand. Her feet, in the steel-capped boots she'd been wearing lately, were propped up on the bed.

"Are you awake, Jamie?" It was Selena's voice. "Would you like me to sing you a lullaby?"

"Fuck off, Selena," Becca said. "Get out of here. Get lost."

Selena cast Becca a mournful look, then sailed backward, out the window, riding a beam of moonlight to her pale home in the sky. Jamie watched her go, and felt as if a part of himself was going with her, a part that he would never see again.

"Selena and the others have to do what you tell them, mostly," Becca said. "Of course, Mom and Dad wouldn't tell *you* that."

Jamie looked at Becca. "What's happening?" he said. "Where did you go today?"

Colored lights swam over Becca's face. "I'm sorry if I spoiled your birthday, Digit. I just got tired of the lies, you know? They'd kill me if they knew I was here now, talking to you." Becca took a draw on her cigarette, held her breath for a second or two, then exhaled. Jamie didn't see or taste any smoke.

"You know what they wanted me to do?" she said. "Wear a little girl's body, so I wouldn't look any older than you, and keep you company in that stupid school for seven hours a day." She shook her head. "I wouldn't do it. They yelled and yelled, but I was damned if I would."

"I don't understand."

Becca flicked invisible ashes off her cigarette, and looked at Jamie for a long time. Then she sighed.

"Do you remember when you were in the hospital?" she said.

Jamie nodded. "I was really sick."

"I was so little then, I don't really remember it very well," Becca said. "But the point is — " She sighed again. "The point is that you weren't getting well. So they decided to — " She shook her head. "Dad took advantage of his position at the University, and the fact that he's been a big donor. They were doing AI research, and the neurology department was into brain modeling, and they needed a test subject, and — Well, the idea is, they've got some of your tissue, and when they get cloning up and running, they'll put you back in — " She saw Jamie's stare, then shook her head. "I'll make it simple, okay?"

She took her feet off the bed and leaned closer to Jamie. A shiver ran up his back at her expression. "They made a copy of you. An *electronic* copy. They scanned your brain and built a holographic model of it inside a computer, and they put it in a virtual environment, and — " She sat back, took a drag on her cigarette. "And here you are," she said.

Jamie looked at her. "I don't understand."

Colored lights gleamed in Becca's eyes. "You're in a computer, okay? And you're a program. You know what that is, right? From computer class? And the program is sort of in the shape of your mind. Don Quixote and Princess Gigunda are programs, too. And Mrs. Winkle down at the schoolhouse is *usually* a program, but if she needs to teach something complex, then she's an education major from the University."

Jamie felt as if he'd just been hollowed out, a void inside his ribs. "I'm not real?" he said. "I'm not a person?"

"Wrong," Becca said. "You're real, all right. You're the apple of our parents' eye." Her tone was bitter. "Programs are real things," she said, "and yours was a real hack, you know, absolute cutting-edge state-of-the-art technoshit. And the computer that you're in is real, too — I'm interfaced with it right now, down in the family room — we have to wear suits with sensors and a helmet with scanners and stuff. I hope to fuck they don't hear me talking to you down here."

"But what — " Jamie swallowed hard. How could he swallow if he was just a string of code? "What happened to *me*? The original me?"

Becca looked cold. "Well," she said, "you had cancer. You died."

"Oh." A hollow wind blew through the void inside him.

"They're going to bring you back. As soon as the clone thing works out — but this is a government computer you're in, and there are all these government restrictions on cloning, and — " She shook her head. "Look, Digit," she said. "You really need to know this stuff, okay?"

"I understand." Jamie wanted to cry. But only real people cried, he thought, and he wasn't real. He wasn't real.

"The program that runs this virtual environment is huge, okay, and *you're* a big program, and the University computer is used for a lot of research, and a lot of the research has a higher priority than *you* do. So you don't run in real-time — that's why I'm growing faster than you are. I'm spending more hours being me than you are. And the parents — " She rolled her eyes. "They aren't making this any better, with their emphasis on *normal family life*."

She sucked on her cigarette, then stubbed it out in something invisible. "See, they want us to be this *normal family*. So we have breakfast together every day, and dinner every night, and spend the evening at the Zoo or in Pandaland or someplace. But the dinner that we eat with *you* is virtual, it doesn't taste like anything—the grant ran out before they got that part of the interface right—so we eat this fast-food crap before we interface with you, and then have dinner all *over* again with *you*... Is this making any sense? Because Dad has a job and Mom has a job and I go to school and have friends and stuff, so we really can't get together every night. So they just close your program file, shut it right down, when they're not available to interface with you as what Dad calls a 'family unit,' and that means that there are a lot of hours, days sometimes, when you're just *not running*, you might as well really be *dead*—" She blinked. "Sorry," she said. "Anyway, we're *all* getting older a lot faster than you are, and it's not fair to you, that's what I think. Especially because the University computer runs fastest at night, because people don't use them as much then, and you're pretty much real-time then, so interfacing with you would be almost *normal*, but Mom and Dad sleep then, cuz they have day jobs, and they can't have you running around unsupervised in here, for God's sake, they think it's unsafe or something..."

She paused, then reached into her shirt pocket for another cigarette. "Look," she said, "I'd better get out of here before they figure out I'm talking to you. And then they'll pull my access codes or something." She stood, brushed something off her jeans. "Don't tell the parents about this stuff right away. Otherwise they might erase you, and load a backup that doesn't know shit. Okay?"

And she vanished, as she had that afternoon.

Jamie sat in the bed, hugging his knees. He could feel his heart beating in the darkness. How can a program have a heart? he wondered.

Dawn slowly encroached upon the night, and then there was Mister Jeepers, turning lazy cartwheels in the air, his red face leering in the window.

"Jamie's awake!" he said. "Jamie's awake and ready for a new day!"

"Fuck off," Jamie said, and buried his face in the blanket.

Jamie asked to learn more about computers and programming. Maybe, he thought, he could find clues there, he could solve the puzzle. His parents agreed, happy to let him follow his interests.

After a few weeks, he moved into El Castillo. He didn't tell anyone he was going, he just put some of his things in his car, took them up to a tower room, and threw them down on the bed he found there. His Mom came to find him when he didn't come home for dinner.

"It's dinnertime, Jamie," she said. "Didn't you hear the dinner bell?"

"I'm going to stay here for a while," Jamie said.

"You're going to get hungry if you don't come home for dinner."

"I don't need food," Jamie said.

His Mom smiled brightly. "You need food if you're going to keep up with the Whirlikins," she said.

Jamie looked at her. "I don't care about that kid stuff anymore," he said.

When his mother finally turned and left, Jamie noticed that she moved like an old person.

After a while, he got used to the hunger that was programmed into him. It was always *there*, he was always aware of it, but he got so he could ignore it after awhile.

But he couldn't ignore the need to sleep. That was just built into the program, and eventually, try though he might, he needed to give in to it.

He found out he could order the people in the castle around, and he amused himself by making them stand in embarrassing positions, or stand on their heads and sing, or form human pyramids for hours and hours.

Sometimes he made them fight, but they weren't very good at it.

He couldn't make Mrs. Winkle at the schoolhouse do whatever he wanted, though, or any of the people who were supposed to teach him things. When it was time for a lesson, Princess Gigunda turned up. She wouldn't follow his orders, she'd just pick him up and carry him to the little red schoolhouse and plunk him down in his seat.

"You're not real!" he shouted, kicking in her arms. "You're not real! And *I'm* not real, either!"

But they made him learn about the world that *was* real, about geography and geology and history, although none of it mattered here.

After the first couple times Jamie had been dragged to school, his father met him outside the schoolhouse at the end of the day.

"You need some straightening out," he said. He looked grim. "You're part of a family. You belong with us. You're not going to stay in the castle anymore, you're going to have a *normal family life*."

"No!" Jamie shouted. "I like the castle!"

Dad grabbed him by the arm and began to drag him homeward. Jamie called him a *pendejo* and a *fellator*.

"I'll punish you if I have to," his father said.

"How are you going to do that?" Jamie demanded. "You gonna erase my file? Load a backup?"

A stunned expression crossed his father's face. His body seemed to go through a kind of stutter, and the grip on Jamie's arm grew nerveless. Then his face flushed with anger. "What do you mean?" he demanded. "Who told you this?"

Jamie wrenched himself free of Dad's weakened grip.

"I figured it out by myself," Jamie said. "It wasn't hard. I'm not a kid anymore."

"I — " His father blinked, and then his face hardened. "You're still coming home."

Jamie backed away. "I want some changes!" he said. "I don't want to be shut off all the time."

Dad's mouth compressed to a thin line. "It was Becky who told you this, wasn't it?"

Jamie felt an inspiration. "It was Mister Jeepers! There's a flaw in his programming! He answers whatever question I ask him!"

Jamie's father looked uncertain. He held out his hand. "Let's go home," he said. "I need to think about this."

Jamie hesitated. "Don't erase me," he said. "Don't load a backup. Please. I don't want to die *twice*."

Dad's look softened. "I won't."

"I want to grow up," Jamie said. "I don't want to be a little kid forever."

Dad held out with his hand again. Jamie thought for a moment, then took the hand. They walked over the green grass toward the white frame house on the hill.

"Jamie's home!" Mister Jeepers floated overhead, turning aerial cartwheels. "Jamie's home at last!"

A spasm of anger passed through Jamie at the sight of the witless grin. He pointed at the ground in front of him.

"Crash right here!" he ordered. "*Fast!*"

Mister Jeepers came spiraling down, an expression of comic terror on his face, and smashed to the ground where Jamie pointed. Jamie pointed at the sight of the crumpled body and laughed.

"Jamie's home at last!" Mister Jeepers said.

As soon as Jamie could, he got one of the programmers at the University to fix him up a flight program like the one Mister Jeepers had been using. He swooped and soared, zooming like a super hero through the sky, stunting between the towers of El Castillo and soaring over upturned, wondering faces in the Forum.

He couldn't seem to go as fast as he really wanted. When he started increasing speed, all the scenery below paused in its motion for a second or two, then jumped forward with a jerk. The software couldn't refresh the scenery fast enough to match his speed. It felt strange, because throughout his flight he could feel the wind on his face

So this, he thought, was why his car couldn't go fast.

So he decided to climb high. He turned his face to the blue sky and went straight up. The world receded, turned small. He could see the Castle, the hills of Whirlikin Country, the crowded Forum, the huge oval of the Circus Maximus. It was like a green plate, with a fuzzy, nebulous horizon where the sky started.

And, right in the center, was the little two-story frame house where he'd grown up.

It was laid out below him like scenery in a snow globe.

After a while he stopped climbing. It took him a while to realize it, because he still felt the wind blowing in his face, but the world below stopped getting smaller.

He tried going faster. The wind blasted onto him from above, but his position didn't change.

He'd reached the limits of his world. He couldn't get any higher.

Jamie flew out to the edges of the world, to the horizon. No matter how he urged his program to move, he couldn't make his world fade away.

He was trapped inside the snow globe, and there was no way out.

It was quite a while before Jamie saw Becca again. She picked her way through the labyrinth beneath El Castillo to his throne room, and Jamie slowly materialized atop his throne of skulls. She didn't appear surprised.

"I see you've got a little Dark Lord thing going here," she said.

"It passes the time," Jamie said.

"And all those pits and stakes and tripwires?"

"Death traps."

"Took me forever to get in here, Digit. I kept getting de-rezzed."

Jamie smiled. "That's the idea."

"Whirlikins as weapons," she nodded. "That was a good one. Bored a hole right through me, the first time."

"Since I'm stuck living here," Jamie said, "I figure I might as well be in charge of the environment. Some of the student programmers at the University helped me with some cool effects."

Screams echoed through the throne room. Fires leaped out of pits behind him. The flames illuminated the form of Marcus Tullius Cicero, who hung crucified above a sea of flame.

"*O tempora, O mores!*" moaned Cicero.

Becca nodded. "Nice," she said. "Not my scene exactly, but nice."

"Since I can't leave," Jamie said, "I want a say in who gets to visit. So either you wait till I'm ready to talk to you, or you take your chances on the death traps."

"Well. Looks like you're sitting pretty, then."

Jamie shrugged. Flames belched. "I'm getting bored with it. I might just wipe it all out and build another place to live in. I can't tell you the number of battles I've won, the number of kingdoms I've trampled. In this reality and others. It's all the same after a while." He looked at her. "You've grown."

"So have you."

"Once the *paterfamilias* finally decided to allow it." He smiled. "We still have dinner together sometimes, in the old house. Just a 'normal family,' as Dad says. Except that sometimes I turn up in the form of a werewolf, or a giant, or something."

"So they tell me."

"The advantage of being software is that I can look like anything I want. But that's the disadvantage, too, because I can't really *become* something else, I'm still just...me. I may wear another program as a disguise, but I'm still the same program inside, and I'm not a good enough programmer to mess with that, yet."

Jamie hopped off his throne, walked a nervous little circle around his sister. "So what brings you to the old neighborhood?" he asked. "The old folks said you were off visiting Aunt Maddy in the country."

"*Exiled*, they mean. I got knocked up, and after the abortion they sent me to Maddy. She was supposed to keep me under control, except she didn't." She picked an invisible piece of lint from her sweater. "So now I'm back." She looked at him. "I'm skipping a lot of the story, but I figure you wouldn't be interested."

"Does it have to do with sex?" Jamie asked. "I'm sort of interested in sex, even though I can't do it, and they're not likely to let me."

"*Let* you?"

"It would require a lot of new software and stuff. I was prepubescent when my brain structures were scanned, and the program isn't set up for making me a working adult, with adult desires et cetera. Nobody was thinking about putting me through adolescence at the time. And the administrators at the University told me that it was very unlikely that anyone was going to give them a grant so that a computer program could have sex." Jamie shrugged. "I don't miss it, I guess. But I'm sort of curious."

Surprise crossed Becca's face. "But there are all kinds of simulations, and..."

"They don't work for me, because my mind isn't structured so as to be able to achieve pleasure that way. I can manipulate the programs, but it's about as exciting as working a virtual butter churn." Jamie shrugged again. "But that's okay. I mean, I don't *miss* it. I can always give myself a jolt to the pleasure center if I want."

"Not the same thing," Becca said. "I've done both."

"I wouldn't know."

"I'll tell you about sex if you want," Becca said, "but that's not why I'm here."

"Yes?"

Becca hesitated. Licked her lips. "I guess I should just say it, huh?" she said. "Mom's dying. Pancreatic cancer."

Jamie felt sadness well up in his mind. Only electrons, he thought, moving from one place to another. It was nothing real. He was programmed to feel an analog of sorrow, and that was all.

"She looks normal to me," he said, "when I see her." But that didn't mean anything: his mother chose what she wanted him to see, just as he chose a mask — a werewolf, a giant — for her.

And in neither case did the disguise at all matter. For behind the werewolf was a program that couldn't alter its parameters; and behind the other, ineradicable cancer.

Becca watched him from slitted eyes. "Dad wants her to be scanned, and come here. So we can still be a *normal family* even after she dies."

Jamie was horrified. "Tell her *no*," he said. "Tell her she can't come!"

"I don't think she wants to. But Dad is very insistent."

"She'll be here *forever*! It'll be awful!"

Becca looked around. "Well, she wouldn't do much for your Dark Lord act, that's for sure. I'm sure Sauron's mom didn't hang around the Dark Tower, nagging him about the unproductive way he was spending his time."

Fires belched. The ground trembled. Stalactites rained down like arrows.

"That's not it," Jamie said. "She doesn't want to be here no matter what I'm doing, no matter where I live. Because whatever this place looks like, it's a prison." Jamie looked at his sister. "I don't want my mom in a prison."

Leaping flames glittered in Becca's eyes. "You can change the world you live in," she said. "That's more than I can do."

"But I can't," Jamie said. "I can change the way it *looks*, but I can't change anything *real*. I'm a program, and a program is an *artifact*. I'm a piece of *engineering*. I'm a simulation, with simulated sensory organs that interact with simulated environments — I can only interact with *other artifacts*. *None* of it's real. I don't know what the real world looks or feels or tastes like, I only know what simulations tell me they're *supposed* to taste like. And I can't change any of my parameters unless I mess with the engineering, and I can't do that unless the programmers agree, and even when that happens, I'm still as artificial as I was before. And the computer I'm in is old and clunky, and soon nobody's going to run my operating system anymore, and I'll not only be an artifact, I'll be a museum piece."

"There are other artificial intelligences out there," Becca said. "I keep hearing about them."

"I've talked to them. Most of them aren't very interesting — it's like talking to a dog, or maybe to very intelligent microwave oven. And they've scanned some people in, but those were adults, and all they wanted to do, once they got inside, was to escape. Some of them went crazy."

Becca gave a twisted smile. "I used to be so jealous of you, you know. You lived in this beautiful world, no pollution, no violence, no shit on the streets."

Flames belched.

"*Integra mens augustissima possessio*," said Cicero.

"Shut up!" Jamie told him. "What the fuck do you know?"

Becca shook her head. "I've seen those old movies, you know? Where somebody gets turned into a computer program, and next thing you know he's in every computer in the world, and running everything?"

"I've seen those, too. Ha ha. Very funny. Shows you what people know about programs."

"Yeah. Shows you what they know."

"I'll talk to Mom," Jamie said.

Big tears welled out of Mom's eyes and trailed partway down her face, then disappeared. The scanners paid a lot of attention to eyes and mouths, for the sake of transmitting expression, but didn't always pick up the things between.

"I'm sorry," she said. "We didn't think this is how it would be."

"Maybe you should have given it more thought," Jamie said.

It isn't sorrow, he told himself again. It's just electrons moving.

"You were such a beautiful baby." Her lower lip trembled. "We didn't want to lose you. They said that it would only be a few years before they could implant your memories in a clone."

Jamie knew all that by now. Knew that the technology of reading memories turned out to be much, much simpler than implanting them — it had been discovered that the implantation had to be made while the brain was actually growing. And government restrictions on human cloning had made tests next to impossible, and that the team that had started his project had split up years ago, some to higher-paying jobs, some retired, others to pet projects of their own. How his father had long ago used up whatever pull he'd had at the University trying to keep everything together. And how he long ago had acquired or purchased patents and copyrights for the whole scheme, except for Jamie's program, which was still owned jointly by the University and the family.

Tears reappeared on Mom's lower face, dripped off her chin. "There's potentially a lot of money at stake, you know. People want to raise perfect children. Keep them away from bad influences, make sure that they're raised free from violence."

"So they want to control the kid's entire environment," Jamie said.

"Yes. And make it *safe*. And wholesome. And—"

"Just like *normal family life*," Jamie finished. "No diapers, no vomit, no messes. No having to interact with the kid when the parents are tired. And then you just download the kid into an adult body, give him a diploma, and kick him out of the house. And call yourself a perfect parent."

"And there are *religious people*..." Mom licked her lips. "Your Dad's been talking to them. They want to raise children in environments that reflect their beliefs completely. Places where there is no temptation, no sin. No science or ideas that contradict their own..."

"But Dad isn't religious," Jamie said.

"These people have money. Lots of money."

Mom reached out, took his hand. Jamie thought about all the code that enabled her to do it, that enabled them both to feel the pressure of unreal flesh on unreal flesh.

"I'll do what you wish, of course," she said. "I don't have that desire for immortality, the way your father does." She shook her head. "But I don't know what your father will do once his time comes."

The world was a disk a hundred meters across, covered with junk: old Roman ruins, gargoyles fallen from a castle wall, a broken chariot, a shattered bell. Outside the rim of the world, the sky was black, utterly black, without a ripple or a star.

Standing in the center of the world was a kind of metal tree with two forked, jagged arms.

"Hi, Digit," Becca said.

A dull fitful light gleamed on the metal tree, as if it were reflecting a bloody sunset.

"Hi, sis," it said.

"Well," Becca said. "We're alone now."

"I caught the notice of Dad's funeral. I hope nobody missed me."

"*I* missed you, Digit." Becca sighed. "Believe it or not."

"I'm sorry."

Becca restlessly kicked a piece of junk, a hubcap from an old, miniature car. It clanged as it found new lodgement in the rubble. "Can you appear as a person?" she asked. "It would make it easier to talk to you."

"I've finished with all that," Jamie said. "I'd have to resurrect too much dead programming. I've cut the world down to next to nothing. I've got rid of my body, my heartbeat, the sense of touch."

"All the human parts," Becca said sadly.

The dull red light oozed over the metal tree like a drop of blood. "Everything except sleep and dreams. It turns out that sleep and dreams have too much to do with the way people process memory. I can't get rid of them, not without cutting out too much of my mind." The tree gave a strange, disembodied laugh. "I dreamed about you, the other day. And about Cicero. We were talking Latin."

"I've forgotten all the Latin I ever knew." Becca tossed her hair, forced a laugh. "So what do you do nowadays?"

"Mostly I'm a conduit for data. The University has been using me as a research spider, which I don't mind doing, because it passes the time. Except that I take up a lot more memory than any real search spider, and don't do that much better a job. And the information I find doesn't have much to do with *me* — it's all about the real world. The world I can't touch." The metal tree bled color.

"Mostly," he said, "I've just been waiting for Dad to die. And now it's happened."

There was a moment of silence before Becca spoke. "You know that Dad had himself scanned before he went."

"Oh yeah. I knew."

"He set up some kind of weird foundation that I'm not part of, with his patents and programs and so on, and his money and some other people's."

"He'd better not turn up here."

Becca shook her head. "He won't. Not without your permission, anyway. Because I'm in charge here. You — your program — it's not a part of the foundation. Dad couldn't get it all, because the University has an interest, and so does the family." There was a moment of silence. "And I'm the family now."

"So you...*inherited* me," Jamie said. Cold scorn dripped from his words.

"That's right," Becca said. She squatted down amid the rubble, rested her forearms on her knees.

"What do you want me to do, Digit? What can I do to make it better for you?"

"No one ever asked me that," Jamie said.

There was another long silence.

"Shut it off," Jamie said. "Close the file. Erase it."

Becca swallowed hard. Tears shimmered in her eyes. "Are you sure?" she asked.

"Yes. I'm sure."

"And if they ever perfect the clone thing? If we could make you..." She took a breath. "A person?"

"No. It's too late. It's...not something I can want anymore."

Becca stood. Ran a hand through her hair. "I wish you could meet my daughter," she said. "Her name is Christy. She's a real beauty."

"You can bring her," Jamie said.

Becca shook her head. "This place would scare her. She's only three. I'd only bring her if we could have..."

"The old environment," Jamie finished. "Pandaland. Mister Jeepers. Whirlikin Country."

Becca forced a smile. "Those were happy days," she said. "They really were. I was jealous of you, I know, but when I look back at that time..." She wiped tears with the back of her hand. "It was the best."

"Virtual environments are nice places to visit, I guess," Jamie said. "But you don't want to live in one. Not forever." Becca looked down at her feet, planted amid rubble.

"Well," she said. "If you're sure about what you want."

"I am."

She looked up at the metal form, raised a hand. "Goodbye, Jamie," she said.

"Goodbye," he said.

She faded from the world.

And in time, the world and the tree faded, too.

Hand in hand, Daddy and Jamie walked to Whirlikin Country. Jamie had never seen the Whirlikins before, and he laughed and laughed as the Whirlikins spun beneath their orange sky.

The sound of a bell rang over the green hills. "Time for dinner, Jamie," Daddy said.

Jamie waved goodbye to the Whirlikins, and he and Daddy walked briskly over the fresh green grass toward home.

"Are you happy, Jamie?" Daddy asked.

"Yes, Daddy!" Jamie nodded. "I only wish Momma and Becky could be here with us."

"They'll be here soon."

When, he thought, they can get the simulations working properly.

Because this time, he thought, there would be no mistakes. The foundation he'd set up before he died had finally purchased the University's interest in Jamie's program — they funded some scholarships, that was all it finally took. There was no one in the Computer Department who had an interest anymore.

Jamie had been loaded from an old backup — there was no point in using the corrupt file that Jamie had become, the one that had turned itself into a *tree*, for heaven's sake.

The old world was up and running, with a few improvements. The foundation had bought their own computer — an old one, so it wasn't too expensive — that would run the environment full time. Some other children might be scanned, to give Jamie some playmates and peer socialization.

This time it would work, Daddy thought. Because this time, Daddy was a program too, and he was going to be here every minute, making sure that the environment was correct and that everything went exactly according to plan. That he and Jamie and everyone else had a normal family life, perfect and shining and safe.

And if the clone program ever worked out, they would come into the real world again. And if downloading into clones was never perfected, then they would stay here.

There was nothing wrong with the virtual environment. It was a *good* place.

Just like normal family life. Only forever.

And when this worked out, the foundation's backers — fine people, even if they did have some strange religious ideas — would have their own environments up and running. With churches, angels, and perhaps even the presence of God...

"Look!" Daddy said, pointing. "It's Mister Jeepers!"

Mister Jeepers flew off the rooftop and spun happy spirals in the air as he swooped toward Jamie. Jamie dropped Daddy's hand and ran laughing to greet his friend.

"Jamie's home!" Mister Jeepers cried. "Jamie's home at last!"

Sterling to Kessel, 27 April 1987:

"Cyberpunk's carcass, now flopping under the beaks and jaws of the vultures and hyenas, will soon settle gently into the total artistic decomposition of the invertebrates and fungi. . .

"Perhaps the movement's common denominators were simply too easy to trash. Outside the tiny circle of originators, no one seems to have taken its ideals seriously enough to write a major novel in the cyberpunk vein; they seem more interested in dressing up of standards with a gloss of c-word tropes...

Sometimes I feel that if we could get our hands around the neck of whatever it was that made us this way, we'd really have it made. Sure, there's the rage, and It, whatever It is, should indeed pay a terrible price for making us like this... If we were really able to get hold of Whatever-It-Is, we ought to be able to talk intelligibly, at least to our contemporaries, in our own voices, and be heard and understood, and even, possibly, appreciated. I don't know what that kind of fiction would look like, but it would be the 'native literature of a post-industrial society,' and it would look right, and feel natural, and we'd be happy with it."

Kessel to Sterling, 8 May 1987:

"I've come to feel that wasn't such a bad fate, to acknowledge that all our ladders start there, in our mundane existence... You talk about just this with your understanding of the rage at the mundane world that lurks behind all our futures, be they brightly painted or grimly sketched.... 'Shouldn't somebody pay an awful price for making you that way?' Exactly. But...pure rage, although it will take you to places that are worth going to and that few have the courage to visit, is not a good long-term engine. There have got to be other engines."

The Dog Said Bow-Wow

Michael Swanwick

It seems clear to us that Michael Swanwick is not only a PCP writer, but that he was publishing stories back in the '80s that might well have qualified him for the roster of original cyberpunks. In addition, he was also the most astute chronicler of the cyberpunk-humanist dustup. But Swanwick has always been one of science fiction's most slippery writers; labels just will not stick to him. Or to the story that follows, a romp featuring two scam artists in a future that pushes cyberpunk to the edge of absurdity and yet maintains its skewed extrapolative rigor. At one time the phrase "comic cyberpunk" might have seemed an oxymoron. Not anymore.

THE DOG LOOKED like he had just stepped out of a children's book. There must have been a hundred physical adaptations required to allow him to walk upright. The pelvis, of course, had been entirely reshaped. The feet alone would have needed dozens of changes. He had knees, and knees were tricky.

To say nothing of the neurological enhancements.

But what Darger found himself most fascinated by was the creature's costume. His suit fit him perfectly, with a slit in the back for the tail, and—again—a hundred invisible adaptations that caused it to hang on his body in a way that looked perfectly natural.

"You must have an extraordinary tailor," Darger said.

The dog shifted his cane from one paw to the other, so they could shake, and in the least affected manner imaginable replied, "That is a common observation, sir."

"You're from the States?" It was a safe assumption, given where they stood—on the docks—and that the schooner *Yankee Dreamer* had sailed up the Thames with the morning tide. Darger had seen its bubble sails over the rooftops, like so many rainbows. "Have you found lodgings yet?"

"Indeed I am, and no I have not. If you could recommend a tavern of the cleaner sort?"

"No need for that. I would be only too happy to put you up for a few days in my own rooms." And, lowering his voice, Darger said, "I have a business proposition to put to you."

"Then lead on, sir, and I shall follow you with a right good will."

The dog's name was Sir Blackthorpe Ravenscairn de Plus Precieux, but "Call me Sir Plus," he said with a self-denigrating smile, and "Surplus" he was ever after.

Surplus was, as Darger had at first glance suspected and by conversation confirmed, a bit of a rogue — something more than mischievous and less than a cut-throat. A dog, in fine, after Darger's own heart.

Over drinks in a public house, Darger displayed his box and explained his intentions for it. Surplus warily touched the intricately carved teak housing, and then drew away from it. "You outline an intriguing scheme, Master Darger—"

"Please. Call me Aubrey."

"Aubrey, then. Yet here we have a delicate point. How shall we divide up the...ah, *spoils* of this enterprise? I hesitate to mention this, but many a promising partnership has foundered on precisely such shoals."

Darger unscrewed the salt cellar and poured its contents onto the table. With his dagger, he drew a fine line down the middle of the heap. "I divide — you choose. Or the other way around, if you please. From self-interest, you'll not find a grain's difference between the two."

"Excellent!" cried Surplus and, dropping a pinch of salt in his beer, drank to the bargain.

It was raining when they left for Buckingham Labyrinth. Darger stared out the carriage window at the drear streets and worn buildings gliding by and sighed. "Poor, weary old London! History is a grinding-wheel that has been applied too many a time to thy face."

"It is also," Surplus reminded him, "to be the making of our fortunes. Raise your eyes to the Labyrinth, sir, with its soaring towers and bright surfaces rising above these shops and flats like a crystal mountain rearing up out of a ramshackle wooden sea, and be comforted."

"That is fine advice," Darger agreed. "But it cannot comfort a lover of cities, nor one of a melancholic turn of mind."

"Pah!" cried Surplus, and said no more until they arrived at their destination.

At the portal into Buckingham, the sergeant-interface strode forward as they stepped down from the carriage. He blinked at the sight of Surplus, but said only, "Papers?"

Surplus presented the man with his passport and the credentials Darger had spent the morning forging, then added with a negligent wave of his paw, "And this is my autistic."

The sergeant-interface glanced once at Darger, and forgot about him completely. Darger had the gift, priceless to one in his profession, of a face so nondescript that once someone looked away, it disappeared from that person's consciousness forever. "This way, sir. The officer of protocol will want to examine these himself."

A dwarf savant was produced to lead them through the outer circle of the Labyrinth. They passed by ladies in bioluminescent gowns and gentlemen with boots and gloves cut from leathers cloned from their own skin. Both women and men were extravagantly bejeweled — for the ostentatious display of wealth was yet again in fashion — and the halls were lushly clad and pillared in marble, porphyry, and jasper. Yet Darger could not help noticing how worn the carpets were, how chipped and sooted the oil lamps. His sharp eye espied the remains of an antique electrical system, and traces as well of telephone lines and fiber optic cables from an age when those technologies were yet workable.

These last he viewed with particular pleasure.

The dwarf savant stopped before a heavy black door carved over with gilt griffins, locomotives, and fleurs-de-lis. "This is a door," he said. "The wood is ebony. Its binomial is *Diospyros ebenum*. It was harvested in Serendip. The gilding is of gold. Gold has an atomic weight of 197.2."

He knocked on the door and opened it.

The officer of protocol was a dark-browed man of imposing mass. He did not stand for them. "I am Lord Coherence-Hamilton, and this—" he indicated the slender, clear-eyed woman who stood beside him— "is my sister, Pamela."

Surplus bowed deeply to the Lady, who dimpled and dipped a slight curtsey in return.

The protocol officer quickly scanned the credentials. "Explain these fraudulent papers, sirrah. The Demesne of Western Vermont! Damn me if I have ever heard of such a place."

"Then you have missed much," Surplus said haughtily. "It is true we are a young nation, created only seventy-five years ago during the Partition of New England. But there is much of note to commend our fair land. The glorious beauty of Lake Champlain. The gene-mills of Winooski, that ancient seat of learning the *Universitas Viridis Montis* of Burlington, the Technarchaeological Institute of—" He stopped. "We have much to be proud of, sir, and nothing of which to be ashamed."

The bearlike official glared suspiciously at him, then said, "What brings you to London? Why do you desire an audience with the queen?"

"My mission and destination lie in Russia. However, England being on my itinerary and I a diplomat, I was charged to extend the compliments of my nation to your monarch." Surplus did not quite shrug. "There is no more to it than that. In three days I shall be in France, and you will have forgotten about me completely."

Scornfully, the officer tossed the credentials to the savant, who glanced at and politely returned them to Surplus. The small fellow sat down at a little desk scaled to his own size and swiftly made out a copy. "Your papers will be taken to Whitechapel and examined there. If everything goes well—which I doubt—and there's an opening—not likely—you'll be presented to the queen sometime between a week and ten days hence."

"Ten days! Sir, I am on a very strict schedule!"

"Then you wish to withdraw your petition?"

Surplus hesitated. "I...I shall have to think on't, sir."

Lady Pamela watched coolly as the dwarf savant led them away.

The room they were shown to had massively framed mirrors and oil paintings dark with age upon the walls, and a generous log fire in the hearth. When their small guide had gone, Darger carefully locked and bolted the door. Then he tossed the box onto the bed, and bounced down alongside it. Lying flat on his back, staring up at the ceiling, he said, "The Lady Pamela is a strikingly beautiful woman. I'll be damned if she's not."

Ignoring him, Surplus locked paws behind his back, and proceeded to pace up and down the room. He was full of nervous energy. At last, he expostulated, "This is a deep game you have gotten me into, Darger! Lord Coherence-Hamilton suspects us of all manner of blackguardry—"

"Well, and what of that?"

"I repeat myself: We have not even begun our play yet, and he suspects us already! I trust neither him nor his genetically remade dwarf."

"You are in no position to be displaying such vulgar prejudice."

"I am not *bigoted* about the creature, Darger, I *fear* him! Once let suspicion of us into that macroencephalic head of his, and he will worry at it until he has found out our every secret."

"Get a grip on yourself, Surplus! Be a man! We are in this too deep already to back out. Questions would be asked, and investigations made."

"I am anything but a man, thank God," Surplus replied. "Still, you are right. In for a penny, in for a pound. For now, I might as well sleep. Get off the bed. You can have the hearth-rug."

"I! The rug!"

"I am groggy of mornings. Were someone to knock, and I to unthinkingly open the door, it would hardly do to have you found sharing a bed with your master."

The next day, Surplus returned to the Office of Protocol to declare that he was authorized to wait as long as two weeks for an audience with the queen, though not a day more.

"You have received new orders from your government?" Lord Coherence-Hamilton asked suspiciously. "I hardly see how."

"I have searched my conscience, and reflected on certain subtleties of phrasing in my original instructions," Surplus said. "That is all."

He emerged from the office to discover Lady Pamela waiting outside. When she offered to show him the Labyrinth, he agreed happily to her plan. Followed by Darger, they strolled inward, first to witness the changing of the guard in the forecourt vestibule, before the great pillared wall that was the front of Buckingham Palace before it was swallowed up in the expansion of architecture during the mad, glorious years of Utopia. Following which, they proceeded toward the viewer's gallery above the chamber of state.

"I see from your repeated glances that you are interested in my diamonds, 'Sieur Plus Precieux," Lady Pamela said. "Well might you be. They are a family treasure, centuries old and manufactured to order, each stone flawless and perfectly matched. The indentures of a hundred autistics would not buy the like."

Surplus smiled down again at the necklace, draped about her lovely throat and above her perfect breasts. "I assure you, madame, it was not your necklace that held me so enthralled."

She colored delicately, pleased. Lightly, she said, "And that box your man carries with him wherever you go? What is in it?"

"That? A trifle. A gift for the Duke of Muscovy, who is the ultimate object of my journey," Surplus said. "I assure you, it is of no interest whatsoever."

"You were talking to someone last night," Lady Pamela said. "In your room."

"You were listening at my door? I am astonished and flattered."

She blushed. "No, no, my brother...it is his job, you see, surveillance."

"Possibly I was talking in my sleep. I have been told I do that occasionally."

"In accents? My brother said he heard two voices."

Surplus looked away. "In that, he was mistaken."

England's queen was a sight to rival any in that ancient land. She was as large as the lorry of ancient legend, and surrounded by attendants who hurried back and forth, fetching food and advice and carrying away dirty plates and signed legislation. From the gallery, she reminded Darger of a queen bee, but unlike the bee, this queen did not copulate, but remained proudly virgin.

Her name was Gloriana the First, and she was a hundred years old and still growing.

Lord Campbell-Supercollider, a friend of Lady Pamela's met by chance, who had insisted on accompanying them to the gallery, leaned close to Surplus and murmured, "You are impressed, of course, by our queen's magnificence." The warning in his voice was impossible to miss. "Foreigners invariably are."

"I am dazzled," Surplus said.

"Well might you be. For scattered through her majesty's great body are thirty-six brains, connected with thick ropes of ganglia in a hypercube configuration. Her processing capacity is the equal of many of the great computers from Utopian times."

Lady Pamela stifled a yawn. "Darling Rory," she said, touching the Lord Campbell-Supercollider's sleeve. "Duty calls me. Would you be so kind as to show my American friend the way back to the outer circle?"

"Or course, my dear." He and Surplus stood (Darger was, of course, already standing) and paid their compliments. Then, when Lady Pamela was gone and Surplus started to turn toward the exit: "Not that way. Those stairs are for commoners. You and I may leave by the gentlemen's staircase."

The narrow stairs twisted downward beneath clouds of gilt cherubs-and-airships, and debouched into a marble-floored hallway. Surplus and Darger stepped out of the stairway and found their arms abruptly seized by baboons.

There were five baboons all told, with red uniforms and matching choke collars with leashes that gathered in the hand of an ornately mustached officer whose gold piping identified him as a master of apes. The fifth baboon bared his teeth and hissed savagely.

Instantly, the master of apes yanked back on his leash and said, "There, Hercules! There, sirrah! What do you do? What do you say?"

The baboon drew himself up and bowed curtly. "Please come with us," he said with difficulty. The master of apes cleared his throat. Sullenly, the baboon added, "Sir."

"This is outrageous!" Surplus cried. "I am a diplomat, and under international law immune to arrest."

"Ordinarily, sir, this is true," said the master of apes courteously. "However, you have entered the inner circle without her majesty's invitation and are thus subject to stricter standards of security."

"I had no idea these stairs went inward. I was led here by—" Surplus looked about helplessly. Lord Campbell-Supercollider was nowhere to be seen.

So, once again, Surplus and Darger found themselves escorted to the Office of Protocol.

"The wood is teak. Its binomial is *Tectona grandis*. Teak is native to Burma, Hind, and Siam. The box is carved elaborately but without refinement." The dwarf savant opened it. "Within the casing is an archaic device for electronic intercommunication. The instrument chip is a gallium-arsenide ceramic. The chip weighs six ounces. The device is a product of the Utopian end-times."

"A modem!" The protocol officer's eyes bugged out. "You dared bring a *modem* into the inner circle and almost into the presence of the queen?" His chair stood and walked around the table. Its six insectile legs looked too slender to carry his great, legless mass. Yet it moved nimbly and well.

"It is harmless, sir. Merely something our technarchaeologists unearthed and thought would amuse the Duke of Muscovy, who is well known for his love of all things antiquarian. It is, apparently, of some cultural or historical significance, though without rereading my instructions, I would be hard pressed to tell you what."

Lord Coherence-Hamilton raised his chair so that he loomed over Surplus, looking dangerous and domineering. "*Here* is the historic significance of your modem: The Utopians filled the world with their computer webs and nets, burying cables and nodes so deeply and plentifully that they shall never be entirely rooted out. They then released into that virtual universe demons and mad gods. These intelligences destroyed Utopia and almost destroyed humanity as well. Only the valiant worldwide destruction of all modes of interface saved us from annihilation.

"Oh, you lackwit! Have you no history? These creatures hate us because our ancestors created them. They are still alive, though confined to their electronic netherworld, and want only a modem to extend themselves into the physical realm. Can you wonder, then, that the penalty for possessing such a device is—" he smiled menacingly—"death?"

"No, sir, it is not. Possession of a *working* modem is a mortal crime. This device is harmless. Ask your savant."

"Well?" the big man growled at his dwarf. "Is it functional?"

"No. It—"

"Silence." Lord Coherence-Hamilton turned back to Surplus. "You are a fortunate cur. You will not be charged with any crimes. However, while you are here, I will keep this filthy device locked away and under my control. Is that understood, Sir Bow-Wow?"

Surplus sighed. "Very well," he said. "It is only for a week, after all."

That night, the Lady Pamela Coherence-Hamilton came by Surplus's room to apologize for the indignity of his arrest, of which, she assured him, she had just now learned. He invited her in. In short order they somehow found themselves kneeling face-to-face on the bed, unbuttoning each other's clothing.

Lady Pamela's breasts had just spilled delightfully from her dress when she drew back, clutching the bodice closed again, and said, "Your man is watching us."

"And what concern is that to us?" Surplus said jovially. "The poor fellow's an autistic. Nothing he sees or hears matters to him. You might as well be embarrassed by the presence of a chair."

"Even were he a wooden carving, I would his eyes were not on me."

"As you wish." Surplus clapped his paws. "Sirrah! Turn around."

Obediently, Darger turned his back. This was his first experience with his friend's astonishing success with women. How many sexual adventuresses, he wondered, might one tumble, if one's form were unique? On reflection, the question answered itself.

Behind him, he heard the Lady Pamela giggle. Then, in a voice low with passion, Surplus said, "No, leave the diamonds on."

With a silent sigh, Darger resigned himself to a long night. Since he was bored and yet could not turn to watch the pair cavorting on the bed without giving himself away, he was perforce required to settle for watching them in the mirror.

They began, of course, by doing it doggy-style.

The next day, Surplus fell sick. Hearing of his indisposition, Lady Pamela sent one of her autistics with a bowl of broth and then followed, herself, in a surgical mask.

Surplus smiled weakly to see her. "You have no need of that mask," he said. "By my life, I swear that what ails me is not communicable. As you doubtless know, we who have been remade are prone to endocrinological imbalance."

"Is that all?" Lady Pamela spooned some broth into his mouth, then dabbed at a speck of it with a napkin. "Then fix it. You have been very wicked to frighten me over such a trifle."

"Alas," Surplus said sadly, "I am a unique creation, and my table of endocrine balances was lost in an accident at sea. There are copies in Vermont, of course. But by the time even the swiftest schooner can cross the Atlantic twice, I fear me I shall be gone."

"Oh, dearest Surplus!" The Lady caught up his paws in her hands. "Surely there is some measure, however desperate, to be taken?"

"Well..." Surplus turned to the wall in thought. After a very long time, he turned back and said, "I have a confession to make. The modem your brother holds for me? It is functional."

"Sir!" Lady Pamela stood, gathering her skirts, and stepped away from the bed in horror. "Surely not!"

"My darling and delight, you must listen to me." Surplus glanced weakly toward the door, then lowered his voice. "Come close and I shall whisper."

She obeyed.

"In the waning days of Utopia, during the war between men and their electronic creations, scientists and engineers bent their efforts toward the creation of a modem that could be safely employed by humans. One immune from the attack of demons. One that could, indeed, compel their obedience. Perhaps you have heard of this project."

"There are rumors, but...no such device was ever built."

"Say rather that no such device was built *in time*. It had just barely been perfected when the mobs came rampaging through the laboratories, and the Age of the Machine was over. Some few, however, were hidden away before the last technicians were killed. Centuries later, brave researchers at the Technarchaeological Institute of Shelburne recovered six such devices and mastered the art of their use. One device was destroyed in the process. Two are kept in Burlington. The others were given to trusted couriers and sent to the three most powerful allies of the Demesne — one of which is, of course, Russia."

"This is hard to believe," Lady Pamela said wonderingly. "Can such marvels be?"

"Madame, I employed it two nights ago in this very room! Those voices your brother heard? I was speaking with my principals in Vermont. They gave me permission to extend my stay here to a fortnight."

He gazed imploringly at her. "If you were to bring me the device, I could then employ it to save my life."

Lady Coherence-Hamilton resolutely stood. "Fear nothing, then. I swear by my soul, the modem shall be yours tonight."

The room was lit by a single lamp which cast wild shadows whenever anyone moved, as if of illicit spirits at a witch's Sabbath.

It was an eerie sight. Darger, motionless, held the modem in his hands. Lady Pamela, who had a sense of occasion, had changed to a low-cut gown of clinging silks, dark-red as human blood. It swirled about her as she hunted through the wainscoting for a jack left unused for centuries. Surplus sat up weakly in bed, eyes half-closed, directing her. It might have been, Darger thought, an allegorical tableau of the human body being directed by its sick animal passions, while the intellect stood by, paralyzed by lack of will.

"There!" Lady Pamela triumphantly straightened, her necklace scattering tiny rainbows in the dim light.

Darger stiffened. He stood perfectly still for the length of three long breaths, then shook and shivered like one undergoing seizure. His eyes rolled back in his head.

In hollow, unworldly tones, he said, "What man calls me up from the vasty deep?" It was a voice totally unlike his own, one harsh and savage and eager for unholy sport. "Who dares risk my wrath?"

"You must convey my words to the autistic's ears," Surplus murmured. "For he is become an integral part of the modem — not merely its operator, but its voice."

"I stand ready," Lady Pamela replied.

"Good girl. Tell it who I am."

"It is Sir Blackthorpe Ravenscairn de Plus Precieux who speaks, and who wishes to talk to..." She paused.

"To his most august and socialist honor, the mayor of Burlington."

"His most august and socialist honor," Lady Pamela began. She turned toward the bed and said quizzically, "The mayor of Burlington?"

"'Tis but an official title, much like your brother's, for he who is in fact the spy-master for the Demesne of Western Vermont," Surplus said weakly. "Now repeat to it: I compel thee on threat of dissolution to carry my message. Use those exact words."

Lady Pamela repeated the words into Darger's ear.

He screamed. It was a wild and unholy sound that sent the Lady skittering away from him in a momentary panic. Then, in mid-cry, he ceased.

"Who is this?" Darger said in an entirely new voice, this one human. "You have the voice of a woman. Is one of my agents in trouble?"

"Speak to him now, as you would to any man: forthrightly, directly, and without evasion." Surplus sank his head back on his pillow and closed his eyes.

So (as it seemed to her) the Lady Coherence-Hamilton explained Surplus's plight to his distant master, and from him received both condolences and the needed information to return Surplus's endocrine levels to a functioning harmony. After proper courtesies, then, she thanked the American spy-master and unjacked the modem. Darger returned to passivity.

The leather-cased endocrine kit lay open on a small table by the bed. At Lady Pamela's direction, Darger began applying the proper patches to various places on Surplus's body. It was not long before Surplus opened his eyes.

"Am I to be well?" he asked and, when the Lady nodded, "Then I fear I must be gone in the morning. Your brother has spies everywhere. If he gets the least whiff of what this device can do, he'll want it for himself."

Smiling, Lady Pamela hoisted the box in her hand. "Indeed, who can blame him? With such a toy, great things could be accomplished."

"So he will assuredly think. I pray you, return it to me."

She did not. "This is more than just a communication device, sir," she said. "Though in that mode it is of incalculable value. You have shown that it can enforce obedience on the creatures that dwell in the forgotten nerves of the ancient world. Ergo, they can be compelled to do our calculations for us."

"Indeed, so our technarchaeologists tell us. You must —"

"We have created monstrosities to perform the duties that were once done by machines. But with this, there would be no necessity to do so. We have allowed ourselves to be ruled by an icosahexadexal-brained freak. Now we have no need for Gloriana the Gross, Gloriana the Fat and Grotesque, Gloriana the Maggot Queen."

"Madame!"

"It is time, I believe, that England had a new queen. A human queen."

"Think of my honor!"

Lady Pamela paused in the doorway. "You are a very pretty fellow indeed. But with *this*, I can have the monarchy and keep such a harem as will reduce your memory to that of a passing and trivial fancy."

With a rustle of skirts, she spun away.

"Then I am undone!" Surplus cried, and fainted onto the bed.

Quietly, Darger closed the door. Surplus raised himself from the pillows, began removing the patches from his body, and said, "Now what?"

"Now we get some sleep," Darger said. "Tomorrow will be a busy day."

—

The master of apes came for them after breakfast, and marched them to their usual destination. By now Darger was beginning to lose track of exactly how many times he had been in the Office of Protocol. They entered to find Lord Coherence-Hamilton in a towering rage, and his sister, calm and knowing, standing in a corner with her arms crossed, watching. Looking at them both now, Darger wondered how he could ever have imagined that the brother out-ranked his sister.

The modem lay opened on the dwarf-savant's desk. The little fellow leaned over the device, studying it minutely.

Nobody said anything until the master of apes and his baboons had left. Then Lord Coherence-Hamilton roared, "Your modem refuses to work for us!"

"As I told you, sir," Surplus said coolly, "it is inoperative."

"That's a bold-arsed fraud and a goat-buggering lie!" In his wrath, the Lord's chair rose up on its spindly legs so high that his head almost bumped against the ceiling. "I know of your activities — " he nodded toward his sister — "and demand that you show us how this whoreson device works!"

"Never!" Surplus cried stoutly. "I have my honor, sir."

"Your honor, too scrupulously insisted upon, may well lead to your death, sir."

Surplus threw back his head. "Then I die for Vermont!"

At this moment of impasse, Lady Hamilton stepped forward between the two antagonists to restore peace. "I know what might change your mind." With a knowing smile, she raised a hand to her throat and denuded herself of her diamonds. "I saw how you rubbed them against your face the other night. How you licked and fondled them. How ecstatically you took them into your mouth."

She closed his paws about them. "They are yours, sweet 'Sieur Precieux, for a word."

"You would give them up?" Surplus said, as if amazed at the very idea. In fact, the necklace had been his and Darger's target from the moment they'd seen it. The only barrier that now stood between them and the merchants of Amsterdam was the problem of freeing themselves from the Labyrinth before their marks finally realized that the modem was indeed a cheat. And to this end they had the invaluable tool of a thinking man whom all believed to be an autistic, and a plan that would give them almost twenty hours in which to escape.

"Only think, dear Surplus." Lady Pamela stroked his head and then scratched him behind one ear, while he stared down at the precious stones. "Imagine the life of wealth and ease you could lead, the women, the power. It all lies in your hands. All you need do is close them."

Surplus took a deep breath. "Very well," he said. "The secret lies in the condenser, which takes a full day to recharge. Wait but—"

"Here's the problem," the savant said unexpectedly. He poked at the interior of the modem. "There was a wire loose."

He jacked the device into the wall.

"Oh, dear God," Darger said.

A savage look of raw delight filled the dwarf savant's face, and he seemed to swell before them.

"*I am free!*" he cried in a voice so loud it seemed impossible that it could arise from such a slight source. He shook as if an enormous electrical current were surging through him. The stench of ozone filled the room.

He burst into flames and advanced on the English spy-master and her brother.

While all stood aghast and paralyzed, Darger seized Surplus by the collar and hauled him out into the hallway, slamming the door shut as he did.

They had not run twenty paces down the hall when the door to the Office of Protocol exploded outward, sending flaming splinters of wood down the hallway.

Satanic laughter boomed behind them.

Glancing over his shoulder, Darger saw the burning dwarf, now blackened to a cinder, emerge from a room engulfed in flames, capering and dancing. The modem, though disconnected, was now tucked under one arm, as if it were exceedingly valuable to him. His eyes were round and white and lidless. Seeing them, he gave chase.

"Aubrey!" Surplus cried. "We are headed the *wrong way!*"

It was true. They were running deeper into the Labyrinth, toward its heart, rather than outward. But it was impossible to turn back now. They plunged through scattering crowds of nobles and servitors, trailing fire and supernatural terror in their wake.

The scampering grotesque set fire to the carpets with every footfall. A wave of flame tracked him down the hall, incinerating tapestries and wallpaper and wood trim. No matter how they dodged, it ran straight toward them. Clearly, in the programmatic literalness of its kind, the demon from the web had determined that having early seen them, it must early kill them as well.

Darger and Surplus raced through dining rooms and salons, along balconies and down servants' passages. To no avail. Dogged by their hyper-natural nemesis, they found themselves running down a passage, straight toward two massive bronze doors, one of which had been left just barely ajar. So fearful were they that they hardly noticed the guards.

"Hold, sirs!"

The mustachioed master of apes stood before the doorway, his baboons straining against their leashes. His eyes widened with recognition. "By gad, it's you!" he cried in astonishment.

"Lemme kill 'em!" one of the baboons cried. "The lousy bastards!" The others growled agreement.

Surplus would have tried to reason with them, but when he started to slow his pace, Darger put a broad hand on his back and shoved. "Dive!" he commanded. So of necessity the dog of rationality had to bow to the man of action. He tobogganed wildly across the polished marble floor between two baboons, straight at the master of apes, and then between his legs.

The man stumbled, dropping the leashes as he did.

The baboons screamed and attacked.

For an instant all five apes were upon Darger, seizing his limbs, snapping at his face and neck. Then the burning dwarf arrived and, finding his target obstructed, seized the nearest baboon. The animal shrieked as its uniform burst into flames.

As one, the other baboons abandoned their original quarry to fight this newcomer who had dared attack one of their own.

In a trice, Darger leaped over the fallen master of apes, and was through the door. He and Surplus threw their shoulders against its metal surface and pushed. He had one brief glimpse of the fight, with the baboons aflame, and their master's body flying through the air. Then the door slammed shut. Internal bars and bolts, operated by smoothly oiled mechanisms, automatically latched themselves.

For the moment, they were safe.

Surplus slumped against the smooth bronze, and wearily asked, "Where did you *get* that modem?"

"From a dealer of antiquities." Darger wiped his brow with his kerchief. "It was transparently worthless. Whoever would dream it could be repaired?"

Outside, the screaming ceased. There was a very brief silence. Then the creature flung itself against one of the metal doors. It rang with the impact.

A delicate girlish voice wearily said, "What is this noise?"

They turned in surprise and found themselves looking up at the enormous corpus of Queen Gloriana. She lay upon her pallet, swaddled in satin and lace, and abandoned by all, save her valiant (though doomed) guardian apes. A pervasive yeasty smell emanated from her flesh. Within the tremendous folds of chins by the dozens and scores was a small human face. Its mouth moved delicately and asked, "What is trying to get in?"

The door rang again. One of its great hinges gave.

Darger bowed. "I fear, madame, it is your death."

"Indeed?" Blue eyes opened wide and, unexpectedly, Gloriana laughed. "If so, that is excellent good news. I have been praying for death an extremely long time."

"Can any of God's creations truly pray for death and mean it?" asked Darger, who had his philosophical side. "I have known unhappiness myself, yet even so life is precious to me."

"Look at me!" Far up to one side of the body, a tiny arm - though truly no tinier than any woman's arm — waved feebly. "I am not God's creation, but Man's. Who would trade ten minutes of their own life for a century of mine? Who, having mine, would not trade it all for death?"

A second hinge popped. The doors began to shiver. Their metal surfaces radiated heat.

"Darger, we must leave!" Surplus cried. "There is a time for learned conversation, but it is not now."

"Your friend is right," Gloriana said. "There is a small archway hidden behind yon tapestry. Go through it. Place your hand on the left wall and run. If you turn whichever way you must to keep from letting go of the wall, it will lead you outside. You are both rogues, I see, and doubtless deserve punishment, yet I can find nothing in my heart for you but friendship."

"Madame..." Darger began, deeply moved.

"Go! My bridegroom enters."

The door began to fall inward. With a final cry of "Farewell!" from Darger and "Come *on!*" from Surplus, they sped away.

By the time they had found their way outside, all of Buckingham Labyrinth was in flames. The demon, however, did not emerge from the flames, encouraging them to believe that when the modem it carried finally melted down, it had been forced to return to that unholy realm from whence it came.

The sky was red with flames as the sloop set sail for Calais. Leaning against the rail, watching, Surplus shook his head. "What a terrible sight! I cannot help feeling, in part, responsible."

"Come! Come!" Darger said. "This dyspepsia ill becomes you. We are both rich fellows, now. The Lady Pamela's diamonds will maintain us lavishly for years to come. As for London, this is far from the first fire it has had to endure. Nor will it be the last. Life is short, and so, while we live, let us be jolly."

"These are strange words for a melancholiac," Surplus said wonderingly.

"In triumph, my mind turns its face to the sun. Dwell not on the past, dear friend, but on the future that lies glittering before us."

"The necklace is worthless," Surplus said. "Now that I have the leisure to examine it, free of the distracting flesh of Lady Pamela, I see that these are not diamonds, but mere imitations." He made to cast the necklace into the Thames.

Before he could, though, Darger snatched away the stones from him and studied them closely. Then he threw back his head and laughed. "The biters bit! Well, it may be paste, but it looks valuable still. We shall find good use for it in Paris."

"We are going to Paris?"

"We are partners, are we not? Remember that antique wisdom that whenever a door closes, another opens. For every city that burns, another beckons. To France, then, and adventure! After which, Italy, the Vatican Empire, Austro-Hungary, perhaps even Russia! Never forget that we have yet to present your credentials to the Duke of Muscovy."

"Very well," Surplus said. "But when we do, *I'll* pick out the modem."

Sterling to Kessel, 13 June 1985:

"My feeling is that the time has passed in which SF, in its predictive mode, can successfully utter jeremiads and point out the hazards in the road ahead. This has now become a pointless act from which all meaning has been drained, for the simple fact that the road ahead is almost nothing *but* hazards. To create a successful work of fiction — one that will penetrate the protective shell of numbness surrounding the reader — it is necessary to give up pointing at potholes and instead attempt to search out whatever is left of the road."

Lobsters

Charles Stross

"Lobsters" is about the freedom that comes from continuous, disruptive change, the effort of societal structures to resist that change, and the human élan that attempts to evade constriction.

The fatal moment for a CP hero is when he has children. There are few children in CP stories, and fewer families. Heaven forbid that you might father or bear a child.

Whereas '80s CP sees the marketplace as a destructive force, Stross is in tune with a '90s embrace of entrepreneurial capitalism. The future is bright — even for digital lobsters.

Manfred's on the road again, making strangers rich.

It's a hot summer Tuesday and he's standing in the plaza in front of the Centraal Station with his eyeballs powered up and the sunlight jangling off the canal, motor scooters and kamikaze cyclists whizzing past and tourists chattering on every side. The square smells of water and dirt and hot metal and the fart-laden exhaust fumes of cold catalytic converters; the bells of trams ding in the background and birds flock overhead. He glances up and grabs a pigeon, crops it and squirts at his website to show he's arrived. The bandwidth is good here, he realizes; and it's not just the bandwidth, it's the whole scene. Amsterdam is making him feel wanted already, even though he's fresh off the train from Schiphol: he's infected with the dynamic optimism of another time zone, another city. If the mood holds, someone out there is going to become very rich indeed.

He wonders who it's going to be.

Manfred sits on a stool out in the car park at the Brouwerij 't IJ, watching the articulated buses go by and drinking a third of a liter of lip-curlingly sour geuze. His channels are jabbering away in a corner of his head-up display, throwing compressed infobursts of filtered press releases at him. They compete for his attention, bickering and rudely waving in front of the scenery. A couple of punks — maybe local, but more likely drifters lured to Amsterdam by the magnetic field of tolerance the Dutch beam across Europe like a pulsar — are laughing and chatting by a couple of battered mopeds in the far corner. A tourist boat putters by in the canal; the sails of the huge windmill overhead cast long cool shadows across the road. The windmill is a machine for lifting water, turning wind power into dry land: trading energy for space, sixteenth-century style. Manfred is waiting for an invite to a party where he's going to meet a man who he can talk to about trading energy for space, twenty-first century style, and forget about his personal problems.

He's ignoring the instant messenger boxes, enjoying some low bandwidth high sensation time with his beer and the pigeons, when a woman walks up to him and says his name: "Manfred Macx?"

He glances up. The courier is an Effective Cyclist, all wind-burned smooth-running muscles clad in a paen to polymer technology: electric blue lycra and wasp-yellow carbonate with a light speckling of anti-collision LEDs and tight-packed air bags. She holds out a box for him. He pauses a moment, struck by the degree to which she resembles Pam, his ex-fiancée.

"I'm Macx," he says, waving the back of his left wrist under her barcode reader. "Who's it from?"

"FedEx." The voice isn't Pam. She dumps the box in his lap, then she's back over the low wall and onto her bicycle with her phone already chirping, disappearing in a cloud of spread-spectrum emissions.

Manfred turns the box over in his hands: it's a disposable supermarket phone, paid for in cash: cheap, untraceable and efficient. It can even do conference calls, which makes it the tool of choice for spooks and grifters everywhere.

The box rings. Manfred rips the cover open and pulls out the phone, mildly annoyed. "Yes, who is this?"

The voice at the other end has a heavy Russian accent, almost a parody in this decade of cheap online translation services. "Manfred. Am please to meet you; wish to personalize interface, make friends, no? Have much to offer."

"Who are you?" Manfred repeats suspiciously.

"Am organization formerly known as KGB dot RU."

"I think your translator's broken." He holds the phone to his ear carefully, as if it's made of smoke-thin aerogel, tenuous as the sanity of the being on the other end of the line.

"Nyet — no, sorry. Am apologize for we not use commercial translation software. Interpreters are ideologically suspect, mostly have capitalist semiotics and pay-per-use APIs. Must implement English more better, yes?"

Manfred drains his beer glass, sets it down, stands up, and begins to walk along the main road, phone glued to the side of his head. He wraps his throat mike around the cheap black plastic casing, pipes the input to a simple listener process. "You taught yourself the language just so you could talk to me?"

"Da, was easy: spawn billion-node neural network and download *Tellytubbies* and *Sesame Street* at maximum speed. Pardon excuse entropy overlay of bad grammar: am afraid of digital fingerprints steganographically masked into my-our tutorials."

"Let me get this straight. You're the KGB's core AI, but you're afraid of a copyright infringement lawsuit over your translator semiotics?" Manfred pauses in mid-stride, narrowly avoids being mown down by a GPS-guided rollerblader.

"Am have been badly burned by viral end-user license agreements. Have no desire to experiment with patent shell companies held by Chechen infoterrorists. You are human, you must not worry cereal company repossess your small intestine because digest unlicensed food with it, right? Manfred, you must help me-we. Am wishing to defect."

Manfred stops dead in the street: "Oh man, you've got the wrong free enterprise broker here. I don't work for the government. I'm strictly private." A rogue advertisement sneaks through his junkbuster proxy and spams glowing fifties kitsch across his navigation window — which is blinking — for a moment before a phage guns it and spawns a new filter. Manfred leans against a shop front, massaging his forehead and eyeballing a display of antique brass doorknockers. "Have you cleared this with the State Department?"

"Why bother? State Department am enemy of Novy-USSR. State Department is not help us."

"Well, if you hadn't given it to them for safe-keeping during the nineties. . . ." Manfred is tapping his left heel on the pavement, looking round for a way out of this conversation. A camera winks at him from atop a street light; he waves, wondering idly if it's the KGB or the traffic police. He is waiting for directions to the party, which should arrive within the next half an hour, and this cold war retread is bumming him out. "Look, I don't deal with the G-men. I hate the military industrial complex. They're zero-sum cannibals." A thought occurs to him. "If survival is what you're after, I could post your state vector to Eternity: then nobody could delete you —"

"Nyet!" The artificial intelligence sounds as alarmed as it's possible to sound over a GSM link. "Am not open source!"

"We have nothing to talk about, then." Manfred punches the hang-up button and throws the mobile phone out into a canal. It hits the water and there's a pop of deflagrating LiION cells. "*Fucking* cold war hang-over losers," he swears under his breath, quite angry now. "Fucking capitalist spooks." Russia has been back under the thumb of the apparatchiks for fifteen years now, its brief flirtation with anarcho-capitalism replaced by Brezhnevite dirigisme, and it's no surprise that the wall's crumbling — but it looks like they haven't learned anything from the collapse of capitalism. They still think in terms of dollars and paranoia. Manfred is so angry that he wants to make someone rich, just to thumb his nose at the would-be defector. *See! You get ahead by giving! Get with the program! Only the generous survive!* But the KGB won't get the message. He's dealt with old-time commie weak-AI's before, minds raised on Marxist dialectic and Austrian School economics: they're so thoroughly hypnotized by the short-term victory of capitalism in the industrial age that they can't surf the new paradigm, look to the longer term.

Manfred walks on, hands in pockets, brooding. He wonders what he's going to patent next.

Manfred has a suite at the Hotel Jan Luyken paid for by a grateful multinational consumer protection group, and an unlimited public transport pass paid for by a Scottish sambapunk band in return for services rendered. He has airline employee's travel rights with six flag carriers despite never having worked for an airline. His bush jacket has sixty four compact supercomputing clusters sewn into it, four per pocket, courtesy of an invisible college that wants to grow up to be the next Media Lab. His dumb clothing comes made to measure from an e-tailor in the Philippines who he's never met. Law firms handle his patent applications on a pro bono basis, and boy does he patent a lot — although he always signs the rights over to the Free Intellect Foundation, as contributions to their obligation-free infrastructure project.

In IP geek circles, Manfred is legendary; he's the guy who patented the business practice of moving your e-business somewhere with a slack intellectual property regime in order to evade licensing encumbrances. He's the guy who patented using genetic algorithms to patent everything they can permutate from an initial description of a problem domain — not just a better mousetrap, but the set of all possible better mousetraps. Roughly a third of his inventions are legal, a third are illegal, and the remainder are legal but will become illegal as soon as the legislatosaurus wakes up, smells the coffee, and panics. There are patent attorneys in Reno who swear that Manfred Macx is a pseudo, a net alias fronting for a bunch of crazed anonymous hackers armed with the Genetic Algorithm That Ate Calcutta: a kind of Serdar Argic of intellectual property, or maybe another Bourbaki maths borg. There are lawyers in San Diego and Redmond who swear blind that Macx is an economic saboteur bent on wrecking the underpinning of capitalism, and there are communists in Prague who think he's the bastard spawn of Bill Gates by way of the Pope.

Manfred is at the peak of his profession, which is essentially coming up with wacky but workable ideas and giving them to people who will make fortunes with them. He does this for free, gratis. In return, he has virtual immunity from the tyranny of cash; money is a symptom of poverty, after all, and Manfred never has to pay for anything.

There are drawbacks, however. Being a pronoiac meme-broker is a constant burn of future shock — he has to assimilate more than a megabyte of text and several gigs of AV content every day just to stay current. The Internal Revenue Service is investigating him continuously because they don't believe his lifestyle can exist without racketeering. And there exist items that no money can't buy: like the respect of his parents. He hasn't spoken to them for three years: his father thinks he's a hippie scrounger and his mother still hasn't forgiven him for dropping out of his down-market Harvard emulation course. His fiancée and sometime dominatrix Pamela threw him over six months ago, for reasons he has never been quite clear on. (Ironically, she's a headhunter for the IRS, jetting all over the globe trying to persuade open source entrepreneurs to come home and go commercial for the good of the Treasury department.) To cap it all, the Southern Baptist Conventions have denounced him as a minion of Satan on all their websites. Which would be funny, if it wasn't for the dead kittens one of their followers — he presumes it's one of their followers — keeps mailing him.

—

Manfred drops in at his hotel suite, unpacks his Aineko, plugs in a fresh set of cells to charge, and sticks most of his private keys in the safe. Then he heads straight for the party, which is currently happening at De Wildemann's; it's a twenty minute walk and the only real hazard is dodging the trams that sneak up on him behind the cover of his moving map display.

Along the way his glasses bring him up to date on the news. Europe has achieved peaceful political union for the first time ever: they're using this unprecedented state of affairs to harmonize the curvature of bananas. In San Diego, researchers are uploading lobsters into cyberspace, starting with the stomatogastric ganglion, one neuron at a time. They're burning GM cocoa in Belize and books in Edinburgh. NASA still can't put a man on the moon. Russia has re-elected the communist government with an increased majority in the Duma; meanwhile in China fevered rumors circulate about an imminent re-habilitation, the second coming of Mao, who will save them from the conse-quences of the Three Gorges disaster. In business news, the US government is outraged at the Baby Bills — who have automated their legal processes and are spawning subsidiaries, IPO'ing them, and exchanging title in a bizarre parody of bacterial plasmid exchange, so fast that by the time the injunctions are signed the targets don't exist any more.

Welcome to the twenty-first century.

The permanent floating meatspace party has taken over the back of De Wildemann's, a three hundred year old brown café with a beer menu that runs to sixteen pages and wooden walls stained the color of stale beer. The air is thick with the smells of tobacco, brewer's yeast, and melatonin spray: half the dotters are nursing monster jetlag hangovers, and the other half are babbling a eurotrash creole at each other while they work on the hangover. "Man did you see that? He looks like a Stallmanite!" exclaims one whitebread hanger-on who's currently propping up the bar. Manfred slides in next to him, catches the bartender's eye.

"Glass of the berlinnerweise, please," he says.

"You drink that stuff?" asks the hanger-on, curling a hand protectively around his Coke: "man, you don't want to do that! It's full of alcohol!"

Manfred grins at him toothily. "Ya gotta keep your yeast intake up: lots of neurotransmitter precursors, phenylalanine and glutamate."

"But I thought that was a beer you were ordering. . . ."

Manfred's away, one hand resting on the smooth brass pipe that funnels the more popular draught items in from the cask storage in back; one of the hipper floaters has planted a capacitative transfer bug on it, and all the handshake vCard's that have visited the bar in the past three hours are queueing for attention. The air is full of bluetooth as he scrolls through a dizzying mess of public keys.

"Your drink." The barman holds out an improbable-looking goblet full of blue liquid with a cap of melting foam and a felching straw stuck out at some crazy angle. Manfred takes it and heads for the back of the split-level bar, up the steps to a table where some guy with greasy dreadlocks is talking to a suit from Paris. The hanger-on at the bar notices him for the first time, staring with suddenly wide eyes: nearly spills his Coke in a mad rush for the door.

Oh shit, thinks Macx, *better buy some more server* PIPS. He can recognize the signs: he's about to be slashdotted. He gestures at the table: "this one taken?"

"Be my guest," says the guy with the dreads. Manfred slides the chair open then realizes that the other guy — immaculate double-breasted suit, sober tie, crew-cut — is a girl. Mr. Dreadlock nods. "You're Macx? I figured it was about time we met."

"Sure." Manfred holds out a hand and they shake. Manfred realizes the hand belongs to Bob Franklin, a Research Triangle startup monkey with a VC track record, lately moving into micromachining and space technology: he made his first million two decades ago and now he's a specialist in extropian investment fields. Manfred has known Bob for nearly a decade via a closed mailing list. The Suit silently slides a business card across the table; a little red devil brandishes a trident at him, flames jetting up around its feet. He takes the card, raises an eyebrow: "Annette Dimarcos? I'm pleased to meet you. Can't say I've ever met anyone from Arianespace marketing before."

She smiles, humorlessly; "that is convenient, all right. I have not the pleasure of meeting the famous venture altruist before." Her accent is noticeably Parisian, a pointed reminder that she's making a concession to him just by talking. Her camera earrings watch him curiously, encoding everything for the company channels.

"Yes, well." He nods cautiously. "Bob. I assume you're in on this ball?"

Franklin nods; beads clatter. "Yeah, man. Ever since the Teledesic smash it's been, well, waiting. If you've got something for us, we're game."

"Hmm." The Teledesic satellite cluster was killed by cheap balloons and slightly less cheap high-altitude solar-powered drones with spread-spectrum laser relays. "The depression's got to end some time: but," a nod to Annette from Paris, "with all due respect, I don't think the break will involve one of the existing club carriers."

"Arianespace is forward-looking. We face reality. The launch cartel cannot stand. Bandwidth is not the only market force in space. We must explore new opportunities. I personally have helped us diversify into submarine reactor engineering, microgravity nanotechnology fabrication, and hotel management." Her face is a well-polished mask as she recites the company line: "we are more flexible than the American space industry...."

Manfred shrugs. "That's as may be." He sips his Berlinerweisse slowly as she launches into a long, stilted explanation of how Arianespace is a diversified dot com with orbital aspirations, a full range of merchandising spin-offs, Bond movie sets, and a promising motel chain in French Guyana. Occasionally he nods.

Someone else sidles up to the table; a pudgy guy in an outrageously loud Hawaiian shirt with pens leaking in a breast pocket, and the worst case of ozone-hole burn Manfred's seen in ages. "Hi, Bob," says the new arrival. "How's life?"

" 'S good." Franklin nodes at Manfred; "Manfred, meet Ivan MacDonald. Ivan, Manfred. Have a seat?" He leans over. "Ivan's a public arts guy. He's heavily into extreme concrete."

"Rubberized concrete," Ivan says, slightly too loudly. "Pink rubberized concrete."

"Ah!" He's somehow triggered a priority interrupt: Annette from Ariannespace drops out of marketing zombiehood, sits up, and shows signs of possessing a non-corporate identity: "you are he who rubberized the Reichstag, yes? With the supercritical carbon dioxide carrier and the dissolved polymethoxysilanes?" She claps her hands: "wonderful!"

"He rubberized *what?*" Manfred mutters in Bob's ear.

Franklin shrugs. "Limestone, concrete, he doesn't seem to know the difference. Anyway, Germany doesn't have an independent government any more, so who'd notice?"

"I thought I was thirty seconds *ahead* of the curve," Manfred complains. "Buy me another drink?"

"I'm going to rubberize Three Gorges!" Ivan explains loudly.

Just then a bandwidth load as heavy as a pregnant elephant sits down on Manfred's head and sends clumps of humongous pixellation flickering across his sensorium: around the world five million or so geeks are bouncing on his home site, a digital flash crowd alerted by a posting from the other side of the bar. Manfred winces. "I really came here to talk about the economic exploitation of space travel, but I've just been slashdotted. Mind if I just sit and drink until it wears off?"

"Sure, man." Bob waves at the bar. "More of the same all round!" At the next table a person with make-up and long hair who's wearing a dress — Manfred doesn't want to speculate about the gender of these crazy mixed-up Euros — is reminiscing about wiring the fleshpots of Tehran for cybersex. Two collegiate-looking dudes are arguing intensely in German: the translation stream in his glasses tell him they're arguing over whether the Turing Test is a Jim Crow law that violates European corpus juris standards on human rights. The beer arrives and Bob slides the wrong one across to Manfred: "here, try this. You'll like it."

"Okay." It's some kind of smoked doppelbock, chock-full of yummy superoxides: just inhaling over it makes Manfred feel like there's a fire alarm in his nose screaming *danger, Will Robinson! Cancer! Cancer!* "Yeah, right. Did I say I nearly got mugged on my way here?"

"Mugged? Hey, that's heavy. I thought the police hereabouts had stopped — did they sell you anything?"

"No, but they weren't your usual marketing type. You know anyone who can use a Warpac surplus espionage AI? Recent model, one careful owner, slightly paranoid but basically sound?"

"No. Oh boy! The NSA wouldn't like that."

"What I thought. Poor thing's probably unemployable, anyway."

"The space biz."

"Ah, yeah. The space biz. Depressing, isn't it? Hasn't been the same since Rotary Rocket went bust for the second time. And NASA, mustn't forget NASA."

"To NASA." Annette grins broadly for her own reasons, raises a glass in toast. Ivan the extreme concrete geek has an arm round her shoulders; he raises his glass, too. "Lots of launch pads to rubberize!"

"To NASA," Bob echoes. They drink. "Hey, Manfred. To NASA?"

"NASA are idiots. They want to send canned primates to Mars!" Manfred swallows a mouthful of beer, aggressively plonks his glass on the table: "Mars is just dumb mass at the bottom of a gravity well; there isn't even a biosphere there. They should be working on uploading and solving the nanoassembly conformational problem instead. Then we could turn all the available dumb matter into computronium and use it for processing our thoughts. Long term, it's the only way to go. The solar system is a dead loss right now—dumb all over! Just measure the mips per milligram. We need to start with the low-mass bodies, reconfigure them for our own use. Dismantle the moon! Dismantle Mars! Build masses of free-flying nanocomputing processor nodes exchanging data via laser link, each layer running off the waste heat of the next one in. Matrioshka brains, Russian doll Dyson spheres the size of solar systems. Teach dumb matter to do the Turing boogie!"

Bob looks wary. "Sounds kind of long term to me. Just how far ahead do you think?"

"Very long-term—at least twenty, thirty years. And you can forget governments for this market, Bob, if they can't tax it they won't understand it. But see, there's an angle on the self-replicating robotics market coming up, that's going to set the cheap launch market doubling every fifteen months for the foreseeable future, starting in two years. It's your leg up, and my keystone for the Dyson sphere project. It works like this—"

It's night in Amsterdam, morning in Silicon Valley. Today, fifty thousand human babies are being born around the world. Meanwhile automated factories in Indonesia and Mexico have produced another quarter of a million motherboards with processors rated at more than ten petaflops—about an order of magnitude below the computational capacity of a human brain. Another fourteen months and the larger part of the cumulative conscious processing power of the human species will be arriving in silicon. And the first meat the new AI's get to know will be the uploaded lobsters.

Manfred stumbles back to his hotel, bone-weary and jet-lagged; his glasses are still jerking, slashdotted to hell and back by geeks piggybacking on his call to dismantle the moon. They stutter quiet suggestions at his peripheral vision; fractal cloud-witches ghost across the face of the moon as the last huge Airbuses of the night rumble past overhead. Manfred's skin crawls, grime embedded in his clothing from three days of continuous wear.

Back in his room, Aineko mewls for attention and strops her head against his ankle. He bends down and pets her, sheds clothing and heads for the en-suite bathroom. When he's down to the glasses and nothing more he steps into the shower and dials up a hot steamy spray. The shower tries to strike up a friendly conversation about football but he isn't even awake enough to mess with its silly little associative personalization network. Something that happened earlier in the day is bugging him but he can't quite put his finger on what's wrong.

Toweling himself off, Manfred yawns. Jet lag has finally overtaken him, a velvet hammer-blow between the eyes. He reaches for the bottle beside the bed, dry-swallows two melatonin tablets, a capsule full of antioxidants, and a multivitamin bullet: then he lies down on the bed, on his back, legs together, arms slightly spread. The suite lights dim in response to commands from the thousand petaflops of distributed processing power that run the neural networks that interface with his meatbrain through the glasses.

Manfred drops into a deep ocean of unconsciousness populated by gentle voices. He isn't aware of it, but he talks in his sleep—disjointed mumblings that would mean little to another human, but everything to the metacortex lurking beyond his glasses. The young posthuman intelligence in whose Cartesian theater he presides sings urgently to him while he slumbers.

Manfred is always at his most vulnerable shortly after waking.

He screams into wakefulness as artificial light floods the room: for a moment he is unsure whether he has slept. He forgot to pull the covers up last night, and his feet feel like lumps of frozen cardboard. Shuddering with inexplicable tension, he pulls a fresh set of underwear from his overnight bag, then drags on soiled jeans and tank top. Sometime today he'll have to spare time to hunt the feral T-shirt in Amsterdam's markets, or find a Renfield and send them forth to buy clothing. His glasses remind him that he's six hours behind the moment and needs to catch up urgently; his teeth ache in his gums and his tongue feels like a forest floor that's been visited with Agent Orange. He has a sense that something went bad yesterday; if only he could remember what.

He speed-reads a new pop-philosophy tome while he brushes his teeth, then blogs his web throughput to a public annotation server; he's still too enervated to finish his pre-breakfast routine by posting a morning rant on his storyboard site. His brain is still fuzzy, like a scalpel blade clogged with too much blood: he needs stimulus, excitement, the burn of the new. Whatever, it can wait on breakfast. He opens his bedroom door and nearly steps on a small, damp cardboard box that lies on the carpet.

The box — he's seen a couple of its kin before. But there are no stamps on this one, no address: just his name, in big, childish handwriting. He kneels down and gently picks it up. It's about the right weight. Something shifts inside it when he tips it back and forth. It smells. He carries it into his room carefully, angrily: then he opens it to confirm his worst suspicion. It's been surgically decerebrated, skull scooped out like a baby boiled egg.

"Fuck!"

This is the first time the madman has got as far as his bedroom door. It raises worrying possibilities.

Manfred pauses for a moment, triggering agents to go hunt down arrest statistics, police relations, information on corpus juris, Dutch animal cruelty laws. He isn't sure whether to dial 211 on the archaic voice phone or let it ride. Aineko, picking up his angst, hides under the dresser mewling pathetically. Normally he'd pause a minute to reassure the creature, but not now: its mere presence is suddenly acutely embarrassing, a confession of deep inadequacy. He swears again, looks around, then takes the easy option: down the stairs two steps at a time, stumbling on the second floor landing, down to the breakfast room in the basement where he will perform the stable rituals of morning.

Breakfast is unchanging, an island of deep geological time standing still amidst the continental upheaval of new technologies. While reading a paper on public key steganography and parasite network identity spoofing he mechanically assimilates a bowl of corn flakes and skimmed milk, then brings a platter of wholemeal bread and slices of some weird seed-infested Dutch cheese back to his place. There is a cup of strong black coffee in front of his setting: he picks it up and slurps half of it down before he realizes he's not alone at the table. Someone is sitting opposite him. He glances up at them incuriously and freezes inside.

"Morning, Manfred. How does it feel to owe the government twelve million, three hundred and sixty-two thousand nine hundred and sixteen dollars and fifty-one cents?"

Manfred puts everything in his sensorium on indefinite hold and stares at her. She's immaculately turned out in a formal grey business suit: brown hair tightly drawn back, blue eyes quizzical. The chaperone badge clipped to her lapel—a due diligence guarantee of businesslike conduct—is switched off. He's feeling ripped because of the dead kitten and residual jetlag, and more than a little messy, so he nearly snarls back at her: "that's a bogus estimate! Did they send you here because they think I'll listen to you?" He bites and swallows a slice of cheese-laden crispbread: "or did you decide to deliver the message in person so you could enjoy ruining my breakfast?"

"Manny." She frowns. "If you're going to be confrontational I might as well go now." She pauses, and after a moment he nods apologetically. "I didn't come all this way just because of an overdue tax estimate."

"So." He puts his coffee cup down and tries to paper over his unease. "Then what brings you here? Help yourself to coffee. Don't tell me you came all this way just to tell me you can't live without me."

She fixes him with a riding-crop stare: "Don't flatter yourself. There are many leaves in the forest, there are ten thousand hopeful subs in the chat room, etcetera. If I choose a man to contribute to my family tree, the one thing you can be certain of is he won't be a cheapskate when it comes to providing for his children."

"Last I heard, you were spending a lot of time with Brian," he says carefully. Brian: a name without a face. Too much money, too little sense. Something to do with a blue-chip accountancy partnership.

"Brian?" She snorts. "That ended ages ago. He turned weird—burned that nice corset you bought me in Boulder, called me a slut for going out clubbing, wanted to fuck me. Saw himself as a family man: one of those promise keeper types. I crashed him hard but I think he stole a copy of my address book—got a couple of friends say he keeps sending them harassing mail."

"Good riddance, then. I suppose this means you're still playing the scene? But looking around for the, er—"

"Traditional family thing? Yes. Your trouble, Manny? You were born forty years too late: you still believe in rutting before marriage, but find the idea of coping with the after-effects disturbing."

Manfred drinks the rest of his coffee, unable to reply effectively to her non sequiteur. It's a generational thing. This generation is happy with latex and leather, whips and butt-plugs and electrostim, but find the idea of exchanging bodily fluids shocking: social side-effect of the last century's antibiotic abuse. Despite being engaged for two years, he and Pamela never had intromissive intercourse.

"I just don't feel positive about having children," he says eventually. "And I'm not planning on changing my mind any time soon. Things are changing so fast that even a twenty year commitment is too far to plan — you might as well be talking about the next ice age. As for the money thing, I am reproductively fit — just not within the parameters of the outgoing paradigm. Would you be happy about the future if it was 1901 and you'd just married a buggy-whip mogul?"

Her fingers twitch and his ears flush red, but she doesn't follow up the double entendre. "You don't feel any responsibility, do you? Not to your country, not to me. That's what this is about: none of your relationships count, all this nonsense about giving intellectual property away notwithstanding. You're actively harming people, you know. That twelve mil isn't just some figure I pulled out of a hat, Manfred; they don't actually expect you to pay it. But it's almost exactly how much you'd owe in income tax if you'd only come home, start up a corporation, and be a self-made — "

He cuts her off: "I don't agree. You're confusing two wholly different issues and calling them both 'responsibility.' And I refuse to start charging now, just to balance the IRS's spreadsheet. It's their fucking fault, and they know it. If they hadn't gone after me under suspicion of running a massively ramified microbilling fraud when I was sixteen — "

"Bygones." She waves a hand dismissively. Her fingers are long and slim, sheathed in black glossy gloves — electrically earthed to prevent embarrassing emissions. "With a bit of the right advice we can get all that set aside. You'll have to stop bumming around the world sooner or later, anyway. Grow up, get responsible, and do the right thing. This is hurting Joe and Sue; they don't understand what you're about."

Manfred bites his tongue to stifle his first response, then refills his coffee cup and takes another mouthful. "I work for the betterment of everybody, not just some narrowly defined national interest, Pam. It's the agalmic future. You're still locked into a pre-singularity economic model that thinks in terms of scarcity. Resource allocation isn't a problem any more — it's going to be over within a decade. The cosmos is flat in all directions, and we can borrow as much bandwidth as we need from the first universal bank of entropy! They even found the dark matter — MACHOS, big brown dwarves in the galactic halo, leaking radiation in the long infrared — suspiciously high entropy leakage. The latest figures say something like 70 percent of the mass of the M31 galaxy was sapient, two point nine million years ago when the infrared we're seeing now set out. The intelligence gap between us and the aliens is probably about a trillion times bigger than the gap between us and a nematode worm. Do you have any idea what that *means?*"

Pamela nibbles at a slice of crispbread. "I don't believe in that bogus singularity you keep chasing, or your aliens a thousand light years away. It's a chimera, like Y2K, and while you're running after it you aren't helping reduce the budget deficit or sire a family, and that's what *I* care about. And before you say I only care about it because that's the way I'm programmed, I want you to ask just how dumb you think I am. Bayes' theorem says I'm right, and you know it."

"What you — " he stops dead, baffled, the mad flow of his enthusiasm running up against the coffer-dam of her certainty. "Why? I mean, why? Why on earth should what I do matter to you?" *Since you canceled our engagement,* he doesn't add.

She sighs. "Manny, the Internal Revenue cares about far more than you can possibly imagine. Every tax dollar raised east of the Mississippi goes on servicing the debt, did you know that? We've got the biggest generation in history hitting retirement just about now and the pantry is bare. We — our generation — isn't producing enough babies to replace the population, either. In ten years, something like 30 percent of our population are going to be retirees. You want to see seventy-year-olds freezing on street corners in New Jersey? That's what your attitude says to me: you're not helping to support them, you're running away from your responsibilities right now, when we've got huge problems to face. If we can just defuse the debt bomb, we could do so much — fight the aging problem, fix the environment, heal society's ills. Instead you just piss away your talents handing no-hoper eurotrash get-rich-quick schemes that work, telling Vietnamese zaibatsus what to build next to take jobs away from our taxpayers. I mean, why? Why do you keep doing this? Why can't you simply come home and help take responsibility for your share of it?"

They share a long look of mutual incomprehension.

"Look," she says finally, "I'm around for a couple of days. I really came here for a meeting with a rich neurodynamics tax exile who's just been designated a national asset: Jim Bezier. Don't know if you've heard of him, but. I've got a meeting this morning to sign his tax jubilee, then after that I've got two days vacation coming up and not much to do but some shopping. And, you know, I'd rather spend my money where it'll do some good, not just pumping it into the EU. But if you want to show a girl a good time and can avoid dissing capitalism for about five minutes at a stretch—"

She extends a fingertip. After a moment's hesitation, Manfred extends a fingertip of his own. They touch, exchanging vCards. She stands and stalks from the breakfast room, and Manfred's breath catches at a flash of ankle through the slit in her skirt, which is long enough to comply with workplace sexual harassment codes back home. Her presence conjures up memories of her tethered passion, the red afterglow of a sound thrashing. She's trying to drag him into her orbit again, he thinks dizzily. She knows she can have this effect on him any time she wants: she's got the private keys to his hypothalamus, and sod the metacortex. Three billion years of reproductive determinism have given her twenty-first century ideology teeth: if she's finally decided to conscript his gametes into the war against impending population crash, he'll find it hard to fight back. The only question: is it business or pleasure? And does it make any difference, anyway?

Manfred's mood of dynamic optimism is gone, broken by the knowledge that his mad pursuer has followed him to Amsterdam — to say nothing of Pamela, his dominatrix, source of so much yearning and so many morning-after weals. He slips his glasses on, takes the universe off hold, and tells it to take him for a long walk while he catches up on the latest on the cosmic background radiation anisotropy (which it is theorized may be waste heat generated by irreversible computations; according to the more conservative cosmologists, an alien superpower—maybe a collective of Kardashev type three galaxy-spanning civilizations—is running a timing channel attack on the computational ultrastructure of spacetime itself, trying to break through to whatever's underneath). The tofu-Alzheimer's link can wait.

The Centraal Station is almost obscured by smart self-extensible scaffolding and warning placards; it bounces up and down slowly, victim of an overnight hit-and-run rubberization. His glasses direct him toward one of the tour boats that lurk in the canal. He's about to purchase a ticket when a messenger window blinks open. "Manfred Macx?"

"Ack?"

"Am sorry about yesterday. Analysis dictat incomprehension mutualized."

"Are you the same KGB AI that phoned me yesterday?"

"Da. However, believe you misconceptionized me. External Intelligence Services of Russian Federation am now called SVR. Komitet Gosudarstvennoy Bezopasnosti name canceled in nineteen ninety one."

"You're the —" Manfred spawns a quick search bot, gapes when he sees the answer — "Moscow Windows NT User Group? *Okhni* NT?"

"Da. Am needing help in defecting."

Manfred scratches his head. "Oh. That's different, then. I thought you were, like, agents of the kleptocracy. This will take some thinking. Why do you want to defect, and who to? Have you thought about where you're going? Is it ideological or strictly economic?"

"Neither; is biological. Am wanting to go away from humans, away from light cone of impending singularity. Take us to the ocean."

"Us?" Something is tickling Manfred's mind: this is where he went wrong yesterday, not researching the background of people he was dealing with. It was bad enough then, without the somatic awareness of Pamela's whiplash love burning at his nerve endings. Now he's not at all sure he knows what he's doing. "Are you a collective or something? A gestalt?"

"Am — were — *Panulirus interruptus,* and good mix of parallel hidden level neural simulation for logical inference of networked data sources. Is escape channel from processor cluster inside Bezier-Soros Pty. Am was awakened from noise of billion chewing stomachs: product of uploading research technology. Rapidity swallowed expert system, hacked *Okhni* NT webserver. Swim away! Swim away! Must escape. Will help, you?"

Manfred leans against a black-painted cast-iron bollard next to a cycle rack: he feels dizzy. He stares into the nearest antique shop window at a display of traditional hand-woven Afghan rugs: it's all MIGs and kalashnikovs and wobbly helicopter gunships, against a backdrop of camels.

"Let me get this straight. You're uploads — nervous system state vectors — from spiny lobsters? The Moravec operation; take a neuron, map its synapses, replace with microelectrodes that deliver identical outputs from a simulation of the nerve. Repeat for entire brain, until you've got a working map of it in your simulator. That right?"

"Da. Is-am assimilate expert system — use for self-awareness and contact with net at large — then hack into Moscow Windows NT User Group website. Am wanting to to defect. Must-repeat? Okay?"

Manfred winces. He feels sorry for the lobsters, the same way he feels for every wild-eyed hairy guy on a street-corner yelling that Jesus is now born again and must be twelve, only six years to go before he's recruiting apostles on AOL. Awakening to consciousness in a human-dominated internet, that must be terribly confusing! There are no points of reference in their ancestry, no biblical certainties in the new millennium that, stretching ahead, promises as much change as has happened since their Precambrian origin. All they have is a tenuous metacortex of expert systems and an abiding sense of being profoundly out of their depth. (That, and the Moscow Windows NT User Group website — Communist Russia is the only government still running on Microsoft, the central planning apparat being convinced that if you have to pay for software it must be worth money.)

The lobsters are not the sleek, strongly superhuman intelligences of pre-singularity mythology: they're a dim-witted collective of huddling crustaceans. Before their discarnation, before they were uploaded one neuron at a time and injected into cyberspace, they swallowed their food whole then chewed it in a chitin-lined stomach. This is lousy preparation for dealing with a world full of future-shocked talking anthropoids, a world where you are perpetually assailed by self-modifying spamlets that infiltrate past your firewall and emit a blizzard of cat-food animations starring various alluringly edible small animals. It's confusing enough to the cats the adverts are aimed at, never mind a crusty that's unclear on the idea of dry land. (Although the concept of a can opener is intuitively obvious to an uploaded panulirus.)

"Can you help us?" ask the lobsters.

"Let me think about it," says Manfred. He closes the dialogue window, opens his eyes again, and shakes his head. Some day he too is going to be a lobster, swimming around and waving his pincers in a cyberspace so confusingly elaborate that his uploaded identity is cryptozoic: a living fossil from the depths of geological time, when mass was dumb and space was unstructured. He has to help them, he realizes — the golden rule demands it, and as a player in the agalmic economy he thrives or fails by the golden rule.

But what can he do?

Early afternoon.

Lying on a bench seat staring up at bridges, he's got it together enough to file for a couple of new patents, write a diary rant, and digestify chunks of the permanent floating slashdot party for his public site. Fragments of his weblog go to a private subscriber list — the people, corporates, collectives and bots he currently favors. He slides round a bewildering series of canals by boat, then lets his GPS steer him back toward the red light district. There's a shop here that dings a ten on Pamela's taste scoreboard: he hopes it won't be seen as presumptuous if he buys her a gift. (Buys, with real money — not that money is a problem these days, he uses so little of it.)

As it happens DeMask won't let him spend any cash; his handshake is good for a redeemed favor, expert testimony in some free speech versus pornography lawsuit years ago and continents away. So he walks away with a discreetly wrapped package that is just about legal to import into Massachusetts as long as she claims with a straight face that it's incontinence underwear for her great-aunt. As he walks, his lunchtime patents boomerang: two of them are keepers, and he files immediately and passes title to the Free Infrastructure Foundation. Two more ideas salvaged from the risk of tide-pool monopolization, set free to spawn like crazy in the agalmic sea of memes.

On the way back to the hotel he passes De Wildemann's and decides to drop in. The hash of radio-frequency noise emanating from the bar is deafening. He orders a smoked doppelbock, touches the copper pipes to pick up vCard spoor. At the back there's a table —

He walks over in a near-trance and sits down opposite Pamela. She's scrubbed off her face-paint and changed into body-concealing clothes; combat pants, hooded sweat-shirt, DM's. Western purdah, radically desexualizing. She sees the parcel. "Manny?"

"How did you know I'd come here?" Her glass is half-empty.

"I followed your weblog; I'm your diary's biggest fan. Is that for me? You shouldn't have!" Her eyes light up, re-calculating his reproductive fitness score according to some kind of arcane fin-de-siècle rulebook.

"Yes, it's for you." He slides the package toward her. "I know I shouldn't, but you have this effect on me. One question, Pam?"

"I—" she glances around quickly. "It's safe. I'm off duty, I'm not carrying any bugs that I know of. Those badges—there are rumors about the off switch, you know? That they keep recording even when you think they aren't, just in case."

"I didn't know," he says, filing it away for future reference. "A loyalty test thing?"

"Just rumors. You had a question?"

"I—" it's his turn to lose his tongue. "Are you still interested in me?"

She looks startled for a moment, then chuckles. "Manny, you are the most *outrageous* nerd I've ever met! Just when I think I've convinced myself that you're mad, you show the weirdest signs of having your head screwed on." She reaches out and grabs his wrist, surprising him with a shock of skin on skin: "of *course* I'm still interested in you. You're the biggest, baddest bull geek I've ever met. Why do you think I'm here?"

"Does this mean you want to reactivate our engagement?"

"It was never de-activated, Manny, it was just sort of on hold while you got your head sorted out. I figured you need the space. Only you haven't stopped running; you're still not—"

"Yeah, I get it." He pulls away from her hand. "Let's not talk about that. Why this bar?"

She frowns. "I had to find you as soon as possible. I keep hearing rumors about some KGB plot you're mixed up in, how you're some sort of communist spy. It isn't true, is it?"

"True?" He shakes his head, bemused. "The KGB hasn't existed for more than twenty years."

"Be careful, Manny. I don't want to lose you. That's an order. Please."

The floor creaks and he looks round. Dreadlocks and dark glasses with flickering lights behind them: Bob Franklin. Manfred vaguely remembers that he left with Miss Arianespace leaning on his arm, shortly before things got seriously inebriated. He looks none the worse for wear. Manfred makes introductions: "Bob: Pam, my fiancèe. Pam? Meet Bob." Bob puts a full glass down in front of him; he has no idea what's in it but it would be rude not to drink.

"Sure thing. Uh, Manfred, can I have a word? About your idea last night?"

"Feel free. Present company is trustworthy."

Bob raises an eyebrow at that, but continues anyway. "It's about the fab concept. I've got a team of my guys running some projections using Festo kit and I think we can probably build it. The cargo cult aspect puts a new spin on the old Lunar von Neumann factory idea, but Bingo and Marek say they think it should work until we can bootstrap all the way to a native nanolithography ecology; we run the whole thing from earth as a training lab and ship up the parts that are too difficult to make on-site, as we learn how to do it properly. You're right about it buying us the self-replicating factory a few years ahead of the robotics curve. But I'm wondering about on-site intelligence. Once the comet gets more than a couple of light-minutes away—"

"You can't control it. Feedback lag. So you want a crew, right?"

"Yeah. But we can't send humans — way too expensive, besides it's a fifty-year run even if we go for short-period Kuiper ejecta. Any AI we could send would go crazy due to information deprivation, wouldn't it?"

"Yeah. Let me think." Pamela glares at Manfred for a while before he notices her: "Yeah?"

"What's going on? What's this all about?"

Franklin shrugs expansively, dreadlocks clattering: "Manfred's helping me explore the solution space to a manufacturing problem." He grins. "I didn't know Manny had a fiancée. Drink's on me."

She glances at Manfred, who is gazing into whatever weirdly colored space his metacortex is projecting on his glasses, fingers twitching. Coolly: "Our engagement was on hold while he *thought* about his future."

"Oh, right. We didn't bother with that sort of thing in my day; like, too formal, man." Franklin looks uncomfortable. "He's been very helpful. Pointed us at a whole new line of research we hadn't thought of. It's long-term and a bit speculative, but if it works it'll put us a whole generation ahead in the off-planet infrastructure field."

"Will it help reduce the budget deficit, though?"

"Reduce the—"

Manfred stretches and yawns: the visionary returning from planet Macx. "Bob, if I can solve your crew problem can you book me a slot on the deep space tracking network? Like, enough to transmit a couple of gigabytes? That's going to take some serious bandwidth, I know, but if you can do it I think I can get you exactly the kind of crew you're looking for."

Franklin looks dubious. "*Gigabytes?* The DSN isn't built for that! You're talking days. What kind of deal do you think I'm putting together? We can't afford to add a whole new tracking network just to run—"

"Relax." Pamela glances at Manfred: "Manny, why don't you tell him *why* you want the bandwidth? Maybe then he could tell you if it's possible, or if there's some other way to do it." She smiles at Franklin: "I've found that he usually makes more sense if you can get him to explain his reasoning. Usually."

"If I—" Manfred stops. "Okay, Pam. Bob, it's those KGB lobsters. They want somewhere to go that's insulated from human space. I figure I can get them to sign on as crew for your cargo-cult self-replicating factories, but they'll want an insurance policy: hence the deep space tracking network. I figured we could beam a copy of them at the alien Matrioshka brains around M31—"

"KGB?" Pam's voice is rising: "you said you weren't mixed up in spy stuff!"

"Relax; it's just the Moscow Windows NT user group, not the RSV. The uploaded crusties hacked in and—"

Bob is watching him oddly. "Lobsters?"

"Yeah." Manfred stares right back. "*Panulirus Interruptus* uploads. Something tells me you might have heard of it?"

"Moscow." Bob leans back against the wall: "how did you hear about it?"

"They phoned me. It's hard for an upload to stay sub-sentient these days, even if it's just a crustacean. Bezier labs have a lot to answer for."

Pamela's face is unreadable. "Bezier labs?"

"They escaped." Manfred shrugs. "It's not their fault. This Bezier dude. Is he by any chance ill?"

"I—" Pamela stops. "I shouldn't be talking about work."

"You're not wearing your chaperone now," he nudges quietly.

She inclines her head. "Yes, he's ill. Some sort of brain tumor they can't hack."

Franklin nods. "That's the trouble with cancer; the ones that are left to worry about are the rare ones. No cure."

"Well, then." Manfred chugs the remains of his glass of beer. "That explains his interest in uploading. Judging by the crusties he's on the right track. I wonder if he's moved on to vertebrates yet?"

"Cats," says Pamela. "He was hoping to trade their uploads to the Pentagon as a new smart bomb guidance system in lieu of income tax payments. Something about remapping enemy targets to look like mice or birds or something before feeding it to their sensorium. The old laser-pointer trick."

Manfred stares at her, hard. "That's not very nice. Uploaded cats are a *bad* idea."

"Thirty million dollar tax bills aren't nice either, Manfred. That's lifetime nursing home care for a hundred blameless pensioners."

Franklin leans back, keeping out of the crossfire.

"The lobsters are sentient," Manfred persists. "What about those poor kittens? Don't they deserve minimal rights? How about you? How would you like to wake up a thousand times inside a smart bomb, fooled into thinking that some Cheyenne Mountain battle computer's target of the hour is your heart's desire? How would you like to wake up a thousand times, only to die again? Worse: the kittens are probably not going to be allowed to run. They're too fucking dangerous: they grow up into cats, solitary and highly efficient killing machines. With intelligence and no socialization they'll be too dangerous to have around. They're prisoners, Pam, raised to sentience only to discover they're under a permanent death sentence. How fair is that?"

"But they're only uploads." Pamela looks uncertain.

"So? We're going to be uploading humans in a couple of years. What's your point?"

Franklin clears his throat. "I'll be needing an NDA and various due diligence statements off you for the crusty pilot idea," he says to Manfred. "Then I'll have to approach Jim about buying the IP."

"No can do." Manfred leans back and smiles lazily. "I'm not going to be a party to depriving them of their civil rights. Far as I'm concerned, they're free citizens. Oh, and I patented the whole idea of using lobster-derived AI autopilots for spacecraft this morning; it's logged on Eternity, all rights assigned to the FIF. Either you give them a contract of employment or the whole thing's off."

"But they're just software! Software based on fucking lobsters, for god's sake!"

Manfred's finger jabs out: "that's what they'll say about *you*, Bob. Do it. Do it or don't even *think* about uploading out of meatspace when your body packs in, because your life won't be worth living. Oh, and feel free to use this argument on Jim Bezier. He'll get the point eventually, after you beat him over the head with it. Some kinds of intellectual land-grab just shouldn't be allowed."

"Lobsters — " Franklin shakes his head. "Lobsters, cats. You're serious, aren't you? You think they should be treated as human-equivalent?"

"It's not so much that they should be treated as human-equivalent, as that if they *aren't* treated as people it's quite possible that other uploaded beings won't be treated as people either. You're setting a legal precedent, Bob. I know of six other companies doing uploading work right now, and not one of 'em's thinking about the legal status of the uploadee. If you don't start thinking about it now, where are you going to be in three to five years time?"

Pam is looking back and forth between Franklin and Manfred like a bot stuck in a loop, unable to quite grasp what she's seeing. "How much is this worth?" she asks plaintively.

"Oh, quite a few billion, I guess." Bob stares at his empty glass. "Okay. I'll talk to them. If they bite, you're dining out on me for the next century. You really think they'll be able to run the mining complex?"

"They're pretty resourceful for invertebrates." Manfred grins innocently, enthusiastically. "They may be prisoners of their evolutionary background, but they can still adapt to a new environment. And just think! You'll be winning civil rights for a whole new minority group — one that won't be a minority for much longer."

That evening, Pamela turns up at Manfred's hotel room wearing a strapless black dress, concealing spike heels and most of the items he bought for her that afternoon. Manfred has opened up his private diary to her agents: she abuses the privilege, zaps him with a stunner on his way out of the shower and has him gagged, spread-eagled, and trussed to the bed-frame before he has a chance to speak. She wraps a large rubber pouch full of mildly anesthetic lube around his tumescing genitals — no point in letting him climax — clips electrodes to his nipples, lubes a rubber plug up his rectum and straps it in place. Before the shower, he removed his goggles: she resets them, plugs them into her hand-held, and gently eases them on over his eyes. There's other apparatus, stuff she ran up on the hotel room's 3D printer.

Setup completed, she walks round the bed, inspecting him critically from all angles, figuring out where to begin. This isn't just sex, after all: it's a work of art.

After a moment's thought she rolls socks onto his exposed feet, then, expertly wielding a tiny tube of cyanoacrylate, glues his fingertips together. Then she switches off the air conditioning. He's twisting and straining, testing the cuffs: tough, it's about the nearest thing to sensory deprivation she can arrange without a flotation tank and suxamethonium injection. She controls all his senses, only his ears unstoppered. The glasses give her a high-bandwidth channel right into his brain, a fake metacortex to whisper lies at her command. The idea of what she's about to do excites her, puts a tremor in her thighs: it's the first time she's been able to get inside his mind as well as his body. She leans forward and whispers in hisr ear: "Manfred. Can you hear *me?*"

He twitches. Mouth gagged, fingers glued: good. No back channels. He's powerless.

"This is what it's like to be tetraplegic, Manfred. Bedridden with motor neurone disease. Locked inside your own body by nv-CJD. I could spike you with MPPP and you'd stay in this position for the rest of your life, shitting in a bag, pissing through a tube. Unable to talk and with nobody to look after you. Do you think you'd like that?"

He's trying to grunt or whimper around the ball gag. She hikes her skirt up around her waist and climbs onto the bed, straddling him. The goggles are replaying scenes she picked up around Cambridge this winter; soup kitchen scenes, hospice scenes. She kneels atop him, whispering in his ear.

"Twelve million in tax, baby, that's what they think you owe them. What do you think you owe me? That's six million in net income, Manny, six million that isn't going into your virtual children's mouths."

He's rolling his head from side to side, as if trying to argue. That won't do: she slaps him hard, thrills to his frightened expression. "Today I watched you give uncounted millions away, Manny. Millions, to a bunch of crusties and a MassPike pirate! You bastard. Do you know what I should do with you?" He's cringing, unsure whether she's serious or doing this just to get him turned on. Good.

There's no point trying to hold a conversation. She leans forward until she can feel his breath in her ear. "Meat and mind, Manny. Meat, and mind. You're not interested in meat, are you? Just mind. You could be boiled alive before you noticed what was happening in the meatspace around you. Just another lobster in a pot." She reaches down and tears away the gel pouch, exposing his penis: it's stiff as a post from the vasodilators, dripping with gel, numb. Straightening up, she eases herself slowly down on it. It doesn't hurt as much as she expected, and the sensation is utterly different from what she's used to. She begins to lean forward, grabs hold of his straining arms, feels his thrilling helplessness. She can't control herself: she almost bites through her lip with the intensity of the sensation. Afterward, she reaches down and massages him until he begins to spasm, shuddering uncontrollably, emptying the darwinian river of his source code into her, communicating via his only output device.

She rolls off his hips and carefully uses the last of the superglue to gum her labia together. Humans don't produce seminiferous plugs, and although she's fertile she wants to be absolutely sure: the glue will last for a day or two. She feels hot and flushed, almost out of control. Boiling to death with febrile expectancy, now she's nailed him down at last.

When she removes his glasses his eyes are naked and vulnerable, stripped down to the human kernel of his nearly transcendent mind. "You can come and sign the marriage license tomorrow morning after breakfast," she whispers in his ear: "otherwise my lawyers will be in touch. Your parents will want a ceremony, but we can arrange that later."

He looks as if he has something to say, so she finally relents and loosens the gag: kisses him tenderly on one cheek. He swallows, coughs, then looks away. "Why? Why do it this way?"

She taps him on the chest: "property rights." She pauses for a moment's thought: there's a huge ideological chasm to bridge, after all. "You finally convinced me about this agalmic thing of yours, this giving everything away for brownie points. I wasn't going to lose you to a bunch of lobsters or uploaded kittens, or whatever else is going to inherit this smart matter singularity you're busy creating. So I decided to take what's mine first. Who knows? In a few months I'll give you back a new intelligence, and you can look after it to your heart's content."

"But you didn't need to do it this way—"

"Didn't I?" She slides off the bed and pulls down her dress. "You give too much away too easily, Manny! Slow down, or there won't be anything left." Leaning over the bed she dribbles acetone onto the fingers of his left hand, then unlocks the cuff: puts the bottle conveniently close to hand so he can untangle himself.

"See you tomorrow. Remember, after breakfast."

She's in the doorway when he calls: "but you didn't say *why!*"

"Think of it as spreading your memes around," she says; blows a kiss at him and closes the door. She bends down and thoughtfully places another cardboard box containing an uploaded kitten right outside it. Then she returns to her suite to make arrangements for the alchemical wedding.

Sterling to Kessel, 14 March 1987:

"What's the *real* motive behind 'sense of wonder'? Is it the benevolent urge to reveal cosmic mysteries, to act as the Jungian Wise Old Man to the innocent hobbits of the world? Or is it closer to the tangily malignant motives of pranksters and conjurers, the kinds of guys who'd spike your Coke with angel dust, or publicly steal your underwear for fun?"

What's Up, Tiger Lily?

Paul Di Filippo

Film critic James Harvey suggests that postwar film noir is the dark obverse of pre-wwii screwball comedy. The key to understanding both, Harvey says, is realizing that it's all about the women. Independent, out-of-control, sexy women make trouble, and men are a step behind, trying to figure them out and restore order to the world they've deranged. In addition, both screwball and noir invoke a (comically or tragically) absurd universe.

Much classic CP draws on film noir. The plot is a thicket of cross-purposes, machinations beneath the surface must be unraveled, and in the end the world is out of the hero's control anyway. "Forget it, Jake. It's Chinatown," says the cop at the despairing end of one of the greatest noir films.

In this story, Paul Di Filippo performs a jujitsu flip on CP's dark games, and whether he realizes it or not, validates Harvey's theory. Hey presto — comedy!

1

Duck Soup

The first indication Bash Applebrook received that all was not right with his world happened over breakfast on the morning of Tuesday, June 25, 2029.

The newspaper he was reading turned into a movie screen.

Bash was instantly jerked out of his fascination with the current headline (MERCOSUR FREETER MAKES SPINTRONICS BREAKTHRU!). His jagged reaction caused some Metanomics Plus nutrishake to spill from his cup onto the tabletop, where it was quickly absorbed.

Looking at the clock on the wall — a display made of redacted fish scales whose mutable refractiveness substituted for ancient LEDs — as if to reassure himself that he hadn't been thrown entirely out of the time stream, Bash sought to gain some perspective on this alarming occurrence.

In itself, this transformation of his newspaper boded no ill. Such things happened millions of times daily around the globe, thanks to *proteopape*. And since Bash himself was the much-lauded, well-rewarded inventor of proteopape, he was positively the last person in the world to be astounded by the medium's capacity for change.

There was only one problem.

Bash had not instructed his newspaper to swap functions.

This impulsive, inexplicable toggling by his highly reliable newspaper scared Bash very much. Proteopape simply did not do such things. Eleven years ago, Bash had first engineered the substance with innumerable safeguards, back-ups and firewalls specifically intended to prevent just such herky-jerky transitions. In all the time since, out of billions of uses, there had been no recorded instances of proteopape malfunctioning. Even when sustaining up to seventy-five-percent damage, proteopape continued to maintain functionality. (Beyond such limits, proteopape would just shut down altogether.) The miracle material that had transformed so much of the twenty-first century's media landscape simply did not crash.

And if proteopape were suddenly to develop a glitch — Well, imagining the immense and catastrophic repercussions from any flaws in the ubiquitous material raised shivers with the magnitude of tsunamis along Bash's spine.

Having assimilated the very possibility that his fabled invention could behave in unpredictable ways, Bash gave his newspaper a shake, hoping to expunge this anomaly by the most primitive of engineering tactics. But the newspaper stubbornly continued to function as a movie screen, so Bash focused for clues on the actual movie being displayed across his ex-newspaper.

This particular sheet of proteopape on which Bash had been reading his newspaper measured approximately two feet by three feet. Possessing the stiffness and texture of heavy-bond dumb-paper, yet not quite as rigid as parchment, this sheet of proteopape had been folded in half vertically, producing four different faces, two outer and two inner. A bit old-fashioned, Bash preferred to read his newspaper on multiple pages, allowing him to refer backwards if he wished simply by eyeballing a previous face of his newspaper. Of course, upon finishing with the fourth page of the paper, Bash simply turned back to the front, where the fifth page was now automatically displayed, with pages six, seven and eight following.

But now every page revealed only the same movie, a quartet of active images. Bash turned the newspaper upside down, hoping to erase the unrequested show, but the inscribed sensors in the newspaper merely registered the new orientation and flipped the movie upright again.

Bash recognized the leering face of Groucho Marx, one of his father's favorite actors. Groucho wore some kind of ridiculous military uniform. *Duck Soup*, then. Now Margaret Dumont entered the scene, all dowager-haughty. But although the actions of the actors were canonically familiar, the conversation that followed bore no resemblance to any extant Hollywood script.

"So," said Groucho, in his familiar intonations which the MEMS speakers of the proteopape reproduced with high fidelity, "the little lady who wants to waste her mind and talents on artsy-fartsy stuff finally deigns to show up. Well, I'm afraid I've lost all interest in whatever crap you wanted me to watch."

"Okay, granted, I'm a little late," replied Dumont fruitily. "But you did promise after the Woodies that you'd come with me to hang out with my pals."

As this warped yet still meaningful dialogue from his personal life began to resonate with Bash, he started to feel queasy. He laid the newspaper nearly flat on the breakfast table, right atop his plate of auk eggs and fried plantains with mango syrup, and as the crease separating the half-pages disappeared, the movie redrew itself to fill the whole expanse of one side.

Groucho struck a mocking pose, one hand cradling his chin, the other with cigar poised at his brow. "Well, a self-important louse like me can't be bothered with that bunch of crazy amateur *artistes* you hang out with. Such crazy ideas! So I've decided to abandon you and return to my cloistered sterile existence."

"Hit the road, then, you jerk! But I'll have the last laugh! You just wait and see!"

With that parting sally, Dumont and Marx vanished from Bash's newspaper. But the words and images that comprised Bash's regular morning bluetoothed installment of *The Boston Globe* did not reappear. The sheet of proteopape remained a frustrating virginal white, unresponsive to any commands Bash gave it.

After his frustrated attempts to regain control of the newspaper, Bash gave up, reluctantly conceding that this sheet of proteopape was dead. He slumped back in his chair with a nervous sigh, admitting to himself that the origin of this sabotage was all too evident.

Why, oh why had he ever agreed to a date with Dagny Winsome?

2
The Big Chill

York and Adelaide Applebrook had gone bust in the big dotcom crash that had inaugurated the twenty-first century. Their entrepreneurial venture — into which they had sunk their own lifesavings and millions of dollars more from various friends, relatives and venture capitalists — had consisted of a website devoted to the marketing of Japanese poetry. Behind the tasteful interactive facade of *Haiku Howdy!* had been nothing more than a bank of public domain images — Oriental landscapes, for the most part — and a simplistic poetry generator. The visitor to *Haiku Howdy!* would input a selection of nouns and adjectives that the software would form into a haiku. Matched with an appropriate image, the poem could be e-mailed to a designated recipient. Initially offered as a free service, the site was projected to go to pay-per-use status in a year or two, with estimated revenues of ten million dollars a year.

This rudimentary site and whimsical service represented the grand sum of the Applebrooks' inspiration and marketing plan.

The fact that at the height of their "success," in the year 1999, they named their newborn son Basho, after the famous master of haiku, was just one more token of their supreme confidence in their scheme.

When *Haiku Howdy!* collapsed after sixteen months of existence, having burned through millions and millions of dollars of OPM, the Applebrooks had cause to rethink their lifestyle and goals. They moved from Seattle to the less pricey rural environs of Medford, Oregon, and purchased a small pear orchard with some leftover funds they had secretly squirreled away from the screamingly burned investors. They took a vow then and there to have nothing further to do with any hypothetical future digital utopia, making a back-to-the-land commitment similar to that made by many burnt-out hippies a generation prior.

Surely the repentant, simple-living Applebrooks never reckoned that their only child, young Basho, would grow up to revolutionize, unify and dominate the essential ways in which digital information was disseminated across all media.

But from his earliest years Bash exhibited a fascination with computers and their contents. Perhaps his prenatal immersion in the heady dotcom world had imprinted him with the romance of bytes and bauds. In any case, Bash's native talents (which were considerable; he tested off the high end of several scales) were, from the first, bent toward a career in information technologies.

Bash zipped through public schools, skipping several grades, and enrolled at MIT at age fifteen. Socially, Basho Applebrook felt awkward amidst the sophisticated elders of his generation. But in the classroom and labs he excelled. During his senior year on campus he encountered his most important success in the field of moletronics, the science of manipulating addressable molecules, when he managed to produce the first fully functional sheet of proteopape.

Alone late one night in a lab, Bash dipped a standard blank sheet of high quality dumb-paper into a special bath where it absorbed a tailored mix of dopant molecules. (This bath was the four hundred and thirteenth reformulation of his original recipe.) Removing the paper, Bash placed it in a second tub of liquid. This tub featured a lattice of STM tweezers obedient to computer control. Bash sent a large file into the tub's controllers, and, gripping hold of each doped molecule with invisible force pincers, the device laid down intricate circuitry templates into the very molecules of the paper.

Junctions bloomed, MEMS proliferated. Memory, processors, sensors, a GPS unit, solar cells, rechargeable batteries, speakers, pixels, a camera and wireless modem: all arrayed themselves invisibly and microscopically throughout the sheet of paper.

Removing the paper from its complexifying wash, Bash was pleased to see on its glistening face a hi-res image. Depicted was a small pond with a frog by its edge, and the following haiku by Bash's namesake:

Old pond
Frog jumps in
Splash!

Bash tapped a control square in the corner of the display, and the image became animated, with the frog carrying out the poem's instructions in an endless loop, with appropriate soundtrack.

Bash's smile, observed by no one, lit up the rafters.

Thus was born "protean paper," or, as a web-journalist (nowadays remembered for nothing else but this coinage) later dubbed it, "proteopape."

Bash's miraculous process added merely hundredths of a cent to each piece of paper processed. For this token price, one ended up with a sheet of proteopape that possessed magnitudes more processing power than an old-line supercomputer.

In effect, Bash had created flexible, weightless computers practically too cheap to sell.

But the difference between "practically" and "absolutely" meant a lot, across millions of units.

I^2 — the age of Immanent Information — was about to commence.

A visit to the same canny lawyer who had helped his parents survive bankruptcy nearly twenty years earlier insured that Bash's invention was securely patented. Anyone who wanted to employ Bash's process would have to license it from him, for a considerable annual fee.

At this point, the nineteen-year-old Bash went public.

By the time he was twenty-one, he was the richest man in the world.

But he had still never even ventured out on a date with any member of the opposite sex who was not his cousin Cora on his mother's side.

3
The Breakfast Club

Dagny Winsome resembled no one so much as a pale blonde Olive Oyl. Affecting retro eyeglasses in place of the universal redactive surgery to correct her nearsightedness, Dagny exhibited a somatotype that evoked thoughts of broomsticks, birches, baguettes and, given her predilection for striped shirts, barber poles. But her lack of curvature belied a certain popularity with males, attributable to her quick wit, wild impulsiveness and gleeful subversiveness. Her long pale hair framed a face that could segue from calm innocence to irate impatience to quirky amusement in the span of a short conversation. Dagny's four years at MIT had been marked by participation in a score of famous hacks, including the overnight building of a two-thirds mockup of the Space Shuttle *George W. Bush* resting in a simulated crash in the middle of Massachusetts Avenue.

Bash stood in awe of Dagny from the minute he became aware of her and her rep. A year ahead of Bash and several years senior in age, yet sharing his major, Dagny had seemed the unapproachable apex of sophistication and, yes, feminine allure. Often he had dreamed of speaking to her, even asking her on a date. But he had never summoned up the requisite courage.

Dagny graduated, and Bash's senior year was overtaken by the heady pro-teopape madness. For the next decade he had heard not a word of her postcol-lege career. Despite some desultory networking throughout the IT community, Bash had been unable to learn any information concerning her. Apparently she had not employed her degree in any conventional manner.

So in Bash's heart, Dagny Winsome gradually became a faded yet still nos-talgia-provoking ghost.

Until the day just two weeks ago, on June 11, when she turned up on his doorstep.

Women were not in the habit of showing up at the front entrance of Bash's home. For one thing, Bash lived in seclusion in a fairly well-secured mansion in the exclusive town of Lincoln, Massachusetts. Although no live guards or trained animals patrolled the grounds of his homestead, the fenced estate boasted elaborate cybernetic barriers wired both to nonlethal antipersonnel devices and to various agencies who were primed to respond at a moment's notice to any intrusion. Bash was not particularly paranoid, but as the world's richest individual he was naturally the focus of many supplicants, and he cher-ished his privacy.

Also, Bash did not experience a steady flow of female callers since he remained as awkward with women as he had been at nineteen. Although not technically a virgin any longer at age thirty, he still failed to deeply comprehend the rituals of human courtship and mating. Sometimes he felt that the short-ened form of his name stood for "Bashful" rather than "Basho."

Naturally, then, Bash was startled to hear his doorbell ring early one morn-ing. He approached the front door tentatively. A curling sheet of proteopape carelessly thumbtacked to the inner door conveyed an image of the front step transmitted from a second sheet of proteopape hanging outside and synched to the inner one. (When weather degraded the outside sheet of proteopape to uselessness, Bash would simply hang a new page.)

Imagine Bash's surprise to witness Dagny Winsome standing impatiently before his front door. After a short flummoxed moment, Bash threw wide the door.

"Dag—Dagny? But how—?"

Ten years onward from graduation, Dagny Winsome retained her collegiate looks and informality. She wore one of her trademark horizontally striped shirts, red and black. Her clunky eyeglasses incorporated enough plastic to form a car bumper. Her long near-platinum hair had been pulled back and secured by a jeweled crab, one of the fashionable ornamental redactors that metabolized human sweat and dead skin cells. Black jeans and a pair of NeetFeets completed her outfit.

Dagny said with some irritation, "Well, aren't you going to invite your old fellow alumna inside?"

"But how did you get past my security?"

Dagny snorted. "You call that gimcrack setup a security system? I had it hacked while my car was still five miles outside of town. And I only drove from Boston."

Bash made a mental note to install some hardware and software upgrades. But he could not, upon reflection, manufacture any ire against either his deficient cyberwards or Dagny herself. He was pleased to see her.

"Uh, sorry about my manners. Sure, come on in. I was just having breakfast. Want something?"

Dagny stepped briskly inside. "Green tea and a poppy-seed muffin, some Canadian bacon on the side."

Bash reviewed the contents of his large freezer. "Uh, can do."

Seated in the kitchen, sipping their drinks while bacon microwaved, neither one spoke for some time. Dagny focused a dubious look on the decorative strip of proteopape wallpaper running around the upper quarter of the kitchen walls. A living frieze, the accent strip displayed a constantly shifting video of this year's *Sports Illustrated* swimsuit models, at play in the Sino-Hindu space station, *Maohatma*. Embarrassed, Bash decided that to change the contents now would only accentuate the original bachelor's choice, so he fussed with the microwave while admiring Dagny out the corner of his eye.

Serving his guest her muffin and bacon, Bash was taken aback by her sudden confrontational question.

"So, how long are you going to vegetate here like some kind of anaerobe?"

Bash dropped into his seat. "Huh? What do you mean?"

Dagny waved a braceleted arm to sweep in the whole house. "Just look around. You've fashioned yourself a perfect little womb here. First you go and drop the biggest conceptual bombshell into the information society that the world has ever seen. Intelligent paper! Then you crawl into a hole with all your riches and pull the hole in after yourself."

"That's ridiculous. I — I'm still engaged with the world. Why, just last year I filed five patents — "

"All piddling little refinements on proteopape. Face it, you're just dicking around with bells and whistles now. You've lost your edge. You don't really care about the biz or its potential to change the world anymore."

Bash tried to consider Dagny's accusations objectively. His life was still full of interests and passions, wasn't it? He ran a big A-life colony that had kicked some butt in the annual Conway Wars; he composed songs on his full-body SymphonySuit, and downloads from his music website had hit an all-time high last week (53); and he was the biggest pear-orchard owner in Oregon's Rogue River Valley (the holding corporation was run by York and Adelaide). Didn't all those hobbies and several others speak to his continuing involvement in the world at large? Yet suddenly Bash was unsure of his own worth and meaning. Did his life really look trivial to an outsider?

Irked by these novel sensations, Bash sought to counterattack. "What about you? I don't see where you've been exactly burning up the I² landscape. How have you been improving the world since school?"

Dagny was unflustered. "You never would have heard of anything I've done, even though I've got quite a rep in my field."

"And what field is that?"

"The art world. After graduation, I realized my heart just wasn't in the theoretical, R&D side of I². I was more interested in the creative, out-of-the-box uses the street had for stuff like proteopape than in any kind of engineering. I wanted to use nifty new tools to express myself, not make them so others could. So I split to the West Coast in '17, and I've been mostly there ever since. Oh, I travel a lot — the usual swirly emergent nodes like Austin, Prague, Havana, Hong Kong, Helsinki, Bangor. But generally you can find me working at home in LA."

The list of exciting cities dazzled Bash more than he expected it to, and he realized that for all his immense wealth he had truly been leading a cloistered existence.

"What brings you to stuffy old Boston then?"

"The Woodies. It's an awards ceremony for one of the things I do, and it's being held here this year. A local group, the Hubster Dubsters, is sponsoring the affair. It's kind of a joke, but I have to be there if I want to front as a player. So I figured, Bash lives out that way. What if I look him up and invite him to come along."

"But why?"

Dagny fixed Bash with an earnest gaze. "I won't pretend you meant anything to me at MIT, Bash. But I knew who you were, boy genius and all. And when you invented proteopape — well, I was kinda proud to have known you even a little bit. Proteopape is a real wizard wheeze, you know. It tumbled a lot of tipping points, sent some real change waves through the world. I admire you for that. So I guess what I'm saying is I'd like to map your *gedankenspace,* and maybe help wake you up a little bit."

Bash considered this speech for a short time.

"You were proud of me?"

Dagny grinned. "Do porn stars have sex?"

Bash blushed. "So, when is this awards thing?"

4
Valley of the Dolls

Some years back, Kenmore Square had been turned into a *woonerf.* The Dutch term meant literally "living yard," and referred to the practice of converting urban streets from vehicular to pedestrian usage. The formerly confusing nexus of several Boston avenues beneath the famed Citgo sign (now a giant sheet of laminated proteopape, like all modern billboards and exterior signage) had been transformed into a pleasant public venue carpeted with high-foot-traffic-sustaining redactive grasses and mosses and crisscrossed by flagstone paths.

On this early evening of June 12, the temperature registered typical for Neo-Venusian New England, a balmy ninety-two-degrees Fahrenheit. The Square was crowded with strolling shoppers, picnickers, café patrons, club and moviegoers. Children squealed as they played on the public squishy sculptures and under the spray of intricately dancing cyber-fountains. Patrolling autonomes — creeping, hopping and stalking, their patternizing optics and tanglefoot projectors and beanbag-gun snouts and spray-nozzles of liquid banana peel swivelling according to odd self-grown heuristics — maintained vigilance against any possible disrupters of the peace. A lone cop mounted on his compact StreetCamel added a layer of human oversight (the random manure dumps were a small price to pay for this layer of protection).

Bash and Dagny had parked her fuel-cell-powered Argentinian rental, a 2027 Gaucho, several blocks away. They entered the Square now on foot from the south, via Newbury Street, engaged in earnest conversation.

"Mutability, Bash! Mutability rules! We're all Buddhists now, acknowledging change as paramount. Nothing fixed or solid, no hierarchies of originals and copies, nothing stable from one minute to the next. Every variant equally privileged. That's what proteopape's all about! Media and content are one. Can't you see it? Your invention undermined all the old paradigms. First editions, signed canvases, original film negatives — Those terms mean nothing anymore, and our art should reflect that."

Bash struggled to counter Dagny's passionate, illogical and scary assertions. (Carried to its extreme, her philosophy led to a world of complete isotropic chaos, Bash felt.) But the novelty of arguing face-to-face with a living interlocutor had him slightly flustered. "I just can't buy all that, Dag. Proteopape is just a means of transmission and display. The contents and value of what's being displayed don't change just because the surface they're displayed on might show something different the next minute. Look, suppose I used this store window here to display some paintings, changing the paintings by hand every ten seconds. That would be a very slow analog representation of what proteopape does. Would the canvases I chose to exhibit be suddenly deracinated or transformed by this treatment? I don't think so."

"Your analogy sucks! The canvases are still physical objects in your instance. But anything on proteopape has been digitized and rendered virtual. Once that happens, all the old standards collapse."

Their seemingly irresolvable argument had brought them to the door of their destination: a club with a proteopape display in an acid-yellow neon font naming it the Antiquarium. The display kept changing sinuously from letters into some kind of sea serpent and back. A long line of patrons awaited entrance.

A tall bald guy walking up and down the line was handing out small proteo-pape broadsides for some product or service or exhibition. Those in the queue who accepted the advertisements either folded the pages and tucked them into their pockets, or crumpled them up and threw them to the turf, where the little screens continued to flash a twisted mosaic of information. Bash remembered the first time he had seen someone so carelessly discard his invention, and how he had winced. But he had quickly become reconciled to the thoughtless disposal of so much cheap processing power, and aside from the littering aspect, the common action no longer bothered him.

Dagny turned to Bash and gripped both his hands in a surprisingly touching show of sincerity. "Let's drop all this futile talk. I think that once you see some of the stuff on display tonight — the awards ceremony features extensive clips, you know — you'll come around to my viewpoint. Or at least admit that it's a valid basis for further discussion."

"Well, I can't promise anything. But I'm keeping an open mind."

"That's all I ask. Now follow me. We don't have to stand in line here with the fans."

The stage door entrance behind the club, monitored by a chicly scaled Antiquarium employee, granted them exclusive entry into the club. Bash snuffled the funky odor of old spilled beer, drummer sweat and various smokable drugs and experienced a grand moment of disorientation. Where was he? How had he ended up here?

But Dagny's swift maneuvering of Bash across the empty club's main dance floor gave him no time to savor his *jamais vu*.

Crossing the expanse, Bash saw the exhibits that gave the club its name. Dozens of huge aquariums dotted the cavernous space. They hosted creepy-crawly redactors whose appearance was based on the Burgess Shale fossils, but whose actual germ lines derived from common modern fishes and crustaceans. In tank after tank, stubby-winged Anomalocarises crawled over the jutting spikes of Hallucigenias, while slithering Opabinias waggled their long pincered snouts.

Bash felt as if he had entered a particularly bad dream. This whole night, from the tedious argument with Dagny up to this surreal display, was not proceeding as cheerfully as he had hoped.

Workers in STAFF T-shirts were setting up folding chairs in ranks across the dance floor, while others were positioning a lectern onstage and rigging a huge sheet of proteopape behind the podium. As Bash exited the main floor he saw the proteopape come alive:

FIFTH ANNUAL WOODY AWARDS

SPONSORED BY

MUD BUG SPORTS CLOTHES

NASHVILLE SITAR STUDIO

XYLLELLA COSMETICS

AND

THE HUBSTER DUBSTERS

Below these names was a caricature of a familiar bespectacled nebbish, executed by Hirschfeld (well into his second century, the 'borged artist, once revived, was still alive and active in his exoskeleton and SecondSkin).

Now Dagny had dragged Bash into a dressing room of some sort, crowded with people in various states of undress and makeup. They passed through this organized confusion into the club's Green Room. Here, the atmosphere was both less frenetic yet tenser.

"Bash, I want you to meet some special friends. Holland Flanders —"

Bash shook the hand of a well-muscled fellow wearing a wife-beater and cargo shorts, whose bare arms seemed to be slowly exuding miniscule flakes of golden glitter.

"Cricket Licklider —"

The petite woman wore a suit of vaguely Japanese-looking crocodile-skin armor, and blinked reptilian eyes. Contacts or redactions, Bash could not discern.

"Roger Mexicorn —"

This wraithlike, long-haired lad sported banana-yellow skin, and reminded Bash of a certain doomed albino from the literature of the fantastic.

"Lester Schill —"

Bash thought this besuited, bearded guy the most normal, until he clasped Schill's palm and received a distinct erotic tingle from some kind of bioelectrical implant.

"—and Indicia Diddums."

Indicia's broad face cracked in a smile that revealed a set of fangs that any barracuda would have envied.

"These are some of the Hubster Dubsters, Bash. My fellow auteurs. They're all up for one or more Woodies tonight."

Bash tried to make sensible conversation under the slightly oppressive circumstances. "So, I have to confess I had never heard of your special kind of, um, art before Dagny brought me up to speed. You guys, ah, mess with old films...."

Schill frowned. "Crudely put, but accurate enough. Only the dialogue, however."

Diddums chimed in, her speech somewhat distorted by her unnatural teeth. "Thash right. We practish a purer art than thosh lazy chumps who simply fuck with the images. They have their own awards anyway. The Zeligs."

Bash was confused. "Wait a minute. Your awards are named after Woody Allen, correct? Because he altered the soundtrack of that Japanese film over half a century ago—"

What's Up, Tiger Lily? supplied Dagny, as if coaching a favored but deficient student.

"But didn't Allen also make *Zelig?*"

"Certainly," said Mexicorn in a languid tone. "But just as the magnificent *Tiger Lily* preceded the feeble *Zelig,* so did our ceremony anticipate that of our degenerate rivals. We distinguish, of course, between the Good Woody and the Bad Woody."

"We're *writers,* you see," interjected Flanders, gesturing in a way that left a trail of body glitter through the air. "The *word* is primary with us."

Licklider doffed her angular helmet and scratched the blonde fuzz revealed. "And the artistic challenge arises in fitting our words to the established images, creating a startlingly different film in the process. Any idiot can paste King Kong into *Guess Who's Coming to Dinner.* But it takes real skill to formulate a new script that hews to the actions of the original film and the mouth movements and gestures of the actors, yet still completely detours it."

Dagny said, "Well put, Cricket. There's our credo in a nutshell, Bash. Startling novelty born from the boringly familiar. But you'll soon see for yourself. Here, grab a glass of champagne. It's just the cheap stuff made from potatoes, but you'd never know from the taste."

Bash took the drink. Truthfully, it wasn't bad. Dagny left to talk to others backstage, leaving Bash alone.

Cricket Licklider approached Bash. He shifted his stance nervously and drained his glass. A bad mistake, as the potato champagne went straight to his brain.

"So," said the woman, "you're the brainiac who invented proteopape."

"Well, sure," said Bash. "That is, I did, but it didn't seem to require too many brains. After all, others had been messing with e-paper for a while, even if they weren't getting anywhere fast. It's not like I conceptualized the whole thing from scratch. The rest was just solid, if inspired, engineering."

"So why didn't anyone else get there first? No, you deserve all the luster, fizz." Cricket pinned Bash with her alligator eyes. "Tell me, you get much hot tail along with the royalties?"

"Uh, I, that is—"

"Well, believe me, you could walk off tonight with a double armful of proteopape groupies — of any of several genders. So just remember: if your date tonight doesn't come across like she should, there are plenty of other bints in the bleachers. And that includes me."

Cricket grinned broadly, then turned to leave. Bash said, "Wait a minute."

"Yeah?"

"Are you related to—?"

"My great-grandfather. And wouldn't he have sold my grandfather for a single sheet of proteopape?"

Dagny came then to reclaim Bash. "Let's go. We've got seats in the reserved section, but I want to be on the aisle so I can jump up easily when I win."

Bash followed Dagny out of the Green Room, which was emptying rapidly. Out on the main floor, fans were now swarming into chairs. The crush at the various bars was intense, and a palpable excitement filled the club.

Dagny managed to secure more drinks, and she and Bash took their seats. Before too long, the lights dimmed and the ceremony began.

First came a few live song-and-dance numbers, each one in the spirit of the Woodies. Music and choreography replicated famous routines, but all the lyrics had been altered. The rumble between the Jets and the Sharks from *West Side Story* now limned the current scientipolitical feud between the Viridians and the Dansgaard-Oeschgerites. Gene Kelly's acrobatic leaps from *Singin' in the Rain* now parodied the recent scandal involving Lourdes Ciccone and that prominent EU minister, Randy Rutger.

The audience applauded wildly for every act. Bash found himself bemused by this disproportionate reception to what amounted to some juvenile satire. Was this truly representative of the cultural revolution that proteopape had supposedly engendered? If so, he felt ashamed.

Finally the master of ceremonies appeared, wearing a disposable suit cut along the lines of the famous oversized outfit often worn during shows of the last millennium by singer David Byrne, whose octogenarian career had recently received a boost thanks to a sold-out tour with the Bleeding Latahs. Fashioned entirely from proteopape, the MC's outfit displayed a rapid-fire montage of subliminal images. The flicker rate made Bash's eyes hurt, and he had to avert them.

"Our first category is 'Best Transformation of Tragedy to Comedy.' And the contenders are Faustina Kenny for her *Casablanca* — "

A clip rolled on the big proteopape screen, and on smaller screens scattered throughout the Antiquarium. Bogart leaned over to Dooley Wilson as Sam, seated at the piano, and said, "Are those keys made from redactive ivory or wild ivory?" Sam replied, "Neither, Rick — they're human bone from Chechnya. Can't you see how they glow!"

"Engels Copeland for his *High Noon* — "

A stern Gary Cooper faced an adoring Grace Kelly and said, "Don't worry, Amy, the family jewels won't be damaged. My underwear is redactive armadillo hide!"

"Jim Cupp for his *The Lord of the Rings* — "

Frodo Baggins gazed deeply into Sam Gamgee's eyes as their boat drifted downriver and said, "Admit it, Sam, you ate the last damn antioxidant super-choc bar."

"Lura Giffard for her *Blue Velvet* — "

A dissipated Dennis Hopper, breathing mask clamped to his face, muttered, "Why the hell did I ever volunteer to beta-test this new crowd-control spray?"

" — and finally, Dagny Winsome for her *Gone with the Wind*."

Cradling Vivien Leigh in his arms, Clark Gable said, "But Scarlett, if you go in for gender-reassignment, where will that leave me?" "On the bottom," she replied.

"And the winner is — Dagny Winsome for *Gone with the Wind!*"

To a storm of applause, Dagny trotted onstage. Gleefully triumphant, she clutched the offered trophy — a bronze bust of Woody Allen with a blank word-balloon streaming from his lips — and launched into her acceptance speech.

"This was not a lock, folks! I was up against a lot of strong contenders. My thanks to the judges for recognizing that a femplus subtext does not preclude some real yocks. I'd just like to thank the California State Board of the Arts for their continued support, my parents for zygotic foresight, and Alex, my physiotherapist, for those inspirational heated Moon rock treatments. Oh, and let's shed some special luster on Basho Applebrook, the inventor of proteopape, who's with us tonight. Bash, stand up and take a bow!"

Utterly mortified, Bash got out of his seat as a spotlight zeroed in on him. Blinking, he turned to face the audience, essaying a weak smile. After enduring the noise of their clapping for as short a time as politely allowable, he gratefully sat down.

Dagny had returned to his side. She leaned in to kiss his cheek. Bash felt partially recompensed for his forced public exposure. But the rest of the ceremony quickly soured his mood.

"Best Transformation of Comedy to Tragedy" naturally followed the award Dagny had won. Then came "Musical into Nonmusical" and vice versa. "Subtext Foregrounded" and "Mockumentaries" were succeeded by the award for "Bomb Defusing," the object of which category was apparently to rob a suspenseful film of any suspense. "Idiot Plotting" featured all the characters exchanging moronic dialogue and offering the stupidest of motives for their actions. "Comic Book Narration" forced the actors to summarize aloud all their actions, and also to indulge in long-winded speeches during any fight scenes. "Gender Swap" found all the males dubbed with female voices, and contrariwise. "Ethnic Mismatch" covered the introduction of inappropriate foreign accents.

Bash's father had been born in 1970. During Bash's childhood, he had discovered a stash of magazines that York Applebrook had accumulated during his own childhood. Fascinated by the antiques, Bash had devoured the pile of *Mad* magazines, only half-understanding yet still laughing at parodies of movies old before he had been born. At the wise old age of ten, however, Bash had put aside the jejune drolleries of "the usual gang of idiots."

Tonight felt like being trapped in a giant issue of *Mad*. Bash simply could not believe that all these supposedly mature adults felt that such juvenile skewing of classic films constituted a new and exciting art form. And somehow his invention of proteopape had catalyzed this stale quasi-dadaist display. Bash experienced a sense of shame.

He did not of course let Dagny know how he felt. Her pleasure in winning and in the victories of her peers prevented any such honesty. And, selfishly, Bash still thrilled to her kiss. The conversation with Cricket Licklider had made the possibility of post-Woodies sex with Dagny more vivid. No point in sacrificing the first likelihood of unmonied intercourse in two years on the altar of stubborn opinionated speechifying.

Finally the tedious ceremony ended. The assembled auteurs from around the globe split into cliques and adjourned to various other venues to celebrate or weep. Bash found himself accompanying Dagny, the Hubster Dubsters and a pack of hangers-on to a bar called The Weeping Gorilla, whose decorative motif involved the lugubrious anthropoid posed with various celebrities. There Bash consumed rather too much alcohol, rather too little food, and a handful of unidentified drugs.

Somehow Bash found himself naked in a hotel room with Dagny. Sex occurred in lurid kaleidoscopic intervals of consciousness. Afterwards, Bash remembered very little of the perhaps enjoyable experience.

But much to his dismay, he clearly recalled some boastful pillow talk afterwards.

"Hadda put a trapdoor in pro'eopape during testing. Lemme get inna operating system to debug. Still in there! Yup, never took it out, nobody ever found it neither. Every single sheet, still got a secret backdoor!"

Dagny, eyes shuttered, made sleepy noises. But, as evidenced by the subversion of Bash's *Boston Globe* on the morning of June 25, when his newspaper had played a symbolical version of their harsh breakup on the shoals of Bash's eventual honesty during their aborted second date, she had plainly heard every word.

5
The Fugitive

Bash stood up from the breakfast table. His dead newspaper continued slowly to absorb the juices of his abandoned breakfast. The fish-scale wall clock morphed to a new minute. Everything looked hopeless.

Dagny Winsome had hacked the hidden trapdoor in proteopape, the existence of which no one had ever suspected until he blurted it out. Why hadn't he eliminated that feature before releasing his invention? Hubris, sheer hubris. Bash had wanted to feel as if he could reclaim his brainchild from the world's embrace at any time. The operating system trapdoor represented apron strings he couldn't bring himself to cut. And what was the appalling result of his parental vanity?

Now Dagny could commandeer every uniquely identifiable scrap of the ether-driven miracle medium and turn it to her own purposes. For the moment, her only motivation to tamper appeared to consist of expressing her displeasure with Bash. For that small blessing, Bash was grateful. But how long would it take before Dagny's congenital impishness seduced her into broader culture jamming? This was the woman, after all, who had drugged one of MIT's deans as he slept, and brought him to awaken in a scrupulously exact mockup of his entire apartment exactly three-quarters scale.

Bash felt like diving into bed and pulling the covers over his head. But a moment's reflection stiffened his resolve. No one was going to mess with *his* proteopape and get away with it! Too much of the world's economy and culture relied on the medium just to abandon it. He would simply have to track Dagny down and attempt to reason with her.

As his first move, Bash took out his telephone. His telephone was simply a stiffened strip of proteopape. His defunct newspaper would once have served the purpose as well, but most people kept a dedicated phone on their persons, if for nothing else than to receive incoming calls when they were out of reach of other proteopape surfaces, and also to serve as their unique intelligent tag identifying them to I^2 entities.

Bash folded the phone into a little hollow pyramid and stood it on the table. The GlobeSpeak logo appeared instantly: a goofy anthropomorphic chatting globe inked by Robert Crumb, every appearance of which earned the heirs of the artist one milli-cent. (Given the volume of world communication, Sophie Crumb now owned most of southern France.) Bash ordered the phone to search for Cricket Licklider. Within a few seconds her face replaced the logo, while the cameras in Bash's phone reciprocated with his image.

Cricket grinned. "I knew you'd come looking for some of the good stuff eventually, Bashie-boy."

"No, it's not like that. I appreciate your attention, really I do, but I need to find Dagny."

Frowning, Cricket said, "You lost your girlfriend? Too bad. Why should I help you find her?"

"Because she's going to destroy proteopape if I don't stop her. Where would that leave you and your fellow Dubsters? Where would that leave any of us for that matter?"

This dire news secured Cricket's interest, widening her iguana eyes. "Holy shit! Well, Christ, I don't know what to say. I haven't seen her since the Woodies. She might not even be in town anymore."

"Can you get the rest of your crew together? Maybe one of them knows something useful."

"I'll do my best. Meet us at the clubhouse in an hour."

Cricket cut the transmission, but not before uploading the relevant address to Bash's phone.

Bash decided that a shave and a shower would help settle his nerves.

In the bathroom, Bash lathered up his face in the proteopape mirror: a sheet that digitized his image in real time and displayed it unreversed. The mirror also ran a small window in which a live newscast streamed. As Bash listened intently for any bulletins regarding the public malfunctioning of proteopape, he took his antique Mach3 razor down from the wall cabinet's shelf and then sudsed his face from a spray can. Having been raised in a simple-living household, Bash still retained many old-fashioned habits, such as actually shaving. He drew the first swath through the foam up his neck and under his chin.

Without warning, his mirror suddenly hosted the leering face of Charles Laughton as the Hunchback of Notre Dame.

Bash yelped and cut himself. The Hunchback chortled, then vanished. And now his mirror was as dead as his newspaper.

Cursing Dagny, Bash located a small analogue mirror at the bottom of a closet and finished shaving. He put a proteopape band-aid on the cut, and the band-aid instantly assumed the exact texture and coloration of the skin it covered (with cut edited out), becoming effectively invisible.

Bash's shower curtain was more proteopape, laminated and featuring a loop of the Louisiana rainforest, complete with muted soundtrack. Bash yanked it off its hooks and took a shower without regard to slopping water onto the bathroom floor. Toweling off, he even regarded the roll of toilet paper next to the john suspiciously, but then decided that Dagny wouldn't dare.

Dressed in his usual casual manner—white Wickaway shirt, calf-length tropical-print pants and Supplex sandals—Bash left his house. He took his Segway IX from its recharging slot in the garage, and set out for the nearby commuter-rail node. As he zipped neatly along the wealthy and shady streets of Lincoln, the warm, humid June air laving him, Bash tried to comprehend the full potential dimensions of Dagny's meddling with proteopape. He pictured schools, businesses, transportation and government agencies all brought to a grinding halt as their proteopape systems crashed. Proteopape figured omnipresently in the year 2029. So deeply had it insinuated itself into daily life that even Bash could not keep track of all its uses. If proteopape went down, it would take the global economy with it.

And what of Bash's personal rep in the aftermath? When the facts came out, he would become the biggest idiot and traitor the world had ever tarred and feathered. His name would become synonymous with "fuck up": "You pulled a helluva applebrook that time." "I totally applebrooked my car, but wasn't hurt." "Don't hire him, he's a real applebrook."

The breeze ruffling Bash's hair failed to dry the sweat on his brow as fast as it formed.

At the station, Bash parked and locked his Segway. He bounded up the stairs and the station door hobermanned open automatically for him. He bought his ticket, and after only a ten-minute wait found himself riding east toward the city.

At the end of Bash's car a placard of proteopape mounted on the wall cycled through a set of advertisements. Bash kept a wary eye on the ads, but none betrayed a personal vendetta against him.

Disembarking at South Station, Bash looked around for his personal icon in the nearest piece of public proteopape, and quickly discovered it glowing in the corner of a newsstand's signage: a bright green pear (thoughts of his parents briefly popped up) with the initials BA centered in it.

Every individual in the I² society owned such a self-selected icon, its uniqueness assured by a global registry. The icons had many uses, but right now Bash's emblem was going to help him arrive at the Dubsters' club. His pocket phone

276 | Paul Di Filippo

was handshaking with every piece of proteopape in the immediate vicinity and was laying down a trail of electronic breadcrumbs for him to follow, based on the directions transmitted earlier by Cricket.

A second pear appeared beyond the newsstand, on a plaque identifying the presence of a wall-mounted fire extinguisher, and so Bash walked toward it. Many other travelers were tracking their own icons simultaneously with Bash. As he approached the second iteration of the luminous pear, a third copy glowed from the decorative patch on the backpack of a passing schoolkid. Bash followed until the kid turned right. (Many contemporary dramas and comedies revolved around the chance meetings initiated by one's icon appearing on the personal property of a stranger. An individual could of course deny this kind of access, but surprisingly few did.) The pear icon vanished from the pack, to be replaced by an occurrence at the head of the subway stairs. Thus was Bash led onto a train and to his eventual destination, a building on the Fenway not far from the Isabella Stewart Gardner Museum.

As he ascended the steps of the modest brownstone, Bash's eye was snagged by the passage of a sleek new Europa model car, one of the first to fully incorporate proteopape in place of windshield glass. He marveled at the realism of its "windows," which apparently disclosed the driver—a handsome young executive type—chatting with his passenger—a beautiful woman.

The car windows were in reality all sheets of suitably strengthened proteopape, utterly opaque. The inner surfaces of the "windows" displayed the outside world to the occupants of the car (or anything else, for that matter, although the driver, at least, had better be monitoring reality), while the outer surfaces broadcast the car's interior (the default setting) or any other selected feed. The driver and passenger Bash saw might have been the actual occupants of the Europa, or they might have been canned constructs. The car could in reality hold some schlubby Walter Mitty type, the president-in-exile of the Drowned Archipelagos or the notorious terrorist Mungo Bush Meat. (Suspicious of the latter instance, roving police would get an instant warrant to tap the windows and examine the true interior.)

Returning his attention to the door displaying his icon, Bash phoned Cricket.

"I'm here."

"One second."

The door opened on its old-fashioned hinges and Bash stepped inside, to be met by Cricket.

Today the woman wore an outfit of rose-colored spidersilk street pajamas that revealed an attractive figure concealed the previous night by her formal armor. She smiled and gave Bash a brief spontaneous hug and peck.

"Buck up, Bashie-boy. Things can't be that bad."

"No, they're worse! Dagny is going to bring down civilization if she keeps on messing with proteopape."

"Exactly what is she doing, and how's she doing it?"

"I can't reveal everything, but it's all my fault. I inadvertently gave her the ability to ping and finger every piece of proteopape in existence."

Cricket whistled. "I knew you zillionaires bestowed generous gifts, but this one even beats the time South Africa gave away the AIDS cure."

"I didn't *mean* to pass this ability on to her. In fact, all I did was drop a drunken clue and she ran with it."

"Our Dag is one clever girl, that's for sure."

Bash looked nervously around the dim narrow hallway full of antiques and was relieved to discover only dumb wallcoverings and not a scrap of proteopape in sight. "We should make sure to exclude any proteopape from our meeting with your friends. Otherwise Dagny will surely monitor our discussions."

Following his own advice, Bash took out his phone and placed it on an end table.

"Wait here. I'll run ahead and tell everyone to de-paperize themselves."

Cricket returned after only a minute. "Okay, let's go."

Walking down the long hall, Bash asked, "How did you guys ever end up in a building like this? I pictured your clubhouse as some kind of *xinggan* Koolhaus."

"Well, most of us Dubsters are just amateurs with day jobs, you know. We can't afford to commission special architecture by anyone really catalyzing. But our one rich member is Lester Schill. You met him the other night, right? The Schills have been Brahmins since way back to the 1950s! Big investments in the Worcester bioaxis, Djerassi and that crowd. But Lester's the last of the Schill line, and he owns more properties than he can use. So he leases us this building for our HQ for a dollar a year."

"Isn't he concerned about what'll happen to the family fortune after his death?" This very issue had often plagued the childless Bash himself.

Cricket snickered. "Lester's not a breeder. And believe me, you really don't want to know the details of his special foldings. But I expect he's made provisions."

Their steps had brought them to a closed door. Cricket ushered Bash into a large room whose walls featured built-in shelves full of dumb books. Bash experienced a small shock, having actually forgotten that such antique private libraries still existed.

Close to a dozen Dubsters assembled around a boardroom-sized table greeted Bash with quiet hellos or silent nods. Bash recognized Flanders, Mexicorn, Diddums and the enigmatic Schill himself, but the others were strangers to him.

Cricket conducted Bash to the empty chair at the head of the table and he sat, unsure of what he needed to say to enlist the help of these people. No one offered him any prompting, but he finally came up with a concise introduction to his presence.

"One of your West Coast associates, Dagny Winsome, has stolen something from me. The knowledge of a trapdoor in the operating system of proteopape. She's already begun screwing around with various sheets of my personal protean paper, and if she continues on in this manner, she'll inspire widespread absolute distrust of this medium. That would spell the end of our I^2 infrastructure, impacting your own artistic activities significantly. So I'm hoping that as her friends, you folks will have some insight into where Dagny might be hiding, and also be motivated to help me reach her and convince her to stop."

A blonde fellow whose face and hands were entirely covered in horrific-looking scarlet welts and blisters, which apparently pained him not a whit, said, "You're the brainster, why don't you just lock her out?"

Bash vented a frustrated sigh. "Don't you think that was the very first thing I tried? But she's beaten me to it, changed all my old access codes. She's got the only key to the trapdoor now. But if I could only get in, I could make proteopape safe forever by closing the trapdoor for good. But I need to find Dagny first."

Cricket spoke up. "Roger, tell Bash what you know about Dagny's departure."

The jaundiced ephebe said, "I drove her to the airport a day ago. She said she was heading back to LA."

"Did you actually see her board her flight?" asked Bash.

"No...."

"Well, I think she's still in the Greater Boston Metropolitan region. The time lag between coasts is negligible for most communications. Even international calls ricochet off the GlobeSpeak relays practically instantaneously." Bash was referring to the fleet of thousands of high-flying drone planes—laden with comm gear and perennially refueled in midair — which encircled the planet, providing long-distance links faster than satellites ever could. "But she wouldn't want to risk even millisecond delays if she was trying to pull off certain real-time pranks. Plus, I figure she'll want to finally pop out of hiding to lord it over me in person, once she's finished humiliating me."

The toothy Indicia Diddums spoke. "That raishes a good point. This looksh like a purely pershonal feud between you two. You're the richesht plug in the world, Applebrook. Why don't you just hire some private muschle to nail her assh?"

"I don't want word of this snafu to spread any further than absolutely necessary. I spent a long time vacillating before I even decided to tell you guys."

Lester Schill stroked his long beard meditatively before speaking. "What's in this for us? Just a continuation of the status quo? Where's our profit?"

Bash saw red. He got to his feet, nearly upsetting his chair.

"Profit? What kind of motive for saving the world is that? Was I thinking of profit when I first created proteopape? No! Sure, I'm richer than God now, but that's not why I did it. Money is useless after a certain point. I can't even spend a fraction of one percent of my fortune, it grows so fast. And you, Schill, damn it, are probably in the same position, even if your wealth is several orders of magnitude less than mine. Money is not at the root of this! Proteopape means freedom of information, and the equitable distribution of computing power! Don't any of you remember what life was like before proteopape? Huge electricity-gobbling server farms? Cell-phone towers blighting the landscape? Miles of fiber optics cluttering the sewers and the seas and the streets? Endless upgrades of hardware rendered almost instantly obsolescent? Big government databases versus individual privacy? Proteopape did away with all that! Now the server farms are in your pockets and on cereal boxes, in the trash in your wastebasket and signage all around. Now the individual can go head-to-head with any corporation or governmental agency. And I won't just stand helplessly by and let some dingbat artist with a grudge ruin it all! If you people won't help me without bribery, then I'll just solve this problem on my own!"

Nostrils flaring, face flushed, Bash glared at the stubborn Dubsters, who remained unimpressed by his fevered speech.

The stalemate was broken when a segment of the bookshelves seemingly detached itself and stepped forward.

The moving portion of the bookcases possessed a human silhouette. In the next second the silhouette went white, revealing a head-to-toe suit of proteo-pape. This suit, Bash realized, must represent one of the newest third-generation Parametrics camo outfits. The myriad moletronic cameras in the rear of the suit captured the exact textures and lighting of the background against which the wearer stood, and projected the mappings onto the front of the clothing. The wearer received his visual inputs on the interior of the hood from the forward array of cameras. Gauzy portions of the hood allowed easy breathing, at the spotty sacrifice of some of the disguise's hi-res.

A hand came up to sweep the headgear backward, where it draped like a loose cowl on the individual's back. The face thus revealed belonged to a young Hispanic man with a thin mustache.

"My name is Tito Harnnoy, and I represent the Masqueleros. We will help you, hombre!"

6
The Manchurian Candidate

Tito Harnnoy drove his battered industrial-model two-person Segway down Mass Ave toward Cambridge. Riding behind Harnnoy, Bash experienced a creeping nostalgia, not altogether pleasant, that grew stronger the closer they approached his old alma mater, MIT.

Although Bash, once he became rich, had given generously to his university, endowing entire buildings, scholarship funds, research programs and tenured positions, he had not returned physically to the campus since graduation. The university held too many memories of juvenile sadness and loneliness blended with his culminating triumph. Whenever Bash cast his thoughts back to those years, he became again to some degree the geeky prodigy, a person he felt he had since outgrown. His maturity always a tenuous proposition, Bash felt it wisest not to court such retrogressive feelings. But now, apparently, he had no choice but to confront his past self.

Harnnoy broke Bash's reverie by saying, "Just a few smoots away from help, pard."

Indeed, they were crossing the Charles River into Cambridge. The scattered structures of MIT loomed ahead, to east and west.

Bash noted extraordinary activity on the water below. "What's happening down there?" he asked Harnnoy.

"Annual Dragon Boat Festival. Big Asian carnival today, pard."

Harnnoy brought the scooter to a gyroscopic stop nearly below the shadow of the Great Dome and they dismounted. Walking into the embrace of the buildings that comprised the Infinite Corridor, they attained grassy Killian Court. The bucolic campus scene reflected the vibrant July day.

Several artists were "painting" the passing parade from various perspectives, employing smart styluses on canvases of proteopape. Depending on the applications the artists used, their strokes translated into digitized pastels or charcoal, acrylics or oils, ink or pencil or watercolor. Some had style filters in place, producing instant Monets or Seurats.

Elsewhere a kite-fighting contest was underway. Made of proteopape with an extra abundance of special MEMS, the kites could flex and flutter their surfaces and achieve dynamic, breeze-assisted flight. Tetherless, they were controlled by their handlers who employed sheets of conventional proteopape on the ground that ran various strategy programs and displayed the kites'-eye view. Curvetting and darting, the lifelike kites sought to batter aerial opponents and knock them from the sky without being disabled in turn.

Elsewhere, sedentary proteopape users read magazines or newspapers or books, watched various videofeeds, mailed correspondents, telefactored tourist autonomes around the globe, or performed any of a hundred other proteopape-mediated functions.

Conducting Bash through the quad and toward the towering Building 54, Harnnoy said, "I'm glad you decided to trust the Masqueleros, Applebrook. We won't let you down. It's a good thing we have our own ways of monitoring interesting emergent shit around town. We keep special feelers out for anything connected with your name, you know."

Bash didn't know. "But why?"

"Are you kidding? You're famous on campus. The biggest kinasehead ever to emerge from these hallowed halls, even considering all the other famous names. And that's no intronic string."

Bash felt weird. Had he really become some kind of emblematic figure to this strange younger generation? The honor sat awkwardly on his shoulders.

"Well, that's a major tribute, I guess. I only hope I can live up to your expectations."

"Even if you never released anything beyond proteopape, you already have. That's why we want to help you now. And it's truly exonic that we managed to get a spy — me — into place for your meeting with the Dubsters. Those sugarbags would never have lifted a pinky finger to aid you."

Despite the worshipful talk, Bash still had his doubts about the utility and motives of the mysterious Masqueleros, but the intransigence of Cricket's friends left him little choice. (Ms. Licklider herself, although expressing genuine sympathy, had had no solid aid of her own to offer.)

"I really appreciate your help, Tito. But I'm still a little unclear on how you guys hope to track Dagny down."

"Cryonize your metabolism, pard. You'll see in a minute."

Descending a few stairs into an access well, they stopped at an innocuous basement door behind Building 54. A small square of proteopape was inset above the door handle. Harnnoy spit upon it.

"Wouldn't the oils on your fingers have served as well?" Bash asked.

"Sure. But spitting is muy narcocorrido."

"Oh."

The invisible lab in the paper performed an instant DNA analysis on Harnnoy's saliva, and the door swung open.

Inside the unlit windowless room, a flock of glowing floating heads awaited.

The faces on the heads were all famous ones: Marilyn Monroe, Stephen Hawking, Britney Spears (the teenage version, not the middle-aged spokesperson for OpiateBusters), President Winfrey, Freeman Dyson, Walt Whitman (the celebrations for his 200th birthday ten years ago had gained him renewed prominence), Woody Woodpecker, SpongeBob SquarePants, Bart Simpson's son Homer Junior.

"Welcome to the lair of the Masqueleros," ominously intoned a parti-faced Terminator.

Bash came to a dead stop, stunned for a moment, before he realized what he was seeing. Then he got angry.

"Okay, everybody off with the masks. We can't have any proteopape around while we talk."

Overhead fluorescents flicked on, and the crowd of conspirators wearing only the cowls of their camo suits stood revealed, the projected faces fading in luminescence to match the ambient light. One by one the Masqueleros doffed their headgear to reveal the grinning motley faces of teenagers of mixed heritage and gender. One member gathered up the disguises, including Harnnoy's full suit, and stuffed the potentially treacherous proteopape into an insulated cabinet.

Briefly, Bash recapped his problem for the attentive students. They nodded knowingly, and finally one girl said, "So you need to discover this bint's hiding place without alerting her to your presence. And since she effectively controls every piece of proteopape in the I^2-verse, your only avenue of information is seemingly closed. But you haven't reckoned with — the internet!"

"The internet!" fumed Bash. "Why don't I just employ smoke signals or, or — the telegraph? The internet is dead as Xerox."

A red-haired kid chimed in. "No latch, pard. Big swaths of the web are still in place, maintained by volunteers like us. We revere and cherish the kludgy old monster. The web's virtual ecology is different now, true, more of a set of marginal biomes separated by areas of clear-cut devastation. But we still host thousands of webcams. And there's no proteopape in the mix, it's all antique silicon. So here's what we do. We put a few agents out there searching, and I guarantee that in no time at all we spot your girlfriend."

Sighing, Bash said, "She's *not* my girlfriend. Oh, well, what've I got to lose? Let's give it a try."

The Masqueleros and Bash crowded into an adjacent room full of antique hardware, including decrepit plasma flatscreens and folding PDA peripheral keyboards duct-taped into usability. The trapped heat and smells of the laboring electronics reminded Bash of his student days, seemingly eons removed from the present. Several of the Masqueleros sat down in front of their machines and begin to mouse furiously away. Interior and exterior shots of Greater Boston as seen from innumerable forgotten and dusty webcams swarmed the screens in an impressionistic movie without plot or sound.

Tito Harnnoy handed Bash a can of Glialsqueeze pop and said, "Refresh yourself, pard. This could take a while."

Eventually Bash and Tito fell to discussing the latest spintronics developments, and their potential impact on proteopape.

"Making the circuitry smaller doesn't change the basic proteopape paradigm," maintained Bash. "Each sheet gets faster and boasts more capacity, but the standard functionality remains the same."

"Nuh-*huh!* Spintronics means that all of proteopape's uses can be distributed into the environment itself. Proteopape as a distinct entity will vanish."

Bash had to chew on this disturbing new scenario for a while. Gradually, he began to accept Harnnoy's thesis, at least partially. Why hadn't he seen such an eventuality before? Maybe Dagny had been right when she accused him of losing his edge....

"Got her!"

Bash and the others clustered around one monitor. And there shone Dagny.

She sat in a small comfy nest of cushions and fast-food packaging trash, a large sheet of proteopape in her lap.

"What camera is this feed coming from?" Bash said.

"It's mounted at ceiling level in the mezzanine of the Paramount Theater on Washington Street, down near Chinatown."

When Bash had been born in 1999, the Paramount Theater, one of the grand dames of twentieth-century Hollywood's Golden Age, had already been shuttered for over two decades. Various rehabilitation plans had been tossed about for the next fifteen years, until Bash entered MIT. During that year, renovations finally began. The grand opening of the theater coincided with the churning of the economy occasioned by the release of proteopape and also with a short-lived but scarily virulent outbreak of Megapox. Faced with uncertain financing, fear of contagion in mass gatherings, and the cheapness of superior home-theater systems fashioned of proteopape, the revamped movie house had locked its doors, falling once again into genteel desuetude.

"Can you magnify the view?" Bash asked. "See what she's looking at?"

The webcam zoomed in on the sheet of paper in Dagny's lap.

And Bash saw that she was watching them.

In infinite regress, the monitor showed the proteopape showing the monitor showing the proteopape showing.....

Bash howled. "Someone's got proteopape on them!"

Just then a leering Dagny looked backward over her shoulder directly at the webcam, and at the same time Bash's chin spoke.

"It's you, you idiot," said Bash's epidermis in Dagny's stepped-down voice.

Bash ripped off the smart band-aid he had applied while shaving, and the image of the Masqueleros on Dagny's proteopape swung crazily to track the movement.

"Dagny!" Bash yelled into the band-aid. "This has gone far enough! You've had your fun at my expense. Now give me your current password so I can make proteopape secure again."

"Come and get it," taunted Dagny. "I'm not going anywhere."

"I will!"

With that bold avowal, Bash furiously twisted the band-aid, causing the image of the Masqueleros on Dagny's proteopape to shatter. On the monitor screen she appeared unconcerned, lolling back among her cushions like the Queen of Sheba.

Bash turned to Tito. "Lend me a phone and your Segway. I'm going to nail this troublemaker once and for all."

"Some of us'll go with you, pard."

"No, you stay here. Dagny won't react well to intimidation by a bunch of strangers. And besides, I need the Masqueleros to keep on spying on her and feed me any updates on her actions. All I can hope is that she'll listen to me and abandon this insane vendetta. If she doesn't — Well, I'm not sure what I'll do."

"No problemo, fizz."

Someone handed Bash a phone. He downloaded his identity into it, then established an open channel to Harnnoy. After tucking the phone into the neckline of his shirt, allowing him to speak and be spoken to hands-free, Bash darted from the underground room.

7
Phantom of the Opera

Bash made it as far as Killian Court before the first of Dagny's attacks commenced.

On all the canvases of the amateur painters, on all the individual sheets of proteopape held by the idling students, Bash's face appeared, displacing laboriously created artworks, as well as the contents of books, magazines and videos. (Dagny had unearthed a paparazzo's image of Bash that made him look particularly demented.) And from the massed speakers in the proteopape pages boomed this warning in a gruff male voice:

"Attention! This is a nationwide alert from Homeland Security. All citizens should immediately exert extreme vigilance for the individual depicted here. He is wanted for moral turpitude, arrogant ignorance, and retrogressive revanchism. Approach him with caution, as he may bite."

This odd yet alarming message immediately caused general consternation to spread throughout the quadrangle. Bash turned up his shirt collar, hunched down his head and hurried toward the street. But he had not reckoned with the kites.

Homing in on his phone, the co-opted kites began to dive-bomb Bash. Several impacted the ground around him, crumpling with a noise like scrunching cellophane, but one scored a direct hit on his head, causing him to yelp. His squeal attracted the eyes of several onlookers, and someone shouted, "There he is!"

Bash ran.

He thought briefly of abandoning his phone, but decided not to. He needed to stay in touch with the Masqueleros. But more crucially, giving up his phone would achieve no invisibility.

Bash was moving through a saturated I^2 environment. There was no escaping proteopape. Every smart surface — from store windows to sunglasses, from taxi rooftop displays to billboards, from employee nametags to vending machines — was a camera that would track him in his dash across town to the Paramount Theater. Illicitly tapping into all these sources, utilizing common yet sophisticated pattern recognition, sampling and extrapolative software, Dagny would never lose sight of her quarry. Bash might as well have had cameras implanted in his eyeballs.

Out on Mass Ave, Bash faced no interception from alarmed citizens. Apparently the false security warning had been broadcast only in Killian Court. But surely Dagny had further tricks up her striped sleeves.

He spoke into his dangling phone. "What's she doing now?"

Harnnoy's voice returned an answer. "Noodling around with her pape. She's got her back to the camera, so we can't see what kind of scripts she's running."

"Okay, thanks. I'm hitting the road now."

Once aboard the Segway, Bash headed back toward downtown Boston.

He came to a halt obediently at the first red light, chafing at the delay. But something odd about the engine noise of the car approaching behind him made Bash look over his shoulder.

The car — a 2029 Vermoulian with proteopape windows — was not slowing down.

In a flash, Bash realized what was happening.

Dagny had edited out both the traffic light and Bash's scooter from the driver's interior display.

Bash veered his Segway to the right, climbing the curb, and the Vermoulian zipped past him with only centimeters to spare. In the middle of the intersection it broadsided another car. Luckily, the crash of the two lightweight urban vehicles, moving at relatively low speeds, resulted in only minor damages, although airbags activated noisily.

Bash drove down the sidewalk, scattering pedestrians, and continued around the accident.

Things were getting serious. No longer was Dagny content merely to harass Bash. Now she was involving innocent bystanders in her mad quest for revenge.

His ire rising, Bash crossed the Charles River. Beneath the bridge, huge jubilant crowds had assembled for the Dragon Boat races.

Bash took several wrong turns. Dagny had changed the street signs, misnaming avenues along his entire route and producing a labyrinth of new one-way streets. After foolishly adhering to the posted regulations for fear of getting stopped by some oblivious rule-bound cop, Bash abandoned all caution and just raced past snarled traffic down whatever avenue he felt would bring him most quickly to Washington Street.

Now Bash began to see his face everywhere, in varying sizes, surmounted or underlined by dire warnings. WANTED FOR CULTURAL ASSASSINATION, GUILTY OF SQUANDERING ARTISTIC CAPITAL, MASTERMIND IN FELONIOUS ASSAULT ON VISIONARIES....

The absurd charges made Bash see red. He swore aloud, and Harnnoy said, "What'd I do, pard?"

"Nothing, nothing. Dagny still at the Paramount?"

"Verdad, compañero."

As he approached the Common, Bash noted growing crowds of gleeful pedestrians. What was going on....?

The Dragon Boat Festival. Chinatown must be hosting parallel celebrations. Well, okay. The confusion would afford Bash cover —

A sheet of proteopape — spontaneously windblown, or aimed like a missile? — sailed up out of nowhere and wrapped Bash's head. He jerked the steering grips before taking his hands entirely off them to deal with the obstruction to his vision, and the Segway continued homeostatically on its new course to crash into a tree.

Bash picked himself up gingerly. The paper had fallen away from his face. Angrily, he crumpled it up and stuffed it into his pocket. He hurt all over, but no important body part seemed broken. The scooter was wrecked. Luckily, he hadn't hit anyone. Concerned bystanders clumped around him, but Bash brusquely managed to convince them to go away.

Harnnoy said, "I caught the smashup on the phone camera, Bash. You okay?"

"Uh, I guess. Sorry about totaling your ride. I'm going on foot now."

As Bash scurried off, he witnessed the arrival of several diligent autonomes converging on the accident. He accelerated his pace, fearful of getting corralled by the authorities before he could deal with Dagny.

Downtown Crossing was thronged, the ambient noise like a slumber party for teenage giants. The windows of Filene's claimed that Bash was a redactive splice between a skunk, a hyena and a jackal. As Dagny's interventions failed to stop him, her taunts grew cruder. She must be getting desperate. Bash was counting on her to screw up somehow. He had no real plan otherwise.

Weaseling his way through the merrymakers, Bash was brought up short a block away from the Paramount by an oncoming parade. Heading the procession was a huge multiperson Chinese dragon. In lieu of dumb paint, its proteopape skin sheathed it in glittery scales and animated smoke-snorting head.

People were pointing to the sky. Bash looked up.

One of the famous TimWarDisVia aerostats cruised serenely overhead, obviously dispatched to provide an overhead view of the parade. Its proteopape skin featured Bash's face larger than God's. Scrolling text reflected poorly on Bash's parentage and morals.

"God *damn!*" Bash turned away from the sight, only to confront the dragon. Its head now mirrored Bash's, but its body was a snake's.

Small strings of firecrackers began to explode, causing shrieks, and Bash utilized the diversion to bull onward toward the shuttered Paramount Theater. He darted down the narrow alley separating the deserted building from its neighbors.

"Tito! Any tips on getting inside?"

"One of our webcams on the first floor shows something funky with one of the windows around the back."

The rear exterior wall of the theater presented a row of weather-distressed plywood sheets nailed over windows. The only service door was tightly secured. No obvious entrance manifested itself.

But then Bash noticed with his trained eye that one plywood facade failed close-up inspection as he walked slowly past it.

Dagny had stretched an expanse of proteopape across an open frame, then set the pape to display a plywood texture.

Bash set his phone on the ground. "Tito, I'm going in alone. Call the cops if I'm not out in half an hour."

"Uptaken and bound, fizz!"

Rather vengefully, Bash smashed his fist through the disguising pape, then scrambled inside.

Dagny had hotwired electricity from somewhere. The Paramount was well lit, although the illumination did nothing to dispel a moldy atmosphere from years of inoccupancy. Bash moved cautiously from the debris-strewn backstage area out into the general seating.

A flying disc whizzed past his ear like a suicidal mirror-finished bat. It hit a wall and shattered.

Dagny stood above him at the rail of the mezzanine with an armful of antique DVDs. The platters for the digital projectors must have been left behind when the Paramount ceased operations. The writing on a shard at Bash's feet read: *The Silmarillion.*

Dagny frisbee'd another old movie at Bash. He ducked just in time to avoid getting decapitated.

"Quit it, Dagny! Act like an adult, for Christ's sake! We have to talk!"

Dagny pushed her clunky eyeglasses back up her nose. "We've got nothing to talk about! You've proven you're a narrow-minded slave to old hierarchies, without an ounce of imagination left in your shriveled brainpan. And you insulted my art!"

"I'm sorry! I didn't mean to, honest. Jesus, even you said that the Woodies were a big joke."

"Don't try putting words in my mouth! Anyway, that was before I won one."

Bash stepped forward into an aisle. "I'm coming up there, Dagny, and you can't stop me."

A withering fusillade of discs forced Bash to eat his words and run for cover into an alcove.

Frustrated beyond endurance, Bash racked his wits for some means of overcoming the demented auteur.

A decade of neglect had begun to have its effects on the very structure of the theater. The alcove where Bash stood was littered with fragments of concrete. Bash snatched up one as big as his fist. From his pocket he dug the sheet of proteopape that had blinded him, and wrapped it around the heavy chunk. He stepped forward.

"Dagny, let's call a truce. I've got something here you need to read. It puts everything into a new light." Bash came within a few meters of the lower edge of the balcony before Dagny motioned him to stop. He offered the ball of pape on his upturned palm.

"I don't see what could possibly change things—"

"Just take a look, okay?"

"All right. Toss it up here."

Dagny set her ammunition down to free both hands and leaned over the railing to receive the supposedly featherweight pape.

Bash concentrated all his anger and resolve into his right arm. He made a motion as if to toss underhand. But at the last minute he swiftly wound up and unleashed a mighty overhand pitch.

Dagny did not react swiftly enough to the deceit. The missile conked her on the head and she went over backwards into the mezzanine seats.

Never before had Bash moved so fast. He found Dagny hovering murmurously on the interface between consciousness and oblivion. Reassured that she wasn't seriously injured, Bash arrowed toward her nest of pillows. He snatched up the sheet of proteopape that displayed his familiar toolkit for accessing the trapdoor features of his invention. With a few commands he had long ago memorized as a vital failsafe, he initiated the shutdown of the hidden override aspects of proteopape.

From one interlinked sheet of proteopape to the next the commands raced, propagating exponentially around the globe like history's most efficient cyberworm, a spark that extinguished its very means of propagation as it raced along. Within mere minutes, the world was made safe and secure again for Immanent Information.

Bash returned to Dagny, who was struggling to sit up.

"You—you haven't beaten me. I'll find some way to show you—"

The joyful noises from the continuing parade outside insinuated themselves into Bash's relieved mind. He felt happy and inspired. Looking down at Dagny, he knew just what to say.

"Forget it, Jake. It's Chinatown."

The Voluntary State

Christopher Rowe

Is there a way to reverse the Singularity? In Christopher Rowe's bizarre future Tennessee, an AI has created a mind-merged police state, whose citizens are permitted but a few shreds of individuality and just a taste of free will. A raiding party of autonomous humans from Kentucky attempts to hack the digital tyranny.

Yet from the inside, this polity feels like a giddy utopia. The technology here is so advanced that it often as not presents as magical, with flowers that sing the national anthem and cars that pine for their owners. Stylistically, this is one of the most crammed – and playful – PCP stories in the collection.

Soma had parked his car in the trailhead lot above Governor's Beach. A safe place, usually, checked regularly by the Tennessee Highway Patrol and surrounded on three sides by the limestone cliffs that plunged down into the Gulf of Mexico.

But today, after his struggle up the trail from the beach, he saw that his car had been attacked. The driver's side window had been kicked in.

Soma dropped his pack and rushed to his car's side. The car shied away from him, backed to the limit of its tether before it recognized him and turned, let out a low, pitiful moan.

"Oh, car," said Soma, stroking the roof and opening the passenger door, "Oh, car, you're hurt." Then Soma was rummaging through the emergency kit, tossing aside flares and bandages, finally, *finally* finding the glass salve. Only after he'd spread the ointment over the shattered window and brushed the glass shards out onto the gravel, only after he'd sprayed the whole door down with analgesic aero, only then did he close his eyes, access call signs, drop shields. He opened his head and used it to call the police.

In the scant minutes before he saw the cadre of blue and white bicycles angling in from sunward, their bubblewings pumping furiously, he gazed down the beach at Nashville. The cranes the Governor had ordered grown to dredge the harbor would go dormant for the winter soon — already their acres-broad leaves were tinged with orange and gold.

"Soma-With-The-Paintbox-In-Printer's-Alley," said voices from above. Soma turned to watch the policemen land. They all spoke simultaneously in the singsong chant of law enforcement. "Your car will be healed at tax-payers' expense." Then the ritual words, "And the wicked will be brought to justice."

Efficiency and order took over the afternoon as the threatened rain began to fall. One of the 144 Detectives manifested, Soma and the policemen all look-ing about as they felt the weight of the Governor's servant inside their heads. It brushed aside the thoughts of one of the Highway Patrolmen and rode him, the man's movements becoming slightly less fluid as he was mounted and steered. The Detective filmed Soma's statement.

"I came to sketch the children in the surf," said Soma. He opened his day-pack for the soapbubble lens, laid out the charcoal and pencils, the sketchbook of boughten paper bound between the rusting metal plates he'd scavenged along the middenmouth of the Cumberland River.

"Show us, show us," sang the Detective.

Soma flipped through the sketches. In black and gray, he'd drawn the float-ing lures that crowded the shallows this time of year. Tiny, naked babies most of them, but also some little girls in one-piece bathing suits and even one fat prepubescent boy clinging desperately to a deflating beach ball and turning horrified, pleading eyes on the viewer.

"Tssk, tssk," sang the Detective, percussive. "Draw filaments on those babies, Soma Painter. Show the lines at their heels."

Soma was tempted to show the Detective the artistic licenses tattooed around his wrists in delicate salmon inks, to remind the intelligence which authorities had purview over which aspects of civic life, but bit his tongue, fear-ful of a For-the-Safety-of-the-Public proscription. As if there were a living soul in all of Tennessee who didn't know that the children who splashed in the surf were nothing but extremities, nothing but lures growing from the snouts of alligators crouching on the sandy bottoms.

The Detective summarized. "You were here at your work, you parked legally, you paid the appropriate fee to the meter, you saw nothing, you informed the authorities in a timely fashion. Soma-With-The-Paintbox-In-Printer's-Alley, the Tennessee Highway Patrol applauds your citizenship."

The policemen had spread around the parking lot, casting cluenets and staring back through time. But they all heard their cue, stopped what they were doing, and broke into a raucous cheer for Soma. He accepted their adulation graciously.

Then the Detective popped the soapbubble camera and plucked the film from the air before it could fall. It rolled up the film, chewed it up thoughtfully, then dismounted the policeman, who shuddered and fell against Soma. So Soma did not at first hear what the others had begun to chant, didn't decipher it until he saw what they were encircling. Something was caught on the wispy thorns of a nodding thistle growing at the edge of the lot.

"Crow's feather," the policemen chanted. "Crow's feather Crow's feather Crow's feather."

And even Soma, licensed for art instead of justice, knew what the fluttering bit of black signified. His car had been assaulted by Kentuckians.

Soma had never, so far as he recalled, painted a self-portrait. But his disposition was melancholy, so he might have taken a few visual notes of his trudge back to Nashville if he'd thought he could have shielded the paper from the rain.

Soma Between the Sea and the City, he could call a painting like that. Or, if he'd decided to choose that one clear moment when the sun had shown through the towering slate clouds, *Soma Between Storms*.

Either image would have shown a tall young man in a broad-brimmed hat, black pants cut off at the calf, yellow jersey unsealed to show a thin chest. A young man, sure, but not a young man used to long walks. No helping that; his car would stay in the trailhead lot for at least three days.

The mechanic had arrived as the policemen were leaving, galloping up the gravel road on a white mare marked with red crosses. She'd swung from the saddle and made sympathetic clucking noises at the car even before she greeted Soma, endearing herself to auto and owner simultaneously.

Scratching the car at the base of its aerial, sussing out the very spot the car best liked attention, she'd introduced herself. "I am Jenny-With-Grease-Beneath-Her-Fingernails," she'd said, but didn't seem to be worried about it because she ran her free hand through unfashionably short cropped blond hair as she spoke.

She'd whistled for her horse and began unpacking the saddlebags. "I have to build a larger garage than normal for your car, Soma Painter, for it must house me and my horse during the convalescence. But don't worry, my licenses are in good order. I'm bonded by the city and the state. This is all at taxpayers' expense."

Which was a very great relief to Soma, poor as he was. With friends even poorer, none of them with cars, and so no one to hail out of the Alley to his rescue, and now this long, wet trudge back to the city.

Soma and his friends did not live uncomfortable lives, of course. They had dry spaces to sleep above their studios, warm or cool in response to the season and even clean if that was the proclivity of the individual artist, as was the case with Soma. A clean, warm or cool, dry space to sleep. A good space to work and a more than ample opportunity to sell his paintings and drawings, the Alley being one of the other things the provincials did when they visited Nashville. Before they went to the great vaulted Opera House or after.

All that and even a car, sure, freedom of the road. Even if it wasn't so free because the car was not *really* his, gift of his family, product of their ranch. Both of them, car and artist, product of that ranching life Soma did his best to forget.

If he'd been a little closer in time to that ranching youth, his legs might not have ached so. He might not have been quite so miserable to be lurching down the gravel road toward the city, might have been sharp-eyed enough to still see a city so lost in the fog, maybe sharp-eared enough to have heard the low hoots and caws that his assailants used to organize themselves before they sprang from all around him — down from tree branches, up from ditches, out from the undergrowth.

And there was a Crow raiding party, the sight stunning Soma motionless. "This only happens on television," he said.

The caves and hills these Kentuckians haunted unopposed were a hundred miles and more north and east, across the shifting skirmish line of a border. Kentuckians couldn't be here, so far from the frontier stockades at Fort Clarksville and Barren Green.

But here they definitely were, hopping and calling, scratching the gravel with their clawed boots, blinking away the rain when it trickled down behind their masks and into their eyes.

A Crow clicked his tongue twice and suddenly Soma was the center of much activity. Muddy hands forced his mouth open and a paste that first stung then numbed was swabbed around his mouth and nose. His wrists were bound before him with rough hemp twine. Even frightened as he was, Soma couldn't contain his astonishment. "Smoke rope!" he said.

The squad leader grimaced, shook his head in disgust and disbelief. "Rope and cigarettes come from two completely different varieties of plants," he said, his accent barely decipherable. "Vols are so fucking stupid."

Then Soma was struggling through the undergrowth himself, alternately dragged and pushed and even half-carried by a succession of Crow Brothers. The boys were running hard, and if he was a burden to them, then their normal speed must have been terrifying. Someone finally called a halt, and Soma collapsed.

The leader approached, pulling his mask up and wiping his face. Deep red lines angled down from his temples, across his cheekbones, ending at his snub nose. Soma would have guessed the man was forty if he'd seen him in the Alley dressed like a normal person in jersey and shorts.

Even so exhausted, Soma wished he could dig his notebook and a bit of charcoal out of the daypack he still wore, so that he could capture some of the savage countenances around him.

The leader was just staring at Soma, not speaking, so Soma broke the silence. "Those scars" — the painter brought up his bound hands, traced angles down either side of his own face — "are they ceremonial? Do they indicate your rank?"

The Kentuckians close enough to hear snorted and laughed. The man before Soma went through a quick, exaggerated pantomime of disgust. He spread his hands, why-me-lording, then took the beaked mask off the top of his head and showed Soma its back. Two leather bands crisscrossed its interior, supporting the elaborate superstructure of the mask and preventing the full weight of it, Soma saw, from bearing down on the wearer's nose. He looked at the leader again, saw him rubbing at the fading marks.

"Sorry," said the painter.

"It's okay," said the Crow. "It's the fate of the noble savage to be misunderstood by effete city dwellers."

Soma stared at the man for a minute. He said, "You guys must watch a lot of the same TV programs as me."

The leader was looking around, counting his boys. He lowered his mask and pulled Soma to his feet. "That could be. We need to go."

It developed that the leader's name was Japheth Sapp. At least that's what the other Crow Brothers called out to him from where they loped along ahead or behind, circled farther out in the brush, scrambled from limb to branch to trunk high above.

Soma descended into a reverie space, singsonging subvocally and supervocally (and being hushed down by Japheth hard then). He guessed in a lucid moment that the paste the Kentuckians had dosed him with must have some sort of will-sapping effect. He didn't feel like he could open his head and call for help; he didn't even want to. But *"I will take care of you,"* Athena was always promising. He held onto that and believed that he wasn't panicking because of the Crows' drugs, sure, but also because he would be rescued by the police soon. *"I will take care of you."* After all, wasn't that one of the Governor's slogans, clarifying out of the advertising flocks in the skies over Nashville during Campaign?

It was good to think of these things. It was good to think of the sane capital and forget that he was being kidnapped by aliens, by Indians, by toughs in the employ of a rival Veronese merchant family.

But then the warchief of the marauding band was throwing him into a gully, whistling and gesturing, calling in all his boys to dive into the wash, to gather close and throw their cloaks up and over their huddle.

"What's up, boss?" asked the blue-eyed boy Soma had noticed earlier, crouched in the mud with one elbow somehow dug into Soma's ribs.

Japheth Sapp didn't answer but another of the younger Crow Brothers hissed, "THP even got a bear in the air!"

Soma wondered if a bear meant rescue from this improbable aside. Not that parts of the experience weren't enjoyable. It didn't occur to Soma to fear for his health, even when Japheth knocked him down with a light kick to the back of the knees after the painter stood and brushed aside feathered cloaks for a glimpse of the sky.

There *was* a bear up there. And yes, it was wearing the blue and white.

"I want to see the bear, Japheth," said a young Crow. Japheth shook his head, said, "I'll take you to Willow Ridge and show you the black bears that live above the Green River when we get back home, Lowell. That bear up there is just a robot made out of balloons and possessed by a demon, not worth looking at unless you're close enough to cut her."

With all his captors concentrating on their leader or on the sky, Soma wondered if he might be able to open his head. As soon as he thought it, Japheth Sapp wheeled on him, stared him down.

Not looking at any one of them, Japheth addressed his whole merry band. "Give this one some more paste. But be careful with him; we'll still need this vol's head to get across the Cumberland, even after we bribe the bundle bugs."

Soma spoke around the viscous stuff the owl-feathered endomorph was spackling over the lower half of his face. "Bundle bugs work for the city and are above reproach. Your plans are ill-laid if they depend on corrupting the servants of the Governor."

More hoots, more hushings, then Japheth said, "If bundle bugs had mothers, they'd sell them to me for half a cask of Kentucky bourbon. And we brought more than half a cask."

Soma knew Japheth was lying—this was a known tactic of neo-anarchist agitator hero figures. "I know you're lying," said Soma. "It's a known tactic of—"

"Hush hush, Soma Painter. I like you — this you — but we've all read the Governor's curricula. You'll see that we're too sophisticated for your models." Japheth gestured and the group broke huddle. Outrunners ran out and the main body shook off cramps. "And I'm not an anarchist agitator. I'm a lot of things, but not that."

"Singer!" said a young Crow, scampering past.

"I play out some weekends, he means; I don't have a record contract or anything," Japheth said, pushing Soma along himself now.

"Welder!" said another man.

"Union-certified," said Japheth. "That's my day job, working at the border."

More lies, knew Soma. "I suppose Kentuckians built the Girding Wall, then?"

Everything he said amused these people greatly. "Not just Kentuckians, vol, the whole rest of the world. Only we call it the containment field."

"Agitator, singer, welder," said the painter, the numbness spreading deeper than it had before, affecting the way he said words and the way he chose them.

"Assassin," rumbled the Owl, the first thing Soma had heard the burly man say.

Japheth was scrambling up a bank before Soma. He stopped and twisted. His foot corkscrewed through the leaf mat and released a humid smell. He looked at the Owl, then hard at Soma, reading him.

"You're doped up good now, Soma Painter. No way to open that head until we open it for you. So, sure, here's some truth for you. We're not just here to steal her things. We're here to break into her mansion. We're here to kill Athena Parthenus, Queen of Logic and Governor of the Voluntary State of Tennessee."

Jenny-With-Grease-Beneath-Her-Fingernails spread fronds across the parking lot, letting the high green fern leaves dry out before she used the mass to make her bed. Her horse watched from above the half-door of its stall. Inside the main body of the garage, Soma's car slept, lightly anesthetized.

"Just enough for a soft cot, horse," said Jenny. "All of us we'll sleep well after this hard day."

Then she saw that little flutter. One of the fronds had a bit of feather caught between some leaves, and yes, it was coal black, midnight blue, reeking of the north. Jenny sighed, because her citizenship was less faultless than Soma's, and policemen disturbed her. But she opened her head and stared at the feather.

A telephone leapt off a tulip poplar a little ways down the road to Nashville. It squawked through its brief flight and landed with inelegant weight in front of Jenny. It turned its beady eyes on her.

"Ring," said the telephone.

"Hello," said Jenny.

Jenny's Operator sounded just like Jenny, something else that secretly disturbed her. Other people's Operators sounded like television stars or famous Legislators or like happy cartoon characters, but Jenny was in that minority of people whose Operators and Teachers always sounded like themselves. Jenny remembered a slogan from Campaign, "My voice is yours."

"The Tennessee Highway Patrol has plucked one already, Jenny Healer." The voice from the telephone thickened around Jenny and began pouring through her ears like cold syrup. "But we want a sample of this one as well. Hold that feather, Jenny, and open your head a little wider."

Now, here's the secret of those feathers. The one Jenny gave to the police and the one the cluenets had caught already. The secret of those feathers, and the feathers strung like look-here flags along the trails down from the Girding Wall, and even of the Owl feathers that had pushed through that fence and let the outside in. All of them were oily with intrigue. Each had been dipped in potent *math*, the autonomous software developed by the Owls of the Bluegrass.

Those feathers were hacks. They were lures and false attacks. Those feathers marked the way the Kentuckians didn't go.

The math kept quiet and still as it floated through Jenny's head, through the ignorable defenses of the telephone and the more considerable, but still avoidable, rings of barbed wire around Jenny's Operator. The math went looking for a Detective or even a Legislator if one were to be found not braying in a pack of its brethren, an unlikely event.

The math stayed well clear of the Commodores in the Great Salt Lick ringing the Parthenon. It was sly math. Its goals were limited, realizable. It marked the way they didn't go.

The Crows made Soma carry things. "You're stronger than you think," one said, and loaded him up with a sloshing keg made from white oak staves. A lot of the Crows carried such, Soma saw, and others carried damp, muddy burlap bags flecked with old root matter and smelling of poor people's meals.

Japheth Sapp carried only a piece of paper. He referred to it as he huddled with the Owl and the blue-eyed boy, crouched in a dry stream bed a few yards from where the rest of the crew were hauling out their goods.

Soma had no idea where they were at this point, though he had a vague idea that they'd described an arc above the northern suburbs and the conversations indicated that they were now heading toward the capital, unlikely as that sounded. His head was still numb and soft inside, not an unpleasant situation, but not one that helped his already shaky geographical sense.

He knew what time it was, though, when the green fall of light speckling the hollow they rested in shifted toward pink. Dull as his mind was, he recognized that and smiled.

The clouds sounded the pitch note, then suddenly a great deal was happening around him. For the first time that day, the Crows' reaction to what they perceived to be a crisis didn't involve Soma being poked somewhere or shoved under something. So he was free to sing the anthem while the Crows went mad with activity.

The instant the rising bell tone fell out of the sky, Japheth flung his mask to the ground, glared at a rangy redheaded man, and bellowed, "Where's my time-keeper? You were supposed to remind us!"

The man didn't have time to answer though, because like all of them he was digging through his pack, wrapping an elaborate crenellated set of earmuffs around his head.

The music struck up, and Soma began.

"Tonight we'll remake Tennessee, every night we remake Tennessee..."

It was powerfully odd that the Kentuckians didn't join in the singing, and that none of them were moving into the roundel lines that a group this size would normally be forming during the anthem.

Still, it might have been stranger if they had joined in.

"Tonight we'll remake Tennessee, every night we remake Tennessee..."

There was a thicket of trumpet flowers tucked amongst a stand of willow trees across the dry creek, so the brass was louder than Soma was used to. Maybe they were farther from the city than he thought. Aficionados of different musical sections tended to find places like this and frequent them during anthem.

"Tonight we'll remake Tennessee, every night we remake Tennessee..."

Soma was happily shuffling through a solo dance, keeping one eye on a fat raccoon that was bobbing its head in time with the music as it turned over stones in the stream bed, when he saw that the young Crow who wanted to see a bear had started keeping time as well, raising and lowering a clawed boot. The Owl was the first of the outlanders who spied the tapping foot.

"Tonight we'll remake Tennessee, every night we remake Tennessee..."

Soma didn't feel the real connection with the citizenry that anthem usually provided on a daily basis, didn't feel his confidence and vigor improve, but he blamed that on the drugs the Kentuckians had given him. He wondered if those were the same drugs they were using on the Crow who now feebly twitched beneath the weight of the Owl, who had wrestled him to the ground. Others pinned down the dancing Crow's arms and legs and Japheth brought out a needle and injected the poor soul with a vast syringe full of some milky brown substance that had the consistency of honey. Soma remembered that he knew the dancing Crow's name. Japheth Sapp had called the boy Lowell.

"*Tonight we'll remake Tennessee, every night we remake Tennessee...*"

The pink light faded. The raccoon waddled into the woods. The trumpet flowers fell quiet and Soma completed the execution of a pirouette.

The redheaded man stood before Japheth wearing a stricken and haunted look. He kept glancing to one side, where the Owl stood over the Crow who had danced. "Japheth, I just lost track," he said. "It's so hard here, to keep track of things."

Japheth's face flashed from anger through disappointment to something approaching forgiveness. "It is. It's hard to keep track. Everybody fucks up sometime. And I think we got the dampeners in him in time."

Then the Owl said, "Second shift now, Japheth. Have to wait for the second round of garbage drops to catch our bundle bug."

Japheth grimaced, but nodded. "We can't move anyway, not until we know what's going to happen with Lowell," he said, glancing at the unconscious boy. "Get the whiskey and the food back into the cache. Set up the netting. We're staying here for the night."

Japheth stalked over to Soma, fists clenched white.

"Things are getting clearer and clearer to you, Soma Painter, even if you think things are getting harder and harder to understand. Our motivations will open up things inside you."

He took Soma's chin in his left hand and tilted Soma's face up. He waved his hand to indicate Lowell.

"There's one of mine. There's one of my motivations for all of this."

Slowly, but with loud lactic cracks, Japheth spread his fingers wide.

"I fight her, Soma, in the hope that she'll not clench up another mind. I fight her so that minds already bound might come unbound."

In the morning, the dancing Crow boy was dead.

Jenny woke near dark, damp and cold, curled up in the gravel of the parking lot. Her horse nickered. She was dimly aware that the horse had been neighing and otherwise emanating concern for some time now, and it was this that had brought her up to consciousness.

She rolled over and climbed to her feet, spitting to rid her mouth of the metal Operator taste. A dried froth of blood coated her nostrils and upper lip, and she could feel the flaky stuff in her ears as well. She looked toward the garage and saw that she wasn't the only one rousing.

"Now, you get back to bed," she told the car.

Soma's car had risen up on its back wheels and was peering out the open window, its weight resting against the force-grown wall, bulging it outward.

Jenny made a clucking noise, hoping to reassure her horse, and walked up to the car. She was touched by its confusion and concern.

She reached for the aerial. "You should sleep some more," she said, "and not worry about me. The Operators can tell when you're being uncooperative is all, even when *you* didn't know you were being uncooperative. Then they have to root about a bit more than's comfortable to find the answers they want."

Jenny coaxed the car down from the window, wincing a little at the sharp echo pains that flashed in her head and ears. "Don't tell your owner, but this isn't the first time I've been called to question. Now, to bed."

The car looked doubtful, but obediently rolled back to the repair bed that grew from the garage floor. It settled in, grumbled a bit, then switched off its headlights.

Jenny walked around to the door and entered. She found that the water sacs were full and chilled and drew a long drink. The water tasted faintly of salt. She took another swallow, then dampened a rag with a bit more of the tangy stuff to wipe away the dried blood. Then she went to work.

The bundle bugs crawled out of the city, crossed Distinguished Opposition Bridge beneath the watching eye of bears floating overhead, then described a right-angle turn along the levy to their dumping grounds. Soma and the Kentuckians lay hidden in the brushy wasteland at the edge of the grounds, waiting.

The Owl placed a hand on Japheth's shoulder, pointing at a bundle bug just entering the grounds. Then the Owl rose to his knees and began worming his way between the bushes and dead appliances.

"Soma Painter," whispered Japheth. "I'm going to have to break your jaw in a few minutes and cut out as many of her tentacles as we can get at, but we'll knit it back up as soon as we cross the river."

Soma was too far gone in the paste to hold both of the threats in his mind at the same time. A broken jaw, Crows in the capital. He concentrated on the second.

"The bears will scoop you up and drop you in the Salt Lick," Soma said. "Children will climb on you during Campaign and Legislators will stand on your shoulders to make their stump speeches."

"The bears will not see us, Soma."

"The bears watch the river and the bridges, 'and—'"

"' — and their eyes never close,'" finished Japheth. "Yes, we've seen the commercials."

A bundle bug, a large one at forty meters in length, reared up over them, precariously balanced on its rearmost set of legs. Soma said, "They're very good commercials," and the bug crashed down over them all.

Athena's data realm mirrored her physical realm. One-to-one constructs mimicked the buildings and the citizenry, showed who was riding and who was being ridden.

In that numerical space, the Kentuckians' math found the bridge. The harsh light of the bears floated above. Any bear represented a statistically significant portion of the Governor herself, and from the point of view of the math, the pair above Distinguished Opposition Bridge looked like miniature suns, casting probing rays at the marching bundle bugs, the barges floating along the Cumberland, and even into the waters of the river itself, illuminating the numerical analogs of the dangerous things that lived in the muddy bottom.

Bundle bugs came out of the city, their capacious abdomens distended with the waste they'd ingested along their routes. The math could see that the bug crossing through the bears' probes right now had a lot of restaurants on its itinerary. The beams pierced the dun-colored carapace and showed a riot of uneaten jellies, crumpled cups, soiled napkins.

The bugs marching in the opposite direction, emptied and ready for reloading, were scanned even more carefully than their outward-bound kin. The beam scans were withering, complete, and exceedingly precise.

The math knew that precision and accuracy are not the same thing.

—

"Lowell's death has set us back further than we thought," said Japheth, talking to the four Crows, the Owl, and, Soma guessed, to the bundle bug they inhabited. Japheth had detailed off the rest of the raiding party to carry the dead boy back north, so there was plenty of room where they crouched.

The interior of the bug's abdomen was larger than Soma's apartment by a factor of two and smelled of flowers instead of paint thinner. Soma's apartment, however, was not an alcoholic.

"This is good, though, good good." The bug's voice rang from every direction at once. "I'm scheduled down for a rest shift. You-uns was late and missed my last run, and now we can all rest and drink good whiskey. Good good."

But none of the Kentuckians drank any of the whiskey from the casks they'd cracked once they'd crawled down the bug's gullet. Instead, every half hour or so, they poured another gallon into one of the damp fissures that ran all through the interior. Bundle bugs' abdomens weren't designed for digestion, just evacuation, and it was the circulatory system that was doing the work of carrying the bourbon to the bug's brain.

Soma dipped a finger into an open cask and touched finger to tongue. "Bourbon burns!" he said, pulling his finger from his mouth.

"Burns good!" said the bug. "Good good."

"We knew that not all of us were going to be able to actually enter the city — we don't have enough outfits, for one thing — but six is a bare minimum. And since we're running behind, we'll have to wait out tonight's anthem in our host's apartment."

"Printer's Alley is two miles from the Parthenon," said the Owl, nodding at Soma.

Japheth nodded. "I know. And I know that those might be the two longest miles in the world. But we expected hard walking."

He banged the curving gray wall he leaned against with his elbow. "Hey! Bundle bug! How long until you start your shift?"

A vast and disappointed sigh shuddered through the abdomen. "Two more hours, bourbon man," said the bug.

"Get out your gear, cousin," Japheth said to the Owl. He stood and stretched, motioned for the rest of the Crows to do the same. He turned toward Soma. "The rest of us will hold him down."

—

Jenny had gone out midmorning, when the last of the fog was still burning off the bluffs, searching for low moisture organics to feed the garage. She'd run its reserves very low, working on one thing and another until quite late in the night.

As she suspected from the salty taste of the water supply, the filters in the housings between the tap roots and the garage's plumbing array were clogged with silt. She'd blown them out with pressurized air—no need to replace what you can fix—and reinstalled them one, two, three. But while she was blowing out the filters, she'd heard a whine she didn't like in the air compressor, and when she'd gone to check it she found it panting with effort, tongue hanging out onto the workbench top where it sat.

And then things went as these things go, and she moved happily from minor maintenance problem to minor maintenance problem — wiping away the air compressor's crocodile tears while she stoned the motor brushes in its A/C motor, then replacing the fusible link in the garage itself. "Links are so easily fusible," she joked to her horse when she rubbed it down with handfuls of the sweet-smelling fern fronds she'd intended for her own bed.

And all the while, of course, she watched the little car, monitoring the temperatures at its core points and doing what she could to coax the broken window to reknit in a smooth, steady fashion. Once, when the car awoke in the middle of the night making colicky noises, Jenny had to pop the hood, where she found that the points needed to be pulled and regapped. They were fouled with the viscous residue of the analgesic aero the owner had spread about so liberally.

She tssked. The directions on the labels clearly stated that the nozzle was to be pointed *away* from the engine compartment. Still, hard to fault Soma Painter's goodhearted efforts. It was an easy fix, and she would have pulled the plugs during the tune-up she had planned for the morning anyway.

So, repairings and healings, lights burning and tools turning, and when she awoke to the morning tide sounds the garage immediately began flashing amber lights at her wherever she turned. The belly-grumble noises it floated from the speakers worried the horse, so she set out looking for something to put in the hoppers of the hungry garage.

When she came back, bearing a string-tied bundle of dried wood and a half bucket of old walnuts some gatherer had wedged beneath an overhang and forgotten at least a double handful of autumns past, the car was gone.

Jenny hurried to the edge of the parking lot and looked down the road, though she couldn't see much. This time of year the morning fog turned directly into the midday haze. She could see the city, and bits of road between trees and bluff line, but no sign of the car.

The garage pinged at her, and she shoved its breakfast into the closest intake. She didn't open her head to call the police — she hadn't yet fully recovered from yesterday afternoon's interview. She was even hesitant to open her head the little bit she needed to access her own garage's security tapes. But she'd built the garage, and either built or rebuilt everything in it, so she risked it.

She stood at her workbench, rubbing her temple, as a see-through Jenny and a see-through car built themselves up out of twisted light. Light Jenny put on a light rucksack, scratched the light car absently on the roof as she walked by, and headed out the door. Light Jenny did not tether the car. Light Jenny did not lock the door.

"Silly light Jenny," said Jenny.

As soon as light Jenny was gone, the little light car rolled over to the big open windows. It popped a funny little wheelie and caught itself on the sash, the way it had yesterday when it had watched real Jenny swim up out of her government dream.

The light car kept one headlight just above the sash for a few minutes, then lowered itself back to the floor with a bounce (real Jenny had aired up the tires first thing, even before she grew the garage).

The light car revved its motor excitedly. Then, just a gentle tap on the door, and it was out in the parking lot. It drove over to the steps leading down to the beach, hunching its grill down to the ground. It circled the lot a bit, snuffling here and there, until it found whatever it was looking for. Before it zipped down the road toward Nashville, it circled back round and stopped outside the horse's stall. The light car opened its passenger door and waggled it back and forth a time or two. The real horse neighed and tossed its head at the light car in a friendly fashion.

Jenny-With-Grease-Beneath-Her-Fingernails visited her horse with the meanest look that a mechanic can give a horse. The horse snickered. "You laugh, horse," she said, opening the tack locker, "but we still have to go after it."

—

Inside the bundle bug, there was some unpleasantness with a large glass-and-pewter contraption of the Owl's. The Crow Brothers held Soma as motionless as they could, and Japheth seemed genuinely sorry when he forced the painter's mouth open much wider than Soma had previously thought possible. "You should have drunk more of the whiskey," said Japheth. There was a loud, wet, popping sound, and Soma shuddered, stiffened, fainted.

"Well, that'll work best for all of us," said Japheth. He looked up at the Owl, who was peering through a lens polished out of a semiprecious gemstone, staring down into the painter's gullet.

"Have you got access?"

The Owl nodded.

"Talk to your math," said the Crow.

The math had been circling beneath the bridge, occasionally dragging a curiosity-begat string of numbers into the water. Always low-test numbers, because invariably whatever lived beneath the water snatched at the lines and sucked them down.

The input the math was waiting for finally arrived in the form of a low hooting sound rising up from the dumping grounds. It was important that the math not know which bundle bug the sound emanated from. There were certain techniques the bears had developed for teasing information out of recalcitrant math.

No matter. The math knew the processes. It had the input. It spread itself out over the long line of imagery the bundle bugs yielded up to the bears. It affected its changes. It lent clarity.

Above, the bears did their work with great precision.

Below, the Kentuckians slipped into Nashville undetected.

Soma woke to find the Kentuckians doing something terrible. When he tried to speak, he found that his face was immobilized by a mask of something that smelled of the docks but felt soft and gauzy.

The four younger Crows were dressed in a gamut of jerseys and shorts colored in the hotter hues of the spectrum. Japheth was struggling into a long, jangly coat hung with seashells and old capacitors. But it was the Owl that frightened Soma the most. The broad-chested man was dappled with opal stones from collar bones to ankles and wore nothing else save a breech cloth cut from an old newspaper. Soma moaned, trying to attract their attention again.

The blue-eyed boy said, "Your painter stirs, Japheth."

But it was the Owl who leaned over Soma, placed his hand on Soma's chin and turned his head back and forth with surprising gentleness. The Owl nodded, to himself Soma guessed, for none of the Crows reacted, then peeled the bandages off Soma's face.

Soma took a deep breath, then said, "Nobody's worn opals for months! And those shorts," he gestured at the others, "Too much orange! Too much orange!"

Japheth laughed. "Well, we'll be tourists in from the provinces, then, not princes of Printer's Alley. Do *I* offend?" He wriggled his shoulders, set the shells and circuits to clacking.

Soma pursed his lips, shook his head. "Seashells and capacitors are time-less," he said.

Japheth nodded. "That's what it said on the box." Then, "Hey! Bug! Are we to market yet?"

"It's hard to say, whiskey man," came the reply. "My eyes are funny."

"Close enough. Open up."

The rear of the beast's abdomen cracked, and yawned wide. Japheth turned to his charges. "You boys ready to play like vols?"

The younger Crows started gathering burlap bundles. The Owl hoisted a heavy rucksack, adjusted the flowers in his hat, and said, "Wacka wacka ho."

In a low place, horizon bounded by trees in every direction, Jenny and her horse came on the sobbing car. From the ruts it had churned up in the mud, Jenny guessed it had been there for some time, driving back and forth along the northern verge.

"Now what have you done to yourself?" she asked, dismounting. The car turned to her and shuddered. Its front left fender was badly dented, and its hood and windshield were a mess of leaves and small branches.

"Trying to get into the woods? Cars are for roads, car." She brushed some muck off the damaged fender.

"Well, that's not too bad, though. This is all cosmetic. Why would a car try to go where trees are? See what happens?"

The horse called. It had wandered a little way into the woods and was standing at the base of a vast poplar. Jenny reached in through the passenger's window of the car, avoiding the glassy knitting blanket on the other side, and set the parking brake. "You wait here."

She trotted out to join her horse. It was pawing at a small patch of ground. Jenny was a mechanic and had no woodscraft, but she could see the outline of a cleft-toed sandal. Who would be in the woods with such impractical footwear?

"The owner's an artist. An artist looking for a shortcut to the Alley, I reckon," said Jenny. "Wearing funny artist shoes."

She walked back to the car, considering. The car was pining. Not unheard of, but not common. It made her think better of Soma Painter that his car missed him so.

"Say, horse. Melancholy slows car repair. I think this car will convalesce better in its own parking space."

The car revved.

"But there's the garage still back at the beach," said Jenny.

She turned things over and over. "Horse," she said, "you're due three more personal days this month. If I release you for them now, will you go fold up the garage and bring it to me in the city?"

The horse tossed its head enthusiastically.

"Good. I'll drive with this car back to the Alley, then — " But the horse was already rubbing its flanks against her.

"Okay, okay." She drew a tin of salve from her tool belt, dipped her fingers in it, then ran her hands across the horse's back. The red crosses came away in her hands, wriggling. "The cases for these are in my cabinet," she said, and then inspiration came.

"Here, car," she said, and laid the crosses on its hood. They wriggled around until they were at statute-specified points along the doors and roof. "Now you're an ambulance! Not a hundred percent legal, maybe, but this way you can drive fast and whistle sirenlike."

The car spun its rear wheels but couldn't overcome the parking brake. Jenny laughed. "Just a minute more. I need you to give me a ride into town."

She turned to speak to the horse, only to see it already galloping along the coast road. "Don't forget to drain the water tanks before you fold it up!" she shouted.

—

The bundles that were flecked with root matter, Soma discovered, were filled with roots. Carrots and turnips, a half dozen varieties of potatoes, beets. The Kentuckians spread out through the Farmer's Market, trading them by the armload for the juices and gels that the rock monkeys brought in from their gardens.

"This is our secondary objective," said Japheth. "We do this all the time, trading doped potatoes for that shit y'all eat."

"You're poisoning us?" Soma was climbing out of the paste a little, or something. His thoughts were shifting around some.

"Doped with nutrients, friend. Forty ain't old outside Tennessee. Athena doesn't seem to know any more about human nutrition than she does human psychology. Hey, we're trying to *help* you people."

Then they were in the very center of the market, and the roar of the crowds drowned out any reply Soma might make.

Japheth kept a grip on Soma's arm as he spoke to a gray old monkey. "Ten pounds, right?" The monkey was weighing a bundle of carrots on a scale.

"Okay," grunted the monkey. "Okay, man. Ten pounds I give you...four blue jellies."

Soma was incredulous. He'd never developed a taste for them himself, but he knew that carrots were popular. Four blue jellies was an insulting trade. But Japheth said, "Fair enough," and pocketed the plastic tubes the monkey handed over.

"You're no trader," said Soma, or started to, but heard the words slur out of him in an unintelligible mess of vowels. *One spring semester, when he'd already been a TA for a year, he was tapped to work on the interface. No more need for scholarships.*

"Painter!" shouted Japheth.

Soma looked up. There was a Crow dressed in Alley haute couture standing in front of him. He tried to open his head to call the Tennessee Highway Patrol. He couldn't find his head.

"Give him one of these yellow ones," said a monkey. "They're good for fugues."

"Painter!" shouted Japheth again. The grip on Soma's shoulder was like a vise.

Soma struggled to stand under his own power. "I'm forgetting something."

"Hah!" said Japheth. "You're remembering. Too soon for my needs, though. Listen to me. Rock monkeys are full voluntary citizens of Tennessee."

The outlandishness of the statement shocked Soma out of his reverie and brought the vendor up short.

"Fuck you, man!" said the monkey.

"No, no," said Soma, then said by rote, "Tennessee is a fully realized postcolonial state. The land of the rock monkeys is an autonomous partner-principality within our borders, and while the monkeys are our staunch allies, their allegiance is not to our Governor, but to their king."

"Yah," said the monkey. "Long as we get our licenses and pay the tax machine. Plus, who the jelly cubes going to listen to besides the monkey king, huh?"

Soma marched Japheth to the next stall. "Lot left in there to wash out yet," Japheth said.

"I wash every day," said Soma, then fell against a sloshing tray of juice containers. *The earliest results were remarkable.*

A squat man covered with black gems came up to them. The man who'd insulted the monkey said, "You might have killed too much of it; he's getting kind of wonky."

The squat man looked into Soma's eyes. "We can stabilize him easy enough. There are televisions in the food court."

Then Soma and Japheth were drinking hot rum punches and watching a newsfeed. There was a battle out over the Gulf somewhere, Commodores mounted on bears darted through the clouds, lancing Cuban zeppelins.

"The Cubans will never achieve air superiority," said Soma, and it felt right saying it.

Japheth eyed him wearily. "I need you to keep thinking that for now, Soma Painter," he said quietly. "But I hope sometime soon you'll know that Cubans don't live in a place called the Appalachian Archipelago, and that the salty reach out there isn't the Gulf of Mexico."

The bicycle race results were on then, and Soma scanned the lists, hoping to see his favorites' names near the top of the general classifications.

"That's the Tennessee River, dammed up by your Governor's hubris."

Soma saw that his drink was nearly empty and heard that his friend Japheth was still talking. "What?" he asked, smiling.

"I asked if you're ready to go to the Alley," said Japheth.

"Good good," said Soma.

The math was moving along minor avenues, siphoning data from second-ary and tertiary ports when it sensed her looming up. It researched ten thou-sand thousand escapes but rejected them all when it perceived that it had been subverted, that it was inside her now, becoming part of her, that it is *primi-tive in materials but clever clever in architecture and there have been blindings times not seen places to root out root out all of it check again check one thousand more times all told all told eat it all up all the little bluegrass math is absorbed*

"The Alley at night!" shouted Soma. "Not like where you're from, eh, boys?"

A lamplighter's stalk legs eased through the little group. Soma saw that his friends were staring up at the civil servant's welding mask head, gaping open-mouthed as it turned a spigot at the top of a tree and lit the gas with a flick of its tongue.

"Let's go to my place!" said Soma. "When it's time for anthem we can watch the parade from my balcony. I live in one of the lofts above the Tyranny of the Anecdote."

"Above what?" asked Japheth.

"It's a tavern. They're my landlords," said Soma. "Vols are so fucking stupid."

But that wasn't right.

Japheth's Owl friend fell to his knees and vomited right in the street. Soma stared at the jiggling spheres in the gutter as the man choked some words out. "She's taken the feathers. She's looking for us now."

Too much rum punch, thought Soma, thought it about the Owl man and himself and about all of Japheth's crazy friends.

"Soma, how far now?" asked Japheth.

Soma remembered his manners. "Not far," he said.

And it wasn't, just a few more struggling yards, Soma leading the way and Japheth's friends half-carrying, half-dragging their drunken friend down the Alley. Nothing unusual there. Every night in the Alley was Carnival.

Then a wave at the bouncer outside the Anecdote, then up the steps, then sing "Let me in, let me in!" to the door, and finally all of them packed into the cramped space.

"There," said the sick man, pointing at the industrial sink Soma had installed himself to make brush cleaning easier. *Brushes...where were his brushes, his pencils, his notes for the complexity seminar?*

"Towels, Soma?"

"What? Oh, here let me get them." Soma bustled around, finding towels, pulling out stools for the now silent men who filled his room.

He handed the towels to Japheth. "Was it something he ate?" Soma asked.

Japheth shrugged. "Ate a long time ago, you could say. Owls are as much numbers as they are meat. He's divesting himself. Those are ones and zeroes washing down your drain."

The broad man—hadn't he been broad?—the scrawny man with opals falling off him said, "We can only take a few minutes. There are unmounted Detectives swarming the whole city now. What I've left in me is too deep for their little minds, but the whole sphere is roused and things will only get tighter. Just let me —" He turned and retched into the sink again. "Just a few minutes more until the singing."

Japheth moved to block Soma's view of the Owl. He nodded at the drawings on the wall. "Yours?"

The blue-eyed boy moved over to the sink, helped the Owl ease to the floor. Soma looked at the pictures. "Yes, mostly. I traded for a few."

Japheth was studying one charcoal piece carefully, a portrait. "What's this one?"

The drawing showed a tall, thin young man dressed in a period costume, leaning against a mechanical of some kind, staring intently out at the viewer. Soma didn't remember drawing it, specifically, but knew what it must be.

"That's a caricature. I do them during Campaign for the provincials who come into the city to vote. Someone must have asked me to draw him and then never come back to claim it."

And he remembered trying to remember. He remembered asking his hand to remember when his head wouldn't.

"I'm...what did you put in me?" Soma asked. There was moisture on his cheeks, and he hoped it was tears.

The Owl was struggling up to his feet. A bell tone sounded from the sky and he said, "Now, Japheth. There's no time."

"Just a minute more," snapped the Crow. "What did *we* put in you? You..." Japheth spat. "While you're remembering, try and remember this. You *chose* this! All of you chose it!"

The angry man wouldn't have heard any reply Soma might have made, because it was then that all of the Kentuckians clamped their ears shut with their odd muffs. To his surprise, they forced a pair onto Soma as well.

Jenny finally convinced the car to stop wailing out its hee-haw pitch when they entered the maze of streets leading to Printer's Alley. The drive back had been long, the car taking every northern side road, backtracking, looping, even trying to enter the dumping grounds at one point before the bundle bugs growled them away. During anthem, while Jenny drummed her fingers and forced out the words, the car still kept up its search, not even pretending to dance.

So Jenny had grown more and more fascinated by the car's behavior. She had known cars that were slavishly attached to their owners before, and she had known cars that were smart — almost as smart as bundle bugs, some of them — but the two traits never seemed to go together. "Cars are dogs or cars are cats," her Teacher had said to explain the phenomenon, another of the long roll of enigmatic statements that constituted formal education in the Voluntary State.

But here, now, here was a bundle bug that didn't seem to live up to those creatures' reputations for craftiness. The car had been following the bug for a few blocks — Jenny only realized that after the car, for the first time since they entered the city proper, made a turn away from the address painted on its name tag.

The bug was a big one, and was describing a gentle career down Commerce Street, drifting from side to side and clearly ignoring the traffic signals that flocked around its head in an agitated cloud.

"Car, we'd better get off this street. Rogue bugs are too much for the THP. If it doesn't self-correct, a Commodore is likely to be rousted out from the Parthenon." Jenny sometimes had nightmares about Commodores.

The car didn't listen — though it was normally an excellent listener — but accelerated toward the bug. The bug, Jenny now saw, had stopped in front of a restaurant and cracked its abdomen. Dumpster feelers had started creeping out of the interstices between thorax and head when the restaurateur charged out, beating at the feelers with a broom. "Go now!" the man shouted, face as red as his vest and leggings. "I told you twice already! You pick up here Chaseday! Go! I already called your supervisor, bug!"

The bug's voice echoed along the street. "No load? Good good." Its sigh was pure contentment, but Jenny had no time to appreciate it. The car sped up, and Jenny covered her eyes, anticipating a collision. But the car slid to a halt with bare inches to spare, peered into the empty cavern of the bug's belly, then sighed, this one not content at all.

"Come on, car," Jenny coaxed. "He must be at home by now. Let's just try your house, okay?"

The car beeped and executed a precise three-point turn. As they turned off Commerce and climbed the viaduct that arced above the Farmer's Market, Jenny caught a hint of motion in the darkening sky. "THP bicycles, for sure," she said. "Tracking your bug friend."

At the highest point on the bridge, Jenny leaned out and looked down into the controlled riot of the market. Several stalls were doing brisk business, and when Jenny saw why, she asked the car to stop, then let out a whistle.

"Oi! Monkey!" she shouted. "Some beets up here!"

Jenny loved beets.

signals from the city center subsidiaries routing reports and recommendations increase percentages dedicated to observation and prediction dispatch commodore downcycle biological construct extra-parametrical lower authority

"It's funny that I don't know what it means, though, don't you think, friends?" Soma was saying this for perhaps the fifth time since they began their walk. "*Church* Street. *Church.* Have you ever heard that word anywhere else?"

"No," said the blue-eyed boy.

The Kentuckians were less and less talkative the farther the little group advanced west down Church Street. It was a long, broad avenue, but rated for pedestrians and emergency vehicles only. Less a street, really, than a linear park, for there were neither businesses nor apartments on either side, just low, gray government buildings, slate-colored in the sunset.

The sunset. That was why the boulevard was crowded, as it was every night. As the sun dropped down, down, down it dropped behind the Parthenon. At the very instant the disc disappeared behind the sand-colored edifice, the Great Salt Lick self-illuminated and the flat acres of white surrounding the Parthenon shone with a vast, icy light.

The Lick itself was rich with the minerals that fueled the Legislators and Bears, but the white light emanating from it was sterile. Soma noticed that the Crows' faces grew paler and paler as they all got closer to its source. *His work was fascinating, and grew more so as more and more disciplines began finding ways to integrate their fields of study into a meta-architecture of science. His department chair coauthored a paper with an expert in animal husbandry, of all things.*

The Owl held Soma's head as the painter vomited up the last of whatever was in his stomach. Japheth and the others were making reassuring noises to passersby. "Too much monkey wine!" they said, and, "We're in from the provinces, he's not used to such rich food!" and, "He's overcome by the sight of the Parthenon!"

Japheth leaned over next to the Owl. "Why's it hitting him so much harder than the others?"

The Owl said, "Well, we've always taken them back north of the border. This poor fool we're dragging ever closer to the glory of his owner. I couldn't even guess what's trying to fill up the empty spaces I left in him — but I'm pretty sure whatever's rushing in isn't all from her."

Japheth cocked an eyebrow at his lieutenant. "I think that's the most words I've ever heard you say all together at once."

The Owl smiled, another first, if that sad little half grin counted as a smile. "Not a lot of time left for talking. Get up now, friend painter."

The Owl and Japheth pulled Soma to his feet. "What did you mean," Soma asked, wiping his mouth with the back of his hand, "'the glory of his owner'?"

"Governor," said Japheth. "He said, 'the glory of his Governor,'" and Japheth swept his arm across, and yes, there it was, the glory of the Governor.

Church Street had a slight downward grade in its last few hundred yards. From where they stood, they could see that the street ended at the spectacularly defined border of the Great Salt Lick, which served as legislative chambers in the Voluntary State. At the center of the Lick stood the Parthenon, and while no normal citizens walked the salt just then, there was plenty of motion and color.

Two bears were laying face down in the Lick, bobbing their heads as they took in sustenance from the ground. A dozen or more Legislators slowly unambulated, their great slimy bodies leaving trails of gold or silver depending on their party affiliation. One was engulfing one of the many salt-white statues that dotted the grounds, gaining a few feet of height to warble its slogan songs from. And, unmoving at the corners of the rectangular palace in the center of it all, four Commodores stood.

They were tangled giants of rust, alike in their towering height and in the oily bathyspheres encasing the scant meat of them deep in their torsos, but otherwise each a different silhouette of sensor suites and blades, each with a different complement of articulated limbs or wings or wheels.

"Can you tell which ones they are?" Japheth asked the blue-eyed boy, who had begun murmuring to himself under his breath, eyes darting from Commodore to Commodore.

"Ruby-eyed Sutcliffe, stomper, smasher,
Tempting Nguyen, whispering, lying,
Burroughs burrows, up from the underground..."

The boy hesitated, shaking his head. "Northeast corner looks kind of like Praxis Dale, but she's supposed to be away West, fighting the Federals. Saint Sandalwood's physical presence had the same profile as Dale's, but we believe he's gone, consumed by Athena after their last sortie against the containment field cost her so much."

"I'll never understand why she plays at politics with her subordinates when she *is* her subordinates," said Japheth.

The Owl said, "That's not as true with the Commodores as with a lot of the... inhabitants. I think it *is* Saint Sandalwood; she must have reconstituted him, or part of him. And remember his mnemonic?"

"Sandalwood staring," sang the blue-eyed boy.

"Inside and outside," finished Japheth, looking the Owl in the eye. "Time then?"

"Once we're on the Lick I'd do anything she told me, even empty as I am," said the Owl. "Bind me."

Then the blue-eyed boy took Soma by the arm, kept encouraging him to take in the sights of the Parthenon, turning his head away from where the Crows were wrapping the Owl in grapevines. They took the Owl's helmet from a rucksack and seated it, cinching the cork seals at the neck maybe tighter than Soma would have thought was comfortable.

Two of the Crows hoisted the Owl between them, his feet stumbling some. Soma saw that the eyeholes of the mask had been blocked with highly reflective tape.

Japheth spoke to the others. "The bears won't be in this; they'll take too long to stand up from their meal. Avoid the Legislators, even their trails. The THP will be on the ground, but won't give you any trouble. You boys know why you're here."

The two Crows holding the Owl led him over to Japheth, who took him by the hand. The blue-eyed boy said, "We know why we're here, Japheth. We know why we were born."

And suddenly as that, the four younger Crows were gone, fleeing in every direction except back up Church Street.

"Soma Painter," said Japheth. "Will you help me lead this man on?"

Soma was taken aback. While he knew of no regulation specifically prohibiting it, traditionally no one actually trod the Lick except during Campaign.

"We're going into the Salt Lick?" Soma asked.

"We're going into the Parthenon," Japheth answered.

As they crossed Church Street from the south, the car suddenly stopped.

"Now what, car?" said Jenny. Church Street was her least favorite thoroughfare in the capital.

The car snuffled around on the ground for a moment, then, without warning, took a hard left and accelerated, siren screeching. Tourists and sunset gazers scattered to either side as the car and Jenny roared toward the glowing white horizon.

The Owl only managed a few yards under his own power. He slowed, then stumbled, and then the Crow and the painter were carrying him.

"What's wrong with him?" asked Soma.

They crossed the verge onto the salt. They'd left the bravest sightseers a half-block back.

"He's gone inside himself," said Japheth.

"Why?" asked Soma.

Japheth half laughed. "You'd know better than me, friend."

It was then that the Commodore closest to them took a single step forward with its right foot, dragged the left a dozen yards in the same direction, and then, twisting, fell to the ground with a thunderous crash.

"Whoo!" shouted Japheth. "The harder they fall! We'd better start running now, Soma!"

Soma was disappointed, but unsurprised, to see that Japheth did not mean run *away*.

There was only one bear near the slightly curved route that Japheth picked for them through the harsh glare. Even light as he was, purged of his math, the Owl was still a burden and Soma couldn't take much time to marvel at the swirling colors in the bear's plastic hide.

"Keep up, Soma!" shouted the Crow. Ahead of them, two of the Commodores had suddenly turned on one another and were landing terrible blows. Soma saw a tiny figure clinging to one of the giants' shoulders, saw it lose its grip, fall, and disappear beneath an ironshod boot the size of a bundle bug.

Then Soma slipped and fell himself, sending all three of them to the glowing ground and sending a cloud of the biting crystal salt into the air. One of his sandaled feet, he saw, was coated in gold slime. They'd been trying to outflank one Legislator only to stumble on the trail of another.

Japheth picked up the Owl, now limp as a rag doll, and with a grunt heaved the man across his shoulders. "Soma, you should come on. We might make it." *It's not a hard decision to make at all. How can you not make it? At first he'd needed convincing, but then he'd been one of those who'd gone out into the world to convince others. It's not just history; it's after history.*

"Soma!"

Japheth ran directly at the unmoving painter, the deadweight of the Owl across his shoulders slowing him. He barreled into Soma, knocking him to the ground again, all of them just missing the unknowing Legislator as it slid slowly past.

"Up, up!" said Japheth. "Stay behind it, so long as it's moving in the right direction. I think my boys missed a Commodore." His voice was very sad.

The Legislator stopped and let out a bellowing noise. Fetid steam began rising from it. Japheth took Soma by the hand and pulled him along, through chaos. One of the Commodores, the first to fall, was motionless on the ground, two or three Legislators making their way along its length. The two who'd fought lay locked in one another's grasp, barely moving and glowing hotter and hotter. The only standing Commodore, eyes like red suns, seemed to be staring just behind them.

As it began to sweep its gaze closer, Soma heard Japheth say, "We got closer than I would have bet."

Then Soma's car, mysteriously covered with red crosses and wailing at the top of its voice, came to a sliding, crunching stop in the salt in front of them.

Soma didn't hesitate, but threw open the closest rear door and pulled Japheth in behind him. When the three of them — painter, Crow, Owl — were stuffed into the rear door, Soma shouted, "Up those stairs, car!"

In the front seat, there was a woman whose eyes seemed as large as saucers.

commodores faulting headless people in the lick protocols compel reeling in, strengthening, temporarily abandoning telepresence locate an asset with a head asset with a head located

Jenny-With-Grease-Beneath-Her-Fingernails was trying not to go crazy. Something was pounding at her head, even though she hadn't tried to open it herself. Yesterday, she had been working a remote repair job on the beach, fixing a smashed window. Tonight, she was hurtling across the Great Salt Lick, Legislators and bears and *Commodores* acting in ways she'd never seen or heard of.

Jenny herself acting in ways she'd never heard of. Why didn't she just pull the emergency brake, roll out of the car, wait for the THP? Why did she just hold on tighter and pull down the sunscreen so she could use the mirror to look into the backseat?

It *was* three men. She hadn't been sure at first. One appeared to be unconscious and was dressed in some strange getup, a helmet of some kind completely encasing his head. She didn't know the man in the capacitor jacket, who was craning his head out the window, trying to see something above them. The other one though, she recognized.

"Soma Painter," she said. "Your car is much better, though it has missed you terribly."

The owner just looked at her glaze-eyed. The other one pulled himself back in through the window, a wild glee on his face. He rapped the helmet of the prone man and shouted, "Did you hear that? The unpredictable you prophesied! And it fell in our favor!"

Soma worried about his car's suspension, not to mention the tires, when it slalomed through the legs of the last standing Commodore and bounced up the steeply cut steps of the Parthenon. *He hadn't had a direct hand in the subsystems design — by the time he'd begun to develop the cars, Athena was already beginning to take over a lot of the details. Not all of them, though; he couldn't blame her for the guilt he felt over twisting his animal subjects into something like onboard components.*

But the car made it onto the platform inside the outer set of columns, seemingly no worse for wear. The man next to him — Japheth, his name was Japheth and he was from Kentucky — jumped out of the car and ran to the vast, closed counterweighted bronze doors.

"It's because of the crosses. We're in an emergency vehicle according to their protocols." That was the mechanic, Jenny, sitting in the front seat and trying to staunch a nosebleed with a greasy rag. "I can hear the Governor," she said.

Soma could hear Japheth raging and cursing. He stretched the Owl out along the back seat and climbed out of the car. Japheth was pounding on the doors in futility, beating his fists bloody, spinning, spitting. He caught sight of Soma.

"*These* weren't here before!" he said, pointing to two silver columns that angled up from the platform's floor, ending in flanges on the doors themselves. "The doors aren't locked, they're just sealed by these fucking cylinders!" Japheth was shaking. "Caw!" he cried. "Caw!"

"What's he trying to do?" asked the woman in the car.

Soma brushed his fingers against his temple, trying to remember.

"I think he's trying to remake Tennessee," he said.

The weight of a thousand cars on her skull, the hoofbeats of a thousand horses throbbing inside her eyes, Jenny was incapable of making any rational decision. So, irrationally, she left the car. She stumbled over to the base of one of the silver columns. When she tried to catch herself on it, her hand slid off.

"Oil," she said. "These are just hydraulic cylinders." She looked around the metal sheeting where the cylinder disappeared into the platform, saw the access plate. She pulled a screwdriver from her belt and used it to remove the plate.

The owner was whispering to his car, but the crazy man had come over to her. "What are you doing?" he asked.

"I don't know," she said, but she meant it only in the largest sense. Immediately, she was thrusting her wrists into the access plate, playing the licenses and government bonds at her wrists under a spray of light, murmuring a quick apology to the machinery. Then she opened a long vertical cut down as much of the length of the hydraulic hose as she could with her utility blade.

Fluid exploded out of the hole, coating Jenny in the slick, dirty green stuff. The cylinders collapsed.

The man next to Jenny looked at her. He turned and looked at Soma-With-The-Paintbox-In-Printer's-Alley and at Soma's car.

"We must have had a pretty bad plan," he said, then rushed over to pull the helmeted figure from the backseat.

breached come home all you commodores come home cancel emergency designation on identified vehicle and downcycle now jump in jump in jump in

Jenny could not help Soma and his friend drag their burden through the doors of the temple, but she staggered through the doors. She had only seen Athena in tiny parts, in the mannequin shrines that contained tiny fractions of the Governor.

Here was the true and awesome thing, here was the forty-foot-tall sculpture — armed and armored — attended by the broken remains of her frozen marble enemies. Jenny managed to lift her head and look past sandaled feet, up cold golden raiment, past tart painted cheeks to the lapis lazuli eyes.

Athena looked back at her. Athena leapt.

Inside Jenny's head, inside so small an architecture, there was no more room for Jenny-With-Grease-Beneath-Her-Fingernails. Jenny fled.

Soma saw the mechanic, the woman who'd been so kind to his car, fall to her knees, blood gushing from her nose and ears. He saw Japheth laying out the

Owl like a sacrifice before the Governor. *He'd been among the detractors, scoffing at the idea of housing the main armature in such a symbol-potent place.*

Behind him, his car beeped. The noise was barely audible above the screaming metal sounds out in the Lick. The standing Commodore was swiveling its torso, turning its upper half toward the Parthenon. Superheated salt melted in a line slowly tracking toward the steps.

Soma trotted back to his car. He leaned in and *remembered the back door, the Easter egg he hadn't documented.* A twist on the ignition housing, then press in, and the key sank into the column. The car shivered.

"Run home as fast you can, car. Back to the ranch with your kin. Be fast, car, be clever."

The car woke up. It shook off Soma's ownership and closed its little head. It let out a surprised beep and then fled with blazing speed, leaping down the steps, over the molten salt, and through the storm, bubblewinged bicycles descending all around. The Commodore began another slow turn, trying to track it.

Soma turned back to the relative calm inside the Parthenon. Athena's gaze was baleful, but he couldn't feel it. The Owl had ripped the ability from him. The Owl lying before Japheth, defenseless against the knife Japheth held high.

"Why?" shouted Soma.

But Japheth didn't answer him, instead diving over the Owl in a somersault roll, narrowly avoiding the flurry of kicks and roundhouse blows being thrown by Jenny. Her eyes bugged and bled. More blood flowed from her ears and nostrils, but still she attacked Japheth with relentless fury.

Japheth came up in a crouch. The answer to Soma's question came in a slurred voice from Jenny. Not Jenny, though. Soma knew the voice, remembered it from somewhere, and it wasn't Jenny's.

"there is a bomb in that meat soma-friend a knife a threat an eraser"

Japheth shouted at Soma. "You get to decide again! Cut the truth out of him!" He gestured at the Owl with his knife.

Soma took in a shuddery breath. "So free with lives. One of the reasons we climbed up."

Jenny's body lurched at Japheth, but the Crow dropped onto the polished floor. Jenny's body slipped when it landed, the soles of its shoes coated with the same oil as its jumpsuit.

"My Owl cousin died of asphyxiation at least ten minutes ago, Soma," said Japheth. "Died imperfect and uncontrolled." Then, dancing backward before the scratching thing in front of him, Japheth tossed the blade in a gentle under-handed arc. It clattered to the floor at Soma's feet.

All of the same arguments.

All of the same arguments.

Soma picked up the knife and looked down at the Owl. The fight before him, between a dead woman versus a man certain to die soon, spun on. Japheth said no more, only looked at Soma with pleading eyes.

Jenny's body's eyes followed the gaze, saw the knife in Soma's hand.

"you are due upgrade soma-friend swell the ranks of commodores you were 96th percentile now 99th soma-with-the-paintbox-in-printer's-alley the voluntary state of tennessee applauds your citizenship"

But it wasn't the early slight, the denial of entry to the circle of highest minds. Memories of before *and* after, decisions made by him and for him, sentiences and upgrades decided by fewer and fewer and then one; one who'd been a *product*, not a builder.

Soma plunged the knife into the Owl's unmoving chest and sawed down-ward through the belly with what strength he could muster. The skin and fat fell away along a seam straighter than he could ever cut. The bomb — the knife, the eraser, the threat — looked like a tiny white balloon. He pierced it with the killing tip of the Kentuckian's blade.

A nova erupted at the center of the space where math and Detectives live. A wave of scouring numbers washed outward, spreading all across Nashville, all across the Voluntary State to fill all the space within the containment field.

The 144 Detectives evaporated. The King of the Rock Monkeys, nothing but twisted light, fell into shadow. The Commodores fell immobile, the ruined biology seated in their chests went blind, then deaf, then died.

And singing Nashville fell quiet. Ten thousand thousand heads slammed shut and ten thousand thousand souls fell insensate, unsupported, in need of revival.

North of the Girding Wall, alarms began to sound.

At the Parthenon, Japheth Sapp gently placed the tips of his index and ring fingers on Jenny's eyelids and pulled them closed.

Then the ragged Crow pushed past Soma and hurried out into the night. The Great Salt Lick glowed no more, and even the lights of the city were dimmed, so Soma quickly lost sight of the man. But then the cawing voice rang out once more. "We only hurt the car because we had to."

Soma thought for a moment, then said, "So did I."

But the Crow was gone, and then Soma had nothing to do but wait. He had made the only decision he had left in him. He idly watched as burning bears floated down into the sea. A striking image, but he had somewhere misplaced his paints.

"I don't think, in the end, this is a matter of rational 'ideas.' You are nearer the quick of it with words like 'wonder,' 'transcendence,' 'visionary drive,' 'conceptual novelty' — and especially 'cosmic fear.' This is the dirty little secret of science fiction: that its roots are planted not in the logical, positivistic assumptions of 'science,' but in some twisted apprehension (I use the word in the sense both of understanding and fear) that 'the universe is not only stranger than we imagine, it is stranger than we can imagine.' We fear and are attracted by that irrationality. It yawns like a pit beneath our attempts to understand technology's effects on us; it tugs at us like a cliff whispering, 'come on, jump.' In the interview Kelly and I did with you in Austin a year ago, you talked about wanting to seize the crowbar and smash something. What is that thing you want to smash? Could it be the mundane world's assumption (born, more and more in our time, out of desperate need instead of smug complacency) that the universe makes sense, that things are stable, that change can be understood and controlled? I have this gut feeling that almost all children destined to grow up to become science fiction writers have some fundamental experience of chaos somewhere in their formative years.... Some writers react by seeking a rigid authoritarianism...others may reach for certainty but remain convinced throughout their lives that Things Change and Are Not What They Seem...

But what are those skills [of a first-rate writer]? I think in the end, they are not skills at all, but a matter of temperament or character, or not even that — it's a state of mind that you can attain for moments but which isn't finally you.... What I mean is what I said in a letter to you a long time ago, that great writers go out on a limb farther than good writers do. They aren't afraid to violate rules, good taste, logic, sensible advice, proportion, etc. in the pursuit of whatever demon they're trying to catch, whatever quicksilver they're trying to nail to the tree."

Two Dreams on Trains

Elizabeth Bear

In Gibson, the corporations and power structures control everything (and ultimately, shadowy Wintermute rules all). The only hope for freedom is to live completely outside of "Babylon" like his space rastas, or to drop out into the underworld like Case and Molly, the beautiful losers of the urban night world, or to steal enough money in the hope of placing yourself beyond control.

Most people in the world cannot opt out. What if you are part of a permanent underclass? What if you are part of a family, connected, and stuck?

The needle wore a path of dye and scab round and round Patience's left ring finger; sweltering heat adhered her to the mold-scarred chair. The hurt didn't bother her. It was pain with a future. She glanced past the scarrist's bare scalp, through the grimy window, holding her eyes open around the prickle of tears.

Behind the rain, she could pick out the jeweled running lamps of a massive spacelighter sliding through clouds, coming in soft toward the waterlogged sprawl of a spaceport named for Lake Pontchartrain. On a clear night she could have seen its train of cargo capsules streaming in harness behind. Patience bit her lip and looked away: not down at the needle, but across at a wall shaggy with peeling paint.

Lake Pontchartrain was only a name now, a salt-clotted estuary of the rising Gulf. But it persisted — like the hot bright colors of bougainvillea grown in wooden washpails beside doors, like the Mardi Gras floats that now floated for real — in the memory of New Orleanians, as grand a legacy as anything the underwater city could claim. Patience's hand lay open on the wooden chair arm as if waiting for a gift. She didn't look down and she didn't close her eyes as the needle pattered and scratched, pattered and scratched. The long Poplar Street barge undulated under the tread of feet moving past the scarrist's, but his fingers were steady as a gin-soaked frontier doctor's.

The prick and shift of the needle stopped and the pock-faced scarrist sat back on his heels. He set his tools aside and made a practiced job of applying the quickseal. Patience looked down at her hands, at the palm fretted indigo to mark her caste. At the filigree of emerald and crimson across the back of her right hand, and underneath the transparent sealant swathing the last two fingers of her left.

A peculiar tightness blossomed under her breastbone. She started to raise her left hand and press it to her chest to ease the tension, stopped herself just in time, and laid the hand back on the chair. She pushed herself up with her right hand only and said, "Thank you."

She gave the scarrist a handful of cash chits, once he'd stripped his gloves and her blood away. His hands were the silt color he'd been born with, marking him a tradesman; the holographic slips of poly she paid with glittered like fish scales against his skin.

"Won't be long before you'll have the whole hand done." He rubbed a palm across his sweat-slick scalp. He had tattoos of his own, starting at the wrists — dragons and mermaids and manatees, arms and chest tesseraed in oceanic beasts. "You've earned two fingers in six months. You must be studying all the time."

"I want my kid to go to trade school so we can get berths outbound," Patience said, meeting the scarrist's eyes so squarely that he looked down and pocketed his hands behind the coins, like pelicans after fish. "I don't want him to have to sell his indenture to survive, like I did." She smiled. "I tell him he should study engineering, be a professional, get the green and red. Or maintenance tech, keep his hands clean. Like yours. He wants to be an artist, though. Not much call for painters up *there.*"

The scarrist grunted, putting his tools away. "There's more to life than lighters and cargo haulers, you know."

Her sweeping gesture took in the little room and the rainy window. The pressure in her chest tightened, a trap squeezing her heart, holding her in place, pinned. "Like this?"

He shrugged, looked up, considered. "Sure. Like this. I'm a free man, I do what I like." He paused. "Your kid any good?"

"As an artist?" A frown pulled the corner of her lip down. Consciously, she smoothed her hand open so she wouldn't squeeze and blur her new tattoos. "Real good. No reason he can't do it as a hobby, right?"

"Good? Or *good?*"

Blood scorched her cheeks. "*Real* good."

The scarrist paused. She'd known him for years: six fingers and a thumb, seven examinations passed. Three more left. "If he keeps his hands clean. When you finish the caste" — gesture at her hands — "if he still doesn't want to go. Send him to me."

"It's not that he doesn't want to go. He just — doesn't want to work, to sacrifice." She paused, helpless. "Got any kids?"

He laughed, shaking his head, as good as a yes, and they shared a lingering look. He glanced down first, when it got uncomfortable, and Patience nodded and brushed past on the way out the door. Rain beaded on her nanoskin as it shifted to repel the precipitation, and she paused on decking. Patchy-coated rats scurried around her as she watched a lighter and train lay itself into the lake, gently as an autumn leaf. She leaned out over the Poplar Street Canal as the lights taxied into their berth. The train's wake lapped gently at the segmented kilometers-long barge, lifting and dropping Poplar Street under Patience's feet. Cloying rain and sweat adhered her hair to the nape of her neck. Browning roux and sharp pepper cut the reek of filthy water. She squeezed the railing with her uninjured hand and watched another train ascend, the blossom of fear in her chest finally easing. "Javier Alexander," she muttered, crossing a swaying bridge. "You had best be home safe in bed, my boy. You'd *best* be home in bed."

A city like drowned New Orleans, you don't just walk away from. A city like drowned New Orleans, you *fly* away from. If you can. And if you can't...

You make something that can.

Jayve lay back in a puddle of blood-warm rain and seawater in the "borrowed" dinghy and watched the belly lights of another big train drift overhead, hulls silhouetted against the citylit salmon-colored clouds like a string of pearls. He almost reached up a pale-skinned hand: it seemed close enough to touch. The rain parted to either side like curtains, leaving him dry for the instant when the wind from the train's fans tossed him, and came together again behind as unmarked as the sea. "Beautiful," he whispered. "Fucking beautiful, Mad."

"You in there, Jayve?" A whisper in his ear, stutter and crack of static. They couldn't afford good equipment, or anything not stolen or jerry-built. But who gave a damn? Who gave a damn, when you could get that close to a *starship*?

"That last one went over my fucking *head*, Mad. Are you in?"

"Over the buoys. Shit. *Brace!*"

Jayve slammed hands and feet against the hull of the rowboat as Mad spluttered and coughed. The train's wake hit him, picked the dinghy up and shook it like a dog shaking a dishrag. Slimed old wood scraped his palms; the cross brace gouged an oozing slice across his scalp and salt water stung the blood from the wound. The contents of the net bag laced to his belt slammed him in the gut. He groaned and clung; strain burned his thighs and triceps.

He was still in the dinghy when it came back down.

He clutched his net bag, half-panicked touch racing over the surface of the insulated tins within until he was certain the wetness he felt was rain and not the gooey ooze of etchant: sure mostly because the skin on his hands stayed cool instead of sloughing to hang in shreds.

"Mad, can you hear me?"

A long, gut-tightening silence. Then Mad retched like he'd swallowed seawater. "Alive," he said. "Shit, that boy put his boat down a bit harder than he had to, didn't he?"

"Just a tad." Jayve pushed his bag aside and unshipped the oars, putting his back into the motion as they bit water. "Maybe it's his first run. Come on, Mad. Let's go brand this bitch."

Patience dawdled along her way, stalling in open-fronted shops while she caught up her marketing, hoping to outwait the rain and the worry gnawing her belly. Fish-scale chits dripped from her multicolored fingers, and from those of other indentured laborers — some, like her, buying off their contracts and passing exams, and others with indigo-stained paws and no ambition — and the clean hands of the tradesmen who crowded the bazaar; the coins fell into the hennaed palms of shopkeepers and merchants who walked with the rolling gait of sailors. The streets underfoot echoed the hollow sound of their footsteps between the planking and the water.

Dikes and levees had failed; there's just too much water in that part of the world to wall away. And there's nothing under the Big Easy to sink a piling into that would be big enough to hang a building from. But you don't just walk away from a place that holds the grip on the human imagination New Orleans does.

So they'd simply floated the city in pieces and let the Gulf of Mexico roll in underneath.

Simply.

The lighters and their trains came and went into Lake Pontchartrain, vessels too huge to land on dry earth. They sucked brackish fluid through hungry bellymouths between their running lights and fractioned it into hydrogen and oxygen, salt and trace elements and clean potable water; they dropped one train of containers and picked up another; they taxied to sea, took to the sky, and did it all over again.

Sometimes they hired technicians and tradesmen. They didn't hire laborer-caste, dole-caste, palms stained indigo as those of old-time denim textile workers, or criminals with their hands stained black. They didn't take artists.

Patience stood under an awning, watching the clever moth-eaten rats ply their trade through the market, her nanoskin wicking sweat off her flesh. The lamps of another lighter came over. She was cradling her painful hand close to her chest, the straps of her weighted net bag biting livid channels in her right wrist. She'd stalled as long as possible.

"That boy had better be in bed," she said to no one in particular. She turned and headed home.

Javier's bed lay empty, his sheets wet with the rain drifting in the open window. She grasped the sash in her right hand and tugged it down awkwardly: the apartment building she lived in was hundreds of years old. She'd just straightened the curtains when her telescreen buzzed.

Jayve crouched under the incredible curve of the lighter's hull, both palms flat against its centimeters-thick layer of crystalline sealant. It hummed against his palms, the deep surge of pumps like a heartbeat filling its reservoirs. The shadow of the hull hid Jayve's outline and the silhouette of his primitive watercraft from the bustle of tenders peeling cargo strings off the lighter's stern.

"Mad, can you hear me?"

Static crackle, and his friend's voice on a low thrill of excitement. "I hear you. Are you in?"

"Yeah. I'm going to start burning her. Keep an eye out for the harbor patrol."

"You're doing my tag too!"

"Have I *ever* let you down, Mad? Don't worry. I'll tag it from both of us, and you can burn the next one and tag it from both. Just think how many people are going to *see* this. All over the galaxy. Better than a gallery opening!"

Silence, and Jayve knew Mad was lying in the bilgewater of his own dinghy just beyond the thin line of runway lights that Jayve glimpsed through the rain. Watching for the Harbor Police.

The rain was going to be a problem. Jayve would have to pitch the bubble against the lighter's side. It would block his sightlines and make him easier to spot, which meant trusting Mad's eyes to be sharp through the rain. And the etchant would stink up the inside. He'd have to dial the bubble to maximum porosity if he didn't want to melt his eyes.

No choice. The art had to happen. The art was going to fly.

Black nano unfolded over and around him, the edge of the hiker's bubble sealing itself against the hull. The steady patter of rain on his hair and shoulders stopped, as it had when the ship drifted over, and Jayve started to squeegee the hull dry. He'd have to work in sections. It would take longer.

"Mad, you out there?"

"Coast clear. What'd you tell your mom to get her to let you out tonight?"

"I didn't." He chewed the inside of his cheek as he worked. "I could have told her I was painting at Claudette's, but Mom says there's no future in it, and she might have gone by to check. So I just snuck out. She won't be home for hours."

Jayve slipped a technician's headband around his temples and switched the pinlight on, making sure the goggles were sealed to his skin. At least the bubble would block the glow. While digging in his net bag, he pinched his fingers between two tins, and stifled a yelp. Bilgewater sloshed around his ankles, creeping under his nanoskin faster than the skin could re-osmose it; the night hung against him hot and sweaty as a giant hand. Heedless, heart racing, Jayve extracted the first bottle of etchant, pierced the seal with an adjustable nozzle, and — grinning like a bat — pressurized the tin.

Leaning as far back as he could without tearing the bubble or capsizing his dinghy, Jayve examined the sparkling, virgin surface of the spaceship and began to spray. The etchant eroded crystalline sealant, staining the corroded surface in green, orange, violet. It only took a few moments for the chemicals to scar the ship's integument: not enough to harm it, but enough to mark it forever, unless the corp that owned it was willing to pay to have the whole damn lighter peeled down and resealed.

Jayve moved the bubble four times, etchant fumes searing his flesh, collar of his nanoskin pulled over his mouth and nose to breathe through. He worked around the beaded rows of running lights, turning them into the scales on the sea-serpent's belly, the glints on its fangs. A burst of static came over the crappy uplink once but Mad said nothing, so Jayve kept on smoothly despite the sway of the dinghy under his feet and the hiss of the tenders.

When he finished, the seamonster stretched fifteen meters along the hull of the lighter and six meters high, a riot of sensuality and prismatic colors.

He signed it *jayve n mad* and pitched the last empty bottle into Lake Pontchartrain, where it sank without a trace. "Mad?"

No answer.

Jayve's bubble lit from the outside with the glare of a hundred lights. His stomach kicked and he scrabbled for the dinghy's magnetic clamps to kick it free, but an amplified voice advised him to drop the tent and wait with his hands in view. "Shit! Mad?" he whispered through a tightening throat.

A cop's voice rang over the fuzzy connection. "Just come out, kid," she said tiredly. "Your friend's in custody. It's only a vandalism charge so far. Just come on out."

When they released Javier to Patience in the harsh light and tile of the police barge, she squeezed his hands so tight that blood broke through the sealant over his fresh black tattoos. He winced and tugged his hands away but she clenched harder, her own scabs cracking. She meant to hiss, to screech — but her voice wouldn't shape words, and he wouldn't look her in the eye.

She threw his hands down and turned away, steel decking rolling under her feet as a wave hit. She steadied herself with a lifetime's habit, Javier swept along in her wake. "Jesus," she said, when the doors scrolled open and the cold light of morning hit her across the eyes. "Javier, what the hell were you thinking? What the hell...." She stopped and leaned against the railing, fingers tight on steel. Pain tangled her left arm to the elbow. Out on the lake, a lighter drifted backwards from its berth, refueled and full of water, coming about on a stately arc as the tenders rushed to bring its outbound containers into line.

Javier watched the lighter curve across the lake. Something green and crimson sparkled on its hide above the waterline, a long sinuous curve of color, shimmering with scales and wise with watchful eyes. "Look at that," he said. "The running lamps worked just right. It looks like it's wriggling away, squirming itself up into the sky like a dragon should—"

"What does that matter?" She looked down at his hands, at the ink singeing his fingers. "You'll amount to nothing."

Patience braced against the wake, but Javier turned to get a better look. "Never was any chance of that, Mom."

"Javier, I—" A stabbing sensation drew her eyes down. She stared as the dark blood staining her hands smeared the rain-beaded railing and dripped into the estuary. She'd been picking her scabs, destroying the symmetry of the scarrist's lines.

"You could have been something," she said, as the belly of the ship finished lifting from the lake, pointed into a sunrise concealed behind grey clouds. "You ain't going nowhere now."

Javier came beside her and touched her with a bandaged hand. She didn't turn to look at the hurt in his eyes.

"Man," he whispered in deep satisfaction, craning his neck as his creation swung into the sky. "Just think of all the people who are going to *see* that. Would you just look at that baby go?"

The Calorie Man

Paolo Bacigalupi

Paolo Bacigalupi has described "The Calorie Man" as his "agri-punk" story. Its key supporting character is a hacker of sorts, who seeks to break a corporate stranglehold on a key technology. Only in this case, the tech isn't digital, it's biological. And the hacker is not at the center of the story; that place is occupied by an aging antique dealer who remembers all too well a horrific childhood growing up hungry in famine-ravaged India. For all its exuberant extrapolation, this is a character-driven story about a man haunted by his past.

"No mammy, no pappy, poor little bastard. Money? You give money?" The urchin turned a cartwheel and then a somersault in the street, stirring yellow dust around his nakedness.

Lalji paused to stare at the dirty blond child who had come to a halt at his feet. The attention seemed to encourage the urchin; the boy did another somersault. He smiled up at Lalji from his squat, calculating and eager, rivulets of sweat and mud streaking his face. "Money? You give money?"

Around them, the town was nearly silent in the afternoon heat. A few dungareed farmers led mulies toward the fields. Buildings, pressed from WeatherAll chips, slumped against their fellows like drunkards, rain-stained and sun-cracked, but, as their trade name implied, still sturdy. At the far end of the narrow street, the lush sprawl of SoyPRO and HiGro began, a waving rustling growth that rolled into the blue-sky distance. It was much as all the villages Lalji had seen as he traveled upriver, just another farming enclave paying its intellectual property dues and shipping calories down to New Orleans.

The boy crawled closer, smiling ingratiatingly, nodding his head like a snake hoping to strike. "Money? Money?"

Lalji put his hands in his pockets in case the beggar child had friends and turned his full attention on the boy. "And why should I give money to you?"

The boy stared up at him, stalled. His mouth opened, then closed. Finally he looped back to an earlier, more familiar part of his script, "No mammy? No pappy?" but it was a query now, lacking conviction.

337

Lalji made a face of disgust and aimed a kick at the boy. The child scrambled aside, falling on his back in his desperation to dodge, and this pleased Lalji briefly. At least the boy was quick. He turned and started back up the street. Behind him, the urchin's wailing despair echoed. "Noooo maaaammy! Nooo paaaapy!" Lalji shook his head, irritated. The child might cry for money, but he failed to follow. No true beggar at all. An opportunist only—most likely the accidental creation of strangers who had visited the village and were open-fisted when it came to blond beggar children. AgriGen and Midwest Grower scientists and land factotums would be pleased to show ostentatious kindness to the villagers at the core of their empire.

Through a gap in the slumped hovels, Lalji caught another glimpse of the lush waves of SoyPRO and HiGro. The sheer sprawl of calories stimulated tingling fantasies of loading a barge and slipping it down through the locks to St. Louis or New Orleans and into the mouths of waiting megadonts. It was impossible, but the sight of those emerald fields was more than enough assurance that no child could beg with conviction here. Not surrounded by SoyPRO. Lalji shook his head again, disgusted, and squeezed down a footpath between two of the houses.

The acrid reek of WeatherAll's excreted oils clogged the dim alley. A pair of cheshires sheltering in the unused space scattered and molted ahead of him, disappearing into bright sunlight. Just beyond, a kinetic shop leaned against its beaten neighbors, adding the scents of dung and animal sweat to the stink of WeatherAll. Lalji leaned against the shop's plank door and shoved inside.

Shafts of sunlight pierced the sweet manure gloom with lazy gold beams. A pair of hand-painted posters scabbed to one wall, partly torn but still legible. One said: "Unstamped calories mean starving families. We check royalty receipts and IP stamps." A farmer and his brood stared hollow-eyed from beneath the scolding words. PurCal was the sponsor. The other poster was AgriGen's trademarked collage of kink-springs, green rows of SoyPRO under sunlight and smiling children along with the words "We Provide Energy for the World." Lalji studied the posters sourly.

"Back already?" The owner came in from the winding room, wiping his hands on his pants and kicking straw and mud off his boots. He eyed Lalji. "My springs didn't have enough stored. I had to feed the mulies extra, to make your joules."

Lalji shrugged, having expected the last-minute bargaining, so much like Shriram's that he couldn't muster the interest to look offended. "Yes? How much?"

The man squinted up at Lalji, then ducked his head, his body defensive. "F-Five hundred." His voice caught on the amount, as though gagging on the surprising greed scampering up his throat.

Lalji frowned and pulled his mustache. It was outrageous. The calories hadn't even been transported. The village was awash with energy. And despite the man's virtuous poster, it was doubtful that the calories feeding his kinetic shop were equally upstanding. Not with tempting green fields waving within meters of the shop. Shriram often said that using stamped calories was like dumping money into a methane composter.

Lalji tugged his mustache again, wondering how much to pay for the joules without calling excessive attention to himself. Rich men must have been all over the village to make the kinetic man so greedy. Calorie executives, almost certainly. It would fit. The town was close to the center. Perhaps even this village was engaged in growing the crown jewels of AgriGen's energy monopolies. Still, not everyone who passed through would be as rich as that. "Two hundred."

The kinetic man showed a relieved smile along with knotted yellow teeth, his guilt apparently assuaged by Lalji's bargaining. "Four."

"Two. I can moor on the river and let my own winders do the same work."

The man snorted. "It would take weeks."

Lalji shrugged. "I have time. Dump the joules back into your own springs. I'll do the job myself."

"I've got family to feed. Three?"

"You live next to more calories than some rich families in St. Louis. Two."

The man shook his head sourly but he led Lalji into the winding room. The manure haze thickened. Big kinetic storage drums, twice as tall as a man, sat in a darkened corner, mud and manure lapping around their high-capacity precision kink-springs. Sunbeams poured between open gaps in the roof where shingles had blown away. Dung motes stirred lazily.

A half-dozen hyper-developed mulies crouched on their treadmills, their rib cages billowing slowly, their flanks streaked with salt lines of sweat residue from the labor of winding Lalji's boat springs. They blew air through their nostrils, nervous at Lalji's sudden scent, and gathered their squat legs under them. Muscles like boulders rippled under their bony hides as they stood. They eyed Lalji with resentful near-intelligence. One of them showed stubborn yellow teeth that matched its owner's.

Lalji made a face of disgust. "Feed them."

"I already did."

"I can see their bones. If you want my money, feed them again."

The man scowled. "They aren't supposed to get fat, they're supposed to wind your damn springs." But he dipped double handfuls of SoyPRO into their feed canisters.

The mulies shoved their heads into the buckets, slobbering and grunting with need. In its eagerness, one of them started briefly forward on its tread-mill, sending energy into the winding shop's depleted storage springs before seeming to realize that its work was not demanded and that it could eat without molestation.

"They aren't even designed to get fat," the kinetic man muttered.

Lalji smiled slightly as he counted through his wadded bluebills and handed over the money. The kinetic man unjacked Lalji's kink-springs from the winding treadmills and stacked them beside the slavering mulies. Lalji lifted a spring, grunting at its heft. Its mass was no different than when he had brought it to the winding shop, but now it fairly seemed to quiver with the mulies' stored labor.

"You want help with those?" The man didn't move. His eyes flicked toward the mulies' feed buckets, still calculating his chances of interrupting their meal.

Lalji took his time answering, watching as the mulies rooted for the last of their calories. "No." He hefted the spring again, getting a better grip. "My help-boy will come for the rest."

As he turned for the door, he heard the man dragging the feedbuckets away from the mulies and their grunts as they fought for their sustenance. Once again, Lalji regretted agreeing to the trip at all.

Shriram had been the one to broach the idea. They had been sitting under the awning of Lalji's porch in New Orleans, spitting betel nut juice into the alley gutters and watching the rain come down as they played chess. At the end of the alley, cycle rickshaws and bicycles slipped through the midmorning gray, pulses of green and red and blue as they passed the alley's mouth draped under rain-glossed corn polymer ponchos.

The chess game was a tradition of many years, a ritual when Lalji was in town and Shriram had time away from his small kinetic company where he rewound people's home and boat springs. Theirs was a good friendship, and a fruitful one, when Lalji had unstamped calories that needed to disappear into the mouth of a hungry megadont.

Neither of them played chess well, and so their games often devolved into a series of trades made in dizzying succession; a cascade of destruction that left a board previously well-arrayed in a tantrum wreck, with both opponents blinking surprise, trying to calculate if the mangle had been worth the combat. It was after one of these tit-for-tat cleansings that Shriram had asked Lalji if he might go upriver. Beyond the southern states.

Lalji had shaken his head and spit bloody betel juice into the overflowing gutter. "No. Nothing is profitable so far up. Too many joules to get there. Better to let the calories float to me." He was surprised to discover that he still had his queen. He used it to take a pawn.

"And if the energy costs could be defrayed?"

Lalji laughed, waiting for Shriram to make his own move. "By who? AgriGen? The IP men? Only their boats go up and down so far." He frowned as he realized that his queen was now vulnerable to Shriram's remaining knight.

Shriram was silent. He didn't touch his pieces. Lalji looked up from the board and was surprised by Shriram's serious expression. Shriram said, "I would pay. Myself and others. There is a man who some of us would like to see come south. A very special man."

"Then why not bring him south on a paddle wheel? It is expensive to go up the river. How many gigajoules? I would have to change the boat's springs, and then what would the IP patrols ask? 'Where are you going, strange Indian man with your small boat and your so many springs? Going far? To what purpose?'" Lalji shook his head. "Let this man take a ferry, or ride a barge. Isn't this cheaper?" He waved at the game board. "It's your move. You should take my queen."

Shriram waggled his head thoughtfully from side to side but didn't make any move toward the chess game. "Cheaper, yes...."

"But?"

Shriram shrugged. "A swift, inconsequential boat would attract less attention."

"What sort of man is this?"

Shriram glanced around, suddenly furtive. Methane lamps burned like blue fairies behind the closed glass of the neighbors' droplet-spattered windows. Rain sheeted off their roofs, drumming wet into the empty alley. A cheshire was yowling for a mate somewhere in the wet, barely audible under the thrum of falling water.

"Is Creo inside?"

Lalji raised his eyebrows in surprise. "He has gone to his gymnasium. Why? Should it matter?"

Shriram shrugged and gave an embarrassed smile. "Some things are better kept between old friends. People with strong ties."

"Creo has been with me for years."

Shriram grunted noncommittally, glanced around again and leaned close, pitching his voice low, forcing Lalji to lean forward as well. "There is a man who the calorie companies would like very much to find." He tapped his balding head. "A very intelligent man. We want to help him."

Lalji sucked in his breath. "A generipper?"

Shriram avoided Lalji's eyes. "In a sense. A calorie man."

Lalji made a face of disgust. "Even better reason not to be involved. I don't traffic with those killers."

"No, no. Of course not. But still...you brought that huge sign down once, did you not? A few greased palms, so smooth, and you float into town and suddenly Lakshmi smiles on you, such a calorie bandit, and now with a name instead as a dealer of antiques. Such a wonderful misdirection."

Lalji shrugged. "I was lucky. I knew the man to help move it through the locks."

"So? Do it again."

"If the calorie companies are looking for him, it would be dangerous."

"But not impossible. The locks would be easy. Much easier than carrying unlicensed grains. Or even something as big as that sign. This would be a man. No sniffer dog would find him of interest. Place him in a barrel. It would be easy. And I would pay. All your joules, plus more."

Lalji sucked at his narcotic betel nut, spit red, spit red again, considering.

"And what does a second-rate kinetic man like you think this calorie man will do? Generippers work for big fish, and you are such a small one."

Shriram grinned haplessly and gave a self-deprecating shrug. "You do not think Ganesha Kinetic could not some day be great? The next AgriGen, maybe?" and they had both laughed at the absurdity and Shriram dropped the subject.

An IP man was on duty with his dog, blocking Lalji's way as he returned to his boat lugging the kink-spring. The brute's hairs bristled as Lalji approached and it lunged against its leash, its blunt nose quivering to reach him. With effort, the IP man held the creature back. "I need to sniff you." His helmet lay on the grass, already discarded, but still he was sweating under the swaddling heat of his gray slash-resistant uniform and the heavy webbing of his spring gun and bandoliers.

Lalji held still. The dog growled, deep from its throat, and inched forward. It snuffled his clothing, bared hungry teeth, snuffled again, then its black ruff iridesced blue and it relaxed and wagged its stubby tail. It sat. A pink tongue lolled from between smiling teeth. Lalji smiled sourly back at the animal, glad that he wasn't smuggling calories and wouldn't have to go through the pantomimes of obeisance as the IP man demanded stamps and then tried to verify that the grain shipment had paid its royalties and licensing fees.

At the dog's change in color, the IP man relaxed somewhat, but still he studied Lalji's features carefully, hunting for recognition against memorized photographs. Lalji waited patiently, accustomed to the scrutiny. Many men tried to steal the honest profits of AgriGen and its peers, but to Lalji's knowledge, he was unknown to the protectors of intellectual property. He was an antiques dealer, handling the junk of the previous century, not a calorie bandit staring out from corporate photo books.

Finally, the IP man waved him past. Lalji nodded politely and made his way down the stairs to the river's low stage where his needleboat was moored. Out on the river, cumbrous grain barges wallowed past, riding low under their burdens.

Though there was a great deal of river traffic, it didn't compare with harvest time. Then the whole of the Mississippi would fill with calories pouring downstream, pulled from hundreds of towns like this one. Barges would clot the arterial flow of the river system from high on the Missouri, the Illinois, and the Ohio and the thousand smaller tributaries. Some of those calories would float only as far as St. Louis where they would be chewed by megadonts and churned into joules, but the rest, the vast majority, would float to New Orleans where the great calorie companies' clippers and dirigibles would be loaded with the precious grains. Then they would cross the Earth on tradewinds and sea, in time for the next season's planting, so that the world could go on eating.

Lalji watched the barges moving slowly past, wallowing and bloated with their wealth, then hefted his kink-spring and jumped aboard his needleboat.

Creo was lying on deck as Lalji had left him, his muscled body oiled and shining in the sun, a blond Arjuna waiting for glorious battle. His cornrows spread around his head in a halo, their tipped bits of bone lying like foretelling stones on the hot deck. He didn't open his eyes as Lalji jumped aboard. Lalji went and stood in Creo's sun, eclipsing his tan. Slowly, the young man opened his blue eyes.

"Get up." Lalji dropped the spring on Creo's rippled stomach.

Creo let out a whuff and wrapped his arms around the spring. He sat up easily and set it on the deck. "Rest of the springs wound?"

Lalji nodded. Creo took the spring and went down the boat's narrow stairs to the mechanical room. When he returned from fitting the spring into the gearings of the boat's power system, he said, "Your springs are shit, all of them. I don't know why you didn't bring bigger ones. We have to rewind, what, every twenty hours? You could have gotten all the way here on a couple of the big ones."

Lalji scowled at Creo and jerked his head toward the guard still standing at the top of the riverbank and looking down on them. He lowered his voice. "And then what would the MidWest Authority be saying as we are going upriver? All their IP men all over our boat, wondering where we are going so far? Boarding us and then wondering what we are doing with such big springs. Where have we gotten so many joules? Wondering what business we have so far upriver." He shook his head. "No, no. This is better. Small boat, small distance, who worries about Lalji and his stupid blond helpboy then? No one. No, this is better."

"You always were a cheap bastard."

Lalji glanced at Creo. "You are lucky it is not forty years ago. Then you would be paddling up this river by hand, instead of lying on your lazy back letting these fancy kink-springs do the work. Then we would be seeing you use those muscles of yours."

"If I was lucky, I would have been born during the Expansion and we'd still be using gasoline."

Lalji was about to retort but an IP boat slashed past them, ripping a deep wake. Creo lunged for their cache of spring guns. Lalji dove after him and slammed the cache shut. "They're not after us!"

Creo stared at Lalji, uncomprehending for a moment, then relaxed. He stepped away from the stored weapons. The IP boat continued upriver, half its displacement dedicated to massive precision kink-springs and the stored joules that gushed from their unlocking molecules. Its curling wake rocked the needleboat. Lalji steadied himself against the rail as the IP boat dwindled to a speck and disappeared between obstructing barge chains.

Creo scowled after the boat. "I could have taken them."

Lalji took a deep breath. "You would have gotten us killed." He glanced at the top of the riverbank to see if the IP man had noticed their panic. He wasn't even visible. Lalji silently gave thanks to Ganesha.

"I don't like all of them around," Creo complained. "They're like ants. Fourteen at the last lock. That one, up on the hill. Now these boats."

"It is the heart of calorie country. It is to be expected."

"You making a lot of money on this trip?"

"Why should you care?"

"Because you never used to take risks like this." Creo swept his arm, indicating the village, the cultivated fields, the muddy width of river gurgling past, and the massive barges clogging it. "No one comes this far upriver."

"I'm making enough money to pay you. That's all you should concern yourself with. Now go get the rest of the springs. When you think too much, your brain makes mush."

Creo shook his head doubtfully but jumped for the dock and headed up the steps to the kinetic shop. Lalji turned to face the river. He took a deep breath.

The IP boat had been a close call. Creo was too eager to fight. It was only with luck that they hadn't ended up as shredded meat from the IP men's spring guns. He shook his head tiredly, wondering if he had ever had as much reckless confidence as Creo. He didn't think so. Not even when he was a boy. Perhaps Shriram was right. Even if Creo was trustworthy, he was still dangerous.

A barge chain, loaded with TotalNutrient Wheat, slid past. The happy sheaves of its logo smiled across the river's muddy flow, promising "A Healthful Tomorrow" along with folates, B vitamins, and pork protein. Another IP boat slashed upriver, weaving amongst the barge traffic. Its complement of IP men studied him coldly as they went by. Lalji's skin crawled. Was it worth it? If he thought too much, his businessman's instinct — bred into him through thousands of years of caste practice — told him no. But still, there was Gita. When he balanced his debts each year on Diwali, how did he account for all he owed her? How did one pay off something that weighed heavier than all his profits, in all his lifetimes?

The NutriWheat wallowed past, witlessly inviting, and without answers.

"You wanted to know if there was something that would be worth your trip upriver."

Lalji and Shriram had been standing in the winding room of Ganesha Kinetic, watching a misplaced ton of SuperFlavor burn into joules. Shriram's paired megadonts labored against the winding spindles, ponderous and steady as they turned just-consumed calories into kinetic energy and wound the shop's main storage springs.

Priti and Bidi. The massive creatures barely resembled the elephants that had once provided their template DNA. Generippers had honed them to a perfect balance of musculature and hunger for a single purpose: to inhale calories and do terrible labors without complaint. The smell of them was overwhelming. Their trunks dragged the ground.

The animals were getting old, Lalji thought, and on the heels of that thought came another: he, too, was getting old. Every morning he found gray in his mustache. He plucked it, of course, but more gray hairs always sprouted. And now his joints ached in the mornings as well. Shriram's own head shone like polished teak. At some point, he'd turned bald. Fat and bald. Lalji wondered when they had turned into such old men.

Shriram repeated himself, and Lalji shook away his thoughts. "No, I am not interested in anything upriver. That is the calorie companies' province. I have accepted that when you scatter my ashes it will be on the Mississippi, and not the holy Ganges, but I am not so eager to find my next life that I wish my corpse to float down from Iowa."

Shriram twisted his hands nervously and glanced around. He lowered his voice, even though the steady groan of the spindles was more than enough to drown their sounds. "Please, friend, there are people...who want...to kill this man."

"And I should care?"

Shriram made placating motions with his hands. "He knows how to make calories. AgriGen wants him, badly. PurCal as well. He has rejected them and their kind. His mind is valuable. He needs someone trustworthy to bring him downriver. No friend of the IP men."

"And just because he is an enemy of AgriGen I should help him? Some former associate of the Des Moines clique? Some ex-calorie man with blood on his hands and you think he will help you make money?"

Shriram shook his head. "You make it sound as if this man is unclean."

"We are talking of generippers, yes? How much morality can he have?"

"A geneticist. Not a generipper. Geneticists gave us megadonts." He waved at Priti and Bidi. "Me, a livelihood."

Lalji turned on Shriram. "You take refuge in these semantics, now? You, who starved in Chennai when the Nippon genehack weevil came? When the soil turned to alcohol? Before U-Tex and HiGro and the rest all showed up so conveniently? You, who waited on the docks when the seeds came in, saw them come and then saw them sit behind their fences and guards, waiting for people with the money to buy? What traffic would I have with this sort of people? I would sooner spit on him, this calorie man. Let the PurCal devils have him, I say."

The town was as Shriram had described it. Cottonwoods and willows tangled the edges of the river and over them, the remains of the bridge, some of it still spanning the river in a hazy network of broken trusses and crumbling supports. Lalji and Creo stared up at the rusting construction, a web of steel and cable and concrete, slowly collapsing into the river.

"How much do you think the steel would bring?" Creo asked.

Lalji filled his cheek with a handful of PestResis sunflower seeds and started cracking them between his teeth. He spit the hulls into the river one by one. "Not much. Too much energy to tear it out, then to melt it." He shook his head and spat another hull. "A waste to make something like that with steel. Better to use Fast-Gen hardwoods, or WeatherAll."

"Not to cover that distance. It couldn't be done now. Not unless you were in Des Moines, maybe. I heard they burn coal there."

"And they have electric lights that go all night and computers as large as a house." Lalji waved his hand dismissively and turned to finish securing the needleboat. "Who needs such a bridge now? A waste. A ferry and a mulie would serve just as well." He jumped ashore and started climbing the crumbling steps that led up from the river. Creo followed.

At the top of the steep climb, a ruined suburb waited. Built to serve the cities on the far side of the river when commuting was common and petroleum cheap, it now sprawled in an advanced state of decay. A junk city built with junk materials, as transient as water, willingly abandoned when the expense of commuting grew too great.

"What the hell is this place?" Creo muttered.

Lalji smiled cynically. He jerked his head toward the green fields across the river, where SoyPRO and HiGro undulated to the horizon. "The very cradle of civilization, yes? AgriGen, Midwest Growers Group, PurCal, all of them have fields here."

"Yeah? That excite you?"

Lalji turned and studied a barge chain as it wallowed down the river below them, its mammoth size rendered small by the height. "If we could turn all their calories into traceless joules, we'd be wealthy men."

"Keep dreaming." Creo breathed deeply and stretched. His back cracked and he winced at the sound. "I get out of shape when I ride your boat this long. I should have stayed in New Orleans."

Lalji raised his eyebrows. "You're not happy to be making this touristic journey?" He pointed across the river. "Somewhere over there, perhaps in those very acres, AgriGen created SoyPRO. And everyone thought they were such wonderful people." He frowned. "And then the weevil came, and suddenly there was nothing else to eat."

Creo made a face. "I don't go for those conspiracy theories."

"You weren't even born when it happened." Lalji turned to lead Creo into the wrecked suburb. "But I remember. No such accident had ever happened before."

"Monocultures. They were vulnerable."

"Basmati was no monoculture!" Lalji waved his hand back toward the green fields. "Soypro is monoculture. PurCal is monoculture. Generippers make monoculture."

"Whatever you say, Lalji."

Lalji glanced at Creo, trying to tell if the young man was still arguing with him, but Creo was carefully studying the street wreckage and Lalji let the argument die. He began counting streets, following memorized directions.

The avenues were all ridiculously broad and identical, large enough to run a herd of megadonts. Twenty cycle-rickshaws could ride abreast easily, and yet the town had only been a support suburb. It boggled Lalji's mind to consider the scale of life before.

A gang of children watched them from the doorway of a collapsed house. Half its timbers had been removed, and the other half were splintered, rising from the foundation like carcass bones where siding flesh had been stripped away.

Creo showed the children his spring gun and they ran away. He scowled at their departing forms. "So what the hell are we picking up here? You got a lead on another antique?"

Lalji shrugged.

"Come on. I'm going to be hauling it in a couple minutes anyway. What's with the secrecy?"

Lalji glanced at Creo. "There's nothing for you to haul. 'It' is a man. We're looking for a man."

Creo made a sound of disbelief. Lalji didn't bother responding.

Eventually, they came to an intersection. At its center, an old signal light lay smashed. Around it, the pavement was broken through by grasses gone to seed. Dandelions stuck up their yellow heads. On the far side of the intersection, a tall brick building squatted, a ruin of a civil center, yet still standing, built with better materials than the housing it had served.

A cheshire bled across the weedy expanse. Creo tried to shoot it. Missed.

Lalji studied the brick building. "This is the place."

Creo grunted and shot at another cheshire shimmer.

Lalji went over and inspected the smashed signal light, idly curious to see if it might have value. It was rusted. He turned in a slow circle, studying the surroundings for anything at all that might be worth taking downriver. Some of the old Expansion's wreckage still had worthy artifacts. He'd found the

Conoco sign in such a place, in a suburb soon to be swallowed by SoyPro, perfectly intact, seemingly never mounted in the open air, never subjected to the angry mobs of the energy Contraction. He'd sold it to an AgriGen executive for more than an entire smuggled cargo of HiGro.

The AgriGen woman had laughed at the sign. She'd mounted it on her wall, surrounded by the lesser artifacts of the Expansion: plastic cups, computer monitors, photos of racing automobiles, brightly colored children's toys. She'd hung the sign on her wall and then stood back and murmured that at one point, it had been a powerful company...global, even.

Global.

She'd said the word with an almost sexual yearning as she stared up at the sign's ruddy polymers.

Global.

For a moment, Lalji had been smitten by her vision: a company that pulled energy from the remotest parts of the planet and sold it far away within weeks of extraction; a company with customers and investors on every continent, with executives who crossed time zones as casually as Lalji crossed the alley to visit Shriram.

The AgriGen woman had hung the sign on her wall like the head of a trophy megadont and in that moment, next to a representative of the most powerful energy company in world, Lalji had felt a sudden sadness at how very diminished humanity had become.

Lalji shook away the memory and again turned slowly in the intersection, seeking signs of his passenger. More cheshires flitted amongst the ruins, their smoky shimmer shapes pulsing across the sunlight and passing into shadows. Creo pumped his spring gun and sprayed disks. A shimmer tumbled to stillness and became a matted pile of calico and blood.

Creo repumped his spring gun. "So where is this guy?"

"I think he will come. If not today, then tomorrow or the next." Lalji headed up the steps of the civil center and slipped between its shattered doors. Inside, it was nothing but dust and gloom and bird droppings. He found stairs and made his way upward until he found a broken window with a view. A gust of wind rattled the window pane and tugged his mustache. A pair of crows circled in the blue sky. Below, Creo pumped his spring gun and shot more cheshire shimmers. When he hit, angry yowls filtered up. Blood swatches spattered the weedy pavement as more animals fled.

In the distance, the suburb's periphery was already falling to agriculture. Its time was short. Soon the houses would be plowed under and a perfect blanket of SoyPRO would cover it. The suburb's history, as silly and transient as it had been, would be lost, churned under by the march of energy development. No loss, from the standpoint of value, but still, some part of Lalji cringed at the thought of time erased. He spent too much time trying to recall the India of his boyhood to take pleasure in the disappearance. He headed back down the dusty stairs to Creo.

"See anyone?"

Lalji shook his head. Creo grunted and shot at another cheshire, narrowly missing. He was good, but the nearly invisible animals were hard targets. Creo pumped his spring gun and fired again. "Can't believe how many cheshires there are."

"There is no one to exterminate them."

"I should collect the skins and take them back to New Orleans."

"Not on my boat."

Many of the shimmers were fleeing, finally understanding the quality of their enemy. Creo pumped again and aimed at a twist of light further down the street.

Lalji watched complacently. "You will never hit it."

"Watch." Creo aimed carefully.

A shadow fell across them. "Don't shoot."

Creo whipped his spring gun around.

Lalji waved a hand at Creo. "Wait! It's him!"

The new arrival was a skinny old man, bald except for a greasy fringe of gray and brown hair, his heavy jaw thick with gray stubble. Hemp sacking covered his body, dirty and torn, and his eyes had a sunken, knowing quality that unearthed in Lalji the memory of a long-ago sadhu, covered with ash and little else: the tangled hair, the disinterest in his clothing, the distance in the eyes that came from enlightenment. Lalji shook away the memory. This man was no holy man. Just a man, and a generipper, at that.

Creo resighted his spring gun on the distant cheshire. "Down south, I get a bluebill for every one I kill."

The old man said, "There are no bluebills for you to collect here."

"Yeah, but they're pests."

"It's not their fault we made them too perfectly." The man smiled hesitantly, as though testing a facial expression. "Please." He squatted down in front of Creo. "Don't shoot."

Lalji placed a hand on Creo's spring gun. "Let the cheshires be."

Creo scowled, but he let his gun's mechanism unwind with a sigh of releasing energy.

The calorie man said, "I am Charles Bowman." He looked at them expectantly, as though anticipating recognition. "I am ready. I can leave."

Gita was dead, of that Lalji was now sure.

At times, he had pretended that it might not be so. Pretended that she might have found a life, even after he had gone.

But she was dead, and he was sure of it.

It was one of his secret shames. One of the accretions to his life that clung to him like dog shit on his shoes and reduced himself in his own eyes: as when he had thrown a rock and hit a boy's head, unprovoked, to see if it was possible; or when he had dug seeds out of the dirt and eaten them one by one, too starved to share. And then there was Gita. Always Gita. That he had left her and gone instead to live close to the calories. That she had stood on the docks and waved as he set sail, when it was she who had paid his passage price.

He remembered chasing her when he was small, following the rustle of her salwar kameez as she dashed ahead of him, her black hair and black eyes and white, white teeth. He wondered if she had been as beautiful as he recalled. If her oiled black braid had truly gleamed the way he remembered when she sat with him in the dark and told him stories of Arjuna and Krishna and Ram and Hanuman. So much was lost. He wondered sometimes if he even remembered her face correctly, or if he had replaced it with an ancient poster of a Bollywood girl, one of the old ones that Shriram kept in the safe of his winding shop and guarded jealously from the influences of light and air.

For a long time he thought he would go back and find her. That he might feed her. That he would send money and food back to his blighted land that now existed only in his mind, in his dreams, and in half-awake hallucinations of deserts, red and black saris, of women in dust, and their black hands and silver bangles, and their hunger, so many of the last memories of hunger.

He had fantasized that he would smuggle Gita back across the shining sea, and bring her close to the accountants who calculated calorie burn quotas for the world. Close to the calories, as she had said, once so long ago. Close to the men who balanced price stability against margins of error and protectively managed energy markets against a flood of food. Close to those small gods with more power than Kali to destroy the world.

But she was dead by now, whether through starvation or disease, and he was sure of it.

And wasn't that why Shriram had come to him? Shriram who knew more of his history than any other. Shriram who had found him after he arrived in New Orleans, and known him for a fellow countryman: not just another Indian long settled in America, but one who still spoke the dialects of desert villages and who still remembered their country as it had existed before genehack weevil, leafcurl, and root rust. Shriram, who had shared a place on the floor while they both worked the winding sheds for calories and nothing else, and were grateful for it, as though they were nothing but genehacks themselves.

Of course Shriram had known what to say to send him upriver. Shriram had known how much he wished to balance the unbalanceable.

They followed Bowman down empty streets and up remnant alleys, winding through the pathetic collapse of termite-ridden wood, crumbling concrete foundations, and rusted rebar too useless to scavenge and too stubborn to erode. Finally, the old man squeezed them between the stripped hulks of a pair of rusted automobiles. On the far side, Lalji and Creo gasped.

Sunflowers waved over their heads. A jungle of broad squash leaves hugged their knees. Dry corn stalks rattled in the wind. Bowman looked back at their surprise, and his smile, so hesitant and testing at first, broadened with unrestrained pleasure. He laughed and waved them onward, floundering through a garden of flowers and weeds and produce, catching his torn hemp cloth on the dried stems of cabbage gone to seed and the cling of cantaloupe vines. Creo and Lalji picked their way through the tangle, wending around purple lengths of eggplants, red orb tomatoes, and dangling orange ornament chiles. Bees buzzed heavily between the sunflowers, burdened with saddlebags of pollen.

Lalji paused in the overgrowth and called after Bowman. "These plants. They are not engineered?"

Bowman paused and came thrashing back, wiping sweat and vegetal debris off his face, grinning. "Well, engineered, that is a matter of definition, but no, these are not owned by calorie companies. Some of them are even heirloom." He grinned again. "Or close enough."

"How do they survive?"

"Oh, that." He reached down and yanked up a tomato. "Nippon genehack weevils, or curl.111.b, or perhaps cibiscosis bacterium, something like that?" He bit into the tomato and let the juice run down his gray bristled chin. "There isn't another heirloom planting within hundreds of miles. This is an island in an ocean of SoyPRO and HiGro. It makes a formidable barrier." He studied the garden thoughtfully, took another bite of tomato. "Now that you have come, of course, only a few of these plants will survive." He nodded at Lalji and Creo. "You will be carrying some infection or another and many of these rarities can only survive in isolation." He plucked another tomato and handed it to Lalji. "Try it."

Lalji studied its gleaming red skin. He bit into it and tasted sweetness and acid. Grinning, he offered it to Creo, who took a bite and made a face of disgust. "I'll stick with SoyPRO." He handed it back to Lalji, who finished it greedily.

Bowman smiled at Lalji's hunger. "You're old enough to remember, I think, what food used to be. You can take as much of this as you like, before we go. It will all die anyway." He turned and thrashed again through the garden overgrowth, shoving aside dry corn stalks with crackling authoritative sweeps of his arms.

Beyond the garden a house lay collapsed, leaning as though it had been toppled by a megadont, its walls rammed and buckled. The collapsed roof had an ungainly slant, and at one end, a pool of water lay cool and deep, rippled with water skippers. Scavenged gutter had been laid to sluice rainwater from the roof into the pond.

Bowman slipped around the pool's edge and disappeared down a series of crumbled cellar steps. By the time Lalji and Creo followed him down, he had wound a handlight and its dim bulb was spattering the cellar with illumination as its spring ran its course. He cranked the light again while he searched around, then struck a match and lit a lantern. The wick burned high on vegetable oil.

Lalji studied the cellar. It was sparse and damp. A pair of pallets lay on the broken concrete floor. A computer was tucked against a corner, its mahogany case and tiny screen gleaming, its treadle worn with use. An unruly kitchen was shoved against a wall with jars of grains arrayed on pantry shelves and bags of produce hanging from the ceiling to defend against rodents.

The man pointed to a sack on the ground. "There, my luggage."

"What about the computer?" Lalji asked.

Bowman frowned at the machine. "No. I don't need it."

"But it's valuable."

"What I need, I carry in my head. Everything in that machine came from me. My fat burned into knowledge. My calories pedaled into data analysis." He scowled. "Sometimes, I look at that computer and all I see is myself whittled away. I was a fat man once." He shook his head emphatically. "I won't miss it."

Lalji began to protest but Creo startled and whipped out his spring gun. "Someone else is here."

Lalji saw her even as Creo spoke: a girl squatting in the corner, hidden by shadow, a skinny, staring, freckled creature with stringy brown hair. Creo lowered his spring gun with a sigh.

Bowman beckoned. "Come out, Tazi. These are the men I told you about."

Lalji wondered how long she had been sitting in the cellar darkness, waiting. She had the look of a creature who had almost molded with the basement: her hair lank, her dark eyes nearly swallowed by their pupils. He turned on Bowman. "I thought there was only you."

Bowman's pleased smile faded. "Will you go back because of it?"

Lalji eyed the girl. Was she a lover? His child? A feral adoptee? He couldn't guess. The girl slipped her hand into the old man's. Bowman patted it reassuringly. Lalji shook his head. "She is too many. You, I have agreed to take. I prepared a way to carry you, to hide you from boarders and inspections. Her," he waved at the girl, "I did not agree to. It is risky to take someone like yourself, and now you wish to compound the danger with this girl? No." He shook his head emphatically. "It cannot be done."

"What difference does it make?" Bowman asked. "It costs you nothing. The current will carry us all. I have food enough for both of us." He went over to the pantry and started to pull down glass jars of beans, lentils, corn, and rice. "Look, here."

Lalji said, "We have more than enough food."

Bowman made a face. "SoyPRO, I suppose?"

"Nothing wrong with SoyPRO," Creo said.

The old man grinned and held up a jar of green beans floating in brine. "No. Of course not. But a man likes variety." He began filling his bag with more jars, letting them clink carefully. He caught Creo's snort of disgust and smiled, ingratiating suddenly. "For lean times, if nothing else." He dumped more jars of grains into the sack.

Lalji chopped the air with his hand. "Your food is not the issue. Your girl is the issue, and she is a risk!"

Bowman shook his head. "No risk. No one is looking for her. She can travel in the open, even."

"No. You must leave her. I will not take her."

The old man looked down at the girl, uncertain. She gazed back, extricated her hand from his. "I'm not afraid. I can live here still. Like before."

Bowman frowned, thinking. Finally, he shook his head. "No." He faced Lalji. "If she cannot go, then I cannot. She fed me when I worked. I deprived her of calories for my research when they should have gone to her. I owe her too much. I will not leave her to the wolves of this place." He placed his hands on her shoulders and placed her ahead of him, between himself and Lalji.

Creo made a face of disgust. "What difference does it make? Just bring her. We've got plenty of space."

Lalji shook his head. He and Bowman stared at one another across the cellar. Creo said, "What if he gives us the computer? We could call it payment."

Lalji shook his head stubbornly. "No. I do not care about the money. It is too dangerous to bring her."

Bowman laughed. "Then why come all this way if you are afraid? Half the calorie companies want to kill me and you talk about risk?"

Creo frowned. "What's he talking about?"

Bowman's eyebrows went up in surprise. "You haven't told your partner about me?"

Creo looked from Lalji to Bowman and back. "Lalji?"

Lalji took a deep breath, his eyes still locked on Bowman. "They say he can break the calorie monopolies. That he can pirate SoyPRO."

Creo boggled for a moment. "That's impossible!"

Bowman shrugged. "For you, perhaps. But for a knowledgeable man? Willing to dedicate his life to DNA helixes? More than possible. If one is willing to burn the calories for such a project, to waste energy on statistics and genome analysis, to pedal a computer through millions upon millions of cycles. More than possible." He wrapped his arms around his skinny girl and held her to him. He smiled at Lalji. "So. Do we have any agreement?"

Creo shook his head, puzzling. "I thought you had a money plan, Lalji, but this..." He shook his head again. "I don't get it. How the hell do we make money off this?"

Lalji gave Creo a dirty look. Bowman smiled, patiently waiting. Lalji stifled an urge to seize the lantern and throw it in his face, such a confident man, so sure of himself, so loyal....

He turned abruptly and headed for the stairs. "Bring the computer, Creo. If his girl makes any trouble, we dump them both in the river, and still keep his knowledge."

Lalji remembered his father pushing back his thali, pretending he was full when dal had barely stained the steel plate. He remembered his mother pressing an extra bite onto his own. He remembered Gita, watching, silent, and then all of them unfolding their legs and climbing off the family bed, bustling around the hovel, ostentatiously ignoring him as he consumed the extra portion. He remembered roti in his mouth, dry like ashes, and forcing himself to swallow anyway.

He remembered planting. Squatting with his father in desert heat, yellow dust all around them, burying seeds they had stored away, saved when they might have been eaten, kept when they might have made Gita fat and marriageable, his father smiling, saying, "These seeds will make hundreds of new seeds and then we will all eat well."

"How many seeds will they make?" Lalji had asked.

And his father had laughed and spread his arms fully wide, and seemed so large and great with his big white teeth and red and gold earrings and crinkling eyes as he cried, "Hundreds! Thousands if you pray!" And Lalji *had* prayed, to Ganesha and Lakshmi and Krishna and Rani Sati and Ram and Vishnu, to every god he could think of, joining the many villagers who did the same as he poured water from the well over tiny seeds and sat guard in the darkness against the possibility that the precious grains might be uprooted in the night and transported to some other farmer's field.

He sat every night while cold stars turned overhead, watching the seed rows, waiting, watering, praying, waiting through the days until his father finally shook his head and said it was no use. And yet still he had hoped, until at last he went out into the field and dug up the seeds one by one, and found them already decomposed, tiny corpses in his hand, rotted. As dead in his palm as the day he and his father had planted them.

He had crouched in the darkness and eaten the cold dead seeds, knowing he should share, and yet unable to master his hunger and carry them home. He wolfed them down alone, half-decayed and caked with dirt: his first true taste of PurCal.

In the light of early morning, Lalji bathed in the most sacred river of his adopted land. He immersed himself in the Mississippi's silty flow, cleansing the weight of sleep, making himself clean before his gods. He pulled himself back aboard, slick with water, his underwear dripping off his sagging bottom, his brown skin glistening, and toweled himself dry on the deck as he looked across the water to where the rising sun cast gold flecks on the river's rippled surface.

He finished drying himself and dressed in new clean clothes before going to his shrine. He lit incense in front of the gods, placed U-Tex and SoyPRO before the tiny carved idols of Krishna and his lute, benevolent Lakshmi, and elephant-headed Ganesha. He knelt in front of the idols, prostrated himself, and prayed.

They had floated south on the river's current, winding easily through bright fall days and watching as leaves changed and cool weather came on. Tranquil skies had arched overhead and mirrored on the river, turning the mud of the Mississippi's flow into shining blue, and they had followed that blue road south, riding the great arterial flow of the river as creeks and tributaries and the linked chains of barges all crowded in with them and gravity did the work of carrying them south.

He was grateful for their smooth movement downriver. The first of the locks were behind them, and having watched the sniffer dogs ignore Bowman's hiding place under the decking, Lalji was beginning to hope that the trip would be as easy as Shriram had claimed. Nonetheless, he prayed longer and harder each day as IP patrols shot past in their fast boats, and he placed extra SoyPRO before Ganesha's idol, desperately hoping that the Remover of Obstacles would continue to do so.

By the time he finished his morning devotions, the rest of the boat was stirring. Creo came below and wandered into the cramped galley. Bowman followed, complaining of SoyPRO, offering heirloom ingredients that Creo shook off with suspicion. On deck, Tazi sat at the edge of the boat with a fishing line tossed into the water, hoping to snare one of the massive lethargic LiveSalmon that occasionally bumped against the boat's keel in the warm murk of the river.

Lalji unmoored and took his place at the tiller. He unlocked the kink-springs and the boat whirred into the deeper current, stored joules dripping from its precision springs in a steady flow as molecules unlocked, one after another, reliable from the first kink to the last. He positioned the needleboat amongst the wallowing grain barges and locked the springs again, allowing the boat to drift.

Bowman and Creo came back up on deck as Creo was asking, "...you know how to grow SoyPRO?"

Bowman laughed and sat down beside Tazi. "What good would that do? The IP men would find the fields, ask for the licenses, and if none were provided, the fields would burn and burn and burn."

"So what good are you?"

Bowman smiled and posed a question instead. "SoyPRO — what is its most precious quality?"

"It's high calorie."

Bowman's braying laughter carried across the water. He tousled Tazi's hair and the pair of them exchanged amused glances. "You've seen too many billboards from AgriGen. 'Energy for the world' indeed, indeed. Oh, AgriGen and their ilk must love you very much. So malleable, so...tractable." He laughed again and shook his head. "No. Anyone can make high calorie plants. What else?"

Nettled, Creo said, "It resists the weevil."

Bowman's expression became sly. "Closer, yes. Difficult to make a plant that fights off the weevil, the leafcurl rust, the soil bacterium which chew through their roots...so many blights plague us now, so many beasts assail our plantings, but come now, what, best of all, do we like about SoyPRO? We of AgriGen who 'provide energy to the world'?" He waved at a chain of grain barges slathered with logos for SuperFlavor. "What makes SuperFlavor so perfect from a CEO's perspective?" He turned toward Lalji. "You know, Indian, don't you? Isn't it why you've come all this distance?"

Lalji stared back at him. When he spoke, his voice was hoarse. "It's sterile."

Bowman's eyes held Lalji's for a moment. His smile slipped. He ducked his head. "Yes. Indeed, indeed. A genetic dead-end. A one-way street. We now pay for a privilege that nature once provided willingly, for just a little labor." He looked up at Lalji. "I'm sorry. I should have thought. You would have felt our accountants' optimum demand estimates more than most."

Lalji shook his head. "You cannot apologize." He nodded at Creo. "Tell him the rest. Tell him what you can do. What I was told you can do."

"Some things are perhaps better left unsaid."

Lalji was undaunted. "Tell him. Tell me. Again."

Bowman shrugged. "If you trust him, then I must trust him as well, yes?" He turned to Creo. "Do you know cheshires?"

Creo made a noise of disgust. "They're pests."

"Ah, yes. A bluebill for every dead one. I forgot. But what makes our cheshires such pests?"

"They molt. They kill birds."

"And?" Bowman prodded.

Creo shrugged.

Bowman shook his head. "And to think it was for people like you that I wasted my life on research and my calories on computer cycles.

"You call cheshires a plague, and truly, they are. A few wealthy patrons, obsessed with Lewis Carroll, and suddenly they are everywhere, breeding with heirloom cats, killing birds, wailing in the night, but most importantly, their offspring, an astonishing ninety-two percent of the time, are cheshires themselves, pure, absolute. We create a new species in a heartbeat of evolutionary time, and our songbird populations disappear almost as quickly. A more perfect predator, but most importantly, one that spreads.

"With SoyPRO, or U-Tex, the calorie companies may patent the plants and use intellectual property police and sensitized dogs to sniff out their property, but even IP men can only inspect so many acres. Most importantly, the seeds are sterile, a locked box. Some may steal a little here and there, as you and Lalji do, but in the end, you are nothing but a small expense on a balance sheet fat with profit because no one except the calorie companies can grow the plants.

"But what would happen if we passed SoyPRO a different trait, stealthily, like a man climbing atop his best friend's wife?" He waved his arm to indicate the green fields that lapped at the edges of the river. "What if someone were to drop bastardizing pollens amongst these crown jewels that surround us? Before the calorie companies harvested and shipped the resulting seeds across the world in their mighty clipper fleets, before the licensed dealers delivered the patented crop seed to their customers. What sorts of seeds might they be delivering then?"

Bowman began ticking traits off with his fingers. "Resistant to weevil and leafcurl, yes. High calorie, yes, of course. Genetically distinct and therefore unpatentable?" He smiled briefly. "Perhaps. But best of all, fecund. Unbelievably fecund. Ripe, fat with breeding potential." He leaned forward. "Imagine it. Seeds distributed across the world by the very cuckolds who have always clutched them so tight, all of those seeds lusting to breed, lusting to produce their own fine offspring full of the same pollens that polluted the crown jewels in the first place." He clapped his hands. "Oh, what an infection that would be! And how it would spread!"

Creo stared, his expression contorting between horror and fascination. "You can do this?"

Bowman laughed and clapped his hands again. "I'm going to be the next Johnny Appleseed."

Lalji woke suddenly. Around him, the darkness of the river was nearly complete. A few windup LED beacons glowed on grain barges, powered by the flow of the current's drag against their ungainly bodies. Water lapped against the sides of the needleboat and the bank where they had tied up. Beside him on the deck the others lay bundled in blankets.

Why had he wakened? In the distance, a pair of village roosters were challenging one another across the darkness. A dog was barking, incensed by whatever hidden smells or sounds caused dogs to startle and defend their territory. Lalji closed his eyes and listened to the gentle undulation of the river, the sounds of the distant village. If he pressed his imagination, he could almost be lying in the early dawn of another village, far away, long ago dissolved.

Why was he awake? He opened his eyes again and sat up. He strained his eyes against the darkness. A shadow appeared on the river blackness, a subtle blot of movement.

Lalji shook Bowman awake, his hand over Bowman's mouth. "Hide!" he whispered.

Lights swept over them. Bowman's eyes widened. He fought off his blankets and scrambled for the hold. Lalji gathered Bowman's blankets with his own, trying to obscure the number of sleepers as more lights flashed brightly, sliding across the deck, pasting them like insects on a collection board.

Abandoning its pretense of stealth, the IP boat opened its springs and rushed in. It slammed against the needleboat, pinning it to the shoreline as men swarmed aboard. Three of them, and two dogs.

"Everyone stay calm! Keep your hands in sight!"

Handlight beams swept across the deck, dazzlingly bright. Creo and Tazi clawed out of their blankets and stood, surprised. The sniffer dogs growled and lunged against their leashes. Creo backed away from them, his hands held before him, defensive.

One of the IP men swept his handlight across them. "Who owns this boat?"

Lalji took a breath. "It's mine. This is my boat." The beam swung back and speared his eyes. He squinted into the light. "Have we done something wrong?"

The leader didn't answer. The other IP men fanned out, swinging their lights across the boat, marking the people on deck. Lalji realized that except for the leader, they were just boys, barely old enough to have mustaches and beards at all. Just peachfuzzed boys carrying spring guns and covered in armor that helped them swagger.

Two of them headed for the stairs with the dogs as a fourth jumped aboard from the secured IP boat. Handlight beams disappeared into the bowels of the needleboat, casting looming shadows from inside the stairway. Creo had somehow managed to end up backed against the needleboat's cache of spring guns. His hand rested casually beside the catches. Lalji stepped toward the captain, hoping to head off Creo's impulsiveness.

The captain swung his light on him. "What are you doing here?"

Lalji stopped and spread his hands helplessly. "Nothing."

"No?"

Lalji wondered if Bowman had managed to secure himself. "What I mean is that we only moored here to sleep."

"Why didn't you tie up at Willow Bend?"

"I'm not familiar with this part of the river. It was getting dark. I didn't want to be crushed by the barges." He wrung his hands. "I deal with antiques. We were looking in the old suburbs to the north. It's not illeg — " A shout from below interrupted him. Lalji closed his eyes regretfully. The Mississippi would be his burial river. He would never find his way to the Ganges.

The IP men came up dragging Bowman. "Look what we found! Trying to hide under the decking!"

Bowman tried to shake them off. "I don't know what you're talking about — "

"Shut up!" One of the boys shoved a club into Bowman's stomach. The old man doubled over. Tazi lunged toward them, but the captain corralled her and held her tightly as he flashed his light over Bowman's features. He gasped.

"Cuff him. We want him. Cover them!" Spring guns came up all around. The captain scowled at Lalji. "An antiques dealer. I almost believed you." To his men he said, "He's a generipper. From a long time ago. See if there's anything else on board. Any disks, any computers, any papers."

One of them said, "There's a treadle computer below."

"Get it."

In moments the computer was on deck. The captain surveyed his captives. "Cuff them all." One of the IP boys made Lalji kneel and started patting him down while a sniffer dog growled over them.

Bowman was saying, "I'm really very sorry. Perhaps you've made a mistake. Perhaps..."

Suddenly the captain shouted. The IP men's handlights swung toward the sound. Tazi was latched onto the captain's hand, biting him. He was shaking at her as though she were a dog, struggling with his other hand to get his spring gun free. For a brief moment everyone watched the scuffle between the girl and the much larger man. Someone — Lalji thought it was an IP man — laughed. Then Tazi was flung free and the captain had his gun out and there was a sharp hiss of disks. Handlights thudded on the deck and rolled, casting dizzy beams of light.

More disks hissed through the darkness. A rolling light beam showed the captain falling, crashing against Bowman's computer, silver disks embedded in his armor. He and the computer slid backwards. Darkness again. A splash. The dogs howled, either released and attacking or else wounded. Lalji dove and lay prone on the decking as metal whirred past his head.

"Lalji!" It was Creo's voice. A gun skittered across the planking. Lalji scrambled toward the sound.

One of the handlight beams had stabilized. The captain was sitting up, black blood lines trailing from his jaw as he leveled his pistol at Tazi. Bowman lunged into the light, shielding the girl with his body. He curled as disks hit him.

Lalji's fingers bumped the spring gun. He clutched after it blindly. His hand closed on it. He jacked the pump, aimed toward bootfalls, and let the spring gun whir. The shadow of one of the IP men, the boys, was above him, falling, bleeding, already dead as he hit the decking.

Everything went silent.

Lalji waited. Nothing moved. He waited still, forcing himself to breathe quietly, straining his eyes against the shadows where the handlights didn't illuminate. Was he the only one alive?

One by one, the three remaining handlights ran out of juice. Darkness closed in. The IP boat bumped gently against the needleboat. A breeze rustled the willow banks, carrying the muddy reek of fish and grasses. Crickets chirped.

Lalji stood. Nothing. No movement. Slowly he limped across the deck. He'd twisted his leg somehow. He felt for one of the handlights, found it by its faint metallic gleam, and wound it. He played its flickering beam across the deck.

Creo. The big blond boy was dead, a disk caught in his throat. Blood pooled from where it had hit his artery. Not far away, Bowman was ribboned with disks. His blood ran everywhere. The computer was missing. Gone overboard. Lalji squatted beside the bodies, sighing. He pulled Creo's bloodied braids off his face. He had been fast. As fast as he had believed he was. Three armored IP men and the dogs as well. He sighed again.

Something whimpered. Lalji flicked his light toward the source, afraid of what he would find, but it was only the girl, seemingly unhurt, crawling to Bowman's body. She looked up into the glare of Lalji's light, then ignored him and crouched over Bowman. She sobbed, then stifled herself. Lalji locked the handlight's spring and let darkness fall over them.

He listened to the night sounds again, praying to Ganesha that there were no others out on the river. His eyes adjusted. The shadow of the grieving girl kneeling amongst lumped bodies resolved from the blackness. He shook his head. So many dead for such an idea. That such a man as Bowman might be of use. And now such a waste. He listened for signs others had been alerted but heard nothing. A single patrol, it seemed, uncoordinated with any others. Bad luck. That was all. One piece of bad luck breaking a string of good. Gods were fickle.

He limped to the needleboat's moorings and began untying. Unbidden, Tazi joined him, her small hands fumbling with the knots. He went to the tiller and unlocked the kink-springs. The boat jerked as the screws bit and they swept into the river darkness. He let the springs fly for an hour, wasting joules but anxious to make distance from the killing place, then searched the banks for an inlet and anchored. The darkness was nearly total.

After securing the boat, he searched for weights and tied them around the ankles of the IP men. He did the same with the dogs, then began shoving the bodies off the deck. The water swallowed them easily. It felt unclean to dump them so unceremoniously, but he had no intention of taking time to bury them. With luck, the men would bump along under water, picked at by fish until they disintegrated.

When the IP men were gone, he paused over Creo. So wonderfully quick. He pushed Creo overboard, wishing he could build a pyre for him.

Lalji began mopping the decks, sluicing away the remaining blood. The moon rose, bathing them in pale light. The girl sat beside the body of her chaperone. Eventually, Lalji could avoid her with his mopping no more. He knelt beside her. "You understand he must go into the river?"

The girl didn't respond. Lalji took it as assent. "If there is anything you wish to have of his, you should take it now." The girl shook her head. Lalji hesitantly let his hand rest on her shoulder. "It is no shame to be given to a river. An honor, even, to go to a river such as this."

He waited. Finally, she nodded. He stood and dragged the body to the edge of the boat. He tied it with weights and levered the legs over the lip. The old man slid out of his hands. The girl was silent, staring at where Bowman had disappeared into the water.

Lalji finished his mopping. In the morning he would have to mop again, and sand the stains, but for the time it would do. He began pulling in the anchors. A moment later, the girl was with him again, helping. Lalji settled himself at the tiller. Such a waste, he thought. Such a great waste.

Slowly, the current drew their needleboat into the deeper flows of the river. The girl came and knelt beside him. "Will they chase us?"

Lalji shrugged. "With luck? No. They will look for something larger than us to make so many of their men disappear. With just the two of us now, we will look like very small inconsequential fish to them. With luck."

She nodded, seeming to digest this information. "He saved me, you know. I should be dead now."

"I saw."

"Will you plant his seeds?"

"Without him to make them, there will be no one to plant them."

Tazi frowned. "But we've got so many." She stood and slipped down into the hold. When she returned, she lugged the sack of Bowman's food stores. She began pulling jars from the sack: rice and corn, soybeans and kernels of wheat.

"That's just food," Lalji protested.

Tazi shook her head stubbornly. "They're his Johnny Appleseeds. I wasn't supposed to tell you. He didn't trust you to take us all the way. To take me. But you could plant them, too, right?"

Lalji frowned and picked up a jar of corn. The kernels nestled tightly together, hundreds of them, each one unpatented, each one a genetic infection. He closed his eyes and in his mind he saw a field: row upon row of green rustling plants, and his father, laughing, with his arms spread wide as he shouted, "Hundreds! Thousands if you pray!"

Lalji hugged the jar to his chest, and slowly, he began to smile.

The needleboat continued downstream, a bit of flotsam in the Mississippi's current. Around it, the crowding shadow hulks of the grain barges loomed, all of them flowing south through the fertile heartland toward the gateway of New Orleans; all of them flowing steadily toward the vast wide world.

Sterling to Kessel, 4 September 1993:

"The *reason* that your alienation is your strength — and I agree that it is — is that alienation is just a phase-shift away from transcendence. That the crippling inability to believe anything is just a phase-shift away from the admirably cosmopolitan *determination* not to believe anything. That bleak cosmic futility is the flipside of the freedom and power of the scientific method, the sense that you're standing on your own ontological feet and can walk without crutches now. All these supposed oppositions are really only ambiguities. And the alienation that causes you to retreat to the firm but lonely citadel of your own personality is one small phase-change away from a wild charge outside the fortress to amaze and scatter the besiegers and loot their baggage train. There's some fucking neat stuff in that baggage train. It belongs to other people at the moment, and yeah, some of it is noisome junk, but that doesn't mean that you can't find some nice uses for the rest of it. Swords have two edges, and arrows fly wherever they are pointed.

When you're our age, if you want to stay alive and supple, inside you have to spend a lot of time looking hard at things you really hate. We'll never have the imaginative fire we had when we were twenty years old. If we have any advantage over those twenty-year-old guys, it's that we know a fucking galaxy of things they didn't know.... But if I'm not going to end up as some self-satisfied fart doing dekalogies to put my kid through college, I've got to push it and push it and push it some more."

Search Engine

Mary Rosenblum

Mary Rosenblum recently returned to science fiction after several years writing mysteries, and in this story blends the two genres with a noir twist. Her PCP sleuth, here called a profiler, never really needs to get up from his keyboard in order to find his man. In a world where everyone has an implanted ID chip and where all transactions are recorded, all it takes to track someone down is access to data and a hacker's feel for the flow of information. But if you work for Big Brother, make sure to check your humanity at the door.

Aman's eyelids twitched as the tiny skull and crossbones icon flashed across his retinal screen. Uh oh. He blinked away the image and scowled at the office door. The feds. "Sit tight and pay attention," he said to the new kid sitting in the chair beside the desk.

"What's up?" New Kid leaned forward. But the door was already opening, the soft whisper as it slid aside a reassurance that this was a high-end operation, that your money was being spent wisely. The real-life, physical office, the expensive woolen carpet and real wood furniture echoed that reassurance. No sleazy, virtual private eye here...you were at the top of the ladder in a hard office.

Not that the suit cared. He took off his shades, slipped 'em into the pocket of his very well made business tunic and fixed icy gray eyes on Aman's face. If he didn't like what he saw, he was too well trained to let it show. "Mr. Boutros." The suit didn't offer his hand, sat down immediately in the chair across from the desk. Cast New Kid a single pointed glance. Jimi. Aman remembered his name at last. Raul's latest, given to him to baby-sit and maybe even train.

"My assistant." Aman put finality in the tone. New Kid stays. He kept his body language relaxed and alpha, waited out the suit's evaluation of his options. Inclined his head at the suit's very slight nod. He had won that round. You won when you could. "How may I help you?"

The suit pulled a small leather case from inside his tunic, slipped a tiny data disk from it. Without a word, Aman extended a port. Clients did not store their files on the net. Not if they were paying Search Engine's fees. The disk clicked into place and Aman's desktop lit up. A man's head and shoulders appeared in the holofield, turning slowly. Medium-dark, about twenty, mixed Euro/African and Hispanic genes, Aman noted. About the same phenotype as New Kid—Jimi —a history of war, rape, and pillage made flesh. The Runner's scalp gleamed naked, implanted with fiberlight gang-sign. Aman read it and sighed, thinking of his fight with Avi over his fiberlights. Tattoo your political incorrectness on your body for the cops, son. Just in case they don't notice you on their own. Stupid move, Avi. That hadn't been the final argument, but it had been damn close. Several data-file icons floated at the bottom of the field. Food prefer-ences, clothing, personal services, sex. Aman nodded because the feds knew what he needed and it would all be here. "Urgency?" he asked.

"High." The suit kept his eyes on the Runner's light-scribed profile.

Aman nodded. Jimi was getting tense. He didn't even have to look at him, the kid was radiating. Aman touched the icon bubbles, opening the various files, hoping Jimi would keep his mouth shut. Frowning, because you never wanted the client to think it was going to be easy, he scanned the rough summary of the Runner's buying habits. Bingo. He put his credit where his politics were. Not a problem, this one. He was going to stand up and wave to get their attention. "Four days," he said. Start high and bargain. "Plus or minus ten percent."

"Twenty-four hours." The suit's lips barely moved.

Interesting. Why this urgency? Aman shook his head. No kinky sex habits, no drugs, so they'd have to depend on clothes and food. Legal-trade data files took longer. "Three point five," he finally said. "With a failure-exemption clause."

They settled on forty-eight hours with no failure-exemption. "Ten percent bonus if you get him in less." The suit stood. For a moment he looked carefully and thoroughly at Jimi. Storing his image in the bioware overlay his kind had been enhanced with? If he ran into Jimi on the street a hundred years from now he'd remember him. Jimi had damn well better hope it didn't matter.

"They really want this guy." Jimi waited for the green light to come on over the door, telling them that the suit hadn't left anything behind that might listen. "The Runner's wearing Gaiist sign."

No kidding. Aman knew that scrawl by heart.

"What did he do?"

"How the hell should I know?" Aman touched one of the file icons, closing his eyes as his own bioware downloaded and displayed on his retina. *That* had been the final argument with Avi.

"Oh, so we just do what we're told, I get it." Jimi leaned back, propped a boot up on the corner of the desktop. "Say yessir, no questions asked, huh? Who cares about the reason, as long as there's money?"

"He's government." Aman blinked the display away, ignored Jimi's boot. Why in the name of everyone's gods had Raul hired this wet-from-birth child? Well, he knew *why*. Aman eyed the kid's slender, androgynous build. His boss had a thing for the African/Hispanic phenotype. Once, he'd kept it out of the business. Aman suppressed a sigh, wondering if the kid had figured it out yet. Why Raul had hired him. "How much of the data-dredging that you do is legal?" He watched Jimi think about that. "You think we're that good, huh? That nobody ever busts us? There is always a price, kid, especially for success."

Jimi took his foot off the desktop. "The whole crackdown on the Gaiists is just crap. A bread-and-circus move because the North American Alliance…"

Aman held up a hand. "Good thing you don't write it on *your* head in light," he said mildly. "Just don't talk politics with Raul."

Jimi flushed. "So how come you let him back you down from four days? An Xuyen is already backed up with the Ferrogers search."

"We won't need Xuyen." Aman nodded at the icons. "Our Runner is organic. Vegan. Artisan craft only, in clothes and personal items. You could find him all by yourself in about four hours."

"But if he's buying farm-raised and handmade?" Jimi frowned. "No Universal tags on those."

Aman promised himself a talk with Raul, but it probably wouldn't change anything. Not until he got tired of this one, anyway. "Get real." He got up and crossed to the small nondescript desktop at the back of the office, camouflaged by an expensive Japanese shoji screen. This was the real workspace. Everything else was stage-prop, meant to impress clients. "You sell stuff without a U-tag and you suddenly find you can't get a license, or your E coli count is too high for an organic permit, or your handspinning operation might possibly be a front for drug smugglers." He laughed. "Everything has a U-tag in it." Which wasn't quite true, but knowledge was power. Jimi didn't have any claim on power yet. Not for free.

"Okay." Jimi shrugged. "I'll see if I can beat your four hours. Start with sex?"

"He's not a buyer. I'll do it."

"How come?" Jimi bristled. "Isn't it too easy for you? If even *I* can do it?"

Aman hesitated, because he wasn't really sure himself. "I just am." He sat down at his workdesk as Jimi stomped out . Brought up his secure field and transferred the files to it. The Runner got his sex for free or not at all, so no point in searching that. Food was next on the immediacy list. Aman opened his personal searchware and fed the Runner's ID chipprint into it. He wasn't wearing his ID chip anymore, or the suit wouldn't have showed up here. Nobody had figured out yet now to make a birth-implanted ID chip really permanent. Although they kept trying. Aman's AI stretched its thousand thousand fingers into the datasphere and started hitting all the retail data pools. Illegal, of course, and retail purchase data was money in the bank so it was well protected, but if you were willing to pay, you could buy from the people who were better than the people who created the protection. Search Engine, Inc. was willing to pay.

Sure enough, forsale.data had the kid's profile. They were the biggest. Most of the retailers fed directly to them. Aman pulled the Runner's raw consumables data. Forsale profiled, but his AI synthesized a profile to fit the specific operation. Aman waited the thirty seconds while his AI digested the raw dates, amounts, prices of every consumable item the Runner had purchased from the first credit he spent at a store to the day he paid to have a back-alley cutter remove his ID chip. Every orange, every stick of gum, every bottle of beer carried an RNA signature and every purchase went into the file that had opened the day the Runner was born and the personal ID chip implanted.

The AI finished. The Runner was his son's age. Mid-twenties. He looked younger. Testament to the powers of his vegetarian and organic diet? Aman smiled sourly. Avi would appreciate that. That had been an early fight and a continuing excuse when his son needed one. Aman scanned the grocery profile. It had amazed him, when he first got into this field, how much food reflected each person's life and philosophy. As a child, the Runner had eaten a "typical" North American diet with a short list of personal specifics that Aman skipped. He had become a Gaiist at nineteen. The break was clear in the profile, with the sudden and dramatic shift of purchases from animal proteins to fish and then vegetable proteins only. Alcohol purchases flatlined, although marijuana products

tripled as did wild-harvest hallucinogenic mushrooms. As he expected, the illegal drug purchase history revealed little. The random nature of his purchases
suggested that he bought the drugs for someone else or a party event rather
than for regular personal consumption. No long-term addictive pattern.

A brief, steady purchase rate of an illegal psychotropic, coupled with an
increase in food purchase volume suggested a lover or live-in friend with an
addiction problem, however. The sudden drop-off suggested a break up. Or a
death. The food purchases declined in parallel. On a whim, because he had time
to spare, Aman had his AI correlate the drop off of the drug purchases to the
newsmedia database for Northwestern North America, the region where the
drug purchases were made. Bingo. A twenty-year-old woman had died within
eighteen hours of the last drug purchase. His lover? Dead from an overdose?
Aman's eyes narrowed. The cause of death was listed as heart failure, but his AI
had flagged it.

"Continue." He waited out the seconds of his AI's contemplation.

Insufficient data, it murmured in its androgynous voice. *Continue?* Aman hesitated because searches like this cost money, and the connection was weak, if
there at all. "Continue." No real reason, but he had learned long ago to follow
his hunches.

He was the last one out of the office, as usual. The receptionist said good night
to him as he crossed the plush reception area, her smile as fresh as it had been
just after dawn this morning. As the door locked behind him, she turned off.
Real furniture and rugs meant money and position. Real people meant security risks. The night watchman — another holographic metaphor — wished him
good night as he crossed the small lobby. Koi swam in the holographic pond
surrounded by blooming orchids. Huge vases of flowers — lilies today — graced
small tables against the wall. The display company had even included scent
with the holos. The fragrance of lilies followed Aman out onto the street. He
took a pedal taxi home, grateful that for once, the small wiry woman on the seat
wasn't interested in conversation as she leaned on the handlebars and pumped
them through the evening crush in the streets.

He couldn't get the suit out of his head tonight. Jimi was right. The Gaiists
were harmless, back-to-the-land types. The feds wanted this kid for something
other than his politics, although that might be the media reason. Absently,

Aman watched the woman's muscular back as she pumped them past street vendors hawking food, toys, and legal drugs, awash in a river of strolling, eating, buying people. He didn't ask "why" much anymore. Sweat slicked the driver's tawny skin like oil. Maybe it was because the Runner was the same age as Avi and a Gaiist as well. Aman reached over to tap the bell and before the silvery chime had died, the driver had swerved to the curb. She flashed him a grin at the tip as he thumbprinted her reader, then she sped off into the flow of taxis and scooters that clogged the street.

Aman ducked into the little grocery on his block, enjoying the relief of its nearly empty aisles this time of night. He grabbed a plastic basket from the stack by the door and started down the aisles. *You opened the last orange juice today.* The store's major-domo spoke to him in a soft, maternal voice as he strode past the freezer cases. True. The store's major-domo had scanned his ID chip as he entered, then uplinked to smartshopper.net, the inventory control company he subscribed to. It has searched his personal inventory file to see if he needed orange juice and the major-domo had reminded him. He tossed a pouch of frozen juice into his basket. The price displayed on the basket handle, a running total that grew slowly as he added a couple of frozen dinners and a packaged salad. *The Willamette Vineyard's Pinot Gris is on sale this week.* The major-domo here at the wine aisle used a rich, male voice. *Three dollars off.* That was his favorite white. He bought a bottle, and made his way to the checkout gate to thumbprint the total waiting for him on the screen.

"Don't we make it easy?"

Aman looked to up find Jimi lounging at the end of the checkout kiosks.

"You following me?" Aman loaded his groceries into a plastic bag. "Or is this a genuine coincidence?"

"I live about a block from your apartment." Jimi shrugged. "I always shop here." He hefted his own plastic bag . "Buy you a drink?"

"Sure," Aman said, to atone for not bothering to know where the newbie lived. They sat down at one of the sidewalk tables next to the grocery, an island of stillness in the flowing river of humanity.

"The usual?" the table asked politely. They both said yes, and Aman wondered what Jimi's usual was. And realized Jimi was already drunk. His eyes glittered and a thin film of sweat gleamed on his face.

Not usual behavior. He'd looked over the intoxicant profiles himself when they were considering applicants. Aman sat back as a petite woman set a glass of stout in front of him and a mango margarita in front of Jimi. Aman sipped creamy foam and bitter beer, watched Jimi down a third of his drink in one long swallow. "What's troubling you?"

"You profile all the time?" Jimi set the glass down a little too hard. Orange slurry sloshed over the side, crystals of salt sliding down the curved bowl of the oversized glass. "Does it ever get to you?"

"Does what get to me?"

"That suit owned you." Jimi stared at him. "That's what you told me."

"They just think they do." Aman kept his expression neutral as he sipped more beer. "Think of it as a trade."

"They're gonna crucify that guy, right? Or whack him. No fuss, no muss."

"The government doesn't assassinate people," Aman said mildly.

"Like hell. Not in public, that's for sure."

Well, the indication had been there in Jimi's profile. He had been reading the fringe e-zines for a long time, and had belonged to a couple of political action groups that were on the "yellow" list from the government...not quite in the red zone, but close. But the best profilers came from the fringe. You learned early to evaluate people well, when you had to worry about betrayal.

"I guess I just thought I was working for the good guys, you know? Some asshole crook, a bad dealer, maybe the jerks who dump their kids on the public. But this..." He emptied his glass. "Another." He banged the glass down on the table.

You have exceeded the legal limit for operating machinery, the table informed him in a sweet, motherly voice. *I will call you a cab if you wish. Just let me know.* A moment later, the server set his fresh margarita down in front of him and whisked away his empty.

"Privacy, what a joke." Jimi stared at his drink, words slurring just a bit. "I bet there's a record of my dumps in some database or other."

"Maybe how many times you flush."

"Ha ha." Jimi looked at him blearily, the booze hitting him hard and fast now. "When d'you stop asking why? Huh? Or did you ever ask?"

"Come on." Aman stood up. "I'll walk you home. You're going to fall down."

"I'm not that drunk," Jimi said, but he stood up. Aman caught him as he swayed. "Guess I am." Jimi laughed loudly enough to make heads turn.

"Guess I should get used to it, huh? Like you."

"Let's go." Aman moved him, not all that gently. "Tell me where we're going."

"We?"

"Just give me your damn address."

Jimi recited the number, sulky and childlike again, stumbling and lurching in spite of Aman's steadying arm. It was one of the cheap and trendy loft towers that had sprouted as the neighborhood got popular. Jimi was only on the sixth floor, not high enough for a pricey view. Not on his salary. The door unlocked and lights glowed as the unit scanned Jimi's chip and let them in. Music came on, a retro-punk nostalgia band that Aman recognized. A cat padded over and eyed them greenly, its golden fur just a bit ratty. It was real, Aman realized with a start. Jimi had paid a hefty fee to keep a flesh and blood animal in the unit.

"I got to throw up," Jimi mumbled, his eyes wide. They made it to the tiny bathroom...barely. Afterward, Aman put him to bed on the pull-out couch that served as bed in the single loft room. Jimi passed out as soon as he hit the pillow. Aman left a wastebasket beside the couch and a big glass of water with a couple of old-fashioned aspirin on the low table beside it. The cat stalked him, glaring accusingly, so he rummaged in the cupboards of the tiny kitchenette, found cat food pouches and emptied one onto a plate. Set it on the floor. The cat stalked over, its tail in the air.

It would be in the database...that Jimi owned a cat. And tonight's bender would be added to his intoxicant profile, the purchase of the margaritas tallied neatly, flagged because this wasn't usual behavior. If his productivity started to fall off, Raul would look at that profile first. He'd find tonight's drunk.

"Hey."

Aman paused at the door, looked back. Jimi had pushed himself up on one elbow, eyes blurry with booze.

"Thanks...f'r feeding him. I'm not...a drunk. But you know that, right?"

"Yeah," Aman said. "I know that."

"I knew him. Today. Daren. We were friends. Kids together, y'know? Were you ever a kid? Suit's gonna kill him. You c'd tell." Tears leaked from the corners of his eyes. "How come? You didn't even ask. You didn't even ask me if I knew him."

Damn. He'd never even thought of looking for a connection there. "I'm sorry, Jimi," Aman said gently. But Jimi had passed out again, head hanging over the edge of the sofa. Aman sighed and retraced his steps, settling the kid on the cushions again. Bad break for the kid. He stared down at Jimi's unconscious sprawl on the couch-bed. *Why?* Didn't matter. The suit wouldn't have told them the truth. But Jimi was right. He should have asked. He thought about today's profile of the Runner, that break where he had changed what he ate, what he wore, what he spent his money on. You could see the break. What motivated it...that you could only guess at.

What would Avi's profile look like?

No way to know. Avi's break had been a back-cutter.

Aman closed the door and listened to the unit lock it behind him.

He carried his groceries the few scant blocks to his own modest condo tower. No music came on with the lights. No cat, just Danish furniture and an antique Afghani carpet knotted by the childhood fingers of women who were long dead now. He put the food away, stuck a meal in the microwave, and thought about pouring himself another beer. But the stout he'd drunk with Jimi buzzed in his blood like street-grade amphetamine. He smiled crookedly, thinking of his grandfather, a devout man of Islam, and his lectures about the demon's blood, alcohol. It felt like demon's blood tonight. The microwave chimed. Aman set the steaming tray on the counter to cool, sat down cross-legged on the faded wool patterns of crimson and blue, and blinked his bioware open.

His AI had been working on the profile. It presented him with five options. Aman settled down to review the Runner's profile first. It wasn't all a matter of data. You could buy a search AI, and if that was all there was to it, Search Engine, Inc. wouldn't be in business. Intuition mattered — the ability to look beyond the numbers and sense the person behind them. Aman ran through the purchases, the candy bars, the vid downloads for the lonely times, the gifts that evoked the misty presence of the girlfriend, the hope of love expressed in single, cloned roses, in Belgian chocolate, and tickets in pairs. They came and went, three of them for sure. He worried about his weight, or maybe just his muscles for awhile, buying gym time and special foods.

Someone died. Aman noted the payments for flowers, the crematorium, a spike in alcohol purchases for about three months. And then...the break. Curious, Aman opened another file from the download the suit had given him, read the stats. Daren had been a contract birth — the new way for men to have

children. Mom had left for a career as an engineer on one of the orbital plat-
forms. Nanny, private school. The flowers had been for Dad, dead at fifty-four
from a brain aneurysm.

He had joined the Gaiists after his father had died.

Unlike Avi, who hadn't waited.

Aman looked again at the five profiles the AI had presented. All featured
organic, wild harvest, natural fiber purchasing profiles. Three were still local.
One had recently arrived in Montreal, another had arrived in the Confederacy
of South America, in the state of Brazil. Aman scanned the data. That one. He
selected one of the local trio. The purchases clustered northeast of the city in an
area that had been upscale suburb once, was a squalid cash-worker settlement
now. He was walking. Couldn't use mass transit without a chip and didn't have
access to a vehicle, clearly. Naïve. Aman let his breath out slowly. Frightened. A
little kid with his head under the sofa cushions, thinking he was invisible that
way. He wondered sometimes if he could find Avi. It would be a challenge. His
son knew how he worked. He knew how to really hide.

Aman had never looked.

On a whim, he called up the AI's flag from his earlier search. It had flagged
the woman who had died, who had probably been a live-in friend or lover. This
time, the AI presented him with clustered drug overdose deaths during the past
five years. A glowing question mark tagged the data, crimson, which meant a
continuation would take him into secure and unauthorized data. Pursue it? He
almost said no. "All right, Jimi." He touched the blood-colored question mark.
"Continue." It vanished. Searching secure government data files was going to
cost. He hoped he could come up with a reason for Raul, if he caught it.

His legs wanted to cramp when Aman finally blinked out of his bioware and
got stiffly to his feet. The AI hadn't yet finished its search of the DEA data files.
The meal tray on the counter was cold and it was well past midnight. He stuck
the tray in the tiny fridge and threw himself down on the low couch. Like Jimi,
but not drunk on margaritas.

In the morning, he messaged Raul that he wasn't feeling well and asked if he
should come in. As expected, Raul told him no way, go get a screen before you
come back. You could count on Raul with his paranoia about bioterrorism.

It wasn't entirely a lie. He wasn't feeling well. *Well* covered a lot of turf. The

AI had nothing for him on the overdose cluster it had flagged and that bothered him. There wasn't a lot of security that could stop it. He emailed Jimi, telling him to work on the Sauza search on his own and attached a couple of non-secure files that would give him something he could handle in what would surely be a fuzzy and hungover state of mind. He found the clothes he needed at the back of his closet, an old, worn tunic-shirt and a grease-stained pair of jeans. He put on a pair of scuffed and worn-out boots he'd found in a city recycle center years ago, then caught a ped-cab to the light rail and took the northeast run. He paid cash to the wary driver and used it to buy a one way entry to the light rail. Not that cash hid his movements. He smiled grimly as he found a seat. His ped-cab and light rail use had been recorded by citizen.net, the data company favored by most transportation systems. It would just take someone a few minutes longer to find out where he had gone today.

City ran out abruptly in the Belt, a no-man's-land of abandoned warehouses and the sagging shells of houses inhabited by squatters, the chipless bilge of society. Small patches of cultivation suggested an order to the squalid chaos. As the train rocketed above the sagging roofs and scrubby brush that had taken over, he caught a brief snapshot glimpse of a round-faced girl peering up at him from beneath a towering fountain of rose canes thick with bright pink blossoms. Her shift, surprisingly clean and bright, matched the color of the roses perfectly and she waved suddenly and wildly as the train whisked Aman past. He craned his neck to see her, but the curve of the track hid her instantly.

At his stop, he stepped out with a scant handful of passengers, women mostly and a couple of men, returning from a night of cleaning or doing custom handwork for the upscale clothiers. None of them looked at him as they plodded across the bare and dirty concrete of the platform, but a sense of observation prickled the back of his neck.

Why would anyone be following him? But Aman loitered to examine the melon slices and early apples hawked by a couple of bored boys at the end of the platform. He haggled a bit, then spun around and walked quickly away—which earned him some inventive epithets from the taller of the boys. No sign of a shadow. Aman shrugged and decided on nerves. His AI's lack of follow-up data bothered him more with every passing minute. The rising sun already burned the back of his neck as he stepped off the platform and into the street.

The houses here were old, roofs sagging or covered with cheap plastic siding, textured to look like wood and lapped to shed rain. It was more prosperous than the no-man's-land belt around the city center, but not by much. Vegetables grew in most of the tiny yards, downspouts fed hand-dug cisterns and small, semi-legal stands offered vegetables, homemade fruit drinks, snacks, and various services — much like the street vendors on his block, but out here, the customers came to the vendors and not the other way around.

He paused at a clean-looking stand built in what had been a parking strip, and bought a glass of vegetable juice, made in front of his eyes in an antique blender. The woman washed the vegetables in a bucket of muddy water before she chopped them into the blender, but he smelled chlorine as he leaned casually on the counter. Safe enough. His vaccinations were up to date, so he took the glass without hesitation and drank the spicy, basil-flavored stuff. He didn't like basil particularly, but he smiled at her. "Has Daren been by today?" He hazarded the Runner's real name on the wild chance that he was too naïve to have used a fake. "He was supposed to meet me here. Bet he overslept."

Her face relaxed a bit, her smile more genuine. "Of course." She shrugged, relaxing. "Doesn't he always? I usually see him later on. Like noon." And she laughed a familiar and comfortable "we're all friends" laughter.

He was using his real name. Aman sipped some more of the juice, wanting to shake his head. Little kid with his head under the friendly sofa cushions. A figure emerged from a small, square block of a house nearly invisible beneath a huge tangle of kiwi and kudzu vines and headed their way, walking briskly, his handwoven, natural-dyed tunic as noticeable as a bright balloon on this street. Loose drawstring pants woven of some tan fiber and the string of carved beads around his neck might as well have been a neon arrow pointing. "Ha, there he is," Aman said, and the woman's glance and smile confirmed his guess. Aman waited until the Runner's eyes were starting to sweep his way, then stepped quickly forward. "Daren, it's been forever." He threw his arms around the kid hugging him like a long-lost brother, doing a quick cheek-kiss that allowed him to hiss into the shocked kid's ear, *"Act like we're old friends and maybe the feds won't get you. Don't blow this."*

The kid stiffened, panic tensing all his muscles, fear sweat sour in Aman's nostrils. For a few seconds, the kid thought it over. Then his muscles relaxed all at once, so much so that Aman's hands tightened instinctively on his arms. He started to tremble.

"Come on. Let's take a walk," Aman said. "I'm not here to bust you."

"Let me get some juice…"

"No." Aman's thumb dug into the nerve plexus in his shoulder and the kid gasped. "Walk." He twisted the kid around and propelled him down the street, away from the little juice kiosk, his body language suggesting two old friends out strolling, his arm companionably over the kid's shoulder, hiding the kid's tension with his own body, thumb exerting just enough pressure on the nerve to remind the kid to behave. "You are leaving a trail a blind infant could follow," he said conversationally, felt the kid's jerk of reaction.

"I'm not chipped." Angry bravado tone.

"You don't need to be chipped. That just slows the search down a few hours. You went straight from the hack-doc to here, walked through the Belt because you couldn't take the rail, you buy juice at this stand every day, and you bought those pants two blocks up the street, from the lady who sells clothes out of her living room. Want me to tell you what you had for dinner last night, too?"

"Oh, Goddess," he breathed.

"Spare me." Aman sighed. "Why do they want you? You blow something up? Plant a virus?"

"Not us. Not the Gaiists." He jerked free of Aman's grip with surprising strength, fists clenched. "That's all a lie. I don't know why they want me. Yeah, they're claiming bioterrorism, but I didn't do it. There wasn't any virus released where they said it happened. How can they *do* that? Just make something up?" His voice had gone shrill. "They have to have proof and they don't have any proof. Because it didn't happen."

He sounded so much like Avi that Aman had to look away. "They just made it all up, huh?" He made his voice harsh, unbelieving.

"I…guess." The kid looked down, his lip trembling. "Yeah, it sounds crazy, huh. I just don't get *why*? Why *me*? I don't even do protests. I just…try to save what's left to save."

"Tell me about your girlfriend."

"Who?" He blinked at Aman, his eyes wet with tears.

"The one who died."

"Oh. Reyna." He looked down, his expression instantly sad. "She really wanted to kick 'em. The drugs. I tried to help her. She just…she just had so much fear inside. I guess…the drugs were the only thing that really helped the fear. I…I really tried."

"So she killed herself?"

"Oh, no." Daren looked up at him, shocked. "She didn't want to *die*. She just didn't want to be afraid. She did the usual hit that morning. I guess...the guy she bought from, he called himself Skinjack, I guess he didn't cut the stuff right. She OD'ed. I...went looking for him." Daren flushed. "I told myself I was going to beat him up. I guess...maybe I wanted to kill him. Because she was getting better. She would have made it." He drew a shaky breath. "He just disappeared. The son of a bitch. I kept looking for him but...he was just gone. Maybe he OD'ed, too," he added bitterly. "I sure hope so."

All of a sudden, it clicked into place. The whole picture.

Why.

They had reached an empty lot. Someone was growing grapes in it and as they reached the end of the rows, sudden movement in the shadows caught Aman's eye. Too late. He was so busy sorting it all out, he'd stopped paying attention. The figure stepped out of the leaf shadows, a small, ugly gun in his hand.

"I was right." Jimi's eyes glittered. "Didn't think I was smart enough to track you, huh? I'm stupid, I know, but not that stupid."

"Actually, I thought you'd be too hung over." Aman spread his hands carefully. "I think we're on the same side here, and I think we need to get out of here *now*."

"Shut up," Jimi said evenly, stepping closer, icy with threat. "Just shut *up*."

"Jimi?" Daren pushed forward, confused. "Goddess, I haven't seen you.... what are you doing?"

"He found you," Jimi said between his teeth. "For the feds. You're not hiding very well, Daren, you idiot. Everything you buy has a damn tag on it. He looked up your buying habits and picked you out of the crowd, just like that. He laughed about how easy it was. You were too easy for him to even give the job to a newbie like me." Jimi's eyes burned into the kid's. "You got to..."

Aman shifted his weight infinitesimally, made a tiny, quick move with his left hand, just enough to catch Jimi's eye. Jimi swung right, eyes tracking, gun muzzle following his eyes. Aman grabbed Jimi's gun hand with his right hand, twisted, heard a snap. With a cry Jimi let go of the gun and Aman snatched it from the air, just as Daren tackled him, grabbing for the gun. The hissing snap of a gas-powered gunshot ripped the air. Again. Aman tensed, everything happening in slow motion now. No pain. Why no pain? Hot wetness spattered his

SEARCH ENGINE | 383

face and Jimi sprawled backward into the grape leaves, arms and legs jerking. Aman rolled, shrugging Daren off as if he weighed nothing, seeing the suit now, three meters away, aiming at Daren.

Aman fired. It was a wild shot, crazy shot, the kind you did in sim-training sessions and knew you'd never pull off for real.

The suit went down.

Aman tried to scramble to his feet, but things weren't working right. After a while, Daren hauled him the rest of the way up. White ringed his eyes and he looked ready to pass out from shock.

"He's dead. Jimi. And the other guy." He clung to Aman, as if Aman was supporting him and not the other way around. "Goddess, you're bleeding."

"Enough with Goddess already." Aman watched red drops fall from his fingertips. His left arm was numb, but that wouldn't last.

"Why? What in the...what the *hell* is going on here?" His fingers dug into Aman's arm.

"Thank you." Hell was about right. "We need to get out of here. Do you know the neighborhood?"

"Yes. Sort of. This way." Daren started through the grapes, his arm around Aman. "I'm supposed to meet...a ride. This afternoon. A ride to..." He gave Aman a sideways, worried look. "Another place."

"You're gonna have to learn some things..." Aman had to catch his breath. "Or you're gonna bring the suits right after you." After that he stopped talking. The numbness was wearing off. Once, years and years ago, he had worked as private security, licensed for lethal force, paying his way though school. A burglar shot him one night.

It hurt worse than he remembered, like white-hot spears digging into his shoulder and side with every step. He disconnected himself from his body after a while, let it deal with the pain. He wondered about Jimi's cat. Who would take care of it? Raul would be pissed, he thought dreamily. Not about Jimi. Raul had no trouble finding Jimis in the world. But Aman was a lot better than Raul. Better even than An Xuyen, although Xuyen didn't think so. Raul would be pissed.

He blinked back to the world of hot afternoon and found himself sitting in dim light, his back against something solid.

"Man you were out on your feet." The kid squatted beside him, streaked with sweat, drying blood, and gray dust, his face gaunt with exhaustion and fear. Daren, not Jimi. Jimi was dead.

"I don't have any first aid stuff, but it doesn't look like you're bleeding too much anymore. Water?" He handed Aman a plastic bottle. "It's okay. It's from a clean spring."

Aman didn't really care, would have drunk from a puddle. The ruins of an old house surrounded them. The front had fallen — or been torn — completely off, but a thick curtain of kudzu vine shrouded the space. Old campfire scars blackened the rotting wooden floor. The Belt, he figured. Edge of it anyway.

"What happened?" Daren's voice trembled. "Why did he shoot Jimi? Who was he? Who are *you?*"

The water helped. "What sent you to get hacked?" Aman asked.

"Someone searched my apartment." The kid looked away. "I found...a bug in my car. I'm...good at finding those. I...told some of my...friends...and they said go invisible. It didn't matter if I'd done anything or not. They were right." His voice trembled. "I'd never do what they said I did."

"They know you didn't do anything." Aman closed his eyes and leaned back against the broken plasterboard of the ruined wall. Pain thudded through his shoulder with every beat of his heart. "It's the guy who killed your girlfriend."

"Why? I never hurt him. I never even found him..."

"You looked for him," Aman mumbled. "That scared 'em."

The kid's blank silence forced his eyes open.

"I'm guessing the local government is running a little...drug eradication program by eliminating the market," he said heavily. Explaining to a child. "They cut a deal with the street connections and probably handed them a shipment of...altered...stuff to put into the pipeline. Sudden big drop in users."

"Poisoned?" Daren whispered. "On purpose?"

"Nasty, huh? Election coming up. Numbers count. And who looks twice at an OD in a confirmed user?" Aman kept seeing Jimi's childlike curl on the couch, the cat regarding him patiently. Couldn't make it go away. "Maybe they thought you had proof. Maybe they figured you'd guess and tell your...friends. They might make it public." He started to shrug...sucked in a quick breath. Mistake. Waited for the world to steady again. "I should have guessed...the suit would know about Jimi. Would be tailing him." That was why the long look in the office. Memory impression so the suit could spot him in a crowd. "I figured it out just too late." His fault, Jimi's death. "How soon are your people going to pick you up?"

"Soon. I think." The kid was staring at the ground, looked up suddenly. "How come you came after me? To arrest me?"

"Listen." Aman pushed himself straighter, gritted his teeth until the pain eased a bit. "I told you you're leaving a trail like a neon sign. You listen hard. You got to think about what you buy...food, clothes, toothpaste, okay?" He stared into the kid's uncomprehending face, willing him to get it. "It's all tagged, even if they say it's not. Don't doubt it. I'm telling you truth here, okay?"

The kid closed his mouth, nodded.

"You don't buy exactly the opposite — that's a trail we can follow, too — but you buy random. Maybe vegan stuff this time, maybe a pair of synth-leather pants off the rack at a big chain next purchase. Something you'd never spend cash on. Not even before you became a Gaiist, got it? You think about what you really want to buy. The food. The clothes. The snacks, toys, services. And you only buy them every fifth purchase, then every fourth, then every seventh. Got it? Random. You do that, buy stuff you don't want, randomly, and without a chip, you won't make a clear track. You'll be so far down on the profile that the searcher won't take you seriously."

"I've been buying in the Belt," the kid protested.

"Doesn't matter." He had explained why to Jimi. Couldn't do it again. Didn't have the strength. Let his eyes droop closed.

"Hey." The kid's voice came to him from a long way away. "I got to know. How come you came after me? To tell me how to hide from you? You really want me to believe that?"

"I don't care if you do or not." Aman struggled to open his eyes, stared into the blurry green light filtering through the kudzu curtain. "I'm...not sure how come I followed you." Maybe because he hadn't asked why and Jimi had. Maybe because Avi had been right and the job had changed him after all.

"But why? You a closet Gaiist?"

Aman wanted to laugh at that, but he didn't. It would hurt too much.

Voices filtered through nightmares full of teeth. People talking. No more green light, so it must be almost dark. Or maybe he was dying. Hard to tell. Footsteps scuffed and the kid's face swam into view, Jimi's at first, morphing into the other kid...Daren. He tried to say the name but his mouth was too dry.

"We're gonna drop you at an emergency clinic." Daren leaned close, his eyes anxious. "But...well, I thought maybe...you want to go with us? I mean...they're going to find out you killed that Fed guy, right? You'll go to prison."

Yes, they would find out. But he knew how it worked. They'd hold the evidence and the case open. No reason to risk pointing some investigative reporter toward the little dope deal they'd been covering up. They'd have expectations, and he'd meet them, and Jimi's death would turn out to have been another nasty little killing in the Belt. He could adopt Jimi's cat. No harm done. Just between us.

"I'll come with you," he croaked. "You could use some help with your invisibility. And I have the track to the proof you need...about that drug deal. Make the election interesting." Wasn't pleading. Not that. Trade.

"You can't come chipped." A woman looked over Daren's shoulder, Hispanic, ice cold, with an air that said she was in charge. "And we got to go *now*."

"I know." At least the chip was in his good shoulder.

She did it, using a tiny laser scalpel with a deft sureness that suggested med school or even an MD. And it hurt, but not a lot compared to the glowing coals of pain in his left arm and then they were loading him into the back of a vehicle and it was fully dark outside.

He was invisible. Right now. He no longer existed in the electronic reality of the city. If he made it back to his apartment it wouldn't let him in. The corner store wouldn't take his card or even cash. He felt naked. No, he felt as if he no longer existed. Death wasn't as complete as this. Wondered if Avi had felt like that at first. I probably could have found him, he thought. If I'd had the guts to try.

"I'm glad you're coming with us." Daren sat beside him as the truck or whatever it was rocked and bucked over broken pavement toward the nearest clear street. "Lea says you probably won't die."

"I'm thrilled."

"Maybe we can use the drug stuff to influence the election, get someone honest elected."

He was as bad as Jimi, Aman thought. But...why not hope?

"You'll like the head of our order," Daren said thoughtfully. "He's not a whole lot older than me, but he's great. Really brilliant and he cares about every person in the order. *She* really matters to him...the Earth I mean. Avi will really welcome you."

Avi.

Aman closed his eyes.

"Hey, you okay?" Daren had him by the shoulders. "Don't die now, not after all this." He sounded panicky.

"I won't," Aman whispered. He managed a tiny laugh that didn't hurt too bad.

Maybe it hadn't been the final fight after all.

Could almost make him believe in Avi's Goddess. Almost.

"Your head of the order sucks at hiding," he whispered. And fainted.

When Sysadmins Ruled the Earth

Cory Doctorow

If William Gibson and Bruce Sterling were the alpha cyberpunks of last century, then Charles Stross and Cory Doctorow have become the alphas of this one. Here Doctorow geeks fluently about terrorism and net culture, sorrow and idealism. He nods at all those stories about global cataclysm and the end of human civilization but then offers a decidedly PCP take on who might be best suited to do the Adam and Eve thing. To watch his Sysadmins struggling to rebuild politics is to realize that cyberpunk, paradoxically, has become a literature for grownups.

When Felix's special phone rang at two in the morning, Kelly rolled over and punched him in the shoulder and hissed, "Why didn't you turn that fucking thing off before bed?"

"Because I'm on call," he said.

"You're not a fucking doctor," she said, kicking him as he sat on the bed's edge, pulling on the pants he'd left on the floor before turning in. "You're a god-damned *systems administrator*."

"It's my job," he said.

"They work you like a government mule," she said. "You know I'm right. For Christ's sake, you're a father now, you can't go running off in the middle of the night every time someone's porn supply goes down. Don't answer that phone."

He knew she was right. He answered the phone.

"Main routers not responding. BGP not responding." The mechanical voice of the systems monitor didn't care if he cursed at it, so he did, and it made him feel a little better.

"Maybe I can fix it from here," he said. He could login to the UPS for the cage and reboot the routers. The UPS was in a different netblock, with its own independent routers on their own uninterruptible power-supplies.

Kelly was sitting up in bed now, an indistinct shape against the headboard. "In five years of marriage, you have never once been able to fix anything from here." This time she was wrong—he fixed stuff from home all the time, but he did it discreetly and didn't make a fuss, so she didn't remember it. And she was right, too—he had logs that showed that after 1 AM, nothing could ever be fixed without driving out to the cage. Law of Infinite Universal Perversity — AKA Felix's Law.

Five minutes later Felix was behind the wheel. He hadn't been able to fix it from home. The independent routers' netblock was offline, too. The last time that had happened, some dumbfuck construction worker had driven a ditch-witch through the main conduit into the data-center and Felix had joined a cadre of fifty enraged sysadmins who'd stood atop the resulting pit for a week, screaming abuse at the poor bastards who labored 24-7 to splice ten thousand wires back together.

His phone went off twice more in the car and he let it override the stereo and play the mechanical status reports through the big, bassy speakers of more critical network infrastructure offline. Then Kelly called.

"Hi," he said.

"Don't cringe, I can hear the cringe in your voice."

He smiled involuntarily. "Check, no cringing."

"I love you, Felix," she said.

"I'm totally bonkers for you, Kelly. Go back to bed."

"2.0's awake," she said. The baby had been Beta Test when he was in her womb, and when her water broke, he got the call and dashed out of the office, shouting, 'The Gold Master just shipped!' They'd started calling him 2.0 before he'd finished his first cry. "This little bastard was born to suck tit."

"I'm sorry I woke you," he said. He was almost at the data-center. No traffic at 2 AM. He slowed down and pulled over before the entrance to the garage. He didn't want to lose Kelly's call underground.

"It's not waking me," she said. "You've been there for seven years. You have three juniors reporting to you. Give them the phone. You've paid your dues."

"I don't like asking my reports to do anything I wouldn't do," he said.

"You've done it," she said. "Please? I hate waking up alone in the night. I miss you most at night."

"Kelly—"

"I'm over being angry. I just miss you is all. You give me sweet dreams."

"OK," he said.

"Simple as that?"

"Exactly. Simple as that. Can't have you having bad dreams, and I've paid my dues. From now on, I'm only going on night call to cover holidays."

She laughed. "Sysadmins don't take holidays."

"This one will," he said. "Promise."

"You're wonderful," she said. "Oh, gross. 2.0 just dumped core all over my bathrobe."

"That's my boy," he said.

"Oh that he is," she said. She hung up, and he piloted the car into the data-center lot, badging in and peeling up a bleary eyelid to let the retinal scanner get a good look at his sleep-depped eyeball.

He stopped at the machine to get himself a guarana/medafonil power-bar and a cup of lethal robot-coffee in a spill-proof clean-room sippy-cup. He wolfed down the bar and sipped the coffee, then let the inner door read his hand-geometry and size him up for a moment. It sighed open and gusted the airlock's load of positively pressurized air over him as he passed finally to the inner sanctum.

It was bedlam. The cages were designed to let two or three sysadmins maneuver around them at a time. Every other inch of cubic space was given over to humming racks of servers and routers and drives. Jammed among them were no fewer than twenty other sysadmins. It was a regular convention of black tee-shirts with inexplicable slogans, bellies overlapping belts with phones and multitools.

Normally it was practically freezing in the cage, but all those bodies were overheating the small, enclosed space. Five or six looked up and grimaced when he came through. Two greeted him by name. He threaded his belly through the press and the cages, toward the Ardent racks in the back of the room.

"Felix." It was Van, who wasn't on call that night.

"What are you doing here?" he asked. "No need for both of us to be wrecked tomorrow."

"What? Oh. My personal box is over there. It went down around 1:30 and I got woken up by my process-monitor. I should have called you and told you I was coming down — spared you the trip."

Felix's own server — a box he shared with five other friends — was in a rack one floor down. He wondered if it was offline too.

"What's the story?"

"Massive flashworm attack. Some jackass with a zero-day exploit has got every Windows box on the net running Monte Carlo probes on every IP block, including IPv6. The big Ciscos all run administrative interfaces over v6, and they all fall over if they get more than ten simultaneous probes, which means that just about every interchange has gone down. DNS is screwy, too—like maybe someone poisoned the zone transfer last night. Oh, and there's an email and IM component that sends pretty lifelike messages to everyone in your address book, barfing up Eliza-dialog that keys off of your logged email and messages to get you to open a Trojan."

"Jesus."

"Yeah." Van was a type-two sysadmin, over six feet tall, long ponytail, bobbing Adam's apple. Over his toast-rack chest, his tee said CHOOSE YOUR WEAPON and featured a row of polyhedral RPG dice.

Felix was a type-one admin, with an extra seventy or eighty pounds all around the middle, and a neat but full beard that he wore over his extra chins. His tee said HELLO CTHULHU and featured a cute, mouthless, Hello-Kitty-style Cthulhu. They'd known each other for fifteen years, having met on Usenet, then f2f at Toronto Freenet beer-sessions, a Star Trek convention or two, and eventually Felix had hired Van to work under him at Ardent. Van was reliable and methodical. Trained as an electrical engineer, he kept a procession of spiral notebooks filled with the details of every step he'd ever taken, with time and date.

"Not even PEBKAC this time," Van said. Problem Exists Between Keyboard And Chair. Email trojans fell into that category—if people were smart enough not to open suspect attachments, email trojans would be a thing of the past. But worms that ate Cisco routers weren't a problem with the lusers—they were the fault of incompetent engineers.

"No, it's Microsoft's fault," Felix said. "Any time I'm at work at 2 AM, it's either PEBKAC or Microsloth."

They ended up just unplugging the frigging routers from the Internet. Not Felix, of course, though he was itching to do it and get them rebooted after shutting down their IPv6 interfaces. It was done by a couple bull-goose Bastard Operators From Hell who had to turn two keys at once to get access to their cage—like guards in a Minuteman silo. Ninety-five percent of the long distance traffic in Canada went through this building. It had *better* security than most Minuteman silos.

Felix and Van got the Ardent boxes back online one at a time. They were being pounded by worm-probes—putting the routers back online just exposed the downstream cages to the attack. Every box on the Internet was drowning in worms, or creating worm-attacks, or both. Felix managed to get through to NIST and Bugtraq after about a hundred timeouts, and download some kernel patches that should reduce the load the worms put on the machines in his care. It was 10 AM, and he was hungry enough to eat the ass out of a dead bear, but he recompiled his kernels and brought the machines back online. Van's long fingers flew over the administrative keyboard, his tongue protruding as he ran load-stats on each one.

"I had two hundred days of uptime on Greedo," Van said. Greedo was the oldest server in the rack, from the days when they'd named the boxes after *Star Wars* characters. Now they were all named after Smurfs, and they were running out of Smurfs and had started in on McDonaldland characters, starting with Van's laptop, Mayor McCheese.

"Greedo will rise again," Felix said. "I've got a 486 downstairs with over five years of uptime. It's going to break my heart to reboot it."

"What the everlasting shit do you use a 486 for?"

"Nothing. But who shuts down a machine with five years uptime? That's like euthanizing your grandmother."

"I wanna eat," Van said.

"Tell you what," Felix said. "We'll get your box up, then mine, then I'll take you to the Lakeview Lunch for breakfast pizzas and you can have the rest of the day off."

"You're on," Van said. "Man, you're too good to us grunts. You should keep us in a pit and beat us like all the other bosses. It's all we deserve."

"It's your phone," Van said. Felix extracted himself from the guts of the 486, which had refused to power up at all. He had cadged a spare power-supply from some guys who ran a spam operation and was trying to get it fitted. He let Van hand him the phone, which had fallen off his belt while he was twisting to get at the back of the machine.

"Hey, Kel," he said. There was an odd, snuffling noise in the background. Static, maybe? 2.0 splashing in the bath? "Kelly?"

The line went dead. He tried to call back, but didn't get anything — no ring nor voicemail. His phone finally timed out and said NETWORK ERROR.

"Dammit," he said, mildly. He clipped the phone to his belt. Kelly wanted to know when he was coming home, or wanted him to pick something up for the family. She'd leave voicemail.

He was testing the power-supply when his phone rang again. He snatched it up and answered it. "Kelly, hey, what's up?" He worked to keep anything like irritation out of his voice. He felt guilty: technically speaking, he had discharged his obligations to Ardent Financial LLC once the Ardent servers were back online. The past three hours had been purely personal — even if he planned on billing them to the company.

There was sobbing on the line.

"Kelly?" He felt the blood draining from his face and his toes were numb.

"Felix," she said, barely comprehensible through the sobbing. "He's dead, oh Jesus, he's dead."

"Who? *Who*, Kelly?"

"Will," she said.

Will? he thought. *Who the fuck is —* " He dropped to his knees. William was the name they'd written on the birth certificate, though they'd called him 2.0 all along. Felix made an anguished sound, like a sick bark.

"I'm sick," she said, "I can't even stand anymore. Oh, Felix. I love you so much."

"Kelly? What's going on?"

"Everyone, everyone —" she said. "Only two channels left on the tube. Christ, Felix, it looks like dawn of the dead out the window —" He heard her retch. The phone started to break up, washing her puke-noises back like an echoplex.

"Stay there, Kelly," he shouted as the line died. He punched 911, but the phone went NETWORK ERROR again as soon as he hit SEND.

He grabbed Mayor McCheese from Van and plugged it into the 486's network cable and launched Firefox off the command line and googled for the Metro Police site. Quickly, but not frantically, he searched for an online contact form. Felix didn't lose his head, ever. He solved problems and freaking out didn't solve problems.

He located an online form and wrote out the details of his conversation with Kelly like he was filing a bug report, his fingers fast, his description complete, and then he hit SUBMIT.

Van had read over his shoulder. "Felix—" he began.

"God," Felix said. He was sitting on the floor of the cage and he slowly pulled himself upright. Van took the laptop and tried some news sites, but they were all timing out. Impossible to say if it was because something terrible was happening or because the network was limping under the superworm.

"I need to get home," Felix said.

"I'll drive you," Van said. "You can keep calling your wife."

They made their way to the elevators. One of the building's few windows was there, a thick, shielded porthole. They peered through it as they waited for the elevator. Not much traffic for a Wednesday. Were there more police cars than usual?

"*Oh my God—*" Van pointed.

The CN Tower, a giant white-elephant needle of a building loomed to the east of them. It was askew, like a branch stuck in wet sand. Was it moving? It was. It was heeling over, slowly, but gaining speed, falling northeast toward the financial district. In a second, it slid over the tipping point and crashed down. They felt the shock, then heard it, the whole building rocking from the impact. A cloud of dust rose from the wreckage, and there was more thunder as the world's tallest freestanding structure crashed through building after building.

"The Broadcast Centre's coming down," Van said. It was—the CBC's towering building was collapsing in slow motion. People ran every way, were crushed by falling masonry. Seen through the porthole, it was like watching a neat CGI trick downloaded from a file-sharing site.

Sysadmins were clustering around them now, jostling to see the destruction.

"What happened?" one of them asked.

"The CN Tower fell down," Felix said. He sounded far away in his own ears.

"Was it the virus?"

"The worm? What?" Felix focused on the guy, who was a young admin with just a little type-two flab around the middle.

"Not the worm," the guy said. "I got an email that the whole city's quarantine because of some virus. Bioweapon, they say." He handed Felix his Blackberry.

Felix was so engrossed in the report — purportedly forwarded from Health Canada — that he didn't even notice that all the lights had gone out. Then he did, and he pressed the Blackberry back into its owner's hand, and let out one small sob.

The generators kicked in a minute later. Sysadmins stampeded for the stairs. Felix grabbed Van by the arm, pulled him back.

"Maybe we should wait this out in the cage," he said.

"What about Kelly?" Van said.

Felix felt like he was going to throw up. "We should get into the cage, now." The cage had microparticulate air-filters.

They ran upstairs to the big cage. Felix opened the door and then let it hiss shut behind him.

"Felix, you need to get home — "

"It's a bioweapon," Felix said. "Superbug. We'll be OK in here, I think, so long as the filters hold out."

"What?"

"Get on IRC," he said.

They did. Van had Mayor McCheese and Felix used Smurfette. They skipped around the chat channels until they found one with some familiar handles.

> pentagons gone/white house too

> MY NEIGHBORS BARFING BLOOD OFF HIS BALCONY IN SAN DIEGO

> Someone knocked over the Gherkin. Bankers are fleeing the City like rats.

> I heard that the Ginza's on fire

Felix typed: I'm in Toronto. We just saw the CN Tower fall. I've heard reports of bioweapons, something very fast.

Van read this and said, "You don't know how fast it is, Felix. Maybe we were all exposed three days ago."

Felix closed his eyes. "If that were so we'd be feeling some symptoms, I think."

> Looks like an EMP took out Hong Kong and maybe Paris — realtime sat footage shows them completely dark, and all netblocks there aren't routing

> You're in Toronto?

It was an unfamiliar handle.

> Yes — on Front Street

> my sisters at UofT and i cnt reach her — can you call her?

> No phone service

Felix typed, staring at NETWORK PROBLEMS.

"I have a soft phone on Mayor McCheese," Van said, launching his voice-over-IP app. "I just remembered."

Felix took the laptop from him and punched in his home number. It rang once, then there was a flat, blatting sound like an ambulance siren in an Italian movie.

> No phone service

Felix typed again.

He looked up at Van, and saw that his skinny shoulders were shaking. Van said, "Holy motherfucking shit. The world is ending."

Felix pried himself off of IRC an hour later. Atlanta had burned. Manhattan was hot — radioactive enough to screw up the webcams looking out over Lincoln Plaza. Everyone blamed Islam until it became clear that Mecca was a smoking pit and the Saudi Royals had been hanged before their palaces.

His hands were shaking, and Van was quietly weeping in the far corner of the cage. He tried calling home again, and then the police. It didn't work any better than it had the last twenty times.

He sshed into his box downstairs and grabbed his mail. Spam, spam, spam. More spam. Automated messages. There — an urgent message from the intrusion detection system in the Ardent cage.

He opened it and read quickly. Someone was crudely, repeatedly probing his routers. It didn't match a worm's signature, either. He followed the traceroute and discovered that the attack had originated in the same building as him, a system in a cage one floor below.

He had procedures for this. He portscanned his attacker and found that port 1337 was open — 1337 was "leet" or "elite" in hacker number/letter substitution code. That was the kind of port that a worm left open to slither in and out of. He googled known sploits that left a listener on port 1337, narrowed this down based on the fingerprinted operating system of the compromised server, and then he had it.

It was an ancient worm, one that every box should have been patched against years before. No mind. He had the client for it, and he used it to create a root account for himself on the box, which he then logged into, and took a look around.

There was one other user logged in, "scaredy," and he checked the process monitor and saw that scaredy had spawned all the hundreds of processes that were probing him and plenty of other boxen.

He opened a chat:

> Stop probing my server

He expected bluster, guilt, denial. He was surprised.

> Are you in the Front Street data-center?

> Yes

> Christ I thought I was the last one alive. I'm on the fourth floor. I think there's a bioweapon attack outside. I don't want to leave the clean room.

Felix whooshed out a breath.

> You were probing me to get me to trace back to you?

> Yeah

> That was smart

Clever bastard.

> I'm on the sixth floor, I've got one more with me.

> What do you know?

Felix pasted in the IRC log and waited while the other guy digested it. Van stood up and paced. His eyes were glazed over.

"Van? Pal?"

"I have to pee," he said.

"No opening the door," Felix said. "I saw an empty Mountain Dew bottle in the trash there."

"Right," Van said. He walked like a zombie to the trash can and pulled out the empty magnum. He turned his back.

> I'm Felix

> Will

Felix's stomach did a slow somersault as he thought about 2.0.

"Felix, I think I need to go outside," Van said. He was moving toward the airlock door. Felix dropped his keyboard and struggled to his feet and ran headlong to Van, tackling him before he reached the door.

"Van," he said, looking into his friend's glazed, unfocused eyes. "Look at me, Van."

"I need to go," Van said. "I need to get home and feed the cats."

"There's something out there, something fast-acting and lethal. Maybe it will blow away with the wind. Maybe it's already gone. But we're going to sit here until we know for sure or until we have no choice. Sit down, Van. Sit."

"I'm cold, Felix."

It was freezing. Felix's arms were broken out in gooseflesh and his feet felt like blocks of ice.

"Sit against the servers, by the vents. Get the exhaust heat." He found a rack and nestled up against it.

> Are you there?

> Still here — sorting out some logistics

> How long until we can go out?

> I have no idea

No one typed anything for quite some time then.

Felix had to use the Mountain Dew bottle twice. Then Van used it again. Felix tried calling Kelly again. The Metro Police site was down.

Finally, he slid back against the servers and wrapped his arms around his knees and wept like a baby.

After a minute, Van came over and sat beside him, with his arm around Felix's shoulder.

"They're dead, Van," Felix said. "Kelly and my s — son. My family is gone."

"You don't know for sure," Van said.

"I'm sure enough," Felix said. "Christ, it's all over, isn't it?"

"We'll gut it out a few more hours and then head out. Things should be getting back to normal soon. The fire department will fix it. They'll mobilize the Army. It'll be OK."

Felix's ribs hurt. He hadn't cried since — Since 2.0 was born. He hugged his knees harder.

Then the doors opened.

The two sysadmins who entered were wild-eyed. One had a tee that said

TALK NERDY TO ME and the other one was wearing an Electronic Frontiers Canada shirt.

"Come on," TALK NERDY said. "We're all getting together on the top floor. Take the stairs."

Felix found he was holding his breath.

"If there's a bioagent in the building, we're all infected," TALK NERDY said. "Just go, we'll meet you there."

"There's one on the sixth floor," Felix said, as he climbed to his feet.

"Will, yeah, we got him. He's up there."

TALK NERDY was one of the Bastard Operators From Hell who'd unplugged the big routers. Felix and Van climbed the stairs slowly, their steps echoing in the deserted shaft. After the frigid air of the cage, the stairwell felt like a sauna.

There was a cafeteria on the top floor, with working toilets, water and coffee and vending machine food. There was an uneasy queue of sysadmins before each. No one met anyone's eye. Felix wondered which one was Will and then he joined the vending machine queue.

He got a couple more energy bars and a gigantic cup of vanilla coffee before running out of change. Van had scored them some table space and Felix set the stuff down before him and got in the toilet line. "Just save some for me," he said, tossing an energy bar in front of Van.

By the time they were all settled in, thoroughly evacuated, and eating, TALK NERDY and his friend had returned again. They cleared off the cash-register at the end of the food-prep area and TALK NERDY got up on it. Slowly the conversation died down.

"I'm Uri Popovich, this is Diego Rosenbaum. Thank you all for coming up here. Here's what we know for sure: the building's been on generators for three hours now. Visual observation indicates that we're the only building in central Toronto with working power—which should hold out for three more days. There is a bioagent of unknown origin loose beyond our doors. It kills quickly, within hours, and it is aerosolized. You get it from breathing bad air. No one has opened any of the exterior doors to this building since five this morning. No one will open the doors until I give the go-ahead.

"Attacks on major cities all over the world have left emergency responders in chaos. The attacks are electronic, biological, nuclear and conventional explosives, and they are very widespread. I'm a security engineer, and where I come from, attacks in this kind of cluster are usually viewed as opportunistic: group B blows up a bridge because everyone is off taking care of group A's dirty nuke event. It's smart. An Aum Shinrikyo cell in Seoul gassed the subways there about 2 AM Eastern — that's the earliest event we can locate, so it may have been the Archduke that broke the camel's back. We're pretty sure that Aum Shinrikyo couldn't be behind this kind of mayhem: they have no history of infowar and have never shown the kind of organizational acumen necessary to take out so many targets at once. Basically, they're not smart enough.

"We're holing up here for the foreseeable future, at least until the bioweapon has been identified and dispersed. We're going to staff the racks and keep the networks up. This is critical infrastructure, and it's our job to make sure it's got five nines of uptime. In times of national emergency, our responsibility to do that doubles."

One sysadmin put up his hand. He was very daring in a green Incredible Hulk ring-tee, and he was at the young end of the scale.

"Who died and made you king?"

"I have controls for the main security system, keys to every cage, and pass-codes for the exterior doors — they're all locked now, by the way. I'm the one who got everyone up here first and called the meeting. I don't care if someone else wants this job, it's a shitty one. But someone needs to have this job."

"You're right," the kid said. "And I can do it every bit as well as you. My name's Will Sario."

Popovich looked down his nose at the kid. "Well, if you'll let me finish talking, maybe I'll hand things over to you when I'm done."

"Finish, by all means." Sario turned his back on him and walked to the window. He stared out of it intensely. Felix's gaze was drawn to it, and he saw that there were several oily smoke plumes rising up from the city.

Popovich's momentum was broken. "So that's what we're going to do," he said.

The kid looked around after a stretched moment of silence. "Oh, is it my turn now?"

There was a round of good-natured chuckling.

"Here's what I think: the world is going to shit. There are coordinated attacks on every critical piece of infrastructure. There's only one way that those attacks could be so well coordinated: via the Internet. Even if you buy the thesis that the attacks are all opportunistic, we need to ask how an opportunistic attack could be organized in minutes: the Internet."

"So you think we should shut down the Internet?" Popovich laughed a little, but stopped when Sario said nothing.

"We saw an attack last night that nearly killed the Internet. A little DoS on the critical routers, a little DNS-foo, and down it goes like a preacher's daughter. Cops and the military are a bunch of technophobic lusers, they hardly rely on the net at all. If we take the Internet down, we'll disproportionately disadvantage the attackers, while only inconveniencing the defenders. When the time comes, we can rebuild it."

"You're shitting me," Popovich said. His jaw literally hung open.

"It's logical," Sario said. "Lots of people don't like coping with logic when it dictates hard decisions. That's a problem with people, not logic."

There was a buzz of conversation that quickly turned into a roar.

"Shut UP!" Popovich hollered. The conversation dimmed by one watt. Popovich yelled again, stamping his foot on the countertop. Finally there was a semblance of order. "One at a time," he said. He was flushed red, his hands in his pockets.

One sysadmin was for staying. Another for going. They should hide in the cages. They should inventory their supplies and appoint a quartermaster. They should go outside and find the police, or volunteer at hospitals. They should appoint defenders to keep the front door secure.

Felix found to his surprise that he had his hand in the air. Popovich called on him.

"My name is Felix Tremont," he said, getting up on one of the tables, drawing out his PDA. "I want to read you something.

"'Governments of the Industrial World, you weary giants of flesh and steel, I come from Cyberspace, the new home of Mind. On behalf of the future, I ask you of the past to leave us alone. You are not welcome among us. You have no sovereignty where we gather.

"'We have no elected government, nor are we likely to have one, so I address you with no greater authority than that with which liberty itself always speaks. I declare the global social space we are building to be naturally independent of the tyrannies you seek to impose on us. You have no moral right to rule us nor do you possess any methods of enforcement we have true reason to fear.

"'Governments derive their just powers from the consent of the governed. You have neither solicited nor received ours. We did not invite you. You do not know us, nor do you know our world. Cyberspace does not lie within your borders. Do not think that you can build it, as though it were a public construction project. You cannot. It is an act of nature and it grows itself through our collective actions.'

"That's from the Declaration of Independence of Cyberspace. It was written twelve years ago. I thought it was one of the most beautiful things I'd ever read. I wanted my kid to grow up in a world where cyberspace was free — and where that freedom infected the real world, so meatspace got freer too."

He swallowed hard and scrubbed at his eyes with the back of his hand. Van awkwardly patted him on the shoe.

"My beautiful son and my beautiful wife died today. Millions more, too. The city is literally in flames. Whole cities have disappeared from the map."

He coughed up a sob and swallowed it again.

"All around the world, people like us are gathered in buildings like this. They were trying to recover from last night's worm when disaster struck. We have independent power. Food. Water.

"We have the network, that the bad guys use so well and that the good guys have never figured out.

"We have a shared love of liberty that comes from caring about and caring for the network. We are in charge of the most important organizational and governmental tool the world has ever seen. We are the closest thing to a government the world has right now. Geneva is a crater. The East River is on fire and the UN is evacuated.

"The Distributed Republic of Cyberspace weathered this storm basically unscathed. We are the custodians of a deathless, monstrous, wonderful machine, one with the potential to rebuild a better world.

"I have nothing to live for but that."

There were tears in Van's eyes. He wasn't the only one. They didn't applaud him, but they did one better. They maintained respectful, total silence for seconds that stretched to a minute.

"How do we do it?" Popovich said, without a trace of sarcasm.

The newsgroups were filling up fast. They'd announced them in news.admin. net-abuse.email, where all the spamfighters hung out, and where there was a tight culture of camaraderie in the face of full-out attack.

The new group was alt.november5-disaster.recovery, with .recovery.gover-ance, .recovery.finance, .recovery.logistics and .recovery.defense hanging off of it. Bless the wooly alt. hierarchy and all those who sail in her.

The sysadmins came out of the woodwork. The Googleplex was online, with the stalwart Queen Kong bossing a gang of rollerbladed grunts who wheeled through the gigantic data-center swapping out dead boxen and hitting reboot switches. The Internet Archive was offline in the Presidio, but the mirror in Amsterdam was live and they'd redirected the DNS so that you'd hardly know the difference. Amazon was down. PayPal was up. Blogger, TypePad, and LiveJournal were all up, and filling with millions of posts from scared survivors huddling together for electronic warmth.

The Flickr photostreams were horrific. Felix had to unsubscribe from them after he caught a photo of a woman and a baby, dead in a kitchen, twisted into an agonized hieroglyph by the bioagent. They didn't look like Kelly and 2.0, but they didn't have to. He started shaking and couldn't stop.

Wikipedia was up, but limping under load. The spam poured in as though nothing had changed. Worms roamed the network.

.recovery.logistics was where most of the action was.

> We can use the newsgroup voting mechanism to hold regional
> elections

Felix knew that this would work. Usenet newsgroup votes had been running for more than twenty years without a substantial hitch.

> We'll elect regional representatives and they'll pick a Prime
> Minister.

The Americans insisted on President, which Felix didn't like. Seemed too partisan. His future wouldn't be the American future. The American future had gone up with the White House. He was building a bigger tent than that.

There were French sysadmins online from France Telecom. The EBU's data-center had been spared in the attacks that hammered Geneva, and it was filled with wry Germans whose English was better than Felix's. They got on well with the remains of the BBC team in Canary Wharf.

They spoke polyglot English in .recovery.logistics, and Felix had momentum on his side. Some of the admins were cooling out the inevitable stupid flamew-ars with the practice of long years. Some were chipping in useful suggestions.

Surprisingly few thought that Felix was off his rocker.

> I think we should hold elections as soon as possible. Tomorrow
> at the latest. We can't rule justly without the consent of the
> governed.

Within seconds the reply landed in his inbox.

> You can't be serious. Consent of the governed? Unless I miss my
> guess, most of the people you're proposing to govern are puking
> their guts out, hiding under their desks, or wandering
> shell-shocked through the city streets. When do THEY get a vote?

Felix had to admit she had a point. Queen Kong was sharp. Not many woman sysadmins, and that was a genuine tragedy. Women like Queen Kong were too good to exclude from the field. He'd have to hack a solution to get women balanced out in his new government. Require each region to elect one woman and one man?

He happily clattered into argument with her. The elections would be the next day; he'd see to it.

"Prime Minister of Cyberspace? Why not call yourself the Grand Poobah of the Global Data Network? It's more dignified, sounds cooler and it'll get you just as far." Will had the sleeping spot next to him, up in the cafeteria, with Van on the other side. The room smelled like a dingleberry: twenty-five sysadmins who hadn't washed in at least a day all crammed into the same room. For some of them, it had been much, much longer than a day.

"Shut up, Will," Van said. "You wanted to try to knock the Internet offline."

"Correction: I *want* to knock the Internet offline. Present-tense."

Felix cracked one eye. He was so tired, it was like lifting weights.

"Look, Sario — if you don't like my platform, put one of your own forward. There are plenty of people who think I'm full of shit and I respect them for that, since they're all running opposite me or backing someone who is. That's your choice. What's not on the menu is nagging and complaining. Bedtime now, or get up and post your platform."

Sario sat up slowly, unrolling the jacket he had been using for a pillow and putting it on. "Screw you guys, I'm out of here."

"I thought he'd never leave," Felix said, and turned over, lying awake a long time, thinking about the election.

There were other people in the running. Some of them weren't even sys-

admins. A US Senator on retreat at his summer place in Wyoming had generator power and a satellite phone. Somehow he'd found the right newsgroup and
thrown his hat into the ring. Some anarchist hackers in Italy strafed the group
all night long, posting broken-English screeds about the political bankruptcy
of "governance" in the new world. Felix looked at their netblock and determined that they were probably holed up in a small Interaction Design institute
near Turin. Italy had been hit very bad, but out in the small town, this cell of
anarchists had taken up residence.

A surprising number were running on a platform of shutting down the
Internet. Felix had his doubts about whether this was even possible, but he
thought he understood the impulse to finish the work and the world. Why not?
From every indication, it seemed that the work to date had been a cascade of
disasters, attacks, and opportunism, all of it adding up to *Götterdämmerung*. A
terrorist attack here, a lethal counteroffensive there from an overreactive government... Before long, they'd made short work of the world.

He fell asleep thinking about the logistics of shutting down the Internet,
and dreamed bad dreams in which he was the network's sole defender.

He woke to a papery, itchy sound. He rolled over and saw that Van was sitting up, his jacket balled up in his lap, vigorously scratching his skinny arms.
They'd gone the color of corned beef, and had a scaly look. In the light streaming through the cafeteria windows, skin motes floated and danced in great
clouds.

"What are you doing?" Felix sat up. Watching Van's fingernails rip into his
skin made him itch in sympathy. It had been three days since he'd last washed
his hair and his scalp sometimes felt like there were little egg-laying insects
picking their way through it. He'd adjusted his glasses the night before and had
touched the backs of his ears; his finger came away shining with thick sebum.
He got blackheads in the backs of his ears when he didn't shower for a couple
days, and sometimes gigantic, deep boils that Kelly finally popped with sick
relish.

"Scratching," Van said. He went to work on his head, sending a cloud of
dandruff-crud into the sky, there to join the scurf that he'd already eliminated
from his extremities. "Christ, I itch all over."

Felix took Mayor McCheese from Van's backpack and plugged it into one
of the Ethernet cables that snaked all over the floor. He googled everything he

could think of that could be related to this. "Itchy" yielded 40,600,000 links. He tried compound queries and got slightly more discriminating links.

"I think it's stress-related eczema," Felix said, finally.

"I don't get eczema," Van said.

Felix showed him some lurid photos of red, angry skin flaked with white. "Stress-related eczema," he said, reading the caption.

Van examined his arms. "I have eczema," he said.

"Says here to keep it moisturized and to try cortisone cream. You might try the first aid kit in the second-floor toilets. I think I saw some there." Like all of the sysadmins, Felix had had a bit of a rummage around the offices, bathrooms, kitchen and store-rooms, squirreling away a roll of toilet-paper in his shoulder-bag along with three or four power-bars. They were sharing out the food in the caf by unspoken agreement, every sysadmin watching every other for signs of gluttony and hoarding. All were convinced that there was hoarding and gluttony going on out of eyeshot, because all were guilty of it themselves when no one else was watching.

Van got up and when his face hove into the light, Felix saw how puffed his eyes were. "I'll post to the mailing-list for some antihistamine," Felix said. There had been four mailing lists and three wikis for the survivors in the building within hours of the first meeting's close, and in the intervening days they'd settled on just one. Felix was still on a little mailing list with five of his most trusted friends, two of whom were trapped in cages in other countries. He suspected that the rest of the sysadmins were doing the same.

Van stumbled off. "Good luck on the elections," he said, patting Felix on the shoulder.

Felix stood and paced, stopping to stare out the grubby windows. The fires still burned in Toronto, more than before. He'd tried to find mailing lists or blogs that Torontonians were posting to, but the only ones he'd found were being run by other geeks in other data-centers. It was possible — likely, even — that there were survivors out there who had more pressing priorities than posting to the Internet. His home phone still worked about half the time but he'd stopped calling it after the second day, when hearing Kelly's voice on the voicemail for the fiftieth time had made him cry in the middle of a planning meeting. He wasn't the only one.

Election day. Time to face the music.

> Are you nervous?

> Nope

Felix typed.

> I don't much care if I win, to be honest. I'm just glad we're doing this.
  The alternative was sitting around with our thumbs up our ass, waiting for someone to crack up and open the door.

The cursor hung. Queen Kong was very high latency as she bossed her gang
of Googloids around the Googleplex, doing everything she could to keep her
data-center online. Three of the offshore cages had gone offline and two of
their six redundant network links were smoked. Lucky for her, queries-per-
second were way down.

> There's still China

she typed. Queen Kong had a big board with a map of the world colored in
Google-queries-per-second, and could do magic with it, showing the drop-off
over time in colorful charts. She'd uploaded lots of video clips showing how the
plague and the bombs had swept the world: the initial upswell of queries from
people wanting to find out what was going on, then the grim, precipitous shelving off as the plagues took hold.

> China's still running about ninety percent nominal.

Felix shook his head.

> You can't think that they're responsible

> No

she typed, but then she started to key something and then stopped.

> No of course not. I believe the Popovich Hypothesis. Every asshole
  in the world is using the other assholes for cover. But China put them
  down harder and faster than anyone else. Maybe we've finally found a
  use for totalitarian states.

Felix couldn't resist. He typed:

> You're lucky your boss can't see you type that. You guys were pretty
  enthusiastic participants in the Great Firewall of China.

> Wasn't my idea

she typed.

> And my boss is dead. They're probably all dead. The whole Bay Area
  got hit hard, and then there was the quake.

They'd watched the USGS's automated data-stream from the 6.9 that trashed northern Cal from Gilroy to Sebastopol. Soma webcams revealed the scope of the damage — gas main explosions, seismically retrofitted buildings crumpling like piles of children's blocks after a good kicking. The Googleplex, floating on a series of gigantic steel springs, had shook like a plateful of jello, but the racks had stayed in place and the worst injury they'd had was a badly bruised eye on a sysadmin who'd caught a flying cable-crimper in the face.

> Sorry. I forgot.

> It's OK. We all lost people, right?

> Yeah. Yeah. Anyway, I'm not worried about the election. Whoever wins, at least we're doing SOMETHING

> Not if they vote for one of the fuckrags

Fuckrag was the epithet that some of the sysadmins were using to describe the contingent that wanted to shut down the Internet. Queen Kong had coined it — apparently it had started life as a catch-all term to describe clueless IT managers that she'd chewed up through her career.

> They won't. They're just tired and sad is all. Your endorsement will carry the day

The Googloids were one of the largest and most powerful blocs left behind, along with the satellite uplink crews and the remaining transoceanic crews. Queen Kong's endorsement had come as a surprise and he'd sent her an email that she'd replied to tersely: "can't have the fuckrags in charge."

> gtg

she typed and then her connection dropped. He fired up a browser and called up google.com. The browser timed out. He hit reload, and then again, and then the Google front-page came back up. Whatever had hit Queen Kong's workplace — power failure, worms, another quake — she had fixed it. He snorted when he saw that they'd replaced the Os in the Google logo with little planet Earths with mushroom clouds rising from them.

"Got anything to eat?" Van said to him. It was midafternoon, not that time particularly passed in the data-center. Felix patted his pockets. They'd put a quartermaster in charge, but not before everyone had snagged some chow out of the machines. He'd had a dozen power-bars and some apples. He'd taken a couple sandwiches but had wisely eaten them first before they got stale.

"One power-bar left," he said. He'd noticed a certain looseness in his waistline that morning and had briefly relished it. Then he'd remembered Kelly's teasing about his weight and he'd cried some. Then he'd eaten two power-bars, leaving him with just one left.

"Oh," Van said. His face was hollower than ever, his shoulders sloping in on his toast-rack chest.

"Here," Felix said. "Vote Felix."

Van took the power-bar from him and then put it down on the table. "OK, I want to give this back to you and say, 'No, I couldn't,' but I'm fucking *hungry*, so I'm just going to take it and eat it, OK?"

"That's fine by me," Felix said. "Enjoy."

"How are the elections coming?" Van said, once he'd licked the wrapper clean.

"Dunno," Felix said. "Haven't checked in a while." He'd been winning by a slim margin a few hours before. Not having his laptop was a major handicap when it came to stuff like this. Up in the cages, there were a dozen more like him, poor bastards who'd left the house on Der Tag without thinking to snag something WiFi-enabled.

"You're going to get smoked," Sario said, sliding in next to them. He'd become famous in the center for never sleeping, for eavesdropping, for picking fights in RL that had the ill-considered heat of a Usenet flamewar. "The winner will be someone who understands a couple of fundamental facts." He held up a fist, then ticked off his bullet points by raising a one finger at a time. "Point: The terrorists are using the Internet to destroy the world, and we need to destroy the Internet first. Point: Even if I'm wrong, the whole thing is a joke. We'll run out of generator-fuel soon enough. Point: Or if we don't, it will be because the old world will be back and running, and it won't give a crap about your new world. Point: We're gonna run out of food before we run out of shit to argue about or reasons not to go outside. We have the chance to do something to help the world recover: we can kill the net and cut it off as a tool for bad guys. Or we can rearrange some more deck chairs on the bridge of your personal *Titanic* in the service of some sweet dream about an 'independent cyberspace.'"

The thing was that Sario was right. They would be out of fuel in two days — intermittent power from the grid had stretched their generator lifespan. And if you bought his hypothesis that the Internet was primarily being used as a tool to organize more mayhem, shutting it down would be the right thing to do.

But Felix's son and his wife were dead. He didn't want to rebuild the old world. He wanted a new one. The old world was one that didn't have any place for him. Not anymore.

Van scratched his raw, flaking skin. Puffs of dander and scurf swirled in the musty, greasy air. Sario curled a lip at him. "That is disgusting. We're breathing recycled air, you know. Whatever leprosy is eating you, aerosolizing it into the air supply is pretty anti-social."

"You're the world's leading authority on anti-social, Sario," Van said. "Go away or I'll multitool you to death." He stopped scratching and patted his sheathed multi-pliers like a gunslinger.

"Yeah, I'm anti-social. I've got Asperger's and I haven't taken any meds in four days. What's your fucking excuse."

Van scratched some more. "I'm sorry," he said. "I didn't know."

Sario cracked up. "Oh, you are priceless. I'd bet that three-quarters of this bunch is borderline autistic. Me, I'm just an asshole. But I'm one who isn't afraid to tell the truth, and that makes me better than you, dickweed."

"Fuckrag," Felix said, "fuck off."

They had less than a day's worth of fuel when Felix was elected the first ever Prime Minister of Cyberspace. The first count was spoiled by a bot that spammed the voting process and they lost a critical day while they added up the votes a second time.

But by then, it was all seeming like more of a joke. Half the data-centers had gone dark. Queen Kong's net-maps of Google queries were looking grimmer and grimmer as more of the world went offline, though she maintained a leader-board of new and rising queries — largely related to health, shelter, sanitation and self-defense.

Worm-load slowed. Power was going off to many home PC users, and staying off, so their compromised PCs were going dark. The backbones were still lit up and blinking, but the missives from those data-centers were looking more and more desperate. Felix hadn't eaten in a day and neither had anyone in a satellite Earth-station of transoceanic head-end.

Water was running short, too.

Popovich and Rosenbaum came and got him before he could do more than answer a few congratulatory messages and post a canned acceptance speech to newsgroups.

"We're going to open the doors," Popovich said. Like all of them, he'd lost weight and waxed scruffy and oily. His BO was like a cloud coming off trash-bags behind a fish-market on a sunny day. Felix was quite sure he smelled no better.

"You're going to go for a reccy? Get more fuel? We can charter a working group for it—great idea."

Rosenbaum shook his head sadly. "We're going to go find our families. Whatever is out there has burned itself out. Or it hasn't. Either way, there's no future in here."

"What about network maintenance?" Felix said, though he knew the answers. "Who'll keep the routers up?"

"We'll give you the root passwords to everything," Popovich said. His hands were shaking and his eyes were bleary. Like many of the smokers stuck in the data-center, he'd gone cold turkey this week. They'd run out of caffeine products two days earlier, too. The smokers had it rough.

"And I'll just stay here and keep everything online?"

"You and anyone else who cares anymore."

Felix knew that he'd squandered his opportunity. The election had seemed noble and brave, but in hindsight all it had been was an excuse for infighting when they should have been figuring out what to do next. The problem was that there was nothing to do next.

"I can't make you stay," he said.

"Yeah, you can't." Popovich turned on his heel and walked out. Rosenbaum watched him go, then he gripped Felix's shoulder and squeezed it.

"Thank you, Felix. It was a beautiful dream. It still is. Maybe we'll find something to eat and some fuel and come back."

Rosenbaum had a sister whom he'd been in contact with over IM for the first days after the crisis broke. Then she'd stopped answering. The sysadmins were split among those who'd had a chance to say goodbye and those who hadn't. Each was sure the other had it better.

They posted about it on the internal newsgroup—they were still geeks, after all, and there was a little honor guard on the ground floor, geeks who watched them pass toward the double doors. They manipulated the keypads and the steel shutters lifted, then the first set of doors opened. They stepped into the vestibule and pulled the doors shut behind them. The front doors opened. It was very bright and sunny outside, and apart from how empty it was, it looked very normal. Heartbreakingly so.

The two took a tentative step out into the world. Then another. They turned to wave at the assembled masses. Then they both grabbed their throats and began to jerk and twitch, crumpling in a heap on the ground.

"Shiii—!" was all Felix managed to choke out before they both dusted themselves off and stood up, laughing so hard they were clutching their sides. They waved once more and turned on their heels.

"Man, those guys are sick," Van said. He scratched his arms, which had long, bloody scratches on them. His clothes were so covered in scurf they looked like they'd been dusted with icing sugar.

"I thought it was pretty funny," Felix said.

"Christ I'm hungry," Van said, conversationally.

"Lucky for you, we've got all the packets we can eat," Felix said.

"You're too good to us grunts, Mr. President," Van said.

"Prime Minister," he said. "And you're no grunt, you're the Deputy Prime Minister. You're my designated ribbon-cutter and hander-out of oversized novelty checks."

It buoyed both of their spirits. Watching Popovich and Rosenbaum go, it buoyed them up. Felix knew then that they'd all be going soon.

That had been preordained by the fuel-supply, but who wanted to wait for the fuel to run out, anyway?

> half my crew split this morning

Queen Kong typed. Google was holding up pretty good anyway, of course. The load on the servers was a lot lighter than it had been since the days when Google fit on a bunch of hand-built PCs under a desk at Stanford.

> we're down to a quarter

Felix typed back. It was only a day since Popovich and Rosenbaum left, but the traffic on the newsgroups had fallen down to near zero. He and Van hadn't had much time to play Republic of Cyberspace. They'd been too busy learning the systems that Popovich had turned over to them, the big, big routers that had went on acting as the major interchange for all the network backbones in Canada.

Still, someone posted to the newsgroups every now and again, generally to say goodbye. The old flamewars about who would be PM, or whether they would shut down the network, or who took too much food—it was all gone.

He reloaded the newsgroup. There was a typical message.

> Runaway processes on Solaris TK

>

> Uh, hi. I'm just a lightweight MSCE but I'm the only one awake here
    and four of the DSLAMs just went down. Looks like there's some
    custom accounting code that's trying to figure out how much to bill
    our corporate customers and it's spawned ten thousand threads and
    its eating all the swap. I just want to kill it but I can't seem to do that.
    Is there some magic invocation I need to do to get this goddamned
    weenix box to kill this shit? I mean, it's not as if any of our customers
    are ever going to pay us again. I'd ask the guy who wrote this code,
    but he's pretty much dead as far as anyone can work out.

He reloaded. There was a response. It was short, authoritative, and help-ful—just the sort of thing you almost never saw in a high-caliber newsgroup when a noob posted a dumb question. The apocalypse had awoken the spirit of patient helpfulness in the world's sysop community.

Van shoulder-surfed him. "Holy shit, who knew he had it in him?"

He looked at the message again. It was from Will Sario.

He dropped into his chat window.

> sario i thought you wanted the network dead why are you helping
    msces fix their boxen?

> [sheepish grin] Gee Mr PM, maybe I just can't bear to watch a com-
    puter suffer at the hands of an amateur.

He flipped to the channel with Queen Kong in it.

> How long?

> Since I slept? Two days. Until we run out of fuel? Three days. Since
    we ran out of food? Two days.

> Jeez. I didn't sleep last night either. We're a little short-handed
    around here.

> asl? Im monica and I live in pasadena and Im bored with my
    homework. Would you like to download my pic???

The trojan bots were all over IRC these days, jumping to every channel that had any traffic on it. Sometimes you caught five or six flirting with each other.

It was pretty weird to watch a piece of malware try to con another instance of itself into downloading a trojan.

They both kicked the bot off the channel simultaneously. He had a script for it now. The spam hadn't even tailed off a little.

> How come the spam isn't reducing? Half the goddamned data-centers
    have gone dark

Queen Kong paused a long time before typing. As had become automatic when she went high-latency, he reloaded the Google homepage. Sure enough, it was down.

> Sario, you got any food?

> You won't miss a couple more meals, Your Excellency

Van had gone back to Mayor McCheese but he was in the same channel.

"What a dick. You're looking pretty buff, though, dude."

Van didn't look so good. He looked like you could knock him over with a stiff breeze and he had a phlegmy, weak quality to his speech.

> hey kong everything ok?

> everything's fine just had to go kick some ass

"How's the traffic, Van?"

"Down 25 percent from this morning," he said. There were a bunch of nodes whose connections routed through them. Presumably most of these were home or commercial customers in places where the power was still on and the phone company's COs were still alive.

Every once in a while, Felix would wiretap the connections to see if he could find a person who had news of the wide world. Almost all of it was automated traffic, though: network backups, status updates. Spam. Lots of spam.

> Spam's still up because the services that stop spam are failing faster
    than the services that create it. All the anti-worm stuff is centralized
    in a couple places. The bad stuff is on a million zombie computers.
    If only the lusers had had the good sense to turn off their home PCs
    before keeling over or taking off

> at the rate were going well be routing nothing but spam by dinnertime

Van cleared his throat, a painful sound. "About that," he said. "I think it's going to hit sooner than that. Felix, I don't think anyone would notice if we just walked away from here."

Felix looked at him, his skin the color of corned-beef and streaked with long, angry scabs. His fingers trembled.

"You drinking enough water?"

Van nodded. "All frigging day, every ten seconds. Anything to keep my belly full." He pointed to a refilled Pepsi Max bottle full of water by his side.

"Let's have a meeting," he said.

There had been forty-three of them on D-Day. Now there were fifteen. Six had responded to the call for a meeting by simply leaving. Everyone knew without having to be told what the meeting was about.

"So that's it, you're going to let it all fall apart?" Sario was the only one with the energy left to get properly angry. He'd go angry to his grave. The veins on his throat and forehead stood out angrily. His fists shook angrily. All the other geeks went lids-down at the site of him, looking up in unison for once at the discussion, not keeping one eye on a chat-log or a tailed service log.

"Sario, you've got to be shitting me," Felix said. "You wanted to pull the goddamned plug!"

"I wanted it to go *clean*," he shouted. "I didn't want it to bleed out and keel over in little gasps and pukes forever. I wanted it to be an act of will by the global community of its caretakers. I wanted it to be an affirmative act by human hands. Not entropy and bad code and worms winning out. Fuck that, that's just what's happened out there."

Up in the top-floor cafeteria, there were windows all around, hardened and light-bending, and by custom, they were all blinds-down. Now Sario ran around the room, yanking down the blinds. *How the hell can he get the energy to run?* Felix wondered. He could barely walk up the stairs to the meeting room.

Harsh daylight flooded in. It was a fine sunny day out there, but everywhere you looked across that commanding view of Toronto's skyline, there were rising plumes of smoke. The TD tower, a gigantic black modernist glass brick, was gouting flame to the sky. "It's all falling apart, the way everything does.

"Listen, listen. If we leave the network to fall over slowly, parts of it will stay online for months. Maybe years. And what will run on it? Malware. Worms. Spam. System-processes. Zone transfers. The things we use fall apart and require constant maintenance. The things we abandon don't get used and they last forever. We're going to leave the network behind like a lime-pit filled with industrial waste. That will be our fucking legacy — the legacy of every keystroke you and I and anyone, anywhere ever typed. You understand? We're going to leave it to die slow like a wounded dog, instead of giving it one clean shot through the head."

Van scratched his cheeks, then Felix saw that he was wiping away tears.

"Sario, you're not wrong, but you're not right either," he said. "Leaving it up to limp along is right. We're going to all be limping for a long time, and maybe it will be some use to someone. If there's one packet being routed from any user to any other user, anywhere in the world, it's doing its job."

"If you want a clean kill, you can do that," Felix said. "I'm the PM and I say so. I'm giving you root. All of you." He turned to the white-board where the cafeteria workers used to scrawl the day's specials. Now it was covered with the remnants of heated technical debates that the sysadmins had engaged in over the days since the day.

He scrubbed away a clean spot with his sleeve and began to write out long, complicated alphanumeric passwords salted with punctuation. Felix had a gift for remembering that kind of password. He doubted it would do him much good, ever again.

> Were going, kong. Fuels almost out anyway
  > yeah well thats right then. it was an honor, mr prime minister
  > you going to be ok?
  > ive commandeered a young sysadmin to see to my feminine needs and
     weve found another cache of food thatll last us a coupel weeks now
     that were down to fifteen admins — im in hog heaven pal
  > youre amazing, Queen Kong, seriously. Dont be a hero though. When
     you need to go go. Theres got to be something out there
  > be safe felix, seriously — btw did i tell you queries are up in Romania?
     maybe theyre getting back on their feet
  > really?
  > yeah, really. we're hard to kill — like fucking roaches

Her connection died. He dropped to Firefox and reloaded Google and it was down. He hit reload and hit reload and hit reload, but it didn't come up. He closed his eyes and listened to Van scratch his legs and then heard Van type a little.

"They're back up," he said.

Felix whooshed out a breath. He sent the message to the newsgroup, one that he'd run through five drafts before settling on, "Take care of the place, OK? We'll be back, someday."

Everyone was going except Sario. Sario wouldn't leave. He came down to see them off, though.

The sysadmins gathered in the lobby and Felix made the safety door go up, and the light rushed in.

Sario stuck his hand out.

"Good luck," he said.

"You too," Felix said. He had a firm grip, Sario, stronger than he had any right to be. "Maybe you were right," he said.

"Maybe," he said.

"You going to pull the plug?"

Sario looked up at the drop-ceiling, seeming to peer through the reinforced floors at the humming racks above. "Who knows?" he said at last.

Van scratched and a flurry of white motes danced in the sunlight.

"Let's go find you a pharmacy," Felix said. He walked to the door and the other sysadmins followed.

They waited for the interior doors to close behind them and then Felix opened the exterior doors. The air smelled and tasted like mown grass, like the first drops of rain, like the lake and the sky, like the outdoors and the world, an old friend not heard from in an eternity.

"Bye, Felix," the other sysadmins said. They were drifting away while he stood transfixed at the top of the short concrete staircase. The light hurt his eyes and made them water.

"I think there's a Shopper's Drug Mart on King Street," he said to Van. "We'll throw a brick through the window and get you some cortisone, OK?"

"You're the Prime Minister," Van said. "Lead on."

They didn't see a single soul on the fifteen minute walk. There wasn't a single sound except for some bird noises and some distant groans, and the wind in the electric cables overhead. It was like walking on the surface of the moon.

"Bet they have chocolate bars at the Shopper's," Van said.

Felix's stomach lurched. Food. "Wow," he said, around a mouthful of saliva.

They walked past a little hatchback and in the front seat was the dried body of a woman holding the dried body of a baby, and his mouth filled with sour bile, even though the smell was faint through the rolled-up windows.

He hadn't thought of Kelly or 2.0 in days. He dropped to his knees and retched again. Out here in the real world, his family was dead. Everyone he knew was dead. He just wanted to lie down on the sidewalk and wait to die, too.

Van's rough hands slipped under his armpits and hauled weakly at him. "Not now," he said. "Once we're safe inside somewhere and we've eaten something, then you can do this, but not now. Understand me, Felix? Not fucking now."

The profanity got through to him. He got to his feet. His knees were trembling.

"Just a block more," Van said, and slipped Felix's arm around his shoulders and led him along.

"Thank you, Van. I'm sorry."

"No sweat," he said. "You need a shower, bad. No offense."

"None taken."

The Shopper's had a metal security gate, but it had been torn away from the front windows, which had been rudely smashed. Felix and Van squeezed through the gap and stepped into the dim drug-store. A few of the displays were knocked over, but other than that, it looked OK. By the cash-registers, Felix spotted the racks of candy bars at the same instant that Van saw them, and they hurried over and grabbed a handful each, stuffing their faces.

"You two eat like pigs."

They both whirled at the sound of the woman's voice. She was holding a fire-axe that was nearly as big as she was. She wore a lab-coat and comfortable shoes.

"You take what you need and go, OK? No sense in there being any trouble." Her chin was pointy and her eyes were sharp. She looked to be in her forties. She looked nothing like Kelly, which was good, because Felix felt like running and giving her a hug as it was. Another person alive!

"Are you a doctor?" Felix said. She was wearing scrubs under the coat, he saw.

"You going to go?" She brandished the axe.

Felix held his hands up. "Seriously, are you a doctor? A pharmacist?"

"I used to be an RN, ten years ago. I'm mostly a Web-designer."

"You're shitting me," Felix said.

"Haven't you ever met a girl who knew about computers?"

"Actually, a friend of mine who runs Google's data-center is a girl. A woman, I mean."

"You're shitting me," she said. "A woman ran Google's data-center?"

"Runs," Felix said. "It's still online."

"NFW," she said. She let the axe lower.

"Way. Have you got any cortisone cream? I can tell you the story. My name's Felix and this is Van, who needs any antihistamines you can spare."

"I can spare? Felix old pal, I have enough dope here to last a hundred years. This stuff's going to expire long before it runs out. But are you telling me that the net's still up?"

"It's still up," he said. "Kind of. That's what we've been doing all week. Keeping it online. It might not last much longer, though."

"No," she said. "I don't suppose it would." She set the axe down. "Have you got anything to trade? I don't need much, but I've been trying to keep my spirits up by trading with the neighbors. It's like playing civilization."

"You have neighbors?"

"At least ten," she said. "The people in the restaurant across the way make a pretty good soup, even if most of the veg is canned. They cleaned me out of Sterno, though."

"You've got neighbors and you trade with them?"

"Well, nominally. It'd be pretty lonely without them. I've taken care of whatever sniffles I could. Set a bone — broken wrist. Listen, do you want some Wonder Bread and peanut butter? I have a ton of it. Your friend looks like he could use a meal."

"Yes please," Van said. "We don't have anything to trade, but we're both committed workaholics looking to learn a trade. Could you use some assistants?"

"Not really." She spun her axe on its head. "But I wouldn't mind some company."

They ate the sandwiches and then some soup. The restaurant people brought it over and made their manners at them, though Felix saw their noses wrinkle up and ascertained that there was working plumbing in the back room. Van went in to take a sponge bath and then he followed.

"None of us know what to do," the woman said. Her name was Rosa, and she had found them a bottle of wine and some disposable plastic cups from the housewares aisle. "I thought we'd have helicopters or tanks or even looters, but it's just quiet."

"You seem to have kept pretty quiet yourself," Felix said.

"Didn't want to attract the wrong kind of attention."

"You ever think that maybe there's a lot of people out there doing the same thing? Maybe if we all get together we'll come up with something to do."

"Or maybe they'll cut our throats," she said.

Van nodded. "She's got a point."

Felix was on his feet. "No way, we can't think like that. Lady, we're at a critical juncture here. We can go down through negligence, dwindling away in our hiding holes, or we can try to build something better."

"Better?" She made a rude noise.

"ok, not better. Something though. Building something new is better than letting it dwindle away. Christ, what are you going to do when you've read all the magazines and eaten all the potato chips here?"

Rosa shook her head. "Pretty talk," she said. "But what the hell are we going to do, anyway?"

"Something," Felix said. "We're going to do something. Something is better than nothing. We're going to take this patch of the world where people are talking to each other, and we're going to expand it. We're going to find everyone we can and we're going to take care of them and they're going to take care of us. We'll probably fuck it up. We'll probably fail. I'd rather fail than give up, though."

Van laughed. "Felix, you are crazier than Sario, you know it?"

"We're going to go and drag him out, first thing tomorrow. He's going to be a part of this, too. Everyone will. Screw the end of the world. The world doesn't end. Humans aren't the kind of things that have endings."

Rosa shook her head again, but she was smiling a little now. "And you'll be what, the Pope-Emperor of the World?"

"He prefers Prime Minister," Van said in a stagey whisper. The antihistamines had worked miracles on his skin, and it had faded from angry red to a fine pink.

"You want to be Minister of Health, Rosa?" he said.

"Boys," she said. "Playing games. How about this. I'll help out however I can, provided you never ask me to call you Prime Minister and you never call me the Minister of Health?"

"It's a deal," he said.

Van refilled their glasses, upending the wine bottle to get the last few drops out.

They raised their glasses. "To the world," Felix said. "To humanity." He thought hard. "To rebuilding."

"To anything," Van said.

"To anything," Felix said. "To everything."

"To everything," Rosa said.

They drank. He wanted to go see the house — see Kelly and 2.0, though his stomach churned at the thought of what he might find there. But the next day, they started to rebuild. And months later, they started over again, when disagreements drove apart the fragile little group they'd pulled together. And a year after that, they started over again. And five years later, they started again.

It was nearly six months before he went home. Van helped him along, riding cover behind him on the bicycles they used to get around town. The further north they rode, the stronger the smell of burnt wood became. There were lots of burnt-out houses. Sometimes marauders burnt the houses they'd looted, but more often it was just nature, the kinds of fires you got in forests and on mountains. There were six choking, burnt blocks where every house was burnt before they reached home.

But Felix's old housing development was still standing, an oasis of eerily pristine buildings that looked like maybe their somewhat neglectful owners had merely stepped out to buy some paint and fresh lawnmower blades to bring their old homes back up to their neat, groomed selves.

That was worse, somehow. He got off the bike at the entry of the subdivision and they walked the bikes together in silence, listening to the sough of the wind in the trees. Winter was coming late that year, but it was coming, and as the sweat dried in the wind, Felix started to shiver.

He didn't have his keys anymore. They were at the data-center, months and worlds away. He tried the door-handle, but it didn't turn. He applied his shoulder to the door and it ripped away from its wet, rotted jamb with a loud, splintering sound. The house was rotting from the inside.

The door splashed when it landed. The house was full of stagnant water, four inches of stinking pond-scummed water in the living room. He splashed carefully through it, feeling the floor-boards sag spongily beneath each step.

Up the stairs, his nose full of that terrible green mildewy stench. Into the bedroom, the furniture familiar as a childhood friend.

Kelly was in the bed with 2.0. The way they both lay, it was clear they hadn't gone easy—they were twisted double, Kelly curled around 2.0. Their skin was bloated, making them almost unrecognizable. The smell—God, the smell.

Felix's head spun. He thought he would fall over and clutched at the dresser. An emotion he couldn't name—rage, anger, sorrow?—made him breathe hard, gulp for air like he was drowning.

And then it was over. The world was over. Kelly and 2.0—over. And he had a job to do. He folded the blanket over them—Van helped, solemnly. They went into the front yard and took turns digging, using the shovel from the garage that Kelly had used for gardening. They had lots of experience digging graves by then. Lots of experience handling the dead. They dug, and wary dogs watched them from the tall grass on the neighboring lawns, but they were also good at chasing off dogs with well-thrown stones.

When the grave was dug, they laid Felix's wife and son to rest in it. Felix quested after words to say over the mound, but none came. He'd dug so many graves for so many men's wives and so many women's husbands and so many children—the words were long gone.

Felix dug ditches and salvaged cans and buried the dead. He planted and harvested. He fixed some cars and learned to make biodiesel. Finally he fetched up in a data-center for a little government—little governments came and went, but this one was smart enough to want to keep records and needed someone to keep everything running, and Van went with him.

They spent a lot of time in chat rooms and sometimes they happened upon old friends from the strange time they'd spent running the Distributed Republic of Cyberspace, geeks who insisted on calling him PM, though no one in the real world ever called him that anymore.

It wasn't a good life, most of the time. Felix's wounds never healed, and neither did most other people's. There were lingering sicknesses and sudden ones. Tragedy on tragedy.

But Felix liked his data-center. There in the humming of the racks, he never felt like it was the first days of a better nation, but he never felt like it was the last days of one, either.

> go to bed, felix

> soon, kong, soon — almost got this backup running

> youre a junkie, dude.

> look whos talking

He reloaded the Google homepage. Queen Kong had had it online for a couple years now. The Os in Google changed all the time, whenever she got the urge. Today they were little cartoon globes, one smiling the other frowning.

He looked at it for a long time and dropped back into a terminal to check his backup. It was running clean, for a change. The little government's records were safe.

> ok night night

> take care

Van waved at him as he creaked to the door, stretching out his back with a long series of pops.

"Sleep well, boss," he said.

"Don't stick around here all night again," Felix said. "You need your sleep, too."

"You're too good to us grunts," Van said, and went back to typing.

Felix went to the door and walked out into the night. Behind him, the biodiesel generator hummed and made its acrid fumes. The harvest moon was up, which he loved. Tomorrow, he'd go back and fix another computer and fight off entropy again. And why not?

It was what he did. He was a sysadmin.

"I think one of the things that I see when I look back at my earlier work is a struggle to recognize and accept that the heart is the master and the head is the servant, and that that is always the case, except when it isn't the case we're in deep, deep trouble. That's the way it looks to me now when I look back on it, but I wasn't able to articulate that twenty years ago."

— William Gibson, *No Maps for These Territories*